Issued to the Bride:
One Navy SEAL

Cora Seton

Author's Note

Issued to the Bride One Navy SEAL is the first volume in the Brides of Chance Creek series, set in the fictional town of Chance Creek, Montana. To find out more about Brian, Cass, Connor, Sadie, Jack, Logan and Hunter, look for the rest of the books in the series, including:

Issued to the Bride One Airman
Issued to the Bride One Marine
Issued to the Bride One Sniper
Issued to the Bride One Soldier

Also, don't miss Cora Seton's other Chance Creek series, the Cowboys of Chance Creek, the Heroes of Chance Creek, and the SEALs of Chance Creek

The Cowboys of Chance Creek Series:

The Cowboy Inherits a Bride (Volume 0)
The Cowboy's E-Mail Order Bride (Volume 1)
The Cowboy Wins a Bride (Volume 2)
The Cowboy Imports a Bride (Volume 3)
The Cowgirl Ropes a Billionaire (Volume 4)
The Sheriff Catches a Bride (Volume 5)
The Cowboy Lassos a Bride (Volume 6)

The Cowboy Rescues a Bride (Volume 7)

The Cowboy Earns a Bride (Volume 8)

The Cowboy's Christmas Bride (Volume 9)

The Heroes of Chance Creek Series:

The Navy SEAL's E-Mail Order Bride (Volume 1)

The Soldier's E-Mail Order Bride (Volume 2)

The Marine's E-Mail Order Bride (Volume 3)

The Navy SEAL's Christmas Bride (Volume 4)

The Airman's E-Mail Order Bride (Volume 5)

The SEALs of Chance Creek Series:

A SEAL's Oath

A SEAL's Vow

A SEAL's Pledge

A SEAL's Consent

Visit Cora's website at www.coraseton.com

Find Cora on Facebook at facebook.com/CoraSeton

Sign up for my newsletter HERE.

www.coraseton.com/sign-up-for-my-newsletter

Prologue

Four months ago

O N THE FIRST of February, General Augustus Reed entered his office at USSOCOM at MacDill Air Force Base in Tampa, Florida, placed his battered leather briefcase on the floor, sat down at his wide, wooden desk and pulled a sealed envelope from a drawer. It bore the date written in his wife's beautiful script, and the General ran his thumb over the words before turning it over and opening the flap.

He pulled out a single page and began to read.

Dear Augustus,

It's time to think of our daughters' future, beginning with Cass.

The General nodded. Spot on, as usual; he'd been thinking about Cass a lot these days. Thinking about all the girls. They'd run yet another of his overseers off Two Willows, his wife's Montana ranch, several months ago, and he'd been forced to replace him with a man he didn't know. There was a long-standing feud between him and the girls over who should run the place, and the truth was, they were wearing him down. Ten overseers in eleven years; that had to be some kind of a record, and no ranch could function well under those circumstances. Still, he'd be damned if he was going to put a passel of rebellious daughters in charge, even if they were adults now. It took a man's steady hand to run such a large spread.

Unfortunately, it was beginning to come clear that Bob Finchley didn't possess that steady hand. Winter in Chance Creek was always a tricky time, but in the months since Finchley had taken the helm, they'd lost far too many cattle. The General's spies in the area reported the ranch was looking run-down, and his daughters hadn't been seen much in town. The worst were the rumors about Cass and Finchley—that they were dating. The General didn't like that at all—not if the man couldn't run the ranch competently—and he'd asked for confirmation, but so far it hadn't come. Finchley always had a rational explanation for the loss of cattle, and he never said a word about Cass, but the General knew something wasn't right and he was already looking for the man's replacement.

Our daughter runs a tight ship, and I'm sure she's been invaluable on the ranch.

He had to admit what Amelia wrote was true. Cass was an organizational wizard. She kept her sisters, the house and the family accounts in line, and not for the first time he wondered if he should have encouraged

Cass to join the Army back when she had expressed interest. She'd mentioned the possibility once or twice as a teenager, but he'd discouraged her. Not that he didn't think she'd make a good soldier; she'd have made a fine one. It was the thought of his five daughters scattered to the wind that had guided his hand. He couldn't stomach that. He needed his family in one place, and he'd done what it took to keep her home. That wasn't much: a suggestion her sisters needed her to watch over them until they were of age, a mention of tasks undone on the ranch, a hint she and the others would inherit one day and shouldn't she watch over her inheritance? It had done the trick.

Maybe he'd been wrong.

But if Cass had gone, wouldn't the rest of them have followed her?

He'd been able to stop sending guardians for the girls when Cass turned twenty-one five years ago, much to everyone's relief. His daughters had liked those about as little as they liked the overseers. He'd hoped when he dispensed of the guardians, the girls would feel they had enough independence, but that wasn't the case; they still wanted control of the ranch.

Cass is a loving soul with a heart as big as Montana, but she's cautious, too. I'll wager she's beginning to think there isn't a man alive she can trust with it.

The General sighed. His girls hadn't confided in him in years—especially about matters of the heart—something he was glad Amelia couldn't know. The truth was his daughters had spent far too much time as teenagers hatching plots to cast off guardians and overseers to have much of a social life. They'd been obsessed with being independent, and there were stretches of time when they'd managed it—and managed to run the show with no one the wiser for months. In order to pull that off, they'd kept to themselves as much as possible. He'd only recently begun to hear rumblings about men and boyfriends. Unfortunately, none of the girls were picking hardworking men who might make a future at Two Willows; they were picking flashy, fly-by-night troublemakers.

Like Bob Finchley.

He couldn't understand it. He wanted that man out of there. Now. Trouble was, when your daughters ran off so many overseers it made it hard to get a new one to sign on. He had yet to find a suitable replacement.

> *Without a career off the ranch, Cass won't get out much. She might not ever meet the man who's right for her. I want you to step in. Send her a man, Augustus. A good man.*

A good man. Those weren't easy to come by in this world. The right man for Cass would need to be strong to hold his own in a relationship with her. He'd need to be fair and true, or he wouldn't be worthy of her. He'd need some experience ranching.

A lot of experience ranching.

The General stopped to ponder that. He'd read something recently about a man with a lot of experience ranching. A good man who'd gotten into a spot of trouble. He remembered thinking he ought to get a second chance—with a stern warning not to screw up again. A Navy SEAL, wasn't it? He'd look up the document when he was done.

He returned to the letter.

Now here's the hard part, darling. You can't order him to marry Cass any more than you can order Cass to marry him. You're a cunning old codger when you want to be, and it'll take all your deviousness to pull this off. Set the stage. Introduce the players.

Let fate do the rest.

I love you and I always will,
Amelia

Set the stage. Introduce the players.

The General read through the letter a second time, folded it carefully, slid it back into the envelope and added it to the stack in his deep, right-hand bottom drawer. He steepled his hands and considered his options. Amelia was right; he needed to do something to make sure his daughters married well. But they'd rebelled against him for years, so he couldn't simply assign them husbands, as much as he'd like to. They'd never allow the interference.

But if he made them think they'd chosen the right men themselves…

He nodded. That was the way to go about it.

In fact…

The General chuckled. Sometime in the next six

months, his daughters would stage another rebellion and evict Bob Finchley from the ranch. He could just about guarantee it, even if Cass was currently dating the man. Sooner or later he'd go too far trying to boss them around, and Cass and the others would flip their lids.

When they did, he'd be ready for them with a replacement they'd never be able to shake. One trained to combat enemy forces by good ol' Uncle Sam himself. A soldier in the Special Forces might do it. Or maybe even a Navy SEAL...

This wasn't the work of a moment, though. He'd need time to put the players in place. Cass wasn't the only one who'd need a man—a good man—to share her life.

Five daughters.

Five husbands.

Amelia would approve.

The General opened the bottom left-hand drawer of his desk, and mentally counted the remaining envelopes that sat unopened in another stack, all dated in his wife's beautiful script. Ten years ago, after Amelia passed away, Cass had forwarded him a plain brown box filled with envelopes she'd received from the family lawyer. The stack in this drawer had dwindled compared to the opened ones in the other drawer.

What on earth would he do when there were none left?

Chapter One

Present day

NAVY SEAL BRIAN Lake was already at work in the large square office he shared with four other men at USSOCOM when Logan Hughes walked in whistling, plunked himself down at his desk and set a tall takeout cup of coffee near the monitor of his computer. A barrel of a man from Idaho, with biceps as big as cantaloupes, the marine was the type to act first and never ask questions later.

"Hello, baby girl!" Logan kissed the palm of his hand with a loud smack and slapped it against the photograph of a dark-haired young woman with blue eyes that hung on the wall nearby. Then he pulled a breakfast sandwich out of a paper bag and began to eat.

"Don't ever let the General see you do that," Brian warned him. He could only imagine the highly decorated officer's reaction to the gesture. General Augustus Reed—or *the General*, as everyone called him, as if he was the only one there'd ever been—oversaw the Joint Special Task Force for Inter-Branch Communication

Clarity, which comprised the five men who worked in this office, representing four branches of the military.

The room was filled with desks and a large central table, and the General had decorated its walls with a strange mixture of military and personal items. There were charts, graphs, print-outs and maps, as you'd expect, but the General had also seen fit to hang a multitude of framed photographs of Two Willows—his Montana cattle ranch—and his family.

This wasn't completely surprising. In the month since he'd been here, Brian had noticed that all of the rooms the General spent time in contained mementos of his home. No one doubted he loved his family's ranch—and his deceased wife, whose gentle visage stared out of innumerable photographs in the General's office and quarters. There was far more speculation about his daughters, however, all five of whom figured prominently in photographs hung around this room— including Lena Reed, who had the misfortune to hang next to Logan's desk. Everyone at USSOCOM knew about the rift between the General and his daughters. None of the girls—women now—had been seen on the base for years, since Cass Reed, the eldest—and most beautiful in Brian's opinion, with her long, thick waves of blond hair and wide-set blue eyes—had pitched a fit at a military function nine years ago.

Brian and the others had discussed where the General got his photographs, since rumor had it he seldom went home, either. Spies, they'd concluded, only half joking. The General might not be father material, but he was excellent at marshaling his forces and collecting intelligence.

"Don't let him see me eat?" Logan asked, eyes wide with mock confusion.

"For fuck's sake," Lieutenant Jack Sanders said from his desk across the room. "Do you two have to do the same damn routine every morning?"

Jack was in the Special Forces, and a cagier man Brian had never met. As far as he could tell, Sanders had dropped fully grown out of the sky. Brian had looked up all of the other men in the task force when he first arrived, and while several had done what they could to keep a low profile, it was as if Sanders simply didn't exist outside the military. He spoke without a discernible accent, seemed to carry an encyclopedia in his head and never lost his cool. Brian wasn't a man who spooked easily, but when Sanders was around, he kept an eye on him.

"It's tradition," Logan said. "And now that you've interrupted us, we'll have to do it all over again." He turned to the photograph. "Hello, baby girl!" He kissed the palm of his hand and slapped it up against Lena's cheek. "Anyway, don't tell me you've never thought about it."

"About making an ass out of myself? Sure, I've thought about it," Jack said. "I've just managed to restrain myself."

Brian noticed he was staring at the photograph nearest to his own desk, though. Alice Reed, the third-oldest of the General's daughters, stared back at him, her mouth curved into an enigmatic smile, her high cheekbones, crystalline blue eyes and the slight quirk of one eyebrow making her look like an otherworldly creature caught just before she slipped away into the ether. Brian could see the attraction. He had no doubt Alice was stunning in person, but he didn't go for otherworldly or enigmatic. Cass's frank, slightly challenging air as she faced the camera in the photo nearest to him drew his gaze over and over again each day he spent here. The General's oldest daughter was… hot.

More than hot. Sweet, sexy… luscious…

She was as all-American as apple pie, with a mass of wavy blond hair, a sweet, heart-shaped face and a trim body, but it was her mouth that caught Brian's attention. That was a mouth made for kissing—for taking your time with on the way to even better things.

But that didn't make her any more available to him than Lena was to Logan.

"Time to get to work," he said, wanting to distract himself from thoughts of what could never be. Maybe someday he'd find himself a woman like Cass to marry, but first he'd have to get out of the mess he'd gotten himself into. That meant making a good impression here at USSOCOM.

"But so much nicer to stare at the young lassies— not to mention that grand green ranch the General has surrounded us with," Connor O'Riley said in a fake, lilting Irish accent. With hair so dark it was almost black, blue eyes and a healthy sense of humor, Connor was a pararescueman in the Air Force and always had a woman or two on the back burner. "Not sure which I'm more in love with—those thousand head of cattle or little Sadie Reed, here." He did Logan one better and kissed Sadie, an auburn-haired young woman with green eyes, who looked about as Irish as Connor claimed he was, full on her photographed lips. To Brian, Sadie Reed seemed more cautious than her sisters. Wise and innocent all at once, in a way he couldn't make out. Presented with Connor in real life, he had a feeling she might run in the other direction.

Connor, who'd spent as much time around horses as Brian had when he was young, had grown up on a Texas spread so big it could have been its own state. But he wasn't a son of the family who owned it, and wouldn't inherit any part of it. His father had been a foreman, and wanted him to be the same. Connor wanted to be his own man, so he'd joined the Air Force. Like Brian, he dreamed of saving enough money to buy his own spread.

"Two Willows is a sexy bit of property," Logan agreed, taking another large bite of his sandwich.

"Two Willows is a ranch a man could be proud to own."

They all fell silent at Hunter Powell's pronouncement. Another Navy SEAL—and sniper—who outranked Brian and had served longer than he had, Powell came across as a laid-back Southern boy from Louisiana, who spoke in an accent so thick it made up for Sanders's lack of one. Hunter liked to play the good 'ol boy, but he was whip smart and an uncanny shot. Brian wondered how he'd ended up here. Hunter could get downright talkative about military equipment, tactics and so on, but he didn't talk much about his hopes and dreams. Like the rest of them, he'd grown up on a ranch.

Like the rest of them, he hadn't a hope in hell of ever owning one himself.

They'd discovered that commonality in the first week they'd worked together. None of them had been happy to land here at USSOCOM doing desk work. Especially when they quickly realized that work was bogus. JSOC had an arsenal of men and women working on inter-branch communication. Brian and the rest of the task force were redundant.

Useless.

Every morning they entered the office to find more manuals and printouts to look through. They'd been tasked with finding contradictions between them, as if the five elite warriors in the room were little better than copy editors. Brian would have taken on any other job if he could, but that was just it: none of them had a choice.

That was something else they shared in common.

The fact was, they were killing time on the way to being ushered out of the military gently but firmly by an apparatus that had made it all too clear that if they objected, things would get ugly, fast.

Brian had to chuckle privately when he remembered the suspicious way they'd regarded each other when they'd all arrived at USSOCOM. He and Hunter were the only ones from the same military branch, and all five of them had secrets to hide. Still, it didn't take long for them to realize the similarities in their situations. Each of them a highly trained officer in one of the special branches of the military.

Each of them a fuck-up.

"I don't mind working," Jack said. "If the General would give us some real work."

Brian knew what he meant. He'd always considered himself to be diligent in his duties, despite the mistake that had landed him here, but he'd spent more time staring at the photographs of the General's ranch—and at Cass, if he was honest—than he'd spent finding discrepancies. There weren't many to find. These publications had been thoroughly vetted by JSOC already.

Several feet away from him, two large, poster-size frames hung on the wall. One was an aerial shot of the General's ranch. The main house was set back from a two-lane country highway. Behind it stood another structure he figured had to be some kind of large garage. Some distance away was a cluster of buildings that had to be barns, stables, that sort of thing. All around them were large pastures, brushy thickets and pine forests. The second frame held a topographical map of the same area, structures, terrain, roads and trails marked out in detail. How many hours had he stared at those two hangings in the past month?

Far too many. He had no doubt he could traverse the General's ranch blindfolded.

Cass's photograph hung just below the topographical map. Just out of easy reach, although if he leaned forward he could slap a kiss onto her lips with his hand the way Logan had Lena's.

If only he could own a ranch like Two Willows, he thought for the thousandth time. If he had to leave the Navy SEALs, he could find contentment on a place like that. A wife like Cass Reed wouldn't hurt, either.

But neither of those scenarios was likely. He'd recently learned his brother, Grant, was walking the same path as their deadbeat father, who'd lost their ranch when Brian was young. Grant had racked up tens of thousands of dollars in debt and called Brian for help, afraid his wife, Marissa, would leave him if she found out. Brian, like the fool he was, had given his brother a substantial loan, knowing all the while he'd never see that money again. Now he was even further away from his dream of owning property. And Grant had likely gambled most of the money away again. The Lakes didn't attract happiness.

He'd wondered too many times what would happen when his time with the SEALs was up and he had to go back to civilian life.

He wanted land. He wanted a ranch like the one his father had lost. He wanted horses. Cattle. Wide open spaces. A family—

Brian cut off that chain of thoughts.

No ranch for him. Not without another decade or more in the military. A real spread cost a bundle these days. Far more than he'd managed to put away so far—

even before that loan to Grant. No wife, either, until he could give her a good life and keep her safe. Until he could prove to himself he wasn't a fuck-up like his father or brother. Better for him to stay single. In the military.

If only the military wanted him.

"The General can't get angry about me flirting with his daughter if he isn't going to give me anything else to do," Logan said.

"Haven't you worked it out yet?" Connor asked him. "They've put us on a shelf. They're keeping us out of trouble until we're gone. They don't have anything *for* you to do."

"It doesn't make sense." Jack's frustration was clear. "You'd think they'd get what they can from us. Send us somewhere we'd see some real action. Give us a chance to make it up to them."

"That's what I can't understand," Logan said. "I've worked with men who've done far worse than what I did and been promoted—"

"We're here. No use complaining."

Hunter's thick accent wrapped around them like a warm blanket, but his words were stern. Brian knew the man wasn't any happier about being pulled from the action than the rest of them were.

"Nothing makes sense anymore," Logan went on. "I mean, look at this room. Are we fixing the communication problem between branches, or are we preparing to invade the General's ranch? We've got maps, mug shots, dossiers…"

Connor nearly spit out the coffee he'd just taken a sip of. "Shit, he's right. I hadn't thought about it like that." He gestured to all the framed photos and prints on the walls. "Look at all the intel."

"Those aren't dossiers," Jack said scornfully.

"What do you call them then?" Logan pointed at the photo collages positioned around the room. Each of the General's daughters had one—a collection of shots depicting her at various activities. Lena's showed her herding cattle, riding horses, shooting pistols at targets, mucking out a stable. Sadie's were mostly set in the ranch's extensive gardens. Alice seemed to favor sewing. In several she held elaborate costumes out at arm's length, but she was also to be seen reading, dancing and riding. Josephine, the youngest daughter, had an animal with her in every shot, from cats and dogs to chickens, cattle and horses.

Brian had looked at all of them over the course of the month, but it was Cass's that held his attention. Her collage showed a woman who worked hard keeping a home together for her family. Cass cooking at the stove, laughing while seated at the head of a table of friends and family, fixing the lock on a door, repairing the back porch, riding with her sisters, bent over paperwork at a desk, collecting eggs while a chicken looked on.

"He's right," Brian said slowly. Staring at these photos, he'd learned a variety of facts about the ranch's inhabitants and had built impressions of each of them in his mind. He knew the layout of the ranch, knew the network of roads and tracks that crisscrossed it, had a sense of the size of the cattle operation...

"So, what—you think the General is going to send us on a mission to Montana? He's just a family man," Jack said scornfully.

"A family man who never goes home," Hunter said suddenly.

The door burst open just as the rest of them jumped into the argument, and the General himself strode into the room. In the sudden silence, he waved them to the table before they could stand up. "Gather round, men. Sit down, sit down." He took a position standing at the head of the large table and Brian and the others hurried to seat themselves around it. Brian wondered if the rest of them were worried that the General had overheard them.

He sure was. He was working to stop the process that was kicking him out of the military. He wanted to stay—needed to. He hadn't saved up near enough money to buy a ranch.

The General paced while they watched. He seemed to be mulling something over, and must have come to a conclusion, because he turned and nodded once. "Guess what, boys? You've earned yourselves a mission. A special mission." He caught the gaze of each man in turn, his hazel eyes glinting with a mixture of triumph and contempt. "One that fits both the skills the United States military has endowed you with, and the blatant, reckless idiocy you've seen fit to display ever since." He grinned his raffish, trademark grin. "Brace yourselves. Your future's about to slap you upside the head."

Brian swallowed against a sudden sense of unease.

"What's that supposed to mean, sir?" Logan asked.

"That means this mission is permanent. It's a one-way ticket out of the military…without a stop in the stockade."

Several men shifted uncomfortably at this new reminder of the ties that linked them. They'd all made mistakes, but none of them had paid for them…

Yet.

Brian knew that was about to change, regardless of what the General said next. He didn't like the sound of *permanent*. If he couldn't figure out how to stay in the SEALs, he'd never reach his goal. He didn't want to hire on to some civilian security corporation. That wasn't his style at all.

"Are you talking about a suicide mission, sir?" Jack joked, bringing Brian back to the present.

The general's eyes narrowed. "Not suicide, although seeing as none of you wanted to leave the military, maybe it'll seem mighty close. Tell me, Lake, you got a girl?"

"A girl, sir?" Brian sputtered. Why was the General interested in his love life all of a sudden?

"A girl. A woman. Someone to keep you warm at night."

"No, sir." Brian didn't have any of those. Hadn't gotten more than three dates into a relationship in years. He supposed a shrink would blame it on mommy issues. As in, he didn't have one. After his father's gambling had lost them their small ranch, they'd moved into a house in town. Late one Saturday night his mother had run to a convenience mart five blocks from home and walked into a robbery gone wrong. She got shot when the police intervened. His dad lost the two hundred bucks he'd bet on the Raiders. Tough night all around.

"What exactly is this all about, sir?" Connor asked the General, leaning forward and setting his elbows on the table as if to better hear the answer.

"You've heard about my contentious relationship with my daughters." Nearly sixty, Reed still evinced the vigor of a much younger man, but several times in the past few weeks Brian had thought he'd glimpsed something behind his veneer of strength and determination. Something far harder to define. Disquiet, maybe.

Regret.

No one answered him. For the General to speak about his family—and mention a problem regarding his girls—was unprecedented.

The General tapped his finger on the table, a gesture uncharacteristically indecisive. After a moment, he straightened. "Last November I installed a new overseer on my ranch. Name of Bob Finchley. Today I received notice that my girls ran him off. Which means my ranch—one of the largest in Montana—is being over-seen by a passel of women and a bunch of hands I've never met. Hands whose reputations aren't stellar. My girls do their best to keep me out of the loop, but something's rotten in Denmark—this isn't the usual case of them wanting to run the place themselves. Profits are way down. The hands Finchley hired are from out of town—no one can vouch for them. And there are rumblings in Chance Creek I haven't heard before. Crime's up. There's more trouble than usual. I don't know what's going on, but I want to find out."

"Sir, what does this have to do with me?" Brian asked.

"Keep a lid on it and you'll find out," the General snapped. He straightened. "I'm giving you your orders, all of you. You will infiltrate Two Willows, root out every last insurgent who's wormed his way in there, secure the property, impose martial law and marry the natives. Do you understand me?"

Brian stilled. So did all the others. He opened his mouth to speak. Closed it again.

"Sir—what did you just say?" Connor's slow-spoken question caused the General's frown to deepen. Two Willows was the name of the General's ranch. Which meant—if Brian wasn't mistaken—the natives were his daughters.

He swallowed in a suddenly dry throat and willed himself not to turn and look at Cass's photograph. The man had lost his marbles. Possibly overnight. Up until now Reed hadn't demonstrated any kind of mental illness, but this wasn't normal behavior, any way you sliced it.

"You heard me." The General didn't budge. Just stared back at them. Was he enjoying this?

Logan rolled his eyes. "With all due respect, General, it's the twenty-first century—you can't order people to marry."

"Like hell I can't." The General fixed him with a look as sharp as flint. "But not you. Not yet. Lake, you're up first. You'll marry Cass."

"Why do I have to go first... sir?" he added belatedly. He hadn't meant to say any of that out loud. It had slipped out while he struggled to get a hold of his emotions. He hadn't expected to ever get the chance to be in the same place as Cass Reed, let alone have the General order him to marry her. It was one thing to lust over a photograph. Another thing altogether to be presented with a woman and ordered to get hitched.

"Because I said so. You're always eager to scout ahead, right?"

That was a direct hit. Brian had landed in the shithouse for an over-eager move on his last mission in the Middle East. Patience not being his particular virtue, he'd decided, after cooling his heels for ten days with the rest of his team waiting for conditions to be right, to get a look at the situation from a different viewpoint. It was a good move, in that he'd spotted their target and taken him out with one clean shot, but the rest of the mission had been a disaster. Brian and his men had to call in an airstrike to escape, and an unlucky hit took out a nearby market square. It was empty at the time, but that didn't stop the international watchdogs from howling about civilian targets.

Brian rubbed his jaw with his hand. "How the hell am I supposed to make your daughter marry me, sir?" None of this could be real. He'd never asked a more ridiculous question in his life.

The General gave him a long, knowing look before he flipped open a file on the table, and Brian wondered again if the man knew far more about what had gone on in this room over the last few weeks than he'd been letting on. "I'm giving you a cover story. My house needs work. While you're fixing it, you can get the lay of the land and see what's what. Get rid of the ranch hands who are still under Finchley's sway. Woo my daughter. The Navy spent a hell of a lot of money training you, Lake. You'll figure it out. The others will follow."

Shifts in body position and the scraping of chair legs over the linoleum floor belied the general's assurance.

"I don't know about everyone else, but I think I'll sit this square dance out, sir," Connor drawled.

"Oh, really? How about I re-open the investigation into the shitstorm you made out of your last mission? Is that what you want, O'Riley?"

The room went absolutely silent. All of them were waiting for the results of investigations into their conduct. If Connor's had been suspended, did that mean…?

"That's what I thought," the General said. "And yes—for the moment, all investigations have been suspended. I can change that with a single phone call."

Reed sighed gustily. Brian sat tense with the possibility that the investigation—and charges—he'd dreaded for months might disappear. He'd do about anything to make that happen.

"Now listen up," the General went on, each word as harsh as sandpaper over steel. Brian held very still. It was clear the man had reached his limit. "You all don't quite seem to be getting the picture, so let's try this one more time. Each and every one of you is sitting in this room because you've fucked things up in such a major way the US military wants you to go crawl under a rug and disappear. They've handed the problem to me. So I'm holding up a rug, and you're damned well going to crawl under it." He looked them each in the eye in turn. "I'm not asking you to a square dance, ladies. I'm giving you a mission. A final mission. One that will end with the termination of any relationship between you and the US military. But that termination will be honorable. At least on paper. You will take it. You will go to Montana. You will get my ranch in hand. You will marry my daughters. Do you understand me?"

Brian wasn't sure he understood any of this, but that didn't matter, did it? Despite everything, he'd do what the General said if it meant crawling out from under the hell of the investigation into his actions. He'd never meant to do anything to blacken the eye of the United States Navy. If this whole episode could disappear, he'd be one happy man.

But marriage—that was different. Like the General said—it was permanent. Was that fair to a woman like Cass? After all, his father had good as killed his mother, and Grant was about to ruin his wife's life. What if he fucked up like that and took Cass, the sweet woman he only knew from photographs, down with him?

What choice did he have but to give it a shot, though? And who better to try it with than Cass Reed?

If the General wasn't pulling his leg in some massive practical joke, that was.

But the General didn't look like he was joking. And if Brian was honest, Cass's photograph had tempted him since the day he walked in here. The collage that depicted her interests resonated with him as if she'd been handpicked for him.

Clarity crashed over Brian, and he sucked in a breath. It was the other way around, wasn't it? Brian had been handpicked for Cass.

By the General.

Months ago.

Had the others realized that?

It looked like they were beginning to. He saw their surreptitious glances at the General's daughters' photos hung around the room.

"Because when you're done," the General continued, leaning forward again to make his point, "if you haven't figured out the math yet, you'll be my sons-in-law. Which means the five of you stand to inherit one of the biggest, most productive ranches in Chance Creek County, Montana. This mission beginning to look a little more palatable?"

Holy shit. Brian's hands flexed, then clenched. He hadn't taken in that part fully. A fifth of an established ranch with no buy-in costs and no risk? Brian gave Cass's photograph another look. "Yeah," he heard himself say. "It's a little more palatable." He ducked when the General chucked a manual at him. "I mean, it would be an honor to marry your daughter, sir!"

"That's better. Get packed. You leave today." The General strode toward the door.

Brian stood up with the others as he passed them.

"You're crazy," Logan said when the General was gone. "Lake, if you do this you're cracked in the head. No matter the alternative."

Maybe. Or maybe this mission was the answer to all his problems.

CASS REED PLACED the last of the breakfast dishes into the draining rack and let the soapy water out of the sink, eyeing the dripping faucet with resignation. It was worse today, which meant she'd have to pull out her tools, take it apart and find the problem. As if she didn't have enough to do already. Sometimes she felt Two Willows was falling apart faster than she could fix it.

The window on the second-story landing still had a piece of cardboard taped into its frame to replace a missing pane. The tiling in the shower on the first floor had given way, which meant another leak was creating havoc behind the wall. The roof was also leaking in three places that Cass knew of, which reminded her she needed to check the buckets she'd positioned around the attic—there'd been a light rain the previous night. One of these days she'd have to crawl out on the roof and repair the shingles.

Too bad she was afraid of heights.

Things didn't used to be like this—not when her mother was alive. Or maybe they had been and she'd just been too young and oblivious to realize how hard her mother had worked to keep up with the large old house they lived in. Cass wasn't sure. One thing she did know was that at twenty-six, she couldn't stack up to Amelia when it came to handling problems with panache—or parenting her sisters. She'd thanked God when she'd turned twenty-one and persuaded her father to stop sending useless guardians to watch over them. None of the women who'd come to help could fill Amelia's shoes. They were there for an easy paycheck, something the General never seemed to understand.

Cass was the one who'd done the real work around the house since her mother passed away when she was fifteen. As her mother lay dying, she and her sisters had taken turns visiting the hospital and keeping an eye on the ranch. It hadn't occurred to Cass until then that her mother had foreseen what had happened to her, as she'd foreseen so much else over the course of her life; although the stroke had come out of nowhere, her mother had been prepared for it. She seemed peaceful in those last few days, even as all her daughters came apart. Cass had tried so hard to match her serenity, but for the most part she'd failed.

"It's up to you now to keep your sisters and father safe," Amelia had struggled to say in her slurred speech. "You'll have to be the anchor that keeps this family together, and it won't be easy, but you're strong, Cass. Stronger than you know. The key is the ranch. The land. That's where the power is. No matter what happens, you have to stay on the ranch."

"Like you did?"

Amelia had understood immediately what she was asking. Did she need to physically stay on the ranch at all times, like her mother had ever since her father joined the Army? All the girls had been aware of why Amelia stayed within the confines of her property unless the General was by her side. She'd made some sort of pact with God—or maybe with the land itself. If she stayed, the General would survive the dangers he'd faced throughout his career. If she left, all bets were off.

Ridiculous, like everything else that happened at Two Willows. And yet—

Despite a long, dangerous career in the Army, the General was still alive.

Even if her mother wasn't.

"There are five of you to share the burden," Amelia had told her. "But Cass… let it mostly be you. I know Alice feels the things to come far more than you do, but she doesn't have the determination you have. You're the oldest. The strongest. And you love the ranch."

"I do," Cass had assured her. She'd taken on that burden willingly, and her sisters had shared it without question. In the past eleven years there hadn't been a single moment when at least one Reed woman wasn't on the property. Until the General came home, there never would.

Would the General ever come home again?

Cass pushed the question aside. It didn't matter. She was here to stay, anyway. And she needed to keep her sisters in line. She'd struggled mightily to do so when they were teenagers. Now it was a lost cause.

It was her fault, Cass admitted to herself. She'd been distracted ever since their latest overseer had arrived last November. Bob Finchley had tricked her well and thoroughly, and they were all paying for her mistake now. He'd pursued her with a vengeance, and Cass, who'd had little time or opportunity for dating and men before now, had been swept off her feet by his flattery and attention.

Every time she thought about it she wanted to die of humiliation.

She'd believed everything he'd said as he accompanied her day and night. She'd told him all of her hopes and dreams. Confessed everything about her estrangement from her father—and the way he'd squashed her dream of joining the Army when she'd dared to express it, even though she'd known she wouldn't follow through. How could she when she was needed here? But she'd wanted him to say, "Yes, Cass, you'd make a fine soldier."

Of course he hadn't.

That wasn't the worst, though. In the end, she'd slept with Bob—the man who'd been stealing from her family the whole time. It was only luck that led her to discover the fact he was cooking the books. He'd been hinting he meant to propose to her soon—and she would have said yes if she hadn't pieced it all together. She still didn't know if he had meant to marry her and try to eventually take the ranch for himself, or string her along while he siphoned all the cash he could from it before leaving her in the dust.

She wasn't sure which was worse, either. All she knew was she was glad he was gone. Even if he'd left their finances in ruins.

If only Bob had gone farther away, though, she thought as she examined the leaky faucet again. He was still in town, and she thought he might be tracking her movements, because she bumped into him far too often. Several people had congratulated her on her engagement to him in the past week. She wouldn't put it past Bob to have started the rumors himself. She was doing everything she could to dispel them, but it worried her; what was he up to? Between his continued presence in town, her sisters' waywardness and the way the house was falling down around her head, Cass was beginning to think she was losing her mind.

Which wasn't an option. Not today, anyway, she reminded herself firmly, going to the large walk-in pantry where she kept her tool kit on the bottom shelf next to the cleaning supplies and "how to" books.

"I'm off to Westfield," Alice called as she crossed the kitchen on her way to the back door. "Be back for dinner."

Cass exited the pantry in a hurry to confront her. The third oldest at twenty-four, Alice was the beauty of the family. Artistic, almost other-worldly in her appearance, she made men young and old stop and stare. She had a way of sensing things before they happened, too, but for someone with the second sight, Cass thought she was awfully blind to her current boyfriend's faults.

"You'll be at Westfield all that time?" She took in

the garment bags draped over Alice's arm. She must be going to the other ranch for a dress fitting. The women at Westfield kept Alice busy sewing the Regency costumes they wore. Sometimes Cass wished she could go stay at their Jane Austen bed and breakfast and never come home again.

But that wasn't possible.

"I'm going out with Howie afterward." Alice quickly turned to go.

Just as Cass had predicted. "Did he ever explain what he was doing with your car?" Cass knew she was overly suspicious after her own disastrous relationship with Bob, but recently Howie's behavior was raising all kinds of red flags.

"I already told you—he had to pick something up in Silver Falls. It was important. I don't see why you're making such a big fuss."

"Why didn't he take his truck?"

"It was in the shop."

Cass didn't like it. Something wasn't sitting right with her about Howie these days, but she knew from experience Alice wouldn't tolerate an inquisition. Howie was the first man her sister had seriously dated, and she'd fallen for him hard in the past month.

Cass couldn't blame her. Howie was handsome and a lot of fun. If he was secretive now and then, or borrowed her sister's Chevy without asking, who was she to say that was a problem? Still, she worried. None of them knew what they were doing around men. The General treated them like something he'd found on the bottom of his shoe. He alternated between ignoring them and imposing his will from USSOCOM headquarters as if they were a rogue nation he'd been tasked with governing since they couldn't be trusted to govern themselves.

"See you later." Alice slipped away and shut the back door behind her. Cass stood in kitchen, her arms crossed over her chest and raised her eyes to the high, whitewashed ceiling. "Mama, if you've got any ideas, now's the time to let me in on them. Because I don't know how to get her away from that man."

She got no answer, aside from the ticking of the grandfather clock in the central hall. She was alone in this mess, just as she'd been since she was fifteen.

Time to fix that faucet.

But before she could return to the task, Sadie, who was twenty-two, clattered down the stairs and called out, "I'm going shopping. I'll be back by dinner time. Need anything?"

Cass's shoulders slumped. Shopping—again? Sadie did that a lot these days, and it terrified Cass—they didn't have money to spare. She knew she should tell her sisters that, but so far she hadn't been able to make herself confess. She was the one in charge of the budget, and she was the one who'd been sleeping with the man who'd stolen more than thirty grand from their coffers, from what Cass could piece together. She needed to tell her sisters. And the General, for that matter. But what if the General took the ranch away from them? He'd threatened to do that several times before, and she couldn't let that happen. This was their home. Two Willows was special. They needed it. The General needed it, too, though he didn't seem to realize that.

"What are you shopping for?" she asked Sadie.

"Shoes. My garden clogs are gone. I've looked for them everywhere."

"Garden clogs don't up and disappear on their own. Look again."

"I have. Seriously, Cass—I've looked everywhere I can think of. So has Lena. They're gone."

Cass shook her head, but given how much food her sister provided from the plot she tended, plus the extra income she made from the farm stand produce and the herbal cures she sold to passersby, she guessed her sister needed a new pair. But Cass's gut told her Sadie wasn't being entirely truthful. She had no doubt her sister would come home with new garden clogs, but how many more bags would she carry into the house?

She hadn't been able to force herself to confront her sister about her overspending yet, as much as she needed to. Why would Sadie shop like that except to fill the hole inside her where her parents' love should have been? Her mother was gone and the General might as well be dead, too, for all the attention he gave them. Her once calm, confident, sweet little sister had turned herself inside out chasing Mark Pendergrass, a handsome but hard-edged young man Cass would have banned from Two Willows if she could.

Cass kept grasping for the right thing to say to show

Sadie she was worth so much more than that, but her words always fell on deaf ears. "Easy for you to say," Sadie had retorted the last time Cass told her she didn't need new clothes to look beautiful. "You and Alice are the pretty ones. The rest of us have to fight to get a man."

"No," Cass had wanted to tell her. "That's all wrong." But Sadie was young; her friends shopped and dressed up to attract men. Who was she to put Sadie down? When the credit card bills came due, Cass paid them from their dwindling funds. And racked her brains for other ways to save money.

"Anything else?" Cass found herself saying, despite her resolutions to keep quiet.

"I might buy some other things," Sadie admitted.

"What other things?"

"Clothes, all right? A dress. For tonight."

"Because…?" Cass wasn't sure why she was asking. There was only one thing Sadie would want to do on a Friday night: go out on the town with Mark.

"I work hard. I deserve some new things once in a while." Sadie tossed her auburn curls over her shoulder. Cass read something else in her expression, though. Not just defiance. Guilt.

That was even worse.

Of course Sadie deserved nice things. They all did. But Cass knew this wasn't about fulfilling a feminine desire for something pretty. This was about Sadie trying to keep the attention of a man who picked up and discarded women without thinking twice. Sadie had floated on air the night Mark first asked her to dance at the local watering hole. She'd been desperate ever since to keep him from moving on to his next conquest. She'd taken to wearing sky-high heels, tight clothes and so much war paint Cass had to strangle the urge to march her into a bathroom and scrub it off every time she saw her. Sadie deserved so much better than Mark.

But the heart wanted what the heart wanted.

Cass knew that better than anyone else.

Sadie waited, almost as if she hoped Cass would save her from herself. Amelia would have known exactly what to say to convince Sadie to turn her back on Mark, but Cass couldn't think of anything she hadn't tried before. "I hope you find something lovely," was all she could come up with. Maybe Sadie would catch the attention of some other man when she wore her new dress. A better man.

A man who would stay.

Sadie nodded, her expression tight, and slipped out of the house before Cass could say more. The screen door banged shut behind her. Seconds later a motor started and Sadie drove away in her battered old Ford.

Cass waited for the sound to fade away. Fix the sink, she reminded herself. That was one job she knew she could do. She had a manual. She had tools. When she was done, the faucet would work again.

Unlike anything else.

She had just started on the task when Jo, the baby of the family at twenty-one, came down the stairs, followed by Tabitha, her white cat. While Sadie had been all dolled up for her trip into Billings, Jo was still in her pajamas. Cass knew she'd been up early to do her chores in the barns, but then she'd come home and gone back to bed. Amelia would never have tolerated that kind of behavior.

"Hey, are there any eggs left?" Jo asked breezily as Tabitha headed for her food dish in the corner. "I want some French toast."

"I just finished cleaning up. What time did you get in last night?"

"Don't try to parent me. I'm too old for that." Jo headed for the refrigerator. She brought out the eggs and butter, then found a loaf of bread. Cass bit back the urge to scream. She'd just gotten the place clean again.

"You'd better wash up after yourself."

"Yes, sir." Jo snapped an ironic salute and went back to perusing the contents of the fridge. Cass sighed. Jo used to be someone she could count on. Always a bit of a smart-ass, she used to ally herself with Cass against the others when they were being truly out of control. Now she was every bit as headstrong as they were. It made Cass wish for the days when a batch of kittens could keep Jo occupied for weeks.

Cass consulted the plumbing manual. It wasn't like she didn't know how to change a washer; she'd done it plenty of times. Still, she wanted to make sure she didn't miss a step.

"You'll have to do without the sink," she told Jo, bending down absentmindedly to pet Tabitha, who was now weaving between her feet.

"Guess I won't be able to wash up after all."

Cass bit back an angry retort. "Where were you last night?" God, she sounded like someone's mother. But with her sisters all acting like children, someone had to take charge.

"With Sean. He was showing me his web cam."

"Web cam." Cass consulted the manual again. She never could force herself to like Sean. There was something weaseley about him she couldn't define. She shooed Tabitha gently away and got to work. "What's he need one of those for?"

"To talk to people. He showed me how to work it. Maybe I'll get one, too."

"You can use the camera in your laptop if you want to video chat," Cass pointed out. They didn't all need to go shopping.

"A web cam has better quality. Anyway, I'm going back to his house in a few minutes. Be back for dinner."

"Don't you have more chores?"

"Already did them."

Jo turned back to her French toast, working quickly and humming to herself. That had to mean she was happy, right? Cass slid a look her way, took in her sister's pajamas, the locks of hair escaping from the messy updo she'd secured with a scrunchie. If anything, Jo looked drawn. Probably had stayed up too late. Probably would again tonight.

"You did your chores in your pajamas?"

"People wear pajamas everywhere these days."

Cass gave up.

Ten minutes later, Cass was deep into her job and she didn't realize Jo had gone until she heard the front door slam. She turned around to see that her sister had left the stove top on, the eggs on the counter and a half-cooked piece of toast still in the pan she'd at least had the presence of mind to move to one of the cool burners.

Cass sighed.

It was going to be one of those days.

By the time dinner rolled around, she'd fixed the sink, pulled enough tiles off the wall of the downstairs bathroom to get an idea of the damage behind it, done five loads of laundry—her own plus the sheets and pillowcases in every bedroom of the house—updated the books for the cattle operation, sighing at the way more money kept going out than came in, and vacuumed all three floors of the house. She'd thrown a pot roast and potatoes in the oven and had even pulled out the tallest ladder they owned and rested it against the back of the house.

She hadn't quite gathered the courage to climb it, though. Instead, she'd remembered she hadn't dusted the front room in a week. By the time that was thoroughly done, dinner required all her attention.

For once, no one's boyfriends followed them home to mooch a meal and her sisters congregated in the kitchen before six, waiting for the oven timer to go off. Jo was setting the table. Lena, the second oldest at twenty-five, was washing up at the sink—her hot-tempered boyfriend, Scott Howell, nowhere to be seen, thank goodness. Alice was perched on top of the refrigerator, as usual, a habit Cass had never been able to break her of despite all her efforts. The high kitchen ceiling allowed her plenty of room to sit cross-legged up there. Her sketch pad in her lap, she leaned against the wall, a dreamy expression on her face. All must be right between her and Howie, Cass thought.

Figured.

"Well? What do you think?" Sadie waltzed into the kitchen in the slinkiest black dress Cass had ever seen, except on a movie screen. A scarlet bra peeked out from its low-cut neckline, and it seemed distinctly possible Sadie wasn't wearing anything underneath it.

"It's great—for a hooker," Lena said flatly.

"You're not going to wear that out," Cass said. "Sadie, that's—"

"I don't look like a hooker." Sadie was furious. "It's a gorgeous dress. The woman in the store said they just got it in."

"Why don't you skip wearing clothes altogether? It'd be about the same thing," Jo joked.

Sadie spun on her heel and left without another word. They heard her pound up the stairs and slam her door.

"She'll get arrested in that thing," Lena predicted. "Just you wait."

"No one gets arrested for looking sexy," Jo contradicted. "Who knows, maybe Mark will keep his eyes on her for once instead of hitting on the barmaid."

"He doesn't do that in front of her, does he?" Cass

asked, horrified. No wonder Sadie was making such a spectacle of herself.

"Yes, he does," Jo said. "And worse."

"Well, I hope Sean's not like that."

"Sean's all about me. He thinks I'm beautiful. That's why he wants to—"

"Incoming," Alice said suddenly.

All of them turned toward her, used to her predictive abilities.

"Well? Who is it?" Cass asked impatiently. If it was Mark, she'd give him a piece of her mind no matter what Sadie thought of it.

"I don't know." Alice shook her head, her expression distant, as if she was listening to something only she could hear. "A man." She began to climb down from the refrigerator, a maneuver only Alice could manage so gracefully. A step on the counter, a leap to the floor and she was striding toward the front door. The others followed her, Cass shutting the oven door.

"What's going on?" Sadie asked sulkily when she rejoined them in jeans and a low-cut blouse.

"Someone's coming," Cass told her.

The front door was propped open to let in the breeze and the five of them gathered together behind the screen door to look outside. They waited patiently even though there was no sign of a car on the drive.

"Now," Alice said, a couple of minutes later. Sure enough, Cass spotted a trail of dust that meant a vehicle was making its way down the lane to their house.

"It's a truck, but I don't recognize it." Sadie craned

her neck to see.

"Must be someone we don't know."

Cass felt a twinge of unease. "Why are they coming here?" she asked Alice. Sometimes her sister got flashes about those things, too.

"I'm not sure… something…" Alice shook her head, then turned to Cass in surprise. "He's here for you."

"For me?" They watched as the metallic blue GMC pulled up in front of the house and after a moment, a man got out. He retrieved a bag from the back of the truck, and shut the tailgate. As he stood looking at the house, Cass had the chance to take him in. He was tall, muscular, with dark hair, blue eyes and a strong jaw. Something stirred within Cass she'd thought had died when she discovered Bob's theft—a curl of carnal interest she immediately squashed. She didn't need another man in her life, but this one was so good-looking she'd have to be a saint not to notice him. He was easy in his body, with a confidence that made her curious to get to know him better. He wore faded jeans, cowboy boots that had seen better days, a crisp, white shirt and a hat that was too new for Cass's taste. This was a man both at home on a ranch and a stranger to it. Cass couldn't get a clear read on him. But there was something else about him she recognized immediately, even as she struggled to get her reaction to him under control.

"Military," Lena said under her breath.

"Did something happen to the General?" Jo asked

Alice.

"No."

Cass let out a breath, not knowing why she'd held it. She cared as little for the General as he did for them. Still, if Alice said he was alive, then he was alive, and that was good. She wasn't ready to lose another parent.

"He's coming," Sadie hissed.

As one, all of them except Alice sprang back from the door and hurried into the front room, where Lena took up a position on the rug in front of the coffee table, and got back to tinkering with a lawnmower motor she'd been repairing for the last several days. Sadie and Jo grabbed magazines and plopped themselves on the couch on the far side of the room. Tabitha appeared from the kitchen and hopped up onto Jo's lap. Cass sat down at her desk and reached for a pen.

Their ruse was silly—their dinner was all ready to be served in the kitchen. Cass didn't know why it felt so important to act like this, but it did. She didn't want this man—this stranger—to think she'd been waiting for him.

When footsteps climbed the front steps, Alice opened the screen door. "Welcome to Two Willows. You must be looking for Cass."

Chapter Two

THAT WAS ALICE. Brian recognized her from the photos from the task force office. Behind her he spotted Jo and Sadie sitting on a sofa, and Lena dismantling some kind of engine on a paper-draped coffee table. It wasn't until he shifted his gaze to the woman seated at the desk that he spotted his quarry.

Cass Reed. Twenty-six, homemaker extraordinaire, ex-girlfriend to a departed Two Willows overseer—

Sweet as shoefly pie on a summer's day.

As Cass got to her feet and started toward him, Brian's pulse kicked up a notch. She was every bit as beautiful as he'd known she would be. Even more attractive in real life than she'd been in the photograph he'd stared at this past month. Her silky blond hair hung in waves down her back. Her wide, blue eyes watched him suspiciously from under long lashes. Her mouth— God, her mouth—made him hungry to taste her.

And that body—that curvy, wonderful body… She was wearing jean shorts and a simple top. Her long legs were bare, sun-kissed and distracting. She wore nothing on her feet and Brian flashed back to his early childhood, before his father's gambling had taken over everything—long, carefree summer days on the family's ranch he hadn't thought about in years.

This was the kind of woman he'd missed during his time with the SEALs. Sure, there were pretty girls in bars all over the world ready to take him for a ride, but they lacked what Cass had—that open, fresh, healthy country glow that told a man this was a woman you could make a life with.

Not for the first time Brian wondered why the General would send a man like him—a headstrong fuck-up—to marry his daughter. Cass could have anyone she wanted.

His mission was to make sure she wanted him. Brian decided on the spot he'd give it his all.

"You're right." He removed his hat, shifted it to the hand that held his bag and pushed inside without waiting for an invitation. "I'm here for Cass."

"That's me." Cass held out a hand and looked him over curiously as he shook it firmly.

"I'm Brian Lake." He found himself loath to let her go. But he did. Last thing he wanted was to scare her off before he'd even started. "The General sent me. I'm here to fix the house."

"The house?" Lena said. "Aren't you here to take over the overseer position?"

"No. Just here to fix the house," Brian told her. The General had prepared him for this line of questioning. *If I start by sending another overseer they'll never go for it*, he'd told Brian back at USSOCOM. *They'll foment a rebellion the likes of which hasn't seen since the Civil War. We've got to be sneakier than that. I've got friends who drive by from time to time. They say the place is going to the dogs.*"

Cass's expression hardened. "I see. I'm sorry he sent you all this way for nothing. As you can see, the house is fine."

The General had told him to expect this. "Beg pardon, ma'am, but I'm not asking. I'm telling. The General sent me here to fix the place up, and I'm not leaving until this house is shipshape."

There was a pause as the women took this in.

"You're in the Army?" Lena asked, not bothering to get up.

"No, the Navy. I'm a SEAL."

If he'd hoped that would garner him some respect he was wrong.

"How'd you get mixed up with the General?" Sadie asked suspiciously.

"USSOCOM business." He hoped that stifled any further interest.

"USSOCOM's business is fixing my house?" Cass asked.

"It is for now." Brian dropped his bag on the floor. "I'll be staying awhile." The General had told him to go in guns blazing. *Don't give them an inch. They'll tear you apart*, he'd warned Brian.

"Like hell," Lena said.

"You're not staying here," Cass added.

"Yes, I am." Brian didn't budge, and he made use of every inch of his height to tower over Cass. She glared back at him. "He said if you don't like it, you all can move out."

Just as the General had predicted, that sent a shock wave through them. *They're attached to the ranch*, the General had said. *Wait and see. They stick close to home, just like their mother used to.*

Cass studied him a moment longer, but she must have seen he couldn't be budged. "Fine. You can stay in the guest room—after I call my father to make sure you are who you say you are."

"I'll ring him myself." The General had predicted this, too. He pulled out his phone, tapped on it a few times and handed it to Cass. She took it with a frown.

"It's me," she said into the phone after a moment. "There's a man here." She hesitated. "Yes. Yes. That's right. I've got it all under control, you know—" Another pause. "Fine. But the minute the repairs are done, he's out. Got it?"

She handed the phone back without cutting the connection. Brian lifted it to his ear. "Lake here, General."

"Don't let those girls of mine scare you off. Eyes on the prize. That's some mighty fine ranch land, isn't it?"

"Yes, it is." A mighty fine woman, too, he thought, looking Cass over again. A mighty pissed off one, by the looks of things. "You sure this is where you want me?"

"Don't get all mealy-mouthed, Lake. You don't like Cass, you tell me straight out."

"It's not that," Brian rushed to tell him.

The General chuckled, letting him know he'd betrayed far too much. "Yeah, I thought you might see something you liked there. Make sure she finds you interesting, too. No marriage, no share in the ranch. Got it?"

"Yeah, I got it." Brian hung up on him, disconcerted by the way the General had seen through him. "We good here?" he asked Cass.

She blinked. "That's not the way I would phrase it, but I'm satisfied you're the minion my father meant to send to annoy me. I don't know why I bothered to check. He does this all the time." She turned on her heel and led the way to the staircase.

"He's done this before?" The General had never mentioned that. Brian grabbed the handles of his bag and followed Cass. "Sent you a man?"

She stopped short on the second step and when she turned to face him they were eye to eye. "He's never sent me a *man*," she said waspishly. "He's sent plenty of workers, though. We always run them off. Eventually."

"He's just trying to help, you know."

She made an exasperated sound and continued up the steps. "He's trying to control us, you mean."

"I'm here to fix the house," he said to her retreating back.

She didn't answer until they'd reached a pleasant bedroom on the second floor and she'd ushered him inside. "Then we won't have to put up with each other for very long."

Before he could say another word, she was gone.

When Cass came downstairs again, her sisters had reconvened in the kitchen. "Where are you going?" Alice asked from her perch atop the refrigerator as Cass passed through the room toward the back door.

"What about dinner?" Sadie asked.

"Go ahead without me. I need some fresh air."

"Hey—do you know where the repair manual I left on the coffee table got to? It's gone," Lena called after her.

"Haven't seen it." Cass walked right out the back door, clattered down the three steps that led from the back porch and strode off toward the small shed she'd claimed years ago for her own. It wasn't nearly as big as the carriage house Alice used for her sewing room, or as light as the glass greenhouse where Sadie retreated to when she needed to be alone. It wasn't as pungent as the barns and stables where Lena and Jo spent most of their time, thank God. It was a square, windowless, tidy shed lined with shelves from floor to ceiling, with a large central wooden table— the perfect surface for all kinds of projects.

And if once in a while those projects involved a small amount of pyrotechnics, how was anyone to know?

Cass unlocked the building, switched on the bright overhead light and gathered what she needed. She didn't have time for anything fancy. Matches, bottle rockets. That was enough. She flicked off the light again, shut and locked the door, and made a beeline to her truck. Following the familiar rutted track toward one of the ranch's farthest pastures, she parked, got out, set the bottle rockets on a flat stone and lit their fuses.

Cass calmly strode back to the truck, leaned against the driver's side door and crossed her arms, waiting for them to go off.

Five.

Four.

Three.

Two.

One.

They popped off one after another in crisp, satisfying explosions, allowing her pent-up exasperation to release and drain away. There. That was better.

Time to go home and face the interloper with a clear head.

She'd have him out of here in no time.

Chapter Three

"**S**HE'LL BE BACK in about…" Lena pulled out her phone and checked it. "Six minutes."

"Where the hell did she run off to?" Brian asked. He stood in the corner of the kitchen, feeling outnumbered, four sets of female eyes sizing him up. The General was right. This had all the undercurrents of an insurgency about to turn hot.

"Just a walk before dinner." Sadie shrugged and as if to belie her words, a truck pulled into the packed-dirt parking area in front of the carriage house and Cass got out.

"A walk?" Brian echoed.

"Walk, drive… what's the difference?" Alice said from up on top of the refrigerator. She climbed down from her perch and went to wash her hands. The other women moved around the room with the ease of familiarity, getting the meal to the table, pouring drinks and settling themselves into their seats. Cass walked in, hung her purse from a hook near the door and headed for the sink. After washing and drying her hands, she slid into a chair at the head of the table.

Which is when Brian realized there was no place set for him.

All five women watched him curiously and once again Brian caught a glimpse of wicked defiance beneath their placid expressions. He'd been in tight situations many times, but none quite so awkward—or as deviously undermining to his authority. He was too well bred to dump one of the women out of their chairs, or to demand to be served—or even to grab a plate and help himself. But he was too versed in conflict to walk away, either. This was a test. If he failed it, he might as well leave right now.

And Brian had decided he wanted to stay. Every move Cass made fascinated him. He couldn't say what it was—some combination of sweetness, sexiness and rank insubordination that pierced straight through his defenses. He wanted to get to know her better, and the ranch had already worked its magic on him. He felt more alive right now than he had since he left his SEAL team.

He went to the cupboard, pulled out another plate, eased his way between the chairs Cass and Lena occupied and stabbed a baked potato with the serving fork that lay in the dish. He transferred a healthy serving of the roast to the plate, too. After adding a helping of green beans, he handed it to Jo. She caught the plate just before he dropped it in front of her and he swiped her empty one out from under it. He went back to serving before anyone could say a word.

As he expected, none of the others protested his

actions out loud. That wasn't their way. He served each of them in turn, and himself last, grabbed some silverware from a drawer near the sink and took his heavily laden plate to one of the spare chairs.

"This is good," he said a minute later, after he'd dug in.

"Cass made it," Jo told him proudly.

"Cass, you are a hell of a cook."

They subsided into silence again and the others finally began to eat.

When a few minutes had passed, Brian decided to stir things up a little. After a month at USSOCOM, he needed some action, and he wouldn't get anywhere until he got them talking.

"Here's what I don't understand. I'm sitting at a table with five beautiful women. How come none of you has a husband?"

Sadie's mouth dropped open. Two spots of color appeared high on Cass's cheeks. "That's none of your business."

"Maybe we've learned men aren't worth the trouble." Lena leaned forward, fork high in her hand as if she meant to stab someone. "Besides, I have a boyfriend. Who knows where it's going?"

"It better not be heading toward matrimony," Cass snapped at her.

"It can go wherever I want it to," Lena retorted.

"I'll marry when the right man asks me," Sadie said.

Alice blinked and frowned. "Husband?" She sounded as if she didn't understand the word.

"Some people think marriage is obsolete," Jo said loftily, shoveling her fork into her green beans.

Cass turned on her. "Who says that? Sean?"

"Maybe."

Brian watched them bicker. This was too much fun. It was like launching a hand grenade into a wasps' nest.

"You're way older than any of us." Alice turned to him suddenly. "Why aren't you married?"

"Who's to say I'm not?" he countered, although her accusation stung. He wasn't *way* older. Maybe five or six years older than Cass.

"Are you?" Cass asked.

Was that a flash of disappointment in her eyes? Of course it wasn't, he chided himself. He was a stranger to her. He'd have to remedy that as fast as he could. "Not yet. But I will be soon." Cass nodded and concentrated on her food.

"Who's the lucky lady?" Lena asked sardonically.

"She's sitting at this table." He wanted to take back the words as soon as he'd said them. What the hell had made him set off a bomb like that? How many times did leaping before he looked have to get him in trouble before he finally learned?

"What?" Sadie said.

"Who?" Jo demanded, looking from one to another of her sisters.

"You're an idiot." Lena cut a bite-size chunk off her slice of roast beef. Cass just stared at him, fork and knife suspended above her plate.

"It's Cass, isn't it?" Alice said suddenly. "I saw—"

She bit off her words and busied herself with her food as the rest of them turned to stare at her.

"What did you see?" Cass demanded.

"Nothing. I saw him coming here—looking for you. That's all." Alice popped a hunk of beef into her mouth and chewed.

"That had better be all," Cass told her with a shake of her head. "Don't be so gullible. Mr. Lake's just having you on."

"No. I'm not," Brian told her firmly, deciding to throw caution to the wind one last time. "Alice is right. I didn't just come to fix the house. I came to marry you."

IN ALL HER years of interacting with ranch hands, Cass had dealt with angry men, lazy men, suspicious men and stupid men, but she'd never dealt with a proposal from a stranger. Not even Bob had tried that.

"Mr. Lake—"

"Brian."

"Mr. Lake—"

"At least call me Lieutenant. Or you could just say sir."

"Mr. Lake, I don't know how it is where you come from, but around here a man gets to know a woman before he asks her to marry him."

"Who said I was asking?"

Cass blinked and tried again. "I never said I had any interest—"

"Again, I'm not asking you to marry me, Cass. Not now. I'm just letting you know my intentions. Where I come from, that's the honorable thing to do." Brian took a bite of his beef and closed his eyes. "Heavenly. I'm going to be one spoiled man when we tie the knot."

Cass stood up, dropped her utensils on her plate, caught her napkin before it slipped to the floor and slammed it on the table.

"Cass," Lena warned.

"I'm fine," Cass snapped, but she ached to head out on the range with a bushel basket of fireworks. Some M-80s ought to do it. They were hard to find, not like in the old days when any stupid teenager could blow things up if he wanted to. Cass felt sure that was all for the best. Most people weren't careful like she was. Still, at times like these she wished the drugstore stocked them. Next to the pads and tampons would be appropriate.

Instead, she went to the sink and poured herself a glass of water, even though she already had one.

When she sat back down, she refused to meet Brian's gaze. She wasn't going to let him get to her, no matter what he said.

"So you're a sailor, huh?" Lena said, sizing him up. "What's wrong; Army wouldn't take you?"

"Army didn't have the specialty I wanted."

"And what was that?"

"Explosives. I like to blow shit up."

Cass choked on the water she'd just drunk. Sadie thumped her on the back.

"What a coincidence," Lena said. "Cass likes—"

"Dessert. Chocolate." Cass stood up again and carried her plate to the sink. "Sadie, help clear the table."

"I've barely started eating."

"Take a load off, Cass. I'll do the dishes tonight. When I'm done."

Everyone fell silent at Brian's pronouncement and Cass stared at him. What the hell was the General up to now? Sending them an explosives expert who did dishes, too?

A ripple of unease ran through her. She didn't like the idea of the SEAL staying in the house. If he knew about explosions, would he figure out what she was doing when she went off on her own? Would she have to stop turning to fireworks when she got angry? She hated the thought of censoring herself. Without that outlet for her feelings, she'd actually have to...feel them.

To hell with that.

When she didn't answer, he just smiled. It shouldn't have affected her, but it did, sending a tide of heat through her body that left her uncomfortable and flushed.

"You can help dry," he offered. "It'll be like playing house."

Cass barely bit back a curse, and she had to work hard through the rest of the meal and the cleanup afterward not to lose her cool. Her sisters seemed to think it was all a big joke and she was glad when they scattered and left her and Brian to finish up.

She thought she'd never seen a sight as sexy as the muscular man elbows deep in sudsy water. Their dishes looked fragile in his large hands but he worked carefully and didn't chip any of them.

She was drying the last pan when Brian said, "See, we're perfectly compatible. We'll be married in no time."

Cass hung up the pan and threw her towel on the counter. "All right. That's it," she said.

"That's what?" He pulled the plug from the sink and let the water drain out.

"Let's go. Now." She headed for the door.

"Where are we going?"

"You'll see." She led the way outside, across the yard and through Sadie's garden toward a tall clipped wall of an evergreen hedge, not looking back to see if he followed. She knew he was behind her. Could sense his steady gaze on the back of her head.

It was a measure of their family's moral code that very few of Chance Creek's citizens had ever gotten lost in the Two Willows hedge maze, because it was entirely capable of baffling unsuspecting wanderers. Even as little children, before their mother had died, their father's prolonged absences had given Cass and her sisters such a deep understanding of what it meant to be left behind that they had tacitly decided no one would ever feel that kind of pain on their watch. They had escorted each new visitor through the maze in an orderly and thorough fashion—Cass remembered holding her friends' hands—until the guest had memorized the way and could be trusted to explore the maze on his or her own.

Amelia had planted the maze as a child and tended it

as long as she lived. Sadie had taken over when she passed, the way she took over all the gardens on the ranch. The maze remained as it had ever been, the shrubbery as tall as the roof of the house, but precisely clipped into passages that never changed. You would think that between their pedantic method of revealing its secrets and the number of times she'd traced the paths it held, the maze would hold no more magic for her.

You'd be wrong.

Because something was special in that part of the ranch. Even newcomers remarked on an uncanny sense that things were different here.

Brian stopped at the entrance to the maze. "You've got to be kidding me. I've never seen one of these on private property before."

"In!" Cass pointed toward the opening.

"What's going on?" Sadie, clippers in hand, popped out from the passage that branched off to the left.

"Jesus, Sadie, don't do that!" Cass put a hand to her heart. "I'm taking Mr. Lake to the standing stone. Time to sort this out."

"Ooh. I want to come." Sadie lay the clippers down and stripped off her gardening gloves.

"We didn't ask for company." But her sister ignored her protests and Cass decided to be grateful Lena, Alice and Jo weren't here, too.

"You think you can lose me in there?" Brian demanded.

"I won't give you the chance. We've got an appointment to keep."

Brian raised an eyebrow, but allowed her to escort him through the tall evergreen shrubbery to the center of the maze, where a large, rectangular obelisk stood. The standing stone had inspired Amelia to plant the maze around it all those years ago. No one knew who'd decided to wedge the large piece of granite vertically into the ground, or how they'd carried it here from Silver Falls, twenty miles away, where it must have been quarried. All that had happened so long ago the story hadn't been passed down. What had been transmitted from generation to generation was the stone's uncanny ability to answer questions.

The stone didn't speak, of course. And its answers didn't always come clear at first, but they did come, and often in a smack-you-in-the-face kind of way. The Reeds had learned not to enter the exercise lightly and they warned their friends to exercise caution, as well.

But strangers were fair game.

"After all, any grown-up knows not to ask a question you don't really want an answer to," Alice had once said.

"Nice rock," Brian said, clearly unimpressed.

"Go ahead. Ask." Cass folded her arms over her chest again.

"Ask what?" Brian cocked his head.

"Ask the standing stone if you and I are going to get married."

"You think it's going to answer me?" He grinned and Cass shook her head in exasperation. Really, the

SEAL was far too handsome to go around smiling like that. When he did she went all funny inside.

She didn't like that one bit.

"It'll definitely answer," Sadie said helpfully.

"Be specific," Cass directed. "You have to word things carefully. The stone will only be as clear as you are. Ask your question, then wait for an answer."

"You're putting me on."

Cass had a feeling Brian could be stubborn when he wanted to. Sadie jumped to her rescue. "If you ask and don't get an answer, Cass'll let you kiss her."

Cass turned on her, but before she could lay into Sadie, Brian laughed out loud. "You're on." He faced the stone, and as angry as Cass was, she decided she wanted to see what happened next, although she took a step away from Brian just in case he tried to steal that kiss before the stone could give its response. SEALs were trained to be sneaky, after all.

"I'll get you for that later," she murmured to Sadie.

Sadie shrugged.

"Oh great and wonderful Standing Stone, in your wisdom, nobility and…" Brian thought a moment. "And rectangular-ness, please reveal to me the truth. Will I marry the fair Cass?" He ended with a little flourish, like a bow mixed with a gyrating dance step.

Sadie gaped at him. "You are so going to pay for that, you know."

"Sweetie, I've fought in battles where bad guys were shooting back at me. This guy's solid…" He rapped on the stone. "But he's immobile. I'm not worried."

Cass could only shake her head. "Well, that's that. Now it's just a matter of time."

"Time until what? Until we kiss?"

He was truly insufferable, Cass thought. Hot, but insufferable. Thank goodness his time at Two Willows was temporary. They'd put up with him until he fixed the house, then wave good-bye as he went back to wherever he came from. All this marriage talk was insufferable.

"Come on," she said, and led the way back out. When they exited the maze and started toward the house, the light breeze that had been playing around all day kicked up into a fiercer gust, and Cass had just lifted a hand to push her hair out of her eyes when a stiff square of paper slapped against Brian's cheek. He yelped in surprise, then chuckled as he peeled it off his face. "What the heck is this?"

"It's an invitation." Sadie was by his side in an instant, tiny next to his hulking frame. She took it from his hand and straightened the well-worn paper. "A wedding invitation. From Boone and Riley Rudman's wedding last spring. I was looking for this. I wanted to add it to my keepsake album and couldn't find it."

"How on earth did it get out here?" Cass asked.

But Sadie had stopped in her tracks, her mouth open. "You… you two *are* going to get married," she said.

Despite the warmth of the day, delicate chills traced a path down Cass's spine. She knew without looking that Brian had drawn nearer. He took the invitation from Sadie's hands.

"This is my answer?"

"That's how it usually works. The clearer the answer, the surer you can be it'll come true."

"Not this time," Cass said. She snatched the invitation back. "This is about Boone and Riley's wedding. Not mine." But even as she spoke, her heart sank. If someone else had received this kind of answer, she would have counseled them the exact same way Sadie had. She met her sister's gaze and silently pleaded with her to agree, but Sadie simply shook her head.

Cass knew Sadie was right. This had happened to her so many times in the past. To other people, too. Children and grown-ups alike standing just the way she was now. Protesting the answer they'd come seeking but didn't expect to get.

Brian took the invitation back from her and held it up. "Seems to me your stone could hardly be any clearer. You and me. Rings. Cake. Presents." He obviously still wasn't taking any of this seriously, but Cass had to. Of course it was silly to believe a stone could answer your questions. But it always did.

And it was always right.

"Sadie—meeting in the pagoda. Now. Tell the others."

Sadie dropped the clippers she'd just picked up and broke into a run before Cass even finished. "You're not invited," Cass told Brian bluntly.

Brian held up his hands in a placating manner. "None of this is my fault. You're the one who told me to ask the stone."

Cass wasn't listening. "Go back to the house and stay there," she said. "Go to bed, or do whatever soldiers do when they're not necessary. I don't want to see you again tonight."

"Sailors. I'm a Navy SEAL, remember?"

"Whoop de do." She should have known he wouldn't listen. As she retraced her steps, he kept pace with her. Cass was far too flustered to think of a way to shake him off. When she spotted Bob Finchley's truck in the driveway, and the man himself striding toward them from the direction of the barns, her heart sank. The last thing she needed was another run-in with him. Didn't he ever call it quits? Why was he on her property at all?

"Evening," he called out when he got near. Dressed in jeans, boots and a t-shirt that had seen better days, a battered brown Stetson on his head, he looked like the quintessential cowboy, something Cass used to find masculine and attractive. Now she saw that on Bob it was just… wrong. It had something to do with his lanky brown hair, the rolling way he walked… and the fact he'd rarely done a lick of real work the entire time he'd been on the ranch.

All her anger rushed up at once. Bad enough he'd stolen from them and played her like a fine violin. Now he was back to gloat?

"What do you want, Bob? Get out of here before I have you arrested," Cass demanded. She wished she could follow through on that threat, but there was no way to do that without letting the General know how badly she'd failed. Bob knew she hadn't told anyone about the stolen money. She was too afraid the General would take the ranch away from her to do that. When she'd first confronted the overseer about it, he'd left the ranch—and stayed away for several weeks—but once Bob figured out there wouldn't be any legal repercussions, he'd started to come back around. Cass didn't know what to do.

"Just came by to say hello to my girl."

"Give me a break."

"How about I give you a kiss instead? Everyone in town is talking about our engagement."

He actually leaned in to try. Cass lifted her hands to shove him away, but before either of them reached the other, Brian stepped between them. "Evening," he said. "Name's Brian Lake. How about you show yourself off the ranch?"

Bob surveyed him. "How about you shove your foot up your ass? Cass, come on. Let's ditch this asshole and go watch the sunset."

"You've got to be fucking kidding me!" Cass saw red. She ached for an M-80. A whole string of them. Maybe—

Bob sidestepped around Brian and confronted her. "Honey, you've got to settle down. I know you're mad. I know you think I did something wrong, but I didn't. I was only planning for our future; yours and mine. We're too good together to throw that away over a little mistake—hey!"

Brian had stepped forward, grabbed Bob's hat and tossed it a dozen feet away.

"What the fuck, man?" Bob went after him, but with a swift series of moves, Brian put him on the ground in a way that left Cass breathless, then stifling a cheer. She recognized that kind of strength and skill from when she used to visit her father on the military bases where he served. Brian knew what he was doing.

Bob had no idea what he was up against.

She refused to admit to herself what a turn on it was to see Brian in action—defending her honor. No one had ever done that before. Bob deserved whatever he got for coming back here to push his luck with her again.

"The lady's not interested. Go back to whatever hole you crawled out from under." Brian pulled Bob up by the front of his shirt and gave him a shove. "Go on."

"You can't treat me like that." Bob backed away. "Whoever the fuck you are."

"Get going."

"This isn't over. And Cass, don't put me off too much longer. You mark my word; you'll want a man like me around the place before too long." He was gone before Cass could answer him, scooping up his hat and climbing back into his truck.

Brian stood next to her, watching as Bob drove off. "Was that joker really your overseer? Your father mentioned the name," he added when she turned a questioning look on him.

"Bob Finchley. In the flesh," Cass said tiredly. "I

kicked him out. Didn't like him." She wouldn't tell Brian anything about the embezzled cash. Or about the fact she'd dated him. Considered marrying him, even. Brian would turn right around and tell the General, and then where would she be?

"I can see why."

Chapter Four

"WELL, HOW GOES it?" Connor asked, his face filling Brian's laptop screen. The other men's faces were visible along the bottom of the screen. Jack had called for this video chat. All the men Brian had left behind in Tampa were curious about the state of the mission.

"So far so good. I'm in the house. The General's daughters are tolerating my presence. For the moment, anyway." He didn't want to think about what they were saying out there in the pagoda at the center of Sadie's herb garden. All five of the women had hustled away as soon as he and Cass reached the back door.

"Stay away from us," Cass had said again before they hurried off. He figured he'd give them their privacy. This time.

"That's progress." Logan laced his fingers behind his head. "What about Cass? She someone you want to marry?"

Leave it to Logan to focus on the female angle. "It's a funny thing," Brian said. "On the surface, anyway, I'm not sure I could have picked better. I definitely could have picked worse. The ranch is spectacular, by the way."

Something like yearning rippled through the men's expressions, and once again Brian wondered if the General had known exactly what he was doing when he picked them for the bogus task force. They were all country boys—all men who wanted a ranch someday.

But had he picked them from a larger pool of expendable fuck-ups? Or had he honed in on them and waited for them to make mistakes? Brian filed the problem away for consideration.

"What about the boyfriends?" Jack asked.

"The General was right; Cass kicked Bob Finchley out," he told them, "but he's still sniffing around. I'll keep an eye out for the others."

"Good luck with that." Connor nodded at him.

"Tell us more about the ranch." Logan leaned forward.

"It's everything you might have hoped for—and more." Brian described what he'd seen so far.

"Worth marrying a stranger for?" Jack asked.

"Maybe. The right stranger. Look, these women—they're all a handful in their own way, but they're also smart, attractive... interesting. I don't know if it's enough, but..."

Their faces all told the same story. Curiosity. Skepticism.

Hope.

"The military's made it clear it doesn't want me anymore," Jack summed up for the rest of them. "I'm not good for much else. Maybe I can make a go of ranch-ing."

The others nodded. So they were coming around to the whole idea, Brian mused.

"Has the General told you anything more about when he'll send you here?" he asked.

"Not a word," Logan answered. "He keeps throw-ing more manuals our way. He says it all depends on you. If you screw things up, the whole mission gets scrapped."

Normally when circumstances got tight, adrenaline kicked in and sharpened his brain. This time Brian found his mind racing in circles. Cass was attracted to him, he was sure of it. He was certainly attracted to her. Not in a casual fling kind of way, either. He wanted to get to know this woman. He wasn't used to having any kind of deadline on his pursuit of a relationship, though, and if he was honest, he hadn't pursued a relationship with any of the women he'd dated in the past few years. He'd convinced himself marriage wasn't for him.

So why was it so compelling to picture marrying Cass?

It shouldn't be. Or rather, even if it was, he shouldn't give in to it. It wasn't fair to her. She deserved a man who wouldn't fuck things up. Who wouldn't send her off for groceries alone at ten at night, or gamble away her money and property.

But he'd never do that to her. He knew it with every fiber of his body. If he was married to a woman like Cass he'd dedicate his life to keeping her safe—to making her world—and her ranch—a paradise.

"No pressure." Connor grinned.

"Yeah, no pressure," Brian echoed uneasily, surprised by the strength of his convictions. After all, he was sure neither his father nor brother set out intending to destroy their wives. "All right; I'll keep you in the loop."

"I DON'T UNDERSTAND why we have to wait for Wye," Lena said.

"Because I need an impartial observer." Apart from her mouthful of a name, Wyoming Smith was as open and uncomplicated as any person Cass had ever known, a perfect antidote to her family's labyrinthine secrets. Cass held one of the white painted posts of the open-air pagoda and watched for her friend. "There she is." She relaxed a little when Wye's Volkswagen Beetle trundled around the side of the house down the driveway and parked near the other vehicles by the carriage house. A moment later Wye climbed out and waved. Cass waved back.

"What's the emergency?" Wye asked when she reached them. She sat down on the built-in slatted bench next to Sadie, across from Cass. Her curly light brown hair was caught in a sensible ponytail. Like Cass, she was dressed in jean shorts, paired with a pretty blue top and white Keds.

"Cass is getting married," Lena said. "To a Navy SEAL."

"Am not."

"That's what the stone says," Jo put in.

Wye rolled her eyes and Cass wanted to hug her for it. "You ladies and your stone. It's an inanimate object. It can't predict the future."

"And yet it does," Alice said. As usual, tendrils of her long hair had escaped her updo, but she looked like she'd just walked out of a boho fashion shoot, and Cass suppressed an almost automatic surge of jealousy. Alice's otherworldly beauty was an outward manifestation of the link she had with their mother. Amelia had been beautiful, too, and both of them sensed things before they happened. It was uncanny how well Amelia had organized everything before her death. Afterward, they'd found her detailed instructions for how everything in the house worked, the Christmas presents she'd purchased and wrapped in the weeks before the stroke took her, the box of letters she'd left with the lawyer for their father. Cass had forwarded those to the General since he'd never come home after the funeral.

So many times she'd wondered what they said, and she hated her father for keeping them to himself. Her sisters didn't know about those letters. Cass had decided it was cruel enough she knew about them. All in order. All dated. The General was still hearing from his wife, but she hadn't had a word from her mother in eleven years.

"Back up. Who's this Navy SEAL? Where did he come from? I thought you were supposed to marry Bob." Wye's last sentence was delivered in a light, teasing tone, and pulled Cass from her melancholy thoughts. Wye knew all about her breakup with Bob—and that the overseer hadn't seemed to want to take the hint and leave her alone.

She didn't know about the money, though. No one but her knew anything about that. Cass couldn't bear to reveal the way Bob had played her, or how she'd nearly lost her family's ranch in her ignorance and desire to be loved. It was a secret she would take to her grave if she could.

"The General sent him to fix the house," Sadie told her. "He took one look at Cass and decided he wanted her."

"Sounds romantic." Wye grinned at Cass.

"Sounds ridiculous," Cass retorted.

"So you don't like him. What's the problem? Oh wait—that's right. The stone said you *have* to marry him."

"It didn't say I have to," Cass said, pleating the hem of her shirt with her fingers. "It said I *would*."

"You always were good at taking orders."

Cass glared at Wye. "I brought you here for help. If I want this kind of crap I'll go hang out with Bob."

"Ouch. Don't get mad at me," Wye told her. "Get mad at the General. He's the one who sent the SEAL. Which makes no sense, by the way. Why wouldn't he send a soldier?"

"Don't try to figure out why the General does what he does. I stopped trying years ago," Cass said.

"Anyway, we're always angry at the General," Lena said practically. "Now we need to figure out what to do with Brian."

"Why not let him fix the house? You've been com-plaining forever about how it's falling down around your ears," Wye pointed out. "If the General sent him, he'll have given him a budget to work with. That's less money out of the cattle earnings. Isn't that a good thing? Seems like cash is a little tight right now."

Cass could have kicked her. Sometimes Wye was far too perceptive for her own good. Cass was trying to solve the problem of the missing money without her sisters knowing about it, and so far Brian hadn't men-tioned anything about a budget. It was going to be tricky enough to fool him about the lost money if he expected the repairs to come out of the cattle income. She didn't need her sisters' attention drawn to it, too. "We can't allow that precedent to be set," she said firmly. "If we accept one SEAL, next he'll send a whole squadron, or team or... whatever."

"Pod," Lena said helpfully.

"I think that's Orcas," Jo said. "Seals run in herds."

"That's cattle," Lena said.

"Seals, too."

"Anyway," Wye went on. "I don't understand why the General is sending anyone. Why doesn't he just let you run things your way? You've always done fine."

Cass didn't answer her. Her secret fear was that somehow the General had figured out what was going on. But there was no way that could have happened—unless Bob had told the man himself, which she highly doubted.

"Because he's so used to ordering people around he can't stand not to," Lena told Wye, growing serious. "Don't you see what he's doing? Brian's just another kind of overseer, and he won't be as easy to get rid of as Bob was. Sure, he says he's here to fix the house, but just you wait. He'll be handing out orders within the week."

"So kick him out," Wye said. "You all are awesome at that. How many overseers have you run off in your time?"

No one answered. Outsiders found it funny when they learned about the girls' attempts to run the ranch themselves when they were younger. But it hadn't been funny at the time; it had been their way of trying to control their future when their mother's death blew everything apart. And a way of expressing their rage at their father's behavior. How could he have not come home—not once—since his wife had died? Especially in those early weeks when they needed him the most? And then to send strangers to run the ranch—to *take care* of them. It wasn't to be borne.

"We're working on it," Lena said.

"We can't get rid of Brian. Remember what the standing stone said," Sadie countered.

"Oh my God! You realize you're giving it the very power you're attributing to it!" Wye shook her head at them. "You are some of the most highly intelligent, capable women I know, but you have the biggest blind spots of anyone I've ever met. A stone can't really predict the future."

Cass sighed. Wye was a good friend, but they'd only gotten to know each other in the past year or so. There was so much she didn't understand. "There's rational, and then there's seeing things with your own eyes. It's not right *some* of the time. It's right *all* of the time. You get used to it and after a while you realize there's no sense fighting fate."

Wye frowned. "So Cass *has* to marry Brian. What else has it said about your futures?"

Cass accepted her sarcasm. She couldn't blame Wye for not getting it. "I'll never leave the ranch," she said quietly. She'd resigned herself to that back when her mother died, though, and it didn't bother her anymore. Maybe at one time she'd thought about joining the Army, but she loved Two Willows, and she'd grown to love caring for it the way her mother had before her. She knew in her heart she might travel now and then, but she'd always come back to her home.

"I'll never leave the ranch," Alice echoed from her seat at the far side of the pagoda. She sounded relieved. Alice drew her heightened sensibilities from the land, just as their mother had, and Cass knew she didn't want to leave it.

"I'll never leave the ranch." Lena was determined. She'd always felt her destiny was to become Two Willows's overseer.

"I'll never leave the ranch." Sadie's answer was thoughtful, and Cass wasn't sure how her sister felt about that. As their chief gardener, she was the most directly attached to the land they lived on, and in the past Cass would have said she'd be happy to stay that way, but recently her infatuation for Mark had distracted her from her work. If he ever got serious about her, Cass felt Sadie could easily be lured away.

"I'll never leave the ranch." Jo grinned impishly. Cass didn't even want to know what was going on in her head—or in Sean's. Sometimes she thought Sean was as determined as Bob to get his hands on their property.

Wye leaned back on the slatted bench. "And you're going to accept that? All of you? Whether you want to stay or not?"

"Two Willows is in our blood, Wye. I know you don't understand—" Cass began. She wasn't sure if it was the location of the house, or the curve of the land, or the mountains far in the distance, or the big Montana sky arcing over all of it. Two Willows got under your skin. It got a grip and didn't let go. The stone had simply spelled out what they all had come to know was true.

Wye forestalled her with a raised hand. She took a moment to think before she spoke, though. "You know, the crazy thing is, I do understand," she said. "I don't know how. I haven't known any of you long enough to have this kind of intuition about you, but I get it," she said. "Honestly, I do. The truth is, you all want to stay as badly as the land wants you to—is that it?"

All of them nodded.

"So what are you going to do about this SEAL problem you're having?"

"We have to find a way to get rid of him." Cass was

firm on that front.

"But—" Sadie began.

"But nothing. The stone said I'd marry him, but it didn't say what would happen if he changed his mind and never asked me."

"You know it doesn't work that way," Sadie said.

"It's going to work that way this time," Cass told her. "If he never asks, then I can't marry him."

"You want to make him dislike you," Wye said.

"Exactly. And I know just how to do it. He's here to help, right? That's why the General sent him?"

Her sisters nodded.

"We won't let him. At all. And we'll document the fact he'd not getting any work done, and make sure the General is very clear about all the ways he's failing his mission. The General will order him back, and that's that—no more SEAL."

"You really think that's going to work?" Wye asked.

"It has to."

BRIAN WOKE EARLY the next morning, but Cass and Lena both beat him downstairs. He came into the kitchen to find Cass cooking a large farm-style breakfast and Lena tinkering with a weed-whacker.

"You need a workshop," he told her.

"Got one. Just busy. Got to fix things when I can," she answered without looking up.

Brian made a mental note to pass that information on to the General. He had a feeling Lena had few weaknesses to exploit. Cass was tough, too, in her own way, but she wore her feelings on her sleeve, while Lena kept hers close to her vest. Brian had learned a few things about Cass in his short time here—like how much she cared about her sisters—and her house.

And that she was superstitious. They all were.

"How long are you going to stay here?" Cass asked him bluntly when he came to survey his breakfast options.

"Forever." He found himself a plate and happily forked a couple of sausages onto it. The hash browns looked terrific, too. This was much better than the food at USSOCOM.

"I'm serious." She elbowed him away from the stove. He ducked around the other side and scooped a generous helping of hash browns onto his plate.

"So am I. Tell me about the house. What needs fixing?" He slipped the spatula from her hand and slid a friend egg onto it. He eased it on top of the rest of his food and handed the spatula back to her.

"Nothing." Cass snatched it from his hand.

"Everything," Lena said at the same time, still bent over the weed-whacker. "The first-floor shower is a mess."

"Don't forget the busted window upstairs," Sadie said as she came into the room. She stopped dead when she noticed Brian there. "Whoops."

Lena looked up. "Right. Whoops."

Uh oh, Brian thought. What were they up to now?

"Food's on the stove," Cass told Sadie. "The shower and window are already taken care of," she told

Brian.

Ah. Of course; Cass didn't want his help with the house. Brian wondered if she thought she could drive him away by refusing to let him take on any tasks and boring him to death. It could work, he decided, given how eager he'd been to leave USSOCOM.

"There's nothing wrong with the house at all," Lena stated firmly.

"You've got to be kidding," Jo said, entering the room, rubbing her hair with a towel, Tabitha following close at her heels. "I just short-circuited the bathroom—again. It happens every time I blow-dry my hair." She, too, stopped in her tracks when she spotted Brian near the stove. "But I fixed it," she stammered. "It's fine now."

"Of course it's fine," Cass said. "Everything is fine. There is not one single thing wrong with this house!"

"Except the roof," Alice murmured, wandering in reading a book. She glanced up. "Hi, Brian."

"For God's sake," Cass exploded. "What is wrong with all of you?"

"Maybe they're hoping I'll actually fix the place." Brian carried his plate over to the table and sat down. Cass looked like she wanted to throw the rest of the breakfast at him. He watched her master her anger, waiting to see if she'd charge off like she had the night before. She took a step toward the door, then whirled to face the stove again.

Brian had the feeling if Cass ever got really mad, she'd be a force to reckon with. Not that he couldn't handle it. But he was beginning to wonder if she ever let her feelings out. Keeping them all bottled up couldn't be easy.

"I'll get started right after breakfast," he added, waiting to see if she'd blow. Cass simply pushed the hash browns and sausages viciously around in the pan with her spatula.

"Aren't you forgetting something?" Lena asked.

"What's that?" Brian tucked into his meal.

Lena waggled her fingers at him. "A ring, Casanova. What kind of fiancé doesn't buy his lady-love a ring?"

"Lena!" Cass's spatula clattered against the cast-iron griddle.

"Just kidding," Lena said sweetly, but when Cass turned away she waggled her fingers at Brian again. "Make it big," she mouthed at him. "Cass likes them really big," she added out loud.

"Lena Reed!" Cass came at her. Lena laughed, grabbed an orange from the bowl on the table and scampered out the back door. "I don't like them… big," Cass said to Brian primly, returning to the stove. "Whatever she meant by that."

Sadie and Jo snorted, then broke into peals of laughter. Even Alice's lips twitched.

Brian couldn't help himself. "Oh, don't worry," he told Cass's sisters. "It'll be big—when Cass agrees to marry me, she'll find that out for herself."

Too late he remembered he wasn't in a war zone joking with his buddies, and Cass wasn't the kind of woman you teased like that. He'd hoped she'd crack a smile, too. Instead, she stiffened, and slowly turned. "I wouldn't marry you if you were the last man on earth. I won't marry, period. Because men are idiots. Reckless, selfish, asinine idiots who make it their life's work to screw everything up and let you down when you need them the most." She dropped the spatula on the counter, turned off all the burners and walked straight out the back door.

Brian's heart sank as he took in the pained expressions of her sisters. Cass had scored a direct hit, as much as he hated to admit it. Maybe all men weren't idiots, but the men in his family were. They were reckless and selfish, too.

And they let their women down.

He never wanted to follow in their footsteps.

Would that happen if he kept pursuing Cass?

WHILE CASS ITCHED to pull out the real pyrotechnics, she didn't want to call attention to herself. Armed with two M-80s this time, she drove past her usual spot, far into the heart of the ranch where no one would think to look for her.

Her hands shook as she readied the firecrackers and lit their fuses. She forced herself to remain calm as she moved the required distance away. She could hardly wait for the explosions to rip away the uncomfortable feelings clawing at her throat. How dare her sisters make fun of her predicament? How dare Brian come and disturb her peace, just when she'd gotten rid of Bob and had things under control... mostly? How dare he joke about marriage while he sat at her table and ate her breakfast, looking like some kind of poster child for the US Navy? Every time he came near she got fluttery and silly, about to go off half-cocked like a firecracker with a short fuse.

One of the M-80s exploded with a bang that made her nerves jump. The second one followed with a satisfying crack. But Cass didn't feel her usual relief. Instead, a longing filled her she could hardly name.

Scratch that.

She knew exactly what it was.

Cass likes them really big. Lena was in deep shit for that remark. She didn't know what had sparked Lena to say it, and she hated the images her words had conjured up.

Brian.

Naked.

Ready for her.

Oh God, she was losing her mind over that stupid man. She needed to get rid of him before her hormones, apparently unleashed at the worst of times, dragged her over the abyss and into some kind of illicit relationship with the SEAL.

He wants to marry you. That's hardly illicit, her mind reasoned with her.

Cass paced in a circle. It was *too* illicit. She'd just proved to herself she wasn't made for marriage—or men. When she thought about what she could have lost if she'd gone on to marry Bob—it simply wasn't worth it.

But Brian is.

No. No, he wasn't. Not in the slightest—

God, she wasn't… attracted to Brian… was she?

Funny how just a few weeks back she had thought Bob was the one. Now she knew how wrong she'd been about him—and Brian's arrival put her crush on Bob in all too stark a perspective. She'd wanted attention before, and Bob had been handy and willing to give it to her. He'd slaked her need for a little romance in her quiet, retiring life.

But Brian affected her far more deeply, eliciting a desire she'd never had to deal with before. The fact he could joke about marriage made the circumstances all too cruel. She'd wanted a husband once—a family.

To have Brian arrive just when she'd decided that those things weren't for her wasn't fair.

But that was life, wasn't it? She headed back to her truck.

Setting off fireworks hadn't fixed any of her problems.

She blamed the Navy SEAL for that.

Chapter Five

As Brian inspected the house, he realized the General wasn't amiss in sending someone to repair it, even if that was a ruse for a far more devious plan. The house was old, and time and weather had taken its toll. He spotted several places where Cass had patched and repaired things that had fallen apart, but it was clear she was struggling to keep up.

It also became clear as he went that while Cass had done a fine job for an amateur armed with basic tools and an impressive set of how-to books, she didn't have the expertise for some of the jobs. Since he didn't share Cass's reluctance to hit her father up for money, and he knew his way around construction work, he figured he could help a lot. He decided to start with the shower Lena had complained about, but when he'd gathered the tools he'd already purchased as part of his cover story, he found Cass there, pulling tiles off the soggy drywall.

"I can take it from here," Brian said, edging into the small room.

Cass glared up at him. "I told you I don't want help. I've got this covered. It was on my list for today."

When she leaned forward over the edge of the tub to pull off another tile, Brian got a wonderful flash of cleavage. Last night he'd had plenty of time to think about Cass and their situation. It was one thing to consider marriage in the abstract. Another thing altogether to meet the woman in question for the first time. He liked everything he saw, and he had to admit the idea of getting intimate with her intrigued him.

He'd had a hard time taking any of this too seriously until he arrived at Two Willows. Now he found himself questioning the way he'd always thought about how people met their partners. He'd seen it as a kind of sifting process—that one part of the brain was always considering and discarding possible mates. Now he really thought about it, however, it occurred to him how few women he'd gotten to know over the course of his adult life. If it was possible to find a life partner in a field so small, what did that mean about love—and marriage?

He wasn't sure.

His case was different, too. Cass wasn't one of the women who'd come into his life by accident; she'd been put there by the General. That meant his field of possible partners included all the women the General knew, too. Other people had set him up once or twice. Brian had tried to add them to the equation. Just how big was his field of possibilities when you took into consideration that friends and family might be searching for him, too?

Love was a strange calculus, he decided. However it

worked, here he was, and here was Cass. And his gut told him she could be the one. Not just because she came with an incredible ranch.

Because she was herself. The woman he was supposed to meet.

The woman for him.

He leaned against the built-in cabinets and watched her work. "Your father sent me here so you wouldn't have to do this stuff."

"The General sent you here to spy on me. Don't even try to pretend otherwise." She reached for another tile. Each inch she stretched forward heightened the view. Was Cass always this prickly, he wondered, or did she soften in a man's arms?

He'd like to find out.

"Isn't it weird to call your father that?"

"The General?" Cass sat back on her heels, her brow furrowed. "We've always called him that."

"Even when you were little?"

"He's been a general for as long as I can remember." She got back to work.

It was Brian's turn to frown. Had the man made his girls call him that? It seemed awfully cold. His dad, as big of a shit as he'd turned out to be, had always been approachable when he was a kid.

He knelt down beside Cass, reached past her and began to peel the tiles quickly off the wall. "I'll get some backerboard to replace this drywall."

"I've already got it."

"Fine. Just tell me where it is and I'll take care of it.

Why don't you go take a rest?"

She shouldered him aside, grabbed the tiles from his hands and dropped them in the box she was using to collect them. "I said I'll handle this. *You* go take a rest. You're the guest."

"I don't intend to be for long. I already told you that." He was much bigger, and his shoulders were much wider than hers. It was easy for him to push her gently away. He got back to work until Cass shoved him—hard. He slammed into the vanity and scrambled to regain his balance.

"I fix the house," Cass exclaimed, waving a tile at him. "That's my job and you can't have it!"

Brian kissed her. He didn't mean to. He didn't know why he did it. She was there, she was impassioned and angry, and so damn beautiful he couldn't help himself.

Cass slapped him. The sound reverberated in the small space. She scrambled back, breathing hard. A strand of hair had come down from her ponytail, and he resisted the urge to tuck it behind her ear. The slap hadn't fazed him, but it had shaken her up.

After a long moment, Cass lurched to her feet and pushed past him out the door. He heard her footsteps hurry off toward the kitchen. A moment later, the back door slammed shut.

Where did Cass go when her feelings got the better of her? He'd have to find out one of these days, but that kiss had been enough for now. It had obviously rattled her, and if he was telling the truth, it had shaken him, too. His entire body had reacted to the brush of his mouth over hers. It wasn't just libido. All of his senses had activated. He wanted more of what he'd gotten. A lot more. He hoped he could convince Cass she wanted that, too.

A minute later, without warning, Cass re-entered the room, surprising Brian. He hadn't heard the back door open again, or any footsteps to warn of her approach.

"You can't run me off. Not with your… kisses. This is my job and I'm going to do it." She was flushed and breathing hard as if she'd run back to confront him.

"I wasn't trying to drive you off. I'd prefer it if you stayed," he said honestly.

"I am staying, but you need to go. This is my house, my bathroom, my tile job." Her voice rose with every word.

Uh oh. Was that the glint of tears in her eyes? It was—and Brian didn't deal well with female tears. He found himself on his feet before he knew what he was doing.

"Fine," he said. "I'll check the boiler in the basement. I haven't done that yet. How does it run?"

"I… I don't know," Cass admitted. "It did all right last winter." She recovered herself. "Not that it's any of your business."

"I know, I know—your house, your boiler," Brian said. "Happy tiling."

He escaped from the bathroom before she started to cry. He hadn't pegged Cass as one to indulge in tears, but maybe he was wrong. Maybe that's what she did every time she slipped away.

Once Brian located the stairs to the basement, he pulled a flashlight from his tool box, just in case, flicked on the light and headed down. The lights worked and the boiler seemed functional. It was old, but had a few more years in it. The rest of the room was unremarkable as far as he could see. A washer and dryer, out of date but still working, hunkered in one corner. The far end of the room was cloaked in shadows. Brian clicked on the flashlight, went to check it out and breathed a sigh of relief several minutes later when he found the foundation, while ancient, was holding strong.

He went upstairs, noting jobs as he spotted them, but it wasn't until he reached the attic that he found the worst of the problems. Buckets were positioned around the large, open space, and when he peeked into them they all held water.

Now he had a real job ahead of him.

HE'D KISSED HER. He'd just reached out and kissed her like he had every right to—which according to the standing stone, he did.

Cass fought the urge to toss away the bathroom tiles and drive far out onto the range to express herself more explosively. She was burning through her supplies of fireworks too fast. She had to find another way to regain control. And she had to finish this job before Brian came back. If there was no work for him to do, he couldn't stay long enough to… to do whatever it was the stone thought he would do to win her over.

It galled her that there was even the possibility that

could occur.

But there was.

When she'd walked away from Bob, she'd thought she'd walked away from any desire to be with a man again. The burn of humiliation she felt every time she thought about the overseer was as scorching today as it was when she'd discovered his theft. For a few short months she'd thought Bob was the answer to all her prayers. He'd doted on her, coming by the house every night, spending time with her and her sisters. She'd thought—

Cass bit her lip, ashamed at what she'd thought. After a decade of keeping the General at arm's length, furious at him for what he'd done to her and her sisters, she'd thought maybe it was time to reconcile. Maybe by marrying the man he'd chosen to be overseer she'd bridge the chasm that had formed between them. She'd almost convinced herself the General had handpicked Bob for that very reason.

Which just showed how wrong she was about everything.

She pulled more tiles off the wall and tossed them into the box she'd brought into the bathroom to hold them. What a stupid, stupid plan. What a betrayal of everything she and her sisters had fought to gain until now. After denying them the chance to run the spread themselves—telling them time and time again it took a man to do the job—the General had gone and put a thief into the position, and Bob hadn't just run off with thirty thousand dollars.

He'd stolen first her heart—and then her self-esteem.

How had he fooled her so badly?

Cass couldn't stand knowing she'd been such an easy mark. When she'd thought of the times they'd made love—thankfully there weren't many of them—she wanted to throw up. He'd been siphoning money off the spread right from the start, and she'd been too busy fawning over him to notice.

Now Brian had kissed her and she'd felt a spark that put anything she'd ever felt for Bob to shame.

She wouldn't put up with a rebellion from her body again. Not after what had just happened to her. Hadn't she learned anything from that fiasco?

But the Navy SEAL was unlike any man who'd ever shown an interest in her before.

Not for the first time she cursed the crazy childhood that had kept her so close to home when most young women got to practice dating in casual ways. Maybe if she had a wealth of experience to draw on she wouldn't be so susceptible to every man who gave her a second look. Brian was handsome, but what did that mean at the end of the day? If she wanted a husband—which she damn well didn't—he'd have far more qualities than good looks.

He'd be kind, for one thing. He'd think about other people, not just himself. He'd fall in love with Two Willows and be willing to work with her, rather than dictate to her how it should be run. He'd care about her sisters as well as her. Watching out for them had always been her job, and she'd want a husband who shared that responsibility. Maybe they were as grown up as she was; that didn't mean she'd ever stop worrying about them.

She had to be careful whom she allowed to be close to her. When she'd dated Bob, she'd nearly let him steal the ranch away from all of them. The General would never tolerate that kind of incompetence. He'd follow through on his threat to kick them off the ranch...

Cass didn't know what would happen then. To her and her sisters—and to him.

Maybe his job at USSOCOM wasn't dangerous like his overseas work used to be, but her mother had been adamant. A Reed present at Two Willows every minute of every day until the General came home.

They needed Two Willows. All of them did.

Why couldn't he see that?

Cass swallowed hard and pulled the last tile off the wall. Time to cut away the sopping mess that was the wall, fix the leak and get that backerboard up. If she couldn't stop her hands from shaking, she'd make a mess of that, too, though. She had to forget the past. She'd realized what Bob was up to and had put a stop to it. Her sisters were safe, and she'd do everything she could to keep them that way.

Which meant keeping her distance from Brian, no matter how hot he was. She had to drive him away— now—before he entrenched himself in Two Willows life. She knew the way this ranch worked on people. Like she'd said to Wye, it drew them in. It was never easy to rid themselves of the overseers and hands the

General kept sending to the ranch. People came and wanted to stay. Bob was a prime example of that, although she knew it was the money rather than the landscape that had won his heart.

It all came down to the house, she decided. If she let Brian stay here long enough to fix it up, he'd surely get attached to it—and to the rest of the ranch. She'd make it absolutely clear she didn't need any help. Didn't want it, either. Without anything to do, he'd get bored and go home.

That meant it was time to steady her hands, fix the leak, cut the backerboard and get it on the walls.

She took a deep breath and got back to work.

WHEN BRIAN CAME downstairs later, after determining to the best of his ability the extent of the damage to the roof, he was surprised to find Cass screwing on the last panel of backerboard. The tiles she'd pulled off the walls earlier were gone and her workspace was as clean as it could be under the circumstances. Tools lay on the counter in a neat row on top of a piece of newspaper.

He had to hand it to her; she was a conscientious worker.

"You found the leak?"

"Yep."

"Sure you fixed it all the way?"

"I'm sure."

He studied her work. "This all looks good."

"I'm sure you think you could have done it better." She pulled the drill back and ran a hand over the backerboard.

"Not at all. This looks fine."

"Then you should leave me to it." She didn't even bother to look his way. His earlier kiss had obviously upset her, but he knew if he apologized, he'd lose ground.

"I can do the mudding if you like."

"I don't like. Haven't I made that perfectly clear? There's nothing for you to do here. The General sent you on a fool's errand."

Maybe he had, but Brian wasn't ready to concede defeat yet. "Unfortunately, the General doesn't take it kindly when you don't follow through on his orders, so I think I'll stick around and help fix up the place."

"I really wish you wouldn't."

Damn, this wasn't going well at all. On the one hand he understood her position; like Cass, he preferred to do things his way, on his own. On the other hand, he kept seeing a vision of the future in which he and Cass worked side by side on the ranch. Once the house was fixed up, he'd take his place working the cattle, but there'd always be jobs they could do together. He liked that idea.

If only she could see it, too.

Early days, he told himself. Things would change over time. He'd prove himself to her and she'd open up to him.

He hoped.

For now, a tactical retreat was best. "I'll leave you to this job and I'll tackle the window upstairs."

Cass slammed the drill down on the counter. "When are you going to get it through your thick skull you aren't wanted around here?"

"When are you going to get it that I'm not going anywhere?" he countered. "Look, sweetheart, I know you don't like this situation, but I'm here to stay. You'd better get used to that."

He was blocking the entrance to the small room and Cass looked ready to plow right through him to reach it, but as he watched, she pulled herself together.

"I won't get used to it, and you'd better not either. We've run lots of men off this ranch. You're nothing special."

"That's where you're wrong," Brian countered. "None of the men who've come here before were Navy SEALs." And none of them were trying to get out from under an investigation into their past actions either, he'd wager. He had everything to lose if she didn't marry him. That definitely made this situation special.

Funny. He wasn't doing this to get away from that investigation anymore. Nor was he doing it to please the General. Or win the ranch.

He was doing it for the chance to get to know Cass. Twenty-four hours in and he was smitten. With a woman who hated the sight of him.

Figured.

"Navy SEALs. Hah. Who gives a hoot?" She lunged for the door.

He caught her in his arms. She might hate him, but she was attracted to him, too. That had been obvious when he'd kissed her before. Which he really wanted to do again. "You do, whether you admit it or not." He was taking a risk, but then he loved risks, and the adrenaline thrumming through his veins was like a drug he'd gone without for too long. The surprise on her pretty face triggered an answering rush of heat that blocked out his better nature. He bent down. Brushed his mouth over hers.

Again.

And liked it even better this time.

He expected Cass to protest. Maybe to strike him again.

She didn't. She squeaked as he covered her mouth with his, then moaned the most delicious moan he'd ever heard. It was a signal for more and he gathered her in closer.

He tangled a hand in her ponytail and wrapped his other arm around her waist. She was so pliant in his arms. So soft. So willing.

And then so absolutely rigid.

Brian let her push him away, knowing he'd never force her into anything she didn't want to do. That kiss had told him everything he wanted to know, anyway. He stepped aside and let her escape through the door.

She *was* as attracted to him as he was to her.

Which meant this war might be lengthy, but his victory would be so, so sweet.

When he heard an engine start up outside, though, his gut twisted. He didn't like the idea of Cass driving off in anger.

She was gone by the time he made it out of the house, so he climbed into his truck and followed the cloud of dust kicked up in the wake of her vehicle. He wouldn't intrude—he'd simply make sure she was all right.

He hadn't come here to hurt Cass.

SHE'D MADE A colossal mistake.

Cass drove fast over the rutted dirt track, eager to get as far away from the house as possible.

Brian had kissed her again—and this time she'd kissed him back.

She had no idea why, except for a moment it had felt so good to melt into his arms. Just for that second she hadn't felt so alone—and Cass had never realized how alone she'd felt until then.

She'd run to the shed, gathered whatever came to hand and bolted for her truck, afraid he'd come after her and try it again. It wasn't that she thought he'd try to overpower her; she couldn't say why, but she knew that wasn't the case.

She was afraid she'd let him... again. Because she didn't seem to have any control over herself just now.

Thank God for the empty pastures and the breadth of Two Willows. Out this far, no one would see her—or hear her, either.

When she pulled over and climbed out, a light wind whipped her hair. Far above her a hawk circled and she watched it jealously. What she'd give to fly away right now.

Except that wasn't true, was it? This land was as much a part of her as her stubbornness. She couldn't imagine leaving Two Willows, no matter what happened. Which meant she needed to be smart about what she did next.

But first she had to calm down.

When she opened the door to the truck's passenger side seat she laughed at the assortment of fireworks she'd grabbed back at the shed. There was no rhyme or reason to them, and that was fine; there wasn't any rhyme or reason to how she was feeling these days, either. Her misguided romance with Bob should have soured her on men for life, instead of leaving her so desperately longing for Brian the way she was now.

She set them off one by one, knowing right from the start they wouldn't help this time. They did nothing for the ache inside that made her restless and desperate for something she didn't want to name.

For Brian's touch.

She was in trouble, Cass decided as more of the fireworks shot off. She—

"It's an M-80 kind of day, huh?" Bob said behind her, and Cass whirled around with a shriek she instantly wished she could bite back when she saw the grin on his face. "Didn't mean to startle you."

"What the hell are you doing on my land?"

"Saw you driving hell for leather down that track. Thought I'd come see if something was wrong."

"The only way you could see me was if you were on my land to begin with," she challenged him, cursing her stupidity for letting Bob get her alone like this.

"Not true. That track's visible from the highway about a quarter mile from your house. Didn't you know that?" He grinned his lazy grin again, the one she used to think was sexy. God, how stupid she'd been. "Thought you knew this spread like the back of your hand."

She did know it, and she'd never noticed a place on the highway where you could see the track. Of course, she'd never exactly been looking for it. "Well, I'm fine. So leave."

"Look, Cass, there doesn't have to be this bad blood between us." Bob came closer. Cass backed away. "You don't think I'm husband material anymore, but you're wrong; I'm exactly the kind of man you need."

"How do you figure that?" She didn't want to continue this conversation but Bob stood between her and her truck and she had a feeling he wouldn't let her pass.

"Think about it—why do most women get married?"

Because they're deluded, Cass thought, but she said aloud, "Because they're in love."

"Wrong. They do it for money or they do it for safety. Or they do it for both."

How had she never seen the cold vacancy of his gaze? Had he put on such a good act that he managed to cover it up? Or had she been so grateful for a little male attention she hadn't even noticed? "That's pretty damn cynical."

"It's the truth."

"Well, I don't need your protection, and the last I looked you were stealing money from me, not the other way around."

"Cass, you need to watch your tongue."

She didn't like his silky tone, or the way he reached out and cupped her chin in his hand. She hadn't kept far enough away. Now she was in a real fix. She tried to jerk out of his grasp, but he didn't let go.

"There's trouble coming to Two Willows. You'll want me there when it does, believe me."

"Screw you," she tried to say, but still caught in his tight grip, her words were slurred.

Bob laughed and kissed her. Had his kisses always been so cold and hard? Cass pushed him away and this time he allowed her to break free. She made a break for her truck but with several long strides Bob made it there first and leaned against the door.

"Think about what we could do with this place together." He was acting as if they were having a pleasant conversation on the back porch, rather than a confrontation. His overconfidence burned Cass. What did it say about what he thought of her?

"Like what? Run it into the ground? You were on your way to bankrupting Two Willows."

"Like hell I was. I was building it into something better. Cattle isn't where the money's at, little girl. You're such a child, aren't you? Still waiting for Daddy to come home. Never been out of Chance Creek. What do you know of the world?"

"Plenty!" In her mind, sticks of dynamite began to

explode. Big, satisfying sticks of dynamite.

"A trip or two to a military ball doesn't count. Especially since it hasn't happened in years. Face it, Cass. You're just a little country girl no one else wants. It's me—or it's nobody."

"Brian wants me." The words leaped out of her mouth before she could think what she was saying. All she knew was she had to shut Bob down before her reduced her to tears. He knew all her vulnerable places—because she'd told them to him.

"That washed up Navy SEAL? You think he wants you? It's the ranch he wants, plain and simple. What do you think he's doing here? Why would a guy like that get the General to send him to Montana? Think for once, Cass. This land is worth a lot of money. That's what he wants. Not you."

Bob's words etched across her brain in blazing red colors and she closed her eyes, because she knew it was entirely possible. After all, it was why Bob himself had pursued her. What *would* a man like Brian ever see in her? She was a backwater country girl who knew nothing about anything except running this ranch. She wanted to lash out and hurt Bob as badly as he'd hurt her.

"Brian wants to marry me," she blurted. A flush of heat branded her cheeks as she realized too late Bob wouldn't give a damn about that declaration. It wasn't as if he'd ever loved her.

Right on cue, Bob tilted his head back and laughed long and hard. "Of course he wants to marry you. How else could he get his hands on a fine ranch like Two Willows?"

"That's not why he wants to do it!" God, she had to shut up. She was making a fool out of herself.

"Oh, yeah?" When Bob took a step toward her she backed up. "If he's so hot for you, where is he? And why are you blowing shit up?" He grabbed her hand and tugged her closer. "Where's your ring, for that matter? What kind of an asshole proposes without a ring?"

"He hasn't proposed yet." Even to her ears that sounded weak. She was losing ground fast.

Bob gave her a pitying look. "He wants the ranch, Cass. Guys like that don't fall for girls like you."

"It's what he said."

"And just because he used the M word, you're ready to spread your legs for him and welcome him home, is that it? How about you and me, then? I was going to propose—and you would have said yes, you know you would. How about we fuck for old times' sake. You know I can make you scream." Bob wrapped a hand in her hair and pulled her in for another kiss. Cass tried to shove him away, but he wasn't playing. His mouth on hers revolted her and she couldn't understand what she'd ever seen in him. His hand pawing at her breast made her lash out at him, but she couldn't budge his arm.

"Everything all right here?"

Cass gasped in relief when she heard Brian's voice. Bob let her go and she ran to Brian's side, well past caring about her pride.

"Everything's fine, sailor," Bob drawled. "Why don't you get the hell out of here? I'm talking to Cass."

"Seemed more like you were grappling with her."

"That's one way to describe it. I prefer to think we've got a passionate relationship."

"Yeah? Is that how it is, Cass?" Brian waited for her answer and Cass took in the differences between the two men. Bob's sardonic half-smile, the way he watched Brian out from under heavy eyelids, sizing up the competition. His perpetual slouch. And Brian's forthright manner. The way he waited for her to speak. His calm but ready watchfulness.

"I… I told him I didn't… I didn't want…"

"She said you were going to marry her," Bob cut across her. "She said you'd fallen head over heels for her the minute you met her, and now it's only matter of time before you're down on one knee. I explained to her it was her ranch you're really after. Isn't that right?" His cocky sneer made Cass want to scream. The last thing she wanted Brian to know was that she'd been talking about him to Bob.

He'd think she was interested. Which she wasn't, despite the fact she was using him as a human shield at the moment. She wanted Bob gone. For once in her life she'd hoped a man would back her up, but of course that was too much to expect, Cass realized as Brian turned to assess her. Was Bob right about him? Was he here for the ranch?

Of course he was.

Bob began to chuckle as the seconds ticked by.

"Cass, you're priceless," he said. "I'll see you later—when you come to your senses and realize I'm the only man who's ever really going to want you." He saluted Brian with great exaggeration. "Don't work too hard fixing up my house, sailor."

Brian finally spoke. "Two Willows will never be yours, Finchley. Cass was telling the truth; I do want to marry her. When she's used to that idea I'll put a ring on her finger. But not until she understands it's her I want, not this land."

Brian's words sent a thrill through her veins, but Cass shook her head, unwilling to fall for another man's tricks. What else could he possibly say when confronted with an accusation like that?

"Cass, do you actually believe that crap?" Bob asked. "He came here yesterday, and now he's so in love with you he has to marry you? If you do believe it, you're not the woman I thought you were."

"I don't believe it. I don't believe either of you." Cass headed for her truck, desperate to get away from both men.

"I'm telling the truth," Brian said. "Finchley, get the hell off the General's land."

"Are you speaking for the General now?" Bob laughed. "That ought to make your choice easy, Cass. Fuck him, and you're doing Daddy's lackey. Fuck me and together we'll give the General the finger. We'll take this ranch from him once and for all. That's what you always wanted, right?"

He left before she could find an answer. A moment

later, his truck peeled out and headed down the track. Cass wrenched open the door to her truck and climbed inside. As she started the engine, she noticed Brian bent over the collection of fireworks she'd left on the ground, carefully gathering up the unspent ones. When he straightened, he turned to her, his confusion clear.

Her heart lurched and her foot rose off the gas pedal.

Bob would have left them there, not caring who stumbled on them at some later date. Brian was cautious. Thoughtful. Responsible.

She shook her head. He was a man. A man about to ask how those fireworks had gotten there.

Cass floored the gas and drove away.

"SO, IN OTHER words, you totally blew it?" Logan said when Brian connected with the guys back at USSO-COM via a video link an hour later.

"No, it gave me a chance to tell her the truth—that I'm not there for the ranch, I'm there for her."

"And you expect her to believe that?" Connor said. "This Finchley guy is right; you are there for the ranch."

"No, I'm not. Not anymore." He met the disbelieving gazes of the four other men head-on. "I told you, it's like the General knew how to pick her out for me. Maybe that's hard to believe, but—"

"Yeah, it's hard to believe," Jack said. "Because you've fallen for your own bullshit."

"Watch it."

"You're talking love at first sight. What the hell kind

of grown man believes in that?" Jack pressed.

"You've never seen a woman and wanted her?" Brian challenged him.

"Wanted her? That's a far cry from loving her," Jack returned.

"The real question is, how are you going to get from here to the altar?" Logan asked. "She doesn't seem to want to date you."

The whole conversation unnerved Brian. The last thing he'd ever thought he'd do was debate love with an enigma like Jack. He answered Logan's question instead. "She's attracted to me. That's a start."

"Fix the damn house." Hunter spoke up for the first time, the sniper's sharp gaze contrasting with his lazy drawl. "That's what you're there to do, so do it."

"I'm here to marry Cass." He rubbed his neck, all too conscious of how rapidly things had changed in the past twenty-four hours. Jack was right; he'd come for the chance at the land. And to clear his name. Now Cass filled his every thought.

"You've only been there a day. You've let her know what you're after. You've let her know why. Seems like the only other guy in the picture is an ass. So show her what kind of man you are. What kind of life you're offering her. Let her decide what she wants," Hunter said reasonably.

"What if she doesn't want me?" Brian pushed. "Then what?"

"Then we're all screwed."

The next video call Brian made was to the General,

who answered far more quickly than Brian had expected.

"What's wrong?"

"N… nothing," Brian said, startled by the General's face filling his screen. Hell, had he just stuttered?

"Why are you calling? You married my daughter yet?"

"No. I've been here one day." Shit, he had to get a hold of himself. Stuttering? Explaining himself like a schoolboy? This wasn't him at all. "I've met your daughters and started working on the house. I've got a good idea what it'll take to get it all done. The big job is the roof. It's leaking all over the place. We'll need to take it down to the joists and start over with new plywood." He named a sum to get it done.

The General pursed his lips. "The income from the ranch will cover it. Tell Cass what you need and she'll get it to you."

"I'll do that."

"What else have you seen?"

"Not much. Like I said, it's only been a day." He decided not to mention his run-in with Bob. Yet. Cass wouldn't like it if he did and he wanted her on his side.

The General nodded. "Keep going, then. Report back in a few days."

"Don't you want to hear about your daughters?" Brian asked quickly. Surely the man wanted an update.

"All healthy?"

"Yes."

"Got rid of their boyfriends yet?"

"Not yet—"

"Let me know when you have." The General cut the call.

THANK GOD FOR Wye. She'd taken one look at Cass's face when Cass came to find her at her little house in town, bundled Cass into her restored Volkswagen Beetle, made a single stop at her brother's place and driven far out into the country. They stopped in a pull-out on a little-used road and Wye passed her a paper bag full of cherry bombs. "I know it's not much, but…"

"It's perfect."

Cass got out of the truck and lit them one by one, but it was Wye's presence, not the unsatisfying little pops, that made her feel better as time passed.

"You know someday you're going to have to feel that anger," Wye said when she was done. She had scrambled up to sit on the roof of the Beetle. Cass joined her.

"You'd better hope I never do. I'd end up taking Chance Creek down with me if I ever let it all out."

"I doubt that. People feel things, Cass. They scream, cry, stomp their feet. And then it's over."

But Cass shook her head. "I'm not like that. I'd start screaming and I'd never stop again."

"Because of your father?" Wye asked gently. She'd never pried before and Cass figured she owed her an answer.

"He's part of it. He doesn't love us, Wye," she said tiredly. "He left us as surely as my mother did when she passed away. He bosses us around, sets rules, dictates everything we do, but he doesn't love us."

"I'm sorry," Wye said, pressing her hand. "I hope someday he realizes what he's missing."

Cass had long stopped thinking that was a possibility, and she'd be damned if she'd sit around and feel this pain. She slid down the rounded edge of the roof, landing hard on the dusty ground. She ached for something big to set off. Wye reached down to hand her another paper bag Cass hadn't noticed she'd held in reserve.

"Sorry. It's all I have." Wye shrugged.

Cass opened it and peered inside. More cherry bombs.

They would have to do.

"Cass," Wye called after her as she went to set them off. "Don't waste your life waiting for things to change with your father. You're your own woman. Create the life you want."

Cass nodded, but the irony was she already had the life she wanted. If only the General would get out of her way.

It was nearly dinnertime when Cass got back to the ranch. She parked near the carriage house and went inside to find the kitchen dark and empty. Was it too much to ask that anyone else might think to get a meal on?

"Lena? Alice?"

She heard a scrape and then a thump from down the hall.

That had to be Brian. With a sigh, she decided to take the bull by the horns, and headed for the bathroom. She found Brian smoothing a layer of joint compound over the seams in the backerboard she'd fastened to the wall earlier. Brian had shucked off his t-shirt and tucked its tail in his back pocket. Cass's anger disappeared as she stopped to admire his chiseled muscles and the ripple of his biceps as he worked on, unaware of her presence. The SEAL was... She didn't know what word to use. Hot? That sounded too shallow. Handsome? Too old-fashioned.

Incredible?

Too childish, and what she felt right now wasn't innocent in the least. A hunger for something left unsatisfied for years stirred within her. She wanted to feel those muscles; feel those hands on her. She wanted...

"Oh, hey, Cass." Brian twisted around to look at her. "Didn't see you there."

Caught staring, Cass felt her face heat. "What... Why are you doing that? I told you I would take care of it," she said to cover her embarrassment.

"And I keep telling you the General sent me to help." He stood up and she got the full effect of his low-slung jeans and washboard abs.

Wow, Cass thought. And then, *That could be my husband.*

And then, *no. Absolutely not.*

Although, if Brian was going to work around her house half-naked for the next few days—or weeks—she was going to have a hell of a time not slipping up and saying yes to him.

Brian rubbed his chin with the top of his hand. "I'm afraid I've got some bad news. That roof of yours is a mess. It's going to be a big job to fix it."

"I already knew we'd have to replace it." Her mouth was dry, and her voice was funny when she said the words. Thank goodness Brian didn't seem to notice. What would it feel like to slide her hands over his biceps?

Good. It would feel really good.

"It isn't just the shingles that are damaged, though. Once I've taken them off, I'm going to have to replace all the plywood, too. That makes the job far more difficult and expensive. I talked to the General about it—"

"You called the General?" That bit of information sliced right through the buzz of desire in her veins. "Why did you do that?"

"Because he's footing the bill, right? I needed to get his okay. He said the ranch should be able to cover it, and I should talk to you."

"He did?" Hell, that was going to be a problem.

"He said the cattle operation should be making enough money to cover the cost."

His words hit her like a splash of cold water in the face. Of course it should... but it hadn't since last fall.

She couldn't admit that, though. "How much do you need?"

"For labor and materials?" He named a sum that

made Cass cringe. "But I think you and I could do the job ourselves if you're up for it. That would be a lot cheaper." He named a lower amount, one she might be able to cover if they economized elsewhere. She swallowed hard, thinking about the height of the roof and its steep pitch. Could she even get out on it?

"It's my roof. I'll take care of it," she made herself say, although she didn't have a clue how she'd manage that. She could barely look out the attic windows, and if Brian couldn't do the job alone, how could she possibly do it herself?

"You can't do this one on your own, honey." Brian echoed her thoughts. "You'll need a second set of hands."

Cass's heart sank. She knew exactly where this was leading.

"Luckily you've got me," he added.

She'd walked right into that one.

Brian touched her arm. "This is a beautiful house, Cass. It's got a history I can only guess at but that I hope to hell I'm going to get to know. Let's get her fixed up so you can put away those buckets I found all over the attic. We'll get her right and tight for another hundred years."

"But—" The whole point was *not* to let him help her.

"I'll be right beside you every step of the way."

He was right beside her right now. She could see a pulse beating in his throat. For one strange, almost exhilarating moment, Cass thought about pressing a kiss to it. But that was as crazy as climbing onto Two Willows's roof.

"Think about it. You and me making Two Willows a safe home for your family. I know how much this house means to you. Let me help you."

Help her?

No one helped her. Not with her housework, and not with the repairs Two Willows perpetually needed. Not with raising her sisters or running this ranch the way it was meant to be run.

"I'm not going to marry you," Cass said. He had to know that. She wouldn't let him put himself out if that's what he thought he was going to get.

"I hope you change your mind." Brian touched her hand with his fingertips and Cass held her breath, her heart beating hard. "Whether or not you do, I'm going to fix your house. It needs to be done and I'm the man for the job."

Cass turned around and strode out of the house. She needed to breathe—to put some distance between her and Brian so he couldn't read on her face what he did to her when he was near. Out in the yard, she paced the garden paths until Lena met her coming back from the barns.

"Did you just have sex?" Lena asked bluntly.

Cass turned on her. "Of course not! Why would you say that?"

Lena laughed. "You look like some guy blew your mind."

Chapter Six

BRIAN LEFT CASS alone the rest of the day, finding his way into town and grabbing a burger for dinner. He understood instinctively how big a deal it was for her to accept his help with the roof; possibly a bigger deal than allowing him to kiss her. If there was one thing the Reed women valued, it was their independence.

He woke early the following morning and when he came downstairs he found Lena was the only one up. He thought about his second mandate—getting control of the ranch—and decided he'd work on that today. "I'd love to get a look at the cattle," he told her, serving himself a bowl of cereal.

"Oh, hell. How did I know this was coming?" She pushed her plate away and crossed her arms over her chest. "Don't tell me; you're really the new overseer come to replace Bob."

Brian scratched the back of his neck. He wasn't, and he didn't know if the General planned on one of them being in charge, or if they'd share the work—and the decision making. Taking in Lena's set jaw, he realized he was being just as chauvinistic as she expected him to be. The General had made it clear he meant for the men to be in charge.

Was that fair?

On the ranch his father had lost, men had handled the cattle, but he knew of several husband-and-wife teams who ran things together in the area where he'd grown up. It hadn't really registered when he was a kid. If his father hadn't lost the place when Brian was fourteen he'd probably know more about how those dynamics worked. Men were certainly stronger, and lots of the work on a ranch took the kind of strength women lacked.

Lots of it took brains and organization—and determination.

He bet Lena had plenty of that.

"Look," he said. "I'm just asking a favor. I used to live on a ranch as a kid. Before my father gambled it away."

"I'm not buying your sob story," Lena said.

"It's not a sob story. It's an explanation. I haven't gotten to ride much since I was a teenager, and I miss it like hell."

She studied him. With her no-nonsense hairstyle, and her work clothes on, he could tell she wanted to appear tough, but Lena didn't fool him. She loved this ranch as much as Cass did—maybe more, because she understood the blood, sweat and tears that went into maintaining it. She worked it; Cass just lived on it.

"C'mon. Let's go for a ride so I can really see the

place," he urged her.

"And report back to the General."

"I'm not trying to hide that. He definitely wants an update on the state of the ranch."

"Maybe he should come here himself sometime and see."

Ah. She missed the old man. "When's the last time he was by?"

Lena rolled her eyes. "You're kidding, right?"

He shook his head.

"Wow. All right, come on, then. You're definitely no spy if you don't even know that much."

"Thanks a lot." He dug into his cereal, unconcerned. He'd taken far worse from buddies in the military. When he glanced up again she was waiting by the door. "Oh, you mean right now?" He stood up and took his bowl with him.

"Better bring that back when you're done. Cass'll have a fit."

"I'm done now." He scooped up a last bite and set the bowl on the counter as he followed Lena out the door. "I'm still curious, though. The General has to visit sometimes."

"Does he?" She led the way toward the outbuildings. "Someone should tell him that."

"What's it been, a couple of years?"

"More than that."

"Five? Ten?" Now he was kidding, but the set of Lena's shoulders told him she didn't find it funny. "When was it then?" he asked, becoming serious. He

knew all too well what it felt like to lose one parent—
and have the other let you down.

"I haven't seen my fa—the General since the day we
buried my mother," she told him bluntly. "He was at the
grave site, and then he was gone. The only time I've
seen him since was on the other side of a video screen."

Brian stopped in his tracks. "That can't be right."
The General's wife had died over a decade ago.

Lena kept walking. After a moment Brian strode
quickly after her to catch up. "He's never come back.
Not once?"

She shook her head.

"But you go to him, right? On visits?"

"Cass did a few times. So did Alice. Sadie did once
or twice." She shrugged. "He never asked me. I'm not
exactly cut out to be a spokeswoman for the family."
She must have read his confusion in his expression,
because she added, "He could depend on Cass and
Alice to behave themselves at military functions. At least
for a little while. When he stopped being able to count
on that, the invitations stopped coming."

"Got it." He remembered the rumors around the
base—that Cass had pitched a fit at an event and the
General's daughters had never been seen there again.

Lena tossed her head as if it was all no big deal, but
Brian knew it had to be. Why the hell wouldn't the
General come and see his girls? He wanted to strangle
the man. "It's his loss, you know."

"Whatever." She increased her pace. At the stables,
she led out two horses and Brian helped to saddle them,

filing away the problem of the General's absence to mull over later. He couldn't stop from taking deep breaths to convince himself he was finally back on a ranch, with a ride in front of him and a chance—a small chance—to one day own a part of this. The fragrant stables took him back to his youth. "Did you give me the horse that likes to buck everyone off?" he asked Lena.

"Thought about it," she admitted. "Decided that was too predictable. Instead I gave you the one you'll miss the most when you're gone."

"Ouch."

"You're the one reporting back to the General."

What Brian saw over the next hour left him uneasy. Lena was knowledgeable about every aspect of the ranch and cattle raising, and from the way her sharp gaze scanned the pastures as they rode, he knew she cared about her job.

But some things didn't add up. Broken equipment. Half-assed repair jobs. His gut told him Lena wasn't responsible for the overall air of dilapidation around the place. So who was?

"You're letting maintenance slide," he finally said when he couldn't hold the criticism in anymore.

"Bob kept getting in my way when he was here. Since he's been gone, I've told Cass about every problem, and what I need to fix it. She keeps putting things off. We need to replace the stock we lost last winter, too. But that's a no go, either."

"Cass keeps the books, huh?"

"Bob used to do the business records, but she took

them back over when he left."

"How come you don't do them if you're in charge down here?" They were riding back along a dusty track toward the stables. Brian didn't want to climb off his horse, but he needed to work out what was going on.

"Numbers aren't my thing," Lena said. "I never minded that Cass did them before, but she's never been tightfisted like this until now. I get that Bob didn't leave things in a perfect state, but she's being ridiculous."

He could tell it was an argument she'd had with her sister, but he also figured Cass had her reasons for keeping hold of their money. Come to think of it, she'd wanted to keep costs low on the roof, too. He'd used it to his advantage, thinking she was being thrifty in the way that all ranch people were.

Was there another reason? Was Cass trying to hide money problems from her sister...and the General?

He needed to see those books, he decided, which wouldn't be easy if Cass had control of them. He was pretty sure he could sneak a look at them sometime while Cass wasn't around, but that wouldn't bode well for their future.

Somehow he needed to persuade her to confide in him.

Beside him, Lena heaved a sigh.

He followed the direction of her gaze and saw a herd of cattle in the distance. "Seems like a ranch this size could support more cattle."

"Of course it could. That's what I'm saying," Lena exploded. "If the General would stop fucking around and let me run this place right—"

"What would you do differently?"

"Everything!" For the next fifteen minutes she gave him a scathing play by play of all of Bob's mistakes. "He was a complete ass. He was trying to ruin this ranch, not run it," she finally finished.

Brian nodded. It had been hard to keep his mouth shut while she rattled on. At first, he wanted to defend the General's decision to send an overseer to a spread this large, but he'd met Bob. The man certainly wasn't an improvement on Lena. Brian had counseled himself to let her have her say, and the more she talked, the more he realized she knew as much as any man about how to get the work done. With a passel of willing hands to help with some of the heavy lifting, she'd be an effective overseer herself.

Why didn't the General know that?

"How about the hands? Are they people you trust?"

Lena looked away. Shook her head. "Overseers come and go a lot around here," she said, keeping her gaze on the distant mountains, "but our hands were a more steady lot until Bob fired them all. Thought the General would have something to say to that, but I guess he was busy. Bob replaced them with new guys. There's some of them." She pointed to a knot of men repairing a fence in the pasture they were approaching.

"I think I'll go have a word." Brian urged his horse forward. If Lena didn't like them, there had to be a reason, and the sooner he knew what it was, the sooner he could talk to the General about how to fix it. "Howdy," he called out. "Hot day for work like that."

The men nodded and grunted when he drew near, but they weren't a talkative lot. Brian did his best to exchange the usual chitchat with them, sussing them out. He didn't like the surly way they answered his questions, or the feeling that they'd united in their dislike of him at first sight.

After a few minutes, he turned to go, but the tallest of the lot—Ed—spoke up. "Take a message to your sister," he called to Lena. "Tell her to cool it. She's spooking the cattle."

Lena didn't acknowledge the man, but Brian knew he had to be talking about the fireworks he'd found when he followed Cass. That answered that question: they were Cass's rather than Bob's. But why had she been setting them off? Was that what she did when she was angry? Blew things up? He'd have to keep an eye on that.

He remembered the tidy way they'd been arranged. The lack of vegetation on that part of the ranch. Even when she was pissed off, Cass was careful—so careful she didn't even allow herself to feel the anger that so obviously burned inside her.

Lena quickly turned her horse and rode off the opposite way they'd come, off the main track toward a path that wound toward higher ground. Brian nodded to the men, re-mounted his horse and followed along after her. He didn't mind the detour; he wasn't in a hurry to curtail this ride. Instead, he scanned the countryside as he thought about Cass, noted how things were positioned and wondered where Lena was leading him.

Fifteen minutes later, they wound around an out-cropping to a level crescent of ground backed by a rising slope where targets had been set up.

"Do you shoot?" Brian asked Lena. He knew she did but he figured he wouldn't mention the photo collages back at the base.

"Of course." She lifted the light jacket she wore over her shirt and showed him a shoulder holster.

Brian raised his eyebrows. "That's a lot of firepower. You know how to use that thing?"

She rose to the challenge, slid off her horse and paced to a point some distance from the target. Seconds later, she'd fired all the rounds. She returned the pistol to its holster and Brian went with her to inspect her shots.

"Pretty good."

"It'll do," she said, but he could tell she was pleased with his praise. He hadn't overstated it; that had been a tight grouping. Lena knew what she was doing.

"Want a try?" she offered. "I've got more ammunition in my saddle bags."

"That would feel too much like work," he told her. "The way I see it, I'm on vacation." As they returned to the horses, Brian asked, "Does Cass shoot that well, too?"

Lena laughed. "Of course; we're Reeds, aren't we?"

WHEN CASS GOT up, it was easy to see that Lena had been and gone already, but the half-eaten bowl of cereal

on the counter perplexed her until she realized Brian
must have eaten and left, too. She did a quick tour of
the house to be sure before she ate her own breakfast,
then quickly cleaned the kitchen and put some more
work into the shower.

At noon she was preparing lunch when she spotted
him and Lena walking back from the direction of the
stables. They stopped near the edge of the lawn, talking
together earnestly. She could tell Lena was describing
something by the way she was gesturing. Brian listened
intently, nodding now and then.

Cass couldn't remember Bob ever listening to Lena
like that. In fact, she couldn't remember Lena ever
talking to any man that way. She was fully engaged in
the conversation and so was Brian. Cass knew she
should be happy for both of them to connect with each
other, but instead she felt a twist of pain.

Was that… jealousy?

Jo entered the kitchen behind her. "What's there to
eat?"

"Whatever you feel like making." Cass couldn't take
her eyes off Lena and Brian. Whatever they were talking
about had them both riveted. Lena was talking again,
her gestures wide with whatever she was describing.
Brian said something and Lena laughed, making her
look so girlish Cass's stomach twisted with a longing for
an easier time. She remembered their early days when
she and Lena would laugh and quarrel and make up and
laugh again. That seemed so long ago.

"Since when do I have to cook?"

That got Cass's attention and she turned around. "You're not a child. Time to learn to take care of yourself. I don't know when I became everyone's mother." She didn't mean to sound so exasperated, but her emotions had been yanked around far too much in the time since Brian had arrived.

"You're the one who always says it's more economical if we eat together." Jo headed back out of the room.

"Jo… I'm sorry," Cass called after her. She was right; Cass had always emphasized family meals. She'd read somewhere as a teen they were the key to a happy and healthy family. Back in those days she'd been desperate to find some formula to get it right.

She was still doing that.

Jo stopped in the doorway and Cass, grateful for the chance to smooth over an argument that was entirely her fault, added, "I'll get lunch on in a minute. Would you go see if Sadie and Alice want to join us?"

"Sadie isn't… here." Jo bit her lip guiltily. Cass knew that look. She'd spilled something Sadie wanted kept quiet.

"Where is she?"

"With Mark, I guess."

Cass sighed. Where else? "Okay. Get the others. I'll whip up something to eat."

Jo lingered by the door. "Cass? What do you really think about marriage?"

"I think it's complicated. Why do you ask?" She opened the refrigerator and pulled out fixings for sandwiches. She didn't want to think about marriage.

Not when Brian and Lena were still outside talking. Had Brian's interest shifted to her sister after spending time with her? Not that she cared, she told herself.

"Just wondering. Sean says we make a lot of things far more complicated than they need to be."

Cass looked at her sharply. "Like what?" She didn't like much Sean had to say these days. He seemed determined to flout every one of society's rules, and she had the feeling he'd throw the baby out with the bathwater to make his point.

"Marriage, love, sex… everything. He thinks we shouldn't worry about it so much."

"Sounds like he wants to shirk responsibility." Lots of men were like that these days. Bob, for example.

Although Brian seemed cut from a different cloth.

"That's not it at all," Sadie said. "He wants to share responsibility. He believes that people should help each other as much as they can. Living together, working together—like we do here."

"He likes our living arrangements, does he?" Cass had a feeling she knew where this was headed. Two Willows drew shirkers like a magnet these days. Reaching back into the fridge, she pulled out a packet of bacon. BLTs would make a good lunch.

"He thinks it's great. And he's right—there's room for a lot more people at Two Willows. In a truly sharing situation, people don't need as much privacy."

"I need privacy, and I don't want Sean here all the time." She deposited the ingredients on the counter and turned to pull a frying pan off the hanging rack. She stopped short. "Where's my good pan?"

"You didn't even notice he was here last night!" Jo exploded.

Cass stopped, one hand raised to look through the pans again. "He was here last night?"

"That's right. And he didn't bother you one bit, did he?"

"I'm going to stop you right there," Cass said, selecting a different pan and moving to the counter. "Sean's not moving in, and that's final."

"You don't get to dictate that!"

"Fine—ask the General." Cass had heard enough. As far as she was concerned, if Sean wanted to live with them, he'd better be prepared to pay—not only for his room and board, but also for the annoyance of having to listen to his pronouncements.

"That's not fair! You know the General will say no."

"Because we don't need a freeloader. Don't you see Sean's using you? All that sharing stuff? That's baloney! What's he shared with you?"

"He's shared his heart with me. That's the most important thing, isn't it?"

"No," Cass said sharply, looking up from the stove. "I mean, yes—hearts are important, but so is paying your way. Don't get taken in by him. He obviously wants to take advantage of you."

"Sean said you'd say that. He said you'd do whatever you could to keep us from being happy. He said you were just like the General!" Jo rushed from the room and pounded up the stairs.

Cass leaned against the counter, defeated. Was she just like the General?

She didn't even know anymore.

When Brian arrived back at the house with Lena for lunch, he noticed right away the tension around the table. Jo's eyes were red, as if she'd been crying. Cass's temper was short. Lena, who'd been so talkative all morning, clammed right up when she took in her sisters' moods. Alice was in her own world. Sadie, who arrived right before the meal was served, was watchful.

Brian knew something had happened; he just didn't know what.

He broke the silence that reigned through most of the meal by describing the work that would have to be done on the roof. "Cass is going to help me, but we might need the rest of you to pitch in now and then."

"You're going up on the roof?" Sadie asked her sister with a frown. "But—"

"I'm always up for learning how to take care of our house," Cass cut her off with a significant look Brian wished he understood.

"Why not hire someone to do it?" Lena asked. "With all the money you're refusing to cough up, you should be able to afford it."

Brian waited to see what Cass would say, once more wishing he could get his hands on the record books for the ranch.

"I need to know how to keep up this house; it'll be my job for the rest of my life," Cass answered primly.

"But—"

"If you want to help, too, you're more than welcome."

Lena subsided under Cass's glare, and Brian knew he'd have to wait to learn the state of the ranch's finances.

"I plan to run into town today," he said, ready to move on to a new topic. "Anyone else need anything? I could pick up some things at the store, if you like."

The sisters all put down their forks and stared at him as if one of the cattle had wandered into the kitchen and asked to do the lunch dishes.

"Did I say something wrong?"

"No," Cass said after a moment, still studying him. "I just can't remember when someone offered to help out like that. We usually handle everything ourselves."

"It's just a trip to the store."

"To you, it is," Sadie said quietly.

"I'll come with you if you don't mind," Alice said suddenly. "I have a few boxes I need to ship."

"What about you, Cass? Want to ride along?"

"I've got some things to do here," she told him. "We're low on milk, though. And juice. Could you… could you buy some for me? I'll give you the cash, of course."

"Of course." Brian wasn't sure what was going on. These women lived in a small town; surely they were the recipients of neighborly help from time to time.

He considered what the General had told him of their teenage escapades. They'd spent their time hiding out, hoping not to be caught when they managed to run off the grownups in charge of caring for them and the ranch. That hiding must have changed the way they looked at other people.

No wonder Cass viewed him with such suspicion. Did she think he wanted to steal her independence?

He did, in a way.

Which made the fact she'd asked for this small favor a major step for Cass. He felt almost… honored.

Cass was studying Alice now, and she suddenly stood up and stalked over to the window. "Alice? Where's your car? Did Howie take it again?"

"He didn't take it. I loaned it to him." Alice took a bite of salad, as if dismissing the topic, but Brian's gut told him she was lying, and Cass seemed to realize it, too. He could almost see her sorting through things to say to her sister and discarding them one by one. Alice kept stabbing leaves of lettuce. It was clear she wouldn't be happy about any interference.

"That's all right. I've got my truck and I'm happy to drive today," Brian said. Seeing Cass's concern about Alice's boyfriend had reminded him the General didn't like any of the men his daughters were dating. Time to look into things and see what was what.

He managed to divert the conversation back to the roof for the rest of the meal, but when he had helped Alice load her boxes into the back of his truck, and they were on their way to town, he decided to revisit the topic.

"Tell me about Howie. Sounds like a busy guy."

"He is," Alice said eagerly. "He's a real self-starter. He's always running back and forth to Billings and Bozeman, day and night. He delivers packages for businesses. He does such a good job getting everything where it needs to go on time, he's got direct deliveries cornered."

Brian's shoulders sagged as he took in her words. He just bet Howie did. And he'd bet the small-town boy hadn't beaten UPS and the United States Post Office to take over the distribution of legitimate shipping in the area. As he drove the winding, two-lane highway toward town, he wondered if Alice could really be so innocent as to think he had.

"Day and night, huh?"

"That's right; you've got to give the customer what he wants."

It sounded like she was quoting her boyfriend. "Most businesses operate within normal business hours."

"Not Howie sometimes he's running packages in the wee hours."

Brian's hands tightened on the steering wheel. Didn't the General see the danger of allowing his daughters to remain so innocent? Hadn't he taught them anything about the world?

Or didn't the man care?

It seemed to Brian their father's long absence had caused them to grab hold of any man who came close and hold on for dear life no matter how that man treated them.

"Do you travel much?" He needed more information before pressing her further.

"I'm more of a homebody. I guess I travel in my imagination, but I like it best right here."

"Have you ever spent much time away from Two Willows?" From what he could gather she spent most of her time in her carriage house workshop sewing the costumes she made. Lena mentioned that people commissioned them, and had said Alice was a gifted seamstress.

"No." Alice shrugged. "But I'm content. I can't keep up with my ideas. I finish one project and the next one's ready to go in my mind. Who has the time to leave home?"

Brian found himself wanting to protect her. He knew what he needed to say: *your boyfriend's probably running drugs. Get rid of him!* But somehow he couldn't say it.

He'd only been out of the Navy for a few days and already he'd gone soft.

"What about TV? Surely you watch TV?" There were crime shows all over the place. Didn't she watch them and put two and two together about her boyfriend?

Alice laughed. "Almost none. We don't get reception out here, and cable is expensive."

"What about the cheap movie channels?"

She shook her head. "We're all pretty busy. I guess we've never really been TV people."

Brian rubbed his chin and tried another tack. "If

Howie delivers so many packages, how come he doesn't deliver yours?"

"Oh, he's not that kind of deliveryman," she said airily. "He does direct delivery. I ship things all over the world. He's just running between Chance Creek, Billings and Bozeman."

"That's a lot of deliveries for such a small area," he commented.

For the first time, Alice frowned. "I know." She studied her hands folded in her lap. Brian waited. If she offered even a hint of understanding, he'd fill in the rest of the picture for her. "Cass thinks he's cheating on me," she blurted when he'd almost given up hope.

Brian wanted to bash his head on the steering wheel. "Honey, he's not cheating on you."

"You really don't think so?" She looked so grateful, the words Brian had been about to say died on his lips. Damn it, he'd never had a problem ordering his men around, or talking straight to a subordinate who needed a dressing down.

But this was no warrior to be chewed out.

This was a fragile, lovely woman. Cass's sister. And Alice's expression was so hopeful it unmanned him.

"What's in the packages Howie's delivering?" he managed to ask.

"I don't know. He doesn't, either. They're ready to go when he picks them up."

"You've seen them?"

Alice shifted, and Brian clutched the steering wheel even tighter. Had that asshole really taken his girlfriend along when he delivered drugs?

"I've ridden with him once or twice on a delivery run, but he said his clients didn't like it, so I stopped," Alice said.

Town was coming up, Brian decided this conversation was too important to have while negotiating its busier streets and looking for parking. He pulled off the road and shut off the engine. "What do you think is in the packages, Alice?" he asked gently.

She looked down at her hands clasped in her lap instead of answering. As the seconds ticked away, she shrugged.

"I think you know," Brian said.

"He's a good guy," Alice said, but her attempt to defend him was half-hearted.

"Then why is he using your car to deliver drugs? That's what he's doing, right?"

"Of course not!"

"You realize what's going to happen if he's stopped, don't you?" Brian pressed on. "First, you'll be implicated in the operation. Second, you could lose your car. Is that what you want?"

She was kneading her left hand with her right, but when she noticed him looking, she stopped. Finally, she shook her head. "No. But it won't happen, because Howie wouldn't do that."

"You positive about that?"

Alice bit her lip, and Brian realized she didn't like to lie.

"Alice, are you positive about that?" he asked again.

"No."

Now they were getting somewhere, but it wasn't easy making Cass's sister so miserable. "Why don't you say something to him? Tell him to leave your car alone, at the very least."

"He'd get mad." Her voice was so low he could barely hear her.

Brian nearly asked, *so what?* But he could tell that wouldn't be a welcome question. "Will he hurt you?"

She straightened, shocked. "Of course not."

"Then what are you afraid of?"

"He'll leave me," she said, as if that explained everything. Maybe it did, Brian thought as he passed a hand over his face. As cocky and independent as the Reed girls were, at the core was a vulnerability so raw it made him wince. Their mother had left them. So had their father, in a way. It explained a lot. Plus, they were young. Cass was twenty-six. Alice couldn't be more than twenty-four. Old enough to know better. Young enough to still hope for the best.

Brian reached out and flipped the visor down on the passenger side. He positioned the mirror so Alice could see into it.

"Know what I see when I look at you?" he asked.

She shook her head.

"Someone so beautiful and talented she's on her way to having the world at her doorstep. Is Howie your first serious boyfriend?" Another stab in the dark.

"Yes."

"I guarantee if you walk away from him, another

man is going to come along who knocks your socks off. You'll know him when he makes your life better, not worse."

"How would I meet someone like that? It's like you said, I never go anywhere."

Brian hated to see the pain in her eyes. "But you could. You know that, right?"

"It's not that simple."

No. He was beginning to see nothing was simple with the Reed women. "If you don't want to leave home, then the trick is to keep doing all the things you like doing, and try one or two new things, too. If you act like yourself all the time, you'll attract the right man. It's when you pretend you're someone you're not—like by condoning drug use when you don't agree with it—that you run into trouble." He figured it was time to end the lecture for the day. He started the truck's engine again.

"Howie took my car," Alice blurted. "Without asking. I didn't want to say anything in front of Cass."

Brian understood why. "Let's take care of your boxes and get you home. I'll sort it out later."

He felt good about the exchange as they took care of their errands in town. Alice was more talkative than she'd previously been with him, telling him about her business and the way she created unique costumes for musicals, plays and even movies. He hoped that she'd taken their conversation to heart and that soon Howie, who sounded like a real troublemaker to Brian, would be a thing of the past. They decided to stop for coffee at Linda's Diner before heading back to the ranch.

Alice stopped him just as they reached the entryway. "Trouble."

Old habits had him scanning the street and rooftops. But then he did that anyway, no matter where he was. "I don't see anything."

"Of course you don't." Alice was impatient. "It's a feeling." She held a hand up and Brian waited. "No, it's gone." She turned on him. "If you talk in the middle of it, I lose it."

"I think you've already lost it." He meant it as a joke, but Alice's face fell, and he cursed his flippant tone, realizing he'd just undone all the good work he'd managed earlier. After a moment, she nodded.

"Most people don't believe in hunches." She opened the door and in the time it took for them to be seated, Brian lost his chance to say any more about the topic. He shouldn't have said what he had, but he felt the Reed women's superstitions were part and parcel of what left them naïve and vulnerable to exploitation. He wasn't surprised Alice thought she felt things, raised on a ranch where everyone believed in a mystical stone. He didn't let himself think about the way he was using that same stone to manipulate Cass into marrying him. That was for a good cause, after all.

They settled in a booth near the front window. The coffee, when it came, was good and plain, the way he liked it. Alice sipped an herbal tea, but didn't say much and he knew he'd hurt her feelings. "Look, I didn't mean—" he began, but Alice leaned sideways and craned her neck to see out the window.

"There's Sadie! I can't see who she's with, though."

Brian turned the best he could and just made her out, standing across the street. Whoever she was talking to was out of his line of vision, blocked by a parked truck. As they watched, she turned and walked away.

The waitress appeared again. "Here you go. Two slices of peach pie. Is there anything else I can get you?"

"No, thanks," Alice told her, accepting the dish from the waitress. Brian took his and eyed it appreciatively.

Alice looked out the window again. "She's gone, and there's Mark. I wonder why I sensed trouble—" she broke off. "Probably the usual thing. He flirts with every woman he sees. He's going to break her heart."

Brian filed that information away for later. "Alice, I'm sorry I made fun of you." He needed to make the apology if he wanted her to trust him. He'd feel awful if she stayed with Howie because he'd undercut her again.

"You don't hear it, do you?" she said, cutting into her pie. "It's okay if you don't; I've only met one other person who does."

"Hear what?"

"It's not hearing, exactly." Alice made a face. "It's hard to explain. It's like if you had to tell someone who'd always been blind what seeing was like. It's information. It's so clear. I've wondered and wondered why I can access it but hardly anyone else can, but I finally decided that's not the real question."

"What's the real question?"

"What do I do with it?"

Uncomfortable, Brian asked, "Who's the other person who can hear it?"

Alice smiled. "Rose Johnson. She's married to the sheriff, and she owns Thayer's Jewelers. Everyone buys their engagement rings there. She can tell if your marriage will last, but she doesn't hear much else."

"It's good pie, huh?" Brian said. He was well out of his depth in this conversation, but at least Alice didn't seem hurt anymore.

She smiled, a little sadly. "Yeah, it's good pie."

"DID ALICE GET her packages off?" Cass asked Brian when they met up by his truck later. She'd been sweeping the back porch when he and Alice pulled in. As soon as they parked, Alice hopped out and high-tailed it into the carriage house. Cass, wondering if something was wrong, leaned her broom against the railing and went to investigate.

"Yes. She's a little… unusual… isn't she?" Brian began to unload bags of groceries. "Hope you don't mind. I added some things to the list because I thought we were low."

Cass took the bag he offered her, watched him heft three more into his arms, and followed him to the house, bemused. She couldn't remember a man ever thinking about the state of their groceries. "Alice is… Alice," she said.

"She had some kind of premonition while we were out. That something bad would happen between Sadie and her boyfriend." He sounded skeptical.

"Well, that's pretty predictable," Cass said. "But Alice's premonitions have a good track record."

"As good as the standing stone's?"

"Just about." She followed him inside and began to unpack the groceries.

"Name one thing she's gotten right." He pulled out a loaf of bread and put it away in the pantry. "Did she predict the stock market crash of 2008? The last presidential election?"

"She predicted my mother's death."

Brian stopped short. "Are you serious?"

Cass nodded. "We were out riding, the five of us. It was a school day and that was our *gym class*." She finger quoted the words. "We were homeschooled, you know."

"The General told me that."

"Alice reined up in the middle of the trail and began to cry. We didn't know what had happened. I thought she got stung by a wasp. But she just kept saying, 'Mom's hurt. She's really hurt!' She was completely hysterical, so I stayed with her while Lena and the others rode like hell to get home. Lena got there first, of course. She found my mother at the base of the stairs where she'd fallen."

"Cass—"

"Mom had a stroke. A massive one. There'd been no warning. She was thirty-seven, Brian. She lasted a few more days. At least we got to say good-bye, but still…"

"I'm sorry."

Cass nodded and swallowed past the lump in her throat. Sometimes when she went riding on a crisp, clear fall day she went right back to that time, sitting on her horse next to Alice's, cradling her sister in her arms as best she could.

"I don't know how Alice knows these things. Neither does she. Sometimes she hates it, because people don't believe her, and sometimes the things she knows… well, they're not pleasant. But she always says them out loud. Always. Even the bad things. Just in case someday she can stop them from happening."

Brian leaned his forehead against the doorjamb. "Hell. I'm an ass. Someday I guess I'll learn to keep my mouth shut." He straightened. "I lost my mom young, too, you know."

Cass hadn't known that. "Was she sick?"

"No. Walked into a robbery at a convenience store. Wrong place at the wrong time."

She read the pain in his features, and suddenly that lump filled Cass's throat again.

"I'm sorry, too."

"Yeah, well…" He shrugged. "We're a little alike, you know. I'm not a big fan of my dad, either. Mom wouldn't have been there if he hadn't been too busy gambling all their money away. He'd already lost our ranch; you'd think he might have been a little more careful about his wife." He turned away, but not before she saw his anguish. "Gotta go bring in the rest of the bags," Brian said and left the house again.

They *were* alike, Cass realized. Except his story was

worse. She supposed she preferred a distant, workaholic father to a neglectful gambling addict.

Her thoughts churned over what she knew about Brian. The way he'd lost his mother. The way he kept trying to do things for her. She busied herself putting away the groceries, uncomfortable with the feelings welling up inside her. She didn't know why she was so emotional these days. It was silly. Nothing had changed.

Except Brian was here.

And he was changing everything.

"It's good to talk about it," he said, coming in behind her. "I didn't think that would be the case."

"We used to talk about Mom a lot," she told him. "But not so much anymore."

"Do you find it hard to remember her? What she sounded like? Things like that?" He leaned against the counter and watched her empty the bags.

"When I start feeling like that I pull out the letter she left me and read it again." She must have done it a thousand times. "It helps."

"What did she say in the letter?"

"To take care of my sisters and keep them together. That was what she wanted most. To keep up the ranch, since it's our inheritance. It was hers, you know. The Griffiths have always lived here. They were from Wales originally, if you can believe it. That's where Alice's gift comes from."

"And why there's a standing stone out there?"

"Maybe." She smiled. "This really is a special place to us. Mom always told us it was important to keep this link to our past. She would trot us outside every year on the summer solstice, and take us through the maze to the stone. We had to take off our shoes and feel the ground under our soles. She was careful about us wearing shoes the rest of the time, this being a ranch and all, but at that time of year she wanted to make sure we were connected to the land. That's always stuck with me. We still do it." The memory of her mother was so clear and bittersweet, Cass found herself blinking against the sting of tears. "I loved her so much. And I love this house—and the ranch. If I lost it—Brian, I don't know what I'd do. Her memory is everywhere here. It would be like losing her all over again."

Brian didn't say a word. Instead, he tugged her into an embrace, his arms a haven from the loneliness that always swept over her when she thought of her mother's passing. Cass knew she shouldn't have said anything. She kept spilling her guts to the enemy.

She settled against him, breathing in his warm, male scent. Brian didn't feel like an enemy at the moment.

Which was more terrifying than anything else.

"THE NIGHT MY mother died I was asleep in my bedroom," Brian told Cass. "I'd gone upstairs early because I hated it when Dad gambled on the game. He always drank, too. If he won, he crowed about it like he was the one who'd scored the touchdowns. When he lost—well, you didn't want to be around to see that. Besides, we'd already lost so much because of him."

Cass shifted in Brian's arms. He kept his hold on

her light, but she didn't push away, so he went on.

"I always wonder what would have happened if Mom had woken me up and asked me to go along—or go for her. I would have. I was young and skinny, but I was tall. Less of a mark than she was after dark."

"You might have been killed instead," Cass murmured.

"Yeah. Maybe. Maybe not, too. I was always quick. Always strong. Things would have been different if she hadn't died."

Cass nodded against his shoulder. She felt so right in his arms he wondered why they hadn't met until now. He should have known her all his life.

"The cops woke me and my younger brother up. Dad was bawling in the living room. Bawling. Never seen the man cry before or since. I knew something was really wrong, and when they told me—" Christ, what a night that had been. Brian struggled to keep his voice even. "I hit him. I fucking hit him as hard as I could. He just sat there and took it. Said, 'Go on. I deserve it.'" Brian broke off. "Shit. Why the fuck couldn't he have gone to get the fucking milk?"

Cass's arms snaked around his neck and it was her turn to comfort him. Brian had never told this to anyone. He'd never even talked about it with Grant. He wondered how much his brother remembered of that night. "Nothing worked after that. Dad never got over it. Ended up on disability. Still lives in a dinky little apartment in Wyoming."

"What about your brother?"

"Grant? He's a chip off the old block. He's got a lovely wife. Two kids. He's about to lose them, he's being such an idiot." Brian released Cass and walked away. "I couldn't stop Dad and I can't stop him, either. He called me a couple of months ago—he'd taken a second mortgage on the house. Couldn't make the payments. Too busy gambling his income away every weekend. Marissa doesn't know. I lent him what I could. You can bet I'll never see that money again."

"I'm sorry." Cass watched him pace the room. "Are you… are you a gambler too?"

He shook his head. "Not like that. Not with money. I just take chances with my life. Part of the job description as a SEAL."

"That's different, don't you think?"

"I don't know." He really didn't. "What I do know is that I'll do everything I can to make sure you don't lose this ranch. I can't give you your mother back, but I can do that much. I know what it feels like to lose your home, and I don't want that for you."

Cass crossed the room, took his face in her hands and kissed him.

"I'M SORRY." CASS backed away from Brian only moments after she'd begun the kiss. "I… I don't know why I did that." Emotion had gotten control of her again. Brian's raw explanation of his past and his pledge to save her ranch had broken past all her defenses and tugged her right across the room.

"Don't be sorry." Brian pursued her, caught her

hand in his and hesitated. "I'm going to kiss you again."
He waited for her to stop him.

But she didn't. And when he leaned down and
pressed his mouth against hers, she found herself up on
her tiptoes to meet him. She kissed him back hungrily,
desperate to prolong the connection his words had
forged between them.

She'd always wanted this kind of understanding
from a man. She'd hoped Bob would bring it to their
relationship, but he'd never been capable of it.

Brian was. His hands slid under her hair as he deep-
ened the kiss, and Cass strained up to be closer to him.
Holding on to his wide shoulders, balancing on her toes,
she experienced his touch with her whole body. She
wanted more.

So much more.

She wanted this closeness to go on and on. Could
she possibly allow Brian into her life?

Could she marry him?

She pulled back, breathing heavily. Brian stepped
closer, dropped his hands to the small of her back and
enclosed her in a true embrace, seeking her mouth
again. She let him find it, loving the feel of his muscled
arms around her. She was safe here. She could relax.

She could let him tease her, igniting a burning hunger inside her she hoped someday he'd quench with his
body.

Cass knew she was sliding into the same dangerous
territory she'd sworn she'd never enter again with any
man, but she had no resistance to Brian. Maybe she'd

been premature in promising to forego love forevermore. Brian was different than Bob.

Different than any man she'd met before.

And she wanted him.

It was as simple as that. Life was complicated, and maybe she'd get hurt again, but she couldn't help think the risk was worth it. Maybe if she knew ahead of time she'd end up disappointed she could simply enjoy the ride.

Her heart told her that wasn't likely, but Cass wasn't willing to listen anymore. Lost in the sensations of Brian's hands stroking her back, she simply let him kiss her, and enjoyed every minute of it.

Part of her hoped he'd sweep her off her feet and carry her upstairs, but all too soon, Brian backed away. "It's getting close to dinnertime," he said, his voice husky. "Everyone will come home soon. I've got an idea. How about I pick up some pizzas and a movie? Think your sisters would like that?"

Cass didn't know. They rarely watched television and they never ordered in.

"Leave it all to me," he said and kissed her forehead. "Go relax for a minute. I'll handle everything."

He urged her toward the stairs, and Cass did as she was told, her lips buzzing from that intoxicating kiss. Her life was changing whether she was ready or not.

And she kind of liked it.

PIZZA. HE NEEDED pizza. And a good movie that would give him an excuse to cuddle Cass on the couch.

A quick check of their TV told him streaming wasn't an option. He needed to find a DVD somewhere—if they still existed. He made his way back to town, found a couple of movies at a run-down video store and picked up the pizzas he'd ordered on the way.

Just as Brian suspected it might be, the take-out food was a big hit with the Reed women. "It's not that we don't eat out," Alice explained, happily munching a slice after they took their customary places at the table. "It's just that we never order in."

"And we don't usually have someone to go get it for us," Jo continued. "No one delivers out here."

They happily consumed the food and were sitting around the kitchen table in a post-carb hangover when someone knocked on the front door.

"Who is it?" Jo asked Alice.

Alice stretched back and patted her stomach. "I'm far too full to get messages from the beyond."

"It's probably for you," Cass told Sadie. "Your customers miss you, you know. You're so busy with Mark all the time you're hardly around."

Sadie's cheeks pinked. "I've caught up with all my orders." She got up and answered the door. When she returned, she was followed by a tall, husky man. "Cab's here for you," she said to Lena.

"Howdy, folks. Sorry to interrupt your meal," the man said. Dressed in a sheriff's uniform, he was an intimidating sight. Six foot four if he was an inch, Brian estimated. Well over two hundred pounds.

"Sit down and have a slice, Sheriff." Cass immediately rose to fetch a plate.

"Don't mind if I do."

Brian waited until the man had sat down to reach over the table and offer his hand. "Brian Lake. I'm visiting Two Willows."

"The General sent him," Sadie explained. "He's fixing our house."

"Good to meet you. I'm Cab Johnson. County sheriff." The sheriff assessed him momentarily and Brian felt that he'd been categorized and summed up in that brief glance. Cab nodded, as if filing him away for future reference. He took the plate Cass handed him and helped himself to a slice. It was only after he'd taken a bite, chewed and swallowed that he addressed Lena. "Seen that boyfriend of yours lately?"

"Not since yesterday."

"Picked a fight last night at the Boot. Hasn't been seen since. I thought you might know where he is."

Brian watched the women take in this information. Cass looked angry. Jo studied her hands. Alice and Sadie exchanged a glance he couldn't interpret.

No one seemed surprised.

"Like I said, I haven't seen him." Lena helped herself to another slice of pepperoni, unfazed.

"Have you heard from him?"

"No." She took a bite, and washed it down with a swallow of milk.

"How about you give him a call," Cab said conversationally.

"What if I don't want to?" Lena was digging in, but

Brian told himself not to get involved. The sheriff had things under control. He wouldn't want to be interfered with.

"I think you should anyway."

Brian had to hand it to Cab. He might not be a man you'd notice in a crowd except for his size, but he had presence when he wanted to. He could feel Lena's desperation growing.

"Fine." Lena pulled out her phone, tapped it a few times and held it to her ear. "He's not there," she said a moment later and shoved her phone back in her pocket.

Cab put his hand out. Lena stared it at a long time. Just when Brian thought she'd refuse, she pulled her phone out a second time, tapped in her code and passed it to the sheriff.

Brian was impressed.

Cab tapped it a few times. "Yeah. Strange he wouldn't be at *Tilly's Odds and Ends*, seeing as it closed about five years ago." A couple more taps and Cab lifted it to his ear. "Yeah, hey baby to you, too, Scott. Get your ass down to the sheriff's department. I've got a few things to talk over with you." He paused. "I'm not asking; I'm telling. See you in an hour, or I'm going to start knocking on doors." He ended the call and handed back the phone. "Thank you for your cooperation. And thank you for the pizza," he said to Cass. "That hit the spot."

"Would you like a slice for the road, Sheriff?"

"I wouldn't refuse it."

Cass wrapped another slice in several layers of paper

towel. Cab nodded his appreciation. Brian stood up as he made to leave. "I'll walk you out, Sheriff."

He waited until they were out front by the sheriff's cruiser, with Two Willows's front door shut firmly behind him. "This Scott character—he get into fights a lot?"

"Scott Howell's been in jail three times in the past two years. Not the best candidate for a boyfriend. Lena should show him the door."

"Maybe he's had a couple of tough breaks?" Brian hedged.

"He's given out a couple of tough breaks, you mean. Howell likes to fight. He never throws the first punch— he knows better than that—but he draws trouble like sugar draws ants. He'll go out to a bar, rile up some drunk cowboy, let the guy take a swing at him and then defend himself like a prizefighter at a championship. I sure as hell wouldn't let him sniff around any lady friend of mine."

"Thanks for the information."

"Now, don't you go get into trouble sorting this out, either. I'd hate to throw you in jail on your first visit to Chance Creek." The big man's lazy smile had Brian thinking Cab might just look the other way if some of that so-called trouble happened.

"I'll do my best. Hey, have you ever heard of a guy named Mark Pendergrass?" Cass had been awfully worried about Sadie's disappearances these past few days. Might as well learn what he could.

"Well, shit." Cab, who'd been leaning against the

cruiser, straightened. "Don't tell me one of the Reeds is dating him, too?"

"Sadie. And she's not home much these days."

Cab shook his head. "The General oughtta get home once in a while. I know he's busy defending our sovereignty and all that, but a man's got to pay attention to his daughters now and then."

"I'm in full agreement." He was, now that he'd seen the way the wind blew at the ranch.

Cab sighed. "Mark Pendergrass is one of the wiliest little shits I've come across in years. You want to go after the drug trade in this town, go after him. Hell, he *is* the drug trade, in a sense."

"Why don't you stop him?"

"Because the sucker's smart, that's why. He studied chemistry at Montana State. He knows how to stay one step ahead of the Feds. They outlaw one of these fancy new designer drugs and the chemists come up with a new one by tweaking the ingredients a little bit. Pendergrass is one of the best. By the time I have the ability to arrest him for something he's distributing, he's on to the next one." Cab looked at Brian. "Are the Reeds getting into drugs?"

He thought about Alice and Howie. Decided to hold off sharing that information just yet. "Not that I've seen. Nothing in their manner suggests any of them are using."

"You'd know the signs?"

"Yeah." He'd seen what drugs could do. He ran through everything he'd seen so far. "I'd be surprised to find they're involved in any of it." Especially now that he'd warned Alice away from Howie.

"Then get them the hell away from Pendergrass." Cab studied him. "You've got more questions. Lay them on me."

"What about Bob Finchley?"

"Used to be the overseer here? Nothing I can pin on the man directly, but I'd keep an eye on him, too, if I were you." He waited a beat. "His name has been linked with Cass, so that's three of them. You've got two more. Who are Alice and Jo seeing these days?"

"Alice let me know today she's dumping Howie Warner."

"Damn good thing. Been hearing some rumors about him running errands at all hours."

"Yeah." Since Cab already knew about him, he decided to come clean. "Seems he likes to borrow Alice's car, too. He's got it now."

"I'll keep an eye out for it."

Brian racked his brain to remember the name of Jo's boyfriend. He hadn't ever seen the guy, though Lena had told him he was in and out of the house more than Cass suspected. "Sean. Sean Pittsville? I think that's it. Jo's boyfriend."

"Sean Pittson. Can't say I've got any issues with him other than that she could do a hell of a lot better."

"So you're saying none of them are any good?" Just as the General had suspected. Brian wondered if the sheriff was one of his sources.

Cab chuckled sympathetically. "You have your work

cut out for you, don't you?" He narrowed his eyes. "You in the service?"

"Navy SEAL." It wasn't something he normally announced, but he figured Cab would understand.

Cab grinned. "The General knows what he's doing."

Brian sure hoped so.

"You need any help, you give me a holler. Don't be fooled. Things might look two bit and ass-backward around here, but that doesn't mean they can't get dangerous."

"I'll keep my eyes open."

"WHAT IS GOING on with Scott?" Cass asked Lena when the men had left the room.

"I already said I don't know." Lena scooted her chair back and stood up, as if about to leave, but Jo stopped her.

"Can't we have one night without fighting—and without our boyfriends?" She sounded so wistful, Cass immediately regretted attacking Lena. "Brian told me he got us a couple of movies and I want to watch them—all of us together, like old times."

"Do you even remember the old times?" Lena asked her. Cass wanted to smack her. These days Jo was so caught up in Sean, Cass rarely got to spend time with her, and she couldn't remember the last time they'd done something as a family.

Oh, Mom, she thought. *I've really been letting you down, haven't I?* She vowed right then and there she'd make the evening one to remember. Which meant no fighting.

And no boyfriends.

Why Brian's face slid into her mind at that moment, Cass didn't know. He wasn't anyone's boyfriend. Certainly not hers, despite all that kissing earlier.

"I'm good with that," Sadie said, interrupting the crazy permutations of her thoughts.

"Me, too," Alice said.

"Lena?" Jo asked hopefully.

"Sure. Whatever."

"All right." Cass began to gather up the plates. "But Lena—please be careful around Scott. I couldn't stand it if you got hurt." Breaking her vow already, she thought grimly. He was out of control these days, though.

"He's never said boo to me," Lena assured her. "He's just hot tempered. He likes to throw down once in a while."

"That's not normal," Cass said.

"Isn't it? It's what the General does, right? Except when he throws down, thousands of lives are at stake."

Cass frowned. That wasn't the same thing at all. As much as the General infuriated her with the way he treated them, she knew he was good at his job—maybe one of the best. "The difference is, the General doesn't start the wars he's in. He does what he does to keep our country safe," she said hotly.

"I've talked to Scott, okay? I've told him he has to cool it down," Lena told her.

"Tell him again."

"We just agreed to have a night in which we don't fight about our boyfriends," Jo complained.

"All right, I've had my say," Cass told her. "We'll forget all about men and watch the show."

"I'll forget about Scott," Lena said with a smart-aleck grin. "But will you be able to forget about Brian? Got a ring on your finger yet?"

Cass tossed a crust of pizza at her. Lena ducked, and it fell at Brian's feet as he walked into the room. Lena stuck her tongue out at Cass and went back to clearing the table, but she was chuckling, and Cass itched with the desire to toss another crust her way.

Brian scooped the food off the floor and placed it on a dirty plate. "Let's pitch in and get these dishes done. Jo, you make the popcorn. Cass, do you have a blender? I'll get the margaritas going."

"Margaritas?"

"That's right." As soon as she fetched the blender, Brian took over, pulled out the drink mixings he'd bought in town and started whipping up the drinks.

"Are popcorn and margaritas a thing?" Cass asked him when she'd run a sink of soapy water.

"They're our thing now," he told her.

When they were done in the kitchen, they all staked their places on the couch and easy chairs around the television, and Brian set up the movie. The first one was a Hollywood crime thriller that thoroughly engrossed Cass, as much because of the romantic tension between the male and female leads as the complicated twists and turns of the plot. Once she noticed Alice was following the action on screen with wide, troubled eyes, but then she got sucked into the story again and forgot her sister's focus.

She didn't like the scenes that depicted the drug trade in a small town—she doubted any of them did—but the film was so fast-paced it didn't give her time to dwell on that, and besides, the romance was the main thing.

As they drank, ate, laughed and called out comments at the screen, Cass relaxed for the first time in ages. Even Lena seemed to get into the movie, although she kept checking her phone. Brian had taken a spot next to Cass and when their hands touched as they both reached into their bowl of popcorn, a little thrill sparked through her. She decided to stop thinking about all her problems for a few hours and enjoy the evening thoroughly.

After they'd glutted themselves on popcorn, Brian placed the bowl they'd shared on the table, took her hand and stroked her palm with his thumb. The margarita she was sipping mellowed her out. Warm and comfortable, happy in the company of her sisters, Cass allowed him to ease closer. Everywhere they touched—their thighs, hips and shoulders, she was so aware of him, her nerves tingled.

It was still early when the first movie ended, and Jo immediately cried, "Let's watch the other one!" In the rush to refill drinks, take turns in the bathroom and load up the second film, Cass didn't notice Sadie's absence until it started.

"Where's Sadie?" she asked as the intro music soared.

"She went out," Jo said. "Said she'll be back later."

Cass sighed.

Family night had been fun while it lasted.

"Who is she with?" As if she didn't know.

Jo made a face. "Mark, who else? Shh."

It was impossible for Cass to enjoy herself now. Lena was still on her phone, probably checking up on Scott. Sadie was off chasing a man doomed to let her down.

What was she doing flirting on the couch with a man the General had sent to spy on them all?

Cass stood up again on the pretext of fetching a glass of water. When she came back into the room, she hesitated. Brian patted the cushion beside him, but she held back. Her job wasn't to fool around with handsome Navy SEALs. Her job was to watch over her sisters. Time to get her priorities straight.

She nodded and smiled at Brian.

But she took Sadie's empty chair across the room.

Chapter Seven

BACK TO SQUARE one.

The phrase rattled around Brian's brain all the following day as he made arrangements for roofing materials and made a thorough inspection of the ranch's outbuildings. When he showed his list of needed repairs to Lena, she added a few more, but approved it overall.

"Are you going to get the General on board with all that? Maybe he'll cough up the money since Cass won't."

"I'll talk to Cass first." He needed to know why she was being so tight-fisted. But first he needed to know why she'd moved across the room from him last night, and why she'd been avoiding him ever since.

Sadie's absence had something to do with it. She'd snuck out in between films and Cass had immediately stiffened up. Brian understood why, after what Cab had told him. It sounded like Mark was into some heavy stuff. The thing that didn't make sense was why a man like that would date little Sadie Reed.

Brian had been around the block enough times to spot the symptoms of a heavy drug user. Sadie's actions didn't add up. She was far too clear-eyed and present when he was around her to be using the stuff herself. Did she know what her boyfriend was up to? Was she attracted to his bad-boy image?

Or had she settled for what was available to her?

He'd investigate her situation next, he promised himself.

After a quiet, stilted lunch in which Sadie's chair was conspicuously empty, and Cass spent most of her time looking at her plate rather than catch his eye, Brian decided he needed a change of pace. He spent the afternoon in town, walking the streets and getting a feel for the place. He stopped in at the sheriff's office and said hello, scoped out the Dancing Boot and Rafters, two local watering holes, noted on which streets the houses and buildings were up and coming, and on which they were fading into disrepair. As he walked, he listened to conversations, spotted places where grown men congregated although it was mid-afternoon on a weekday. He tried to pick up the vibe of the town.

In the end, he ate dinner at the local burger joint, deciding to give Cass some space. He wasn't sure what he'd learned from his afternoon, except that Chance Creek suffered from the same problems all small towns did.

When he finally drove back to Two Willows and walked into the kitchen around eight, Alice was climbing down from the top of the refrigerator.

"Howie finally texted me," she said, waving her phone. "He's bringing back my car. He just left

Billings."

"Did you think at all about what I said?" Brian asked her.

"Yeah. You're right. I'm done with him. As soon as I get my car back, I'll tell him."

She brushed the wrinkles out of the peasant blouse she wore over a pair of white cut-off jean shorts. Her long, tan legs were encased in a pair of cowboy boots. Howie wouldn't let go of a woman like her easily, Brian thought. Especially not when he felt he could take her car any time he wanted it to cover his tracks.

"Alice—do you trust me?"

She met his gaze and held it, and something told him she wasn't simply looking at him; she was listening, too. "Yes."

"How about you give me your phone and let me deal with Howie?"

"Don't you think I should break up with him myself?" She smiled, but it didn't quite reach her eyes. "Stuff like that is character-building, right?"

"If this was a normal relationship, I'd say yes, but this isn't normal. Howie's running drugs in your car. I'd like to handle it."

She gave him her phone and told him her password. "You realize how unusual this is, right? We Reeds don't trust anyone."

"You trusted Howie," he pointed out. He patted his pockets to make sure he had his keys, and headed for the door again.

"I don't think I ever really trusted him," Alice said,

following him. "I think I thought being with him was better than being alone."

"You won't be alone for long, I promise. Once word gets out that you've ditched Howie, you'll have to beat men off with a stick." He stepped outside. "I'll be back with your car. Don't wait up."

He waited until he was sitting in his truck to pull out her phone and answer Howie's text. Howie's last message had been short.

Just left Billings. On my way. See U soon.

Alice had texted back a smiley face, but nothing else. Brian thought a moment and began to type.

At the Boot with Lena. Pick me up?

He waited until Howie texted back.

Be there by 10.

Brian checked his watch. That gave him nearly an hour and a half. He pulled out and headed toward town. His next stop would be the sheriff's department again.

CASS HAD JUST emptied the dryer, and was on her way upstairs, balancing the basket on her hip, when she got a call from Lena. Brian had barely been around all day. She'd seen Lena and Jo head back to the barn after dinner to do the evening chores. Sadie still hadn't come home, and she peeked out the kitchen window at Alice's workshop. The lights were on out there, so she must be working away on some project or other.

"Could you get away for a while and come down to the Park?" Lena said without preamble when Cass answered her call. There's something going on."

"What kind of something?" Cass turned to look out the window, but the Park, where the hired hands had their trailers, wasn't visible from here. The light was fading and it was a perfect summer evening, but chill traced down her spine nonetheless.

"I don't know. I bumped into three guys in a white Datsun close to there. They were going real slow; trying not to kick up dust. When I tried to flag them down to talk, they swerved around me and took off. I didn't like the look of things. Never seen them before in my life. I want to ask the hands some questions. Could use a little backup."

"Where's Jo?"

"Finishing up at the barn. I don't want her involved in this. I need someone with a level head."

Lena's praise surprised Cass. Her sister generally regarded her with a mixture of exasperation and disdain for favoring household chores over ranch work. "Maybe we should wait for Brian to come back."

"Are you serious? Have you forgotten he works for the General?"

"No. Of course not." But that didn't mean he wouldn't be handy in a situation like this. Cass knew that things between Lena and the hands had been coming to a head for a while. She wished Bob had never come to the ranch, and at the same time realized she couldn't say the same for Brian.

"Look, I get it," Lena said candidly. "He seems like a good guy, but we can't forget who he answers to. If there's trouble, the General will sic another overseer on us before you know it."

"I know. You're right." Cass heard the frustration in her sister's voice and understood it all too well. But she didn't like the idea of strangers driving on the ranch. She liked the idea of confronting the hands even less.

"Are you coming or not?" Lena pushed.

"I'll be there."

As Cass walked down to the Park to meet Lena, she couldn't help wishing that Brian was there despite his connection to the General, but she reminded herself that just a few days ago she hadn't known the man existed. They'd done all right without his help up until now. The hands might be a surly bunch, but at the end of the day, they knew who paid the bills. They wouldn't pull anything that would stop the flow of money. Still, the sun was low in the sky by the time she reached the stables.

"Ready?" Lena asked when Cass met her.

"Ready as I'll ever be. How do you think the hands are going to react when we start poking our noses into their business?"

"They won't like it one bit."

"We should wait until tomorrow. It's getting dark."

"We need to strike while the iron's hot," Lena countered.

They walked on without talking. Cass didn't relish

asking five grown men a bunch of questions they wouldn't want to answer. But Lena had made it clear she thought they should, and Lena didn't act on impulse.

The Park was nothing more than a flat stretch of land about a quarter mile from the barn. Hidden from view by the curve of the land, bushy growth between the trailers provided their inhabitants with even more privacy. The trailers were a motley collection of sizes and vintages. The trailer Bob had lived in during his tenure at Two Willows was the newest and largest. The rest ran from a two-bedroom eighties special to a vintage Airstream that used to be second to last in the line. Bob had hauled away the final trailer a month ago—a dilapidated brown and tan affair that the hands had always used for storage. When Cass had confronted him about taking ranch property, he'd laughed in her face and said he'd hauled it to the dump. "You can't expect anyone to use it; it's not even fit for storage. It was drawing rats. Some people build real houses for their hands, you know."

He'd shamed her into keeping her mouth shut, and looking at the cluster of trailers now, Cass thought again he was right. The people who worked their ranch deserved real homes. Maybe if they had them they could replace the rough single men Bob had hired with hardworking couples. Even families.

Still, before this bunch Cass had mostly felt she'd had a good relationship with the men who worked the ranch. Lena had counted many of them as friends. She'd been furious when Bob had let the last group go, but when Cass urged her to call the General about it, Lena had refused. She hadn't spoken to the General—even on the phone or computer—for years. The most stubborn of the sisters, she'd dug her feet in and the General hadn't made any effort to bridge the gap.

They were almost to the first trailer—traditionally reserved for the most senior hand—when the door opened and Gary Boyd stepped out.

"Who told him he could move in there?" Cass asked Lena. "He's not the overseer."

"Not me."

Cass quickened her pace. Gary braced his hands on the railing of the small built-on porch and waited for them.

"What brings you two lovely ladies down to the Park at this hour?" he called out as they approached.

"We've got a couple of questions for you and the others." Cass had always disliked the man. He had a way of waiting a beat before answering any questions to let you know he was only talking because he'd decided to, not because you outranked him.

"Let 'er rip."

"We need the others here, as well," Lena put in.

"Whatever the lady wants, the lady gets."

Cass didn't know how he managed to make the line suggestive, but he did, and she rolled her eyes as Gary swaggered down the steps of the foreman's trailer, went to its neighbor and rapped his knuckles on the door. "Ed? You in there? The ladies from up at the house have some questions for you. Tell the others to get out here, too."

Ed must have texted the others, because a minute or so later, Cass and Lena were surrounded by the hands. Cass didn't like the feel of this, but she didn't know how to get out of it now.

Lena took command of the situation. "I've been seeing traffic on this ranch I don't understand. I want to know what's going on."

"No crime having a few friends over now and then," Ed said, hitching up his pants and scratching at his waistline.

"A few friends is one thing," Lena said. "But entertaining half the county? Getting high? Or maybe selling something? That's another thing altogether."

Gary leaned in toward her. "See here. You'd better stop throwing around accusations like that."

"If I partake now and then that's no one's business," Ed added. "What're you, the morality patrol?"

"I want to know if you're dealing pot on my ranch," Lena said.

Cass just wanted to leave before things got any uglier. She'd never felt unsafe at Two Willows, but between Bob's threats the other day and the way the hands had circled around them now, she didn't like how this was going.

"Okay. That's fair enough," Gary said suddenly, surprising Cass. "You want to make sure we're not selling pot on your property, we'll give you a tour of our homes. You can look all you want. You're not going to find anything like that here."

After a moment, Ed chuckled. "That's right. But you will find a mess in mine. Not much of a housekeeper. Never thought it was a problem, seeing as it's not much of a house." He turned to lead the way to his trailer. "Me, first." After a moment, Lena and Cass followed him. "Come right on in."

"Lena," Cass said beneath her breath as they moved toward the trailer. This was a dumb idea. A really idiotic idea. What if the men cornered them in there? What if…?

"I'm packing," Lena whispered as they approached the trailer.

Cass nearly stumbled. That was all they needed—a shootout at the O.K. Corral. But it was too late to stop any of this now. Her sister elbowed her way past Gary and Ed and went inside. There was nothing for it but for Cass to follow. As soon as she stepped in the door, she gasped and fought the urge to pinch her nose.

Trash overflowed a small canister near the sink, which was stacked so high with dirty dishes it was impossible to use the tap. Every inch of the place held paper plates, pizza crusts and take-out containers. Flies buzzed around.

"You're supposed to keep the trailer in good condition," Cass told Ed.

"Yeah. I'll get right on that." He smirked at Gary.

"Seen enough?" Gary said.

"Hardly." Lena pulled her phone out of her pocket and began taking photographs. She documented everything. Both men began to get restless. Cass silently begged her sister to hurry up as they made their way through the place. The one bathroom was disgusting. The bedroom was hardly better. When she finally launched herself out the front door again, Cass sucked in deep breaths of fresh air. She'd have to burn her clothes and take a shower when she got home to rid herself of the contamination.

"We'll give you a week to clean that up before I do another inspection. Otherwise you'll find your own accommodations," Lena told Ed.

"You and who else is going to make me?"

"Me and the Board of Health," Lena said tartly. "Next."

Thankfully, the next three trailers were in far better shape, although as they passed through each one, the men whose homes had already been inspected seemed to feel the need to inspect all the others. Trailed by the group, Cass was definitely feeling outnumbered.

"Now yours," Lena told Gary, pointing to one of the eighties specials. "Then we'll take a look at the foreman's trailer. You haven't moved in there, have you? No one gave you permission to do that."

"I haven't moved in," Gary growled at her. "But it should be mine. I was just checking it out."

Gary's trailer wasn't the worst of the lot and wasn't the best, either. Lena kept taking pictures. When she was done, they headed for the newest one. Cass couldn't wait to get this whole thing over with, and she braced herself for what they might find as they approached it.

The trailer was starkly empty, clean as a whistle. Almost eerie. As they walked through the trailer, Cass realized she had underestimated Bob. He was either a far more meticulous man than she'd thought he was, or he'd had something he wanted to hide so badly he'd made a clean sweep of it when he'd left.

When they finally trailed outside again, Lena said, "Ed, get your trailer cleaned up. I'm not joking. I appreciate everyone's cooperation."

Cass fought to keep her steps even as they walked away. She wanted to run from the ugliness of the encounter. She wanted to set off a few sticks of dynamite. The sun was beneath the horizon now. Soon it would be dark. She picked up her pace. "It didn't used to be like that," she said.

"Damn right it didn't. Things need to change around here," Lena said.

BRIAN WAS MORE than a little gratified to find Cab at the station so late when he arrived. The man ushered him into his office for the second time that day, a plain room with a utilitarian desk, a set of filing cabinets and a couple of chairs for guests.

"Have a seat. What can I do for you?" Cab asked, settling his big frame in the chair behind his desk. He laced his fingers behind his neck and leaned back, signaling his readiness to hear anything Brian might have to say.

Brian filled him in on the situation as quickly as he could. "I don't know if there's anything you can do. I intend to meet Howie at the Boot and pass along the message that Alice is no longer interested in dating him."

"He's coming back from a trip right now?" Cab asked.

"That's right."

The sheriff looked thoughtful. "What I'll do is pass the message along and make sure he's got a tail all the way. I'll join in at the county line. If he makes a mistake, we'll pull him over and have a look in the car."

"Alice is concerned she might lose her vehicle," Brian said, but he passed on the make, model and license plate number.

"Nah. That won't happen," Cab assured him as he wrote it down. "Think she's willing to testify about anything she's seen?"

"Maybe. I can't say for sure." Brian hesitated. "Don't suppose you'd let me ride along?"

"Can't do that. But there's nothing I can do to stop a civilian from driving on Montana's beautiful highways."

"Copy that." He was finally in on the action again, even if it was in a supporting role. Brian's pulse quickened and he realized he'd missed this.

"Just remember this isn't a war zone," Cab said as they left the office together.

"I'll keep that in mind."

"ALICE? ARE YOU in here?" Cass, standing at the top of the stairs at the entrance to Alice's studio over the carriage house garages, scanned the large space and finally located her sister at one of the sewing machines at the far end of the room.

She made her way past the cluster of worktables, the racks and racks of completed costumes, and the dress-maker dummies that stood like headless sentries at various points around the room until she reached Alice and tapped her on the shoulder.

Alice, bent over the sewing machine, jumped, which was strange because she wasn't actually sewing at the moment. She held a swath of green fabric in her hands, and had been running it through the machine, but now the needle was stationary and she'd been staring at the wall instead of working.

"Cass." She took a deep breath and recovered herself. "Hi. Is Brian back?"

"Brian? No, not yet. Why?" Jealousy pulsed through Cass, an emotion she was becoming far too familiar with these days. Worry for her sister pushed it aside. Alice was paler than normal, her features drawn. "Are you getting ill?"

"No. Just… feeling like a loser." Alice turned off the machine, balled up the fabric and shoved it into the space between its cabinet and the needle. Cass had never seen her treat a project so carelessly, and her concern grew.

"You're not a loser."

"Really? I let Howie steal my car—a half-dozen times. I let him use it to run drugs to Billings and Bozeman."

Cass's mouth dropped open. She struggled to find her voice. "Drugs? You didn't stop him?"

"How could I?" Alice watched her. "Really, Cass? How could I? Without giving him up?"

"That's just it—why would you want to keep him if he was selling drugs?"

"Not selling; delivering. And I don't know. I fooled myself into believing that wasn't what he was doing. I lied to myself. I lied to you. For a man."

Cass recognized the pain in her sister's voice. "Oh, Alice—"

"No. Let me say it. I was a fool. I was so, so stupid. If Brian hadn't made me see what I was doing—what I was possibly throwing away—"

"Brian?" Cass asked again. "What does he have to do with this?"

"Everything. He's out there right now getting my car back." Alice picked at the rough edge of her jean shorts. "He made me realize I was worth more than Howie."

"Of course you are." Cass fell to her knees and gathered Alice up into her arms. "You're worth so much more than that. You are so special."

"I don't feel very special. I haven't in a long time." Alice extricated herself gently and tucked a strand of Cass's hair behind her ear. "You haven't, either, have you? Or why would you have stuck with Bob for so long?"

Suddenly Cass didn't feel like hiding everything anymore. "You're right. He was awful. Alice, he was—"

She almost spilled the beans about the money, but taking in the dark circles under Alice's eyes, decided it wasn't the time to add to her misery. "He was an ass," she finished instead. "He never loved me. He just wanted the ranch."

"Brian's not like that, you know," Alice said. "I don't feel like running him off the property anymore. He was so kind when he walked me through what Howie had to be doing. He didn't make me feel bad for hiding the truth from myself."

Cass nodded. She silently blessed Brian for making Alice see the light. Of course Howie was mixed up in the drug trade. What else would explain the way his silly business took off? She was ashamed of herself for being so caught up in her own affairs she never investigated what Howie was really doing.

Thank God for Brian.

Thank God the General had sent him.

She had to bite back a laugh; she'd never thought she'd think such a thing.

She didn't know what to make of it, either. She found herself wondering if Brian could help sort out the hands, too.

And the missing money. Maybe if she explained everything that had happened, Brian could pass the news on to the General in a way didn't end up with them losing the ranch.

Unbidden, a memory surfaced. One she thought of far too often. She'd been seventeen, and had attended a military function on the General's command. She hated leaving her sisters behind, especially because of her mother's request that she watch over them, but she'd done so hoping she could persuade him that they were old enough to be on their own now. The last guardian he'd hired to babysit them had developed quite a thing for one of the newer hired hands, and the two of them had indulged in a passionate relationship they carried out at all hours of the night and day—in the family home. Cass had already fielded some awkward questions from Jo, and had tried to reason with the woman to at least keep her escapades out of the house. When she asked the General about the possibility of ditching the guardians altogether, however, he'd laid down the law.

"No guardian, no ranch," he'd thundered. "Two Willows might have belonged to your mother, but that doesn't mean it's yours. I'm the one paying the bills. I'm the one calling the shots. It's my ranch and I say what goes on there. You don't like it—leave."

"What's going on is a whole lot of fucking," Cass had yelled back at him in her horror at the threat he'd made. She and her sisters couldn't leave Two Willows. Her mother was buried there. The standing stone was there. The house was… her haven, for God's sake. If he took away the ranch, Cass hadn't known what she'd do.

The General hadn't slapped her, but he'd wanted to—she'd read it in his eyes—and the desire was as bad as the doing would have been. Her father hated her. She disgusted him. He didn't care what was happening at Two Willows—or for the ranch itself, even if his own safety depended on it. "Your mother didn't raise you to use language like that, and I didn't bring you here to disgrace the family," he told her in a voice taut with rage. "Get changed. You're going home on the first flight. I thought you were my daughter. I don't know who the hell you are."

He'd gotten rid of the guardian, and replaced her with a grim-faced matron of sixty-two, but that hadn't made anything better.

Cass closed her eyes, remembering the shame and pain she'd felt that night, second only to her mother's death and the crushing blow of Bob's treachery when she'd discovered he was siphoning money from the ranch. Her father had made it perfectly clear. They could lose their home at any time—for something as small as a breach of etiquette. Since then she'd held her breath, waiting for the ax to fall.

She pulled herself together. This wasn't about her heart; it was about Alice's.

"Why don't you call it quits for the night and come back to the house?" she asked.

"All right. I'm not getting anything done, anyway."

Darkness had fallen, and the maze loomed large in the light of the moon that was just rising in the east. Both of them hesitated when their path drew near it.

"I'm afraid to ask any questions tonight," Alice said tiredly. "I'm afraid it will tell me I'm destined for a nunnery. At least you've got Brian."

Cass's heart throbbed, but with the memory of her father and Bob's betrayals so fresh in her mind, she didn't dare think of falling in love with another man. "I thought we decided not to let that happen."

"One of us should be happy." Alice squeezed her shoulders. "Why shouldn't it be you?"

WHEN THE FLASHING red lights sprang to life on Cab's cruiser, Brian, lagging behind in his truck, was ready. He kept well back as Howie, in Alice's car ahead of Cab, sped up at first, changed lanes, changed back and finally pulled to the side of the road. Howie had been driving erratically for several miles and Brian wondered what was going on. Was he fiddling with his phone? Getting high? He obviously hadn't noticed the sheriff's cruiser behind him until Cab turned on his lights. Then Howie must have panicked, but quickly realized he couldn't pull off an escape in Alice's old beater.

Brian pulled off the side of the road behind Cab and waited for the sheriff and his deputy to make their initial approach. A few minutes later, Alice's car's doors opened. A thickset man with a scruff of beard and a wiry mop of hair got out of the driver's side. A tall man with dark hair and a square jaw got out of the passenger side. A moment later, Sadie followed suit.

Brian swore. He climbed out of his own truck and strode toward the action. Cab, noticing him, waved him over.

"An unexpected surprise," he murmured, nodding at Sadie, who looked miserable as she stood aside and watched the deputy frisk the men. She hugged her arms across her chest, but that couldn't hide the plunging neckline of the slinky black dress she wore. It didn't fit with her youthful face. Neither did her heavy makeup. She looked like a teenager trying to play the part of a mature woman, but this was far more serious than a youthful prank. "Come on. Maybe she'll talk with a friendly face around."

The sheriff drew Sadie away from the others as backup arrived in the form of two more sheriff's department cruisers.

"Spill it," he said without preamble when they stood some distance down the road.

"I've got nothing to say."

"Sadie, I'm taking it easy on you on account of who your father is. You should by all rights be leaning against that vehicle getting searched, too, on your way to the lockup. So let's try this again. What the fuck were you three doing tonight in your sister's car?"

"We weren't doing anything wrong."

"Really? Because my deputy is about to open those packages we found in the back. Want to fess up before he does? It'll go better for you than if you wait. Looks like a big shipment."

Sadie's gaze darted around them as if she was looking for a way out. Cab must have sensed it, too. He took a step nearer, blocking her escape. "You can't run away from this. Tell me what you know."

"For God's sake. It's just a bunch of pot, okay? Big deal. It's practically legal everywhere anyway."

Brian wasn't buying her bravado. All he could think about was the photo collage back at USSOCOM. Sadie was still young, and maybe she needed to rebel against something, but all of those photos had shown a bright eyed, intelligent woman working from sunup to sundown in her garden, and he'd heard from her sisters how people came from far around for her natural cures. He'd bet his life this foray into criminal activity had far more to do with Mark than her own inclinations.

"You like to partake?" Cab asked her. "If I go look at that garden of yours, will I find you've got a crop growing?"

Sadie's disgusted reaction was too genuine to doubt. Besides, Brian was sure he'd have noticed if the Reeds had a grow-op on their ranch.

"There's no pot on Two Willows. Mom would spin in her grave. We don't need that stuff to feel—" She broke off and shrugged. Brian knew what she meant, though. They had the standing stone, the maze and their family's mythology. They didn't need to smoke to make the world less mundane.

"The thing is, Sadie, I don't have to look in those packages to know they don't contain pot," Cab told her. "So I need to know whatever it is you know."

For the first time, Sadie lost her bravado. "What do you mean they don't contain pot? Of course they do."

"You want to wager money on that? It would be a bad bet." Cab turned and gestured to one of the deputies buzzing around Alice's car. "Art? What've you got?"

The man trotted over. "Meth, pills, coke. You name it, it's in there. Department is going to have a field day."

Sadie lifted a hand to cover her mouth, and shook her head. "That's not true. Mark wouldn't be involved in anything like that."

"Honey, Mark's in it up to his eyeballs," Cab contradicted. "He's the one cooking up half this shit, and he's going down for a good long while if I've got anything to say about it. So what I want to know is how many times you've shot up with him?"

"Never. I swear! I've never done anything like that. I don't even smoke his pot. I mean—I tried it once, but—"

"Art, take her to the station. Get her statement."

A tear snaked down her cheek. "Cab, I swear—I didn't—" Sadie's voice rose in desperation. "Dad—the General," she corrected herself, and Brian's heart ached for her, "He'll be furious. He'll take the ranch. He'll—"

Cab, towering over her, stared down at Sadie for a long moment before softening. "Okay, settle down. You're not going to lose the ranch."

"You don't know that! He's always looking for an excuse—" Her bravado long gone, Sadie's tears ran freely, and Cab touched her arm.

"You swear you never took any of that junk?"

She nodded vigorously. "I swear. Except the pot—just once. I swear on my mother."

"Okay," Cab said. "I'm going to believe you. This time. You go with Art and tell him everything. You don't leave anything out. But if I ever see you near any of these yahoos again, I'll find a way to bust your ass and put you in jail. Because your parents raised you better than that."

Sadie's face crumpled. She turned away and a moment later, her shoulders heaved with her sobs.

Cab exchanged a long look with Brian. "That man has got to come home and clean up the mess he's made," the sheriff said. "If you're in touch with the General, you tell him I said that."

Brian nodded. "Will do."

He took Sadie's arm and Art led the way to a police cruiser where he let Brian install Sadie in the backseat without comment. Brian followed the cruiser in his truck. By the time they left the sheriff's department several hours later, Sadie was a mess. She'd sobbed non-stop through giving her statement, and her shame and embarrassment were far too obvious for any doubt to remain in his mind. She'd participated because she wanted a boyfriend, not for the thrill or for the money. Brian felt for her, but on the other hand, he thought the pain she felt tonight might save her a world of heartache later on. He'd had a private word with Cab, who told him Mark had tried to implicate Sadie in the operation, but Howie had the decency to say she was just along for the ride.

"I'm inclined to believe him," Cab finished up. "But Two Willows keeps cropping up lately when we're talking about the drug trade. That's not good. You'd better look into it."

"I mean to."

He'd get on that as soon as he got Sadie home to her sisters. Alice would be devastated when she found out what had happened tonight.

Cass, too.

He wasn't looking forward to the confrontation to come.

CASS WAS CURLED up on the sofa paging through a magazine when she heard soft footsteps in the hall. She thought it was Alice coming back from the kitchen with the cup of tea she'd gone to get, but instead it was Jo heading toward the stairs, Tabitha pattering along at her heels. At least Sean wasn't with her. She hadn't seen him since she put her foot down about him moving in.

But given what Jo had said, that didn't mean much.

"Good-night," she called.

Jo hesitated, her hand on the bannister. Tabitha kept going. "Night."

When she didn't continue up to her room after the cat, Cass patted the cushion beside her. "Come talk for a minute." She held her breath, wondering if Jo would come, and sent a silent thank you to the universe when she did.

Jo curled up beside her on the sofa like she'd used to do when she was much younger. Cass put an arm around her, grateful to spend a few minutes with her. "What did you do tonight?" she asked.

Jo stiffened under her touch, and immediately Cass wished she could take the question back.

"Not much. Just hung out at Sean's place." Jo kept her face turned away, and plucked a tiny piece of lint from the couch.

"Was he playing video games?" Cass knew sometimes Jo watched him play for hours. She couldn't imagine anything more boring.

"No. Not tonight."

What were the magic words to get her sister to open up to her? Cass wondered. Her mother would have known.

"Is everything all right?"

Jo tensed again. "Yes."

No, it wasn't, Cass knew. "Did you and Sean have an argument?"

"No." Jo sat up, pulled away from her and hugged her arms to her chest. "I wish…"

"What do you wish?" Cass prompted, sitting up, too.

"I wish we were young again. I wish Mom was here."

Cass nodded. "I know, honey. Me, too." When Jo softened against her again, Cass put her arms around her and held on. *Mom*, she thought. *Please—I need help here.*

She was hoping an instruction manual would fall from the sky, or perhaps she'd have some sort of epiphany. Instead, the front door flung open and Brian strode in, followed more slowly by Sadie, who was wearing the hideous, slinky dress she'd tried on for them before. Cass took one look at her smeared makeup and her heart sunk.

"What happened?" She let go of Jo and stood up, the better to brace herself against whatever new calamity was about to unfold.

Brian gestured Sadie forward. "Better just tell

them," he said.

Alice appeared around the corner, cup of tea in hand. "What's going on? Sadie? What's wrong?"

"You didn't sense it?" Sadie asked flatly.

"Sense what?" Alice looked as lost as Cass felt.

A tear slid down Sadie's cheek and she swallowed. Cass could see she'd been crying for some time. "Did Mark do something?" she asked. *Please let him not have hurt her*. She didn't know what she'd do if he had.

"Not exactly," Brian said. "But he was involved in a little business transaction—along with Howie, wasn't he, Sadie?" he prompted. The SEAL looked all too dangerous tonight. He stood behind Sadie, and Cass had the feeling he meant to corral her in the living room until she confessed to whatever had happened.

"We got pulled over," Sadie managed.

"We?" Alice echoed.

"Me and Mark. And Howie."

"Howie? I don't understand." Alice paled. "Why were you with Howie?"

"Because he and Mark… work together," Sadie said. "Mark… He… he fills the orders Howie ships."

This was far worse than Cass had ever imagined. "Drugs?" she asked.

"All kinds, right, Sadie?" Brian prompted.

"I didn't know." Sadie's tears were falling thick and fast. "I feel like an idiot. I thought it was… pot. I know that doesn't excuse it—"

Cass covered her face with her hands, and sank back down on the couch. She had failed. Completely and totally failed. Her mother had trusted her with her sisters' safety and she'd let Amelia down in every way. A tear slid down her own cheek as she fought for control and she scraped it away with the sleeve of her shirt. Nausea clawed its way into her throat. Drugs. Dangerous men. What else had she missed?

"You knew Mark was giving Howie drugs to deliver? And you didn't say anything?" Alice's voice slid higher as she spoke.

"You had to know what was going on," Sadie cried. "I've seen you with him when he was supposed to be delivering. Don't pretend to be innocent!"

Cass looked up at this last bit of information. Alice looked as shocked as she felt. She was breathing fast, her eyes glassy with unshed tears. "You knew I could be in danger and never said a thing?"

"It was Mark's fault, not mine," Sadie retorted, but her flushed face told Cass she was mortified at the outcome of her actions. "It wasn't supposed to be anything serious. Just pot, not pills or...or meth!" Her eyes welled up again. "I hate men. I hate all of them. I will never trust another one as long as I live!"

"I will never trust *anyone* as long as I live! Least of all you!" Alice rushed toward the kitchen and a moment later the back door slammed shut. With a cry, Sadie raced upstairs to her room, and the slam of her bedroom door rattled through the house.

Cass, still breathless with shock, faced Brian. "Meth?"

He nodded.

"But—"

Jo stood up beside her. "I'll go talk to Sadie," she said unevenly.

"Thank you," Cass managed. She didn't think she could talk to anyone right now. Sorrow warred with shame within her. How had everything gone so far astray? If only she and her sisters had kept to themselves, the way they used to, maybe they could have avoided this heartbreak. Maybe Sadie was right; maybe they needed to give up on men.

"Rough night for everyone, huh?" Brian said quietly when they were alone.

"Yeah, you could say that." A thought occurred to her. "How much of this are you going to relay to the General?"

"Cass, come on. You know me better than that."

"No," she said a little wildly. "I don't." Every man they knew was turning out to be trouble. How was she supposed to trust anyone?

He ran a hand through his hair and nodded. "Yeah, I guess you're right. You don't. I want to change that, you know. I want you to know me better than…" He looked around for a comparison. "Better than this house."

"That's pretty well." Despite everything that had happened, Cass had to smile a little. She knew this damn house like the back of her hand. She'd fixed about every part of it, hadn't she?"

If only she knew how to fix this latest disaster.

He moved closer. "The way I see it, we're in this

together. I'm not going to rat you out to the General. I'm glad we found out what was going on before things got worse, though. It bugs me that Howie and Mark were both in on it—both talking to each other without anyone but Sadie knowing."

"It bothers me that Sadie never told Alice. I never figured her for keeping secrets like that."

"Why not? You're keeping a bunch of them, aren't you?"

She sucked in a breath at the accusation. When she didn't answer, he went on. "What's going on with the money? Did Bob take it?"

Cass closed her eyes. She'd wanted so badly for no one to know. Trust Brian to be the one who figured it out. Finally, she nodded. "He stole about thirty grand, near as I can make out."

Brian whistled. "Thought it had to be something like that. Why didn't you turn him in?"

"The General has waited for years for an excuse to take Two Willows from us. I'm not going to hand it to him."

"Wait. Hold up. Take it from you?"

She could tell he didn't believe her. "That's right. He's never wanted us here, not since Mom died."

"But—" Brian broke off. "I don't think you've got that right. He's proud of this ranch."

Cass shook her head at him in disbelief. "Maybe. But he's not proud of us. We can't let him know anything's happened. Promise me, Brian. Or I swear, I will run you off no matter what that takes."

Brian crossed his arms over his chest, wanting her to know that wasn't possible, but in the end he only said, "I'll keep your secrets—if you start being honest with me. If we can find a way to get the ranch back on track without him knowing about it, mum's the word. Otherwise, I've got to tell him about Bob, at least."

"Don't tell him about Alice and Sadie. They won't make the same mistake twice, I guarantee it. I doubt you'll see them with any man after this."

"We'll see about that," Brian said enigmatically. "It's late. Let's talk more tomorrow. You and I had better sit down soon and go through those books."

Chapter Eight

WHEN BRIAN CAME down to find Lena loitering in the kitchen the next morning, he instantly knew she had something she wanted to say to him. Instead of asking her outright, however, he moved to fix himself a simple breakfast of toast and fruit, figuring she'd speak up when she was ready. She fiddled with the calendar hanging on the wall near the refrigerator, then suddenly asked, "Have you ever worked below-decks on a Nimitz-Class?"

"An aircraft carrier?" Somehow he doubted that was really what she wanted to know, but he remembered the weed-whacker she'd been disassembling the first time he met her. She was definitely interested in motors. "I'm a SEAL, not a technician. Sorry." He hid a grin. Was he actually apologizing for being a SEAL? That was a first.

"Ah." Her disappointment was clear, but still she lingered. "You ever deal with insubordination?"

Brian laughed outright. "Hell, yeah. Dished it out a bunch, too."

"Right. Is that why you're here?"

That was a little too close to the mark. "I've gotten

myself into a little trouble now and then," he hedged.

"If you tell someone to do something, and they don't do it, then what? Without asking someone else to take over?"

Brian sat down at the table with his food. "That's always the issue, isn't it? The Navy has some pretty strong built-in fail-safes to stop a mutiny in its tracks. Everyone involved knows what they are. The disincentives outweigh the incentives most of the time. Don't want to find yourself in front of a firing squad, so to speak."

"Makes sense." She hesitated. "See you around."

Her abrupt dismissal of the topic didn't fool him, but again he knew he couldn't push too hard. "Lena, let me know if there's any way I can help… without taking over." He didn't think she'd go for that, but he figured he might as well put it out there. He wondered who was giving her trouble. The hands?

She shrugged. "I'll be in the Park around one," she said, confirming his guess. She left without saying more, but Brian got the message. He decided he'd be in the Park around one, as well. In the meantime, he had an errand to run in town.

An hour and a half later, he stood at the center of the hedge maze and stared up at the standing stone. He had to admit it had a certain presence. About ten feet tall, an irregular rectangle, its surface was rough to the touch—warm from the sun.

The bright sun that had dawned this morning was fading, though, in advance of storm clouds on the horizon. Brian had squinted at them on his way to the maze and judged he had a little time before it hit. Enough for what he wanted to do. Alice had weathered some hard blows in the last few days, and he hadn't been kind when she told him about her premonitions. He wanted to make up for that if he could.

Still, the stone held his attention. Who had decided to erect this monument? Why go through the trouble? That ancestral Welshman, maybe, who'd lived near some megalith in his homeland and wanted to recreate it here?

He didn't believe it really gave answers. When the wedding invitation had slapped him in the face, he'd made use of the incident to give Cass a hard time and press his case, but it seemed to him the card could have been interpreted any number of ways. Since Cass had interpreted it to mean they would marry, did that mean she hoped they would? It was a cheering thought.

Brian placed both hands on the stone's warm surface, drawn to it somehow. He shut his eyes a moment, wanting to feel the rock rather than see it. It had its own strength and his sense was that its presence here was old. It belonged right here on this ranch in a way he wanted to.

Will Two Willows ever be my home?

Brian opened his eyes and pulled back, letting his hands drop to his sides, uncomfortable with what he'd just done. That didn't count, he told himself. He hadn't asked the stone a question—not really. He turned his back on it and faced the bench he'd purchased in town.

He busied himself looking for the perfect location for it. Far back enough to be able to see the standing stone without craning your neck. Close enough to still feel its presence.

There he went again.

Brian told himself to get a grip, but as he adjusted the bench, the back of his neck prickled, as if he was being watched. He checked reluctantly, already knowing no one was there, and wasn't surprised to find himself still alone. When he went back to shifting the bench into place, however, the space between his shoulder blades began to tingle, as if a sniper had him in his sights. If one did, he was a goner, he told himself, but unless that sniper was in a helicopter, there was no way anyone had a bead on him in the heart of the maze. You couldn't see the center from an upper story window in the house or carriage house. He was alone here.

Except for the stone.

A crackle behind him made him spin around. Just the breeze rustling the grass on the pathways... and a bit of trash caught in the lower branches of one of the hedges. He went to pocket it, planning to throw it away later. The faded paper was so windblown and parched he couldn't tell what it once had been. A newspaper article, maybe. Once there had been a paragraph of writing on it, but he couldn't make out any of the words.

Except one.

Yes.

Brian swallowed hard and glanced at the stone,

wondering if it was his answer. He wanted it to be, but that made him just like Cass—seeing what he wanted to see.

Had Cass seen what she wanted to see, though? She'd seemed upset when the stone confirmed he would marry her, and he'd been a stranger at the time. No sane woman would have wanted him then.

Was the stone an independent force?

He was going soft. Brian crumpled up the paper, shoved it in his pocket. Turned back to the bench and adjusted it again.

"You got an answer, didn't you?"

Brian jumped. "When did you get here?" he asked Alice.

"Just now." She nodded at his pocket. "What did it say?"

"Nothing." He smoothed a hand over his jeans.

"What did you ask it?"

She wouldn't let it go, would she? Maybe it was time to trust her a little bit. "It said I'll stay here and make Two Willows my home."

She gazed at him thoughtfully. "You must have asked it if you would, then. Which means you want to."

"You're right," he admitted. Alice might be a little fey, and a little gullible where men were concerned, but she was no dummy.

"Do you love my sister?" She drew closer, caught sight of the bench and her eyes lit up. "Oh, it's beautiful."

"It's for you. An apology. I didn't mean to hurt you

when I doubted your premonitions." He realized they had come true. Sadie had gotten into trouble with Mark. Maybe Alice did see the future sometimes.

Not always, though. She hadn't predicted how things would turn out with Howie.

Shock, incredulity and something else flashed across Alice's face. Something like… gratitude. The tears in her eyes made Brian wince.

"Why are all of you so surprised when someone treats you right?" he asked.

"Because it happens so seldom. I knew a change was coming," she rushed on. "I felt it. Before you even arrived. Now it's happening." Her expression faltered. "I didn't know it would include so much heartache, though."

"How are you doing today?"

She sat down on the bench and ran her hand over the wood. "Okay. A little wiser, I guess. I don't want to think about my problems right now, though." She looked up. "I knew you were here for Cass the day you arrived, you know. I saw a connection between you—a strong one. I didn't say anything because I didn't want to scare either one of you, but you knew it, too, didn't you?"

Brian wasn't sure how to answer that without giving away the General's plan. "I guess that's true. Anyway, I want to stay now. And I want to be with her."

"I'm glad." She smiled a little wistfully. "I feel… I feel like you will be with her."

"You do?"

She nodded. "I wonder if there's someone out there for me?"

"Last night you said you were done with men," he reminded her gently.

"Last night I was."

"I definitely think there's a man out there for you," he said, thinking of Jack. "I think you'll meet him before you know it."

She smiled again. "Now who's having premonitions?"

WHEN CASS SPOTTED the storm clouds piling up in the west, she raced to the attic to make sure she had plenty of buckets and they were positioned under each leak she knew about. Brian had told her he'd ordered shingles, and she hoped they got here before the roof gave out once and for all.

As she made her way downstairs looking for him, she had to admit she was relieved she had someone else to talk to about household problems. Lena was the only other practical person at Two Willows, and she was so tied up with the cattle operation—and the ornery hired hands—she had little time or interest in the state of their home. Which reminded her; she needed to set up a time with Lena to inspect Ed's trailer again, something she wasn't looking forward to at all. This time they'd better bring backup, she decided. She'd talk to Brian about that.

On the second floor, she thought about checking in with Jo, but when she got to her bedroom, it was empty.

Clothes and other items were scattered all over. The bed half-heartedly made, but rumpled. If only Brian could sort her out, too.

She sent a text, got no answer, but that was par for the course with her sister, who compared cell phones to an electronic leash, and consistently turned hers off. Cass headed to the barns next. She spent a half hour looking for her in all the outbuildings, to no avail.

Making her way back toward the house, she didn't see Jo in the gardens or the greenhouse. She headed for the maze next. Jo was just as apt to go there as the rest of them if she needed a chance to think. Cass traced the paths as she had so many times before, thinking of the message she'd gotten the last time she'd come here.

What if the stone was right and Brian really was the man for her? Sometimes she almost believed it. It was hard to allow herself to think about finding a partner when the possibility that she was wrong—that she was doomed to go through life alone—loomed so large. She'd been impressed with the way he'd sorted out Alice's problems with Howie—and rescued Sadie from the trouble she'd gotten herself into. She liked the way he talked to Lena as an equal—not just a girl playing cowboy. She couldn't pretend she wasn't attracted to him.

It took a lot more than that to make a life with a man, though. Cass continued to follow the twists and turns of the paths. Trust, for one thing. Respect. A common vision of the future. Loyalty. He still answered to the General, after all.

She met Alice halfway to the center. "Have you seen Jo?"

"No, but you have to see what Brian's done." She hesitated, frowning suddenly. "Cass…"

"What is it?" Cass stepped closer in concern. Alice had a look on her face she couldn't interpret.

"I don't know. Something—" She broke off and searched Cass's face. "Be careful. But… it's all right if you're not careful." Alice shook her head, obviously as confused as Cass was by this unusual bit of advice. "I don't know why," she said before Cass could speak up. "That's all I'm getting. Have you seen Lena?"

"No. Not lately. Why?"

Alice shook her head again. "I don't know. There's too much coming at me all at once. She shouldn't be with Scott. He's not right for her."

"Of course he's not right for her. If you see her, tell her I said that and you agree. Maybe she'll come to her senses."

"Maybe." Alice hurried on toward the house, leaving Cass to continue, wondering what would happen next. If Alice was sensing trouble, trouble was sure to come sooner or later. She'd talk to Brian, then go after Jo, she decided. And when Jo was in hand, she'd help Alice find Lena—and Sadie. She'd keep her sisters close today, just in case.

A short time later, she rounded the final twist in the path and came to a stop. Brian was bent over a beautiful, rustic wooden bench and as she watched, he gave it a little twist and push, settling it into the ground in what he seemed to feel was the perfect location. He straightened, took a step back, surveyed it and nodded.

Then he flopped down on it, reached into the pocket of his jeans and pulled out a slip of paper. Cass wondered what it was. It had to be meaningful because Brian stared at it a long time before crumpling it up in his fist and sighing. He looked up at the stone. "I hope you're telling the truth."

Cass stilled. Had he asked it a question and received a response? She hadn't expected that. Like most people, he'd treated the whole thing as a big joke, and she couldn't blame him. You had to live with the stone, see it get things right over and over and over again before you stopped trying for logic and just accepted what was.

Suddenly conscious she'd intruded on a private moment, Cass stepped back, but she must have made a sound because Brian was on his feet in an instant.

"Cass? Is something wrong?"

"No. Nothing's wrong." If you didn't count the missing money, the rebellious hands, Alice's premonitions, Jo's disappearance and the multiple buckets even now waiting to catch the leaks from the oncoming storm.

"Good." He glanced at the stone. "Oh, I can leave you alone, if you like…"

"No, I was looking for Jo. I'm not sure where she'd gotten to."

"Are you worried about her?" He gestured to the bench. "Why don't you sit down?"

"Okay." Cass did, admiring its beautiful construction. Brian sat down beside her.

"You don't mind, do you? That I put it here? Seemed like a good place for one." He looked a little sheepish. "After making fun of Alice, I figured it was the least I could do. She seemed to like it."

Cass studied him and wondered again if he was truly a different breed from the men she'd known—or if he was just more devious. She wanted to believe there were good men in the world, but with the year she was having, that was hard.

"It was a lovely thing to do."

"Well, I've waltzed in here and trespassed on your hospitality. I know you don't want me here. Figured I'd better start making myself useful or you'll never change your mind."

His grin made it hard for her to keep hold of her common sense. "Can I ask you something? Why did you take this particular mission?"

He dropped his gaze to his hands resting on his knees. "I didn't have much of a choice. You rarely do with missions, you know."

"Does the Navy really allow Army generals to send their SEALs to Montana?"

"Not usually." Brian sighed. "I fucked up. Big time. Ran a mission wrong, got in a mess of trouble. Navy wanted to keep things as quiet as possible, so I needed to disappear."

"And what better place to disappear to than Chance Creek, Montana?"

"I guess that about sums it up. I'm on my way out

of the military, Cass. I don't know what kind of paperwork they're doing back there, but the end result is I
won't be a SEAL anymore. I need to carve out a new
future."

"So you arrived at Two Willows and decided you'd
like to stay?"

"Something like that. I guess I should tell you… I'd
seen your picture before. Been staring at it for weeks
before I got here."

That set her back. "Really? Where?"

"At the base. Your father's got pictures of you all
over the place. You and your sisters. And your mother.
Most of all your mother."

"He does?" Cass couldn't fathom it.

"I think your dad cares more about you than you
know." He raised up his hands to ward off her protests.
"I don't agree with the way he shows it. I'm just saying."

"We're not talking about the General. We're talking
about you." She needed to keep this conversation on
track. She'd mull over what he'd said about the photographs later when she was alone.

"This ranch pretty much sums up what I've always
wanted. A home. Land. Cattle, because that's in my
blood. When I'm feeling really optimistic, a wife and a
family. I can't stop thinking you're the right woman to
make that family with."

Longing throbbed through Cass, leaving her empty
of everything except the desire to make his words true.
Linking her life to Brian, facing the world with him at
her side, establishing a haven at the ranch for all her

sisters for years to come. She couldn't imagine a better future than that.

Brian reached to cup her chin as he bent to kiss her. A raindrop hit Cass's forehead at the same time, then another, as his mouth brushed hers once, twice, and he wrapped her in an embrace Cass felt like she'd been waiting for her entire life.

"I want you," Brian murmured against her cheek. "More than I've got a right to, given we just met. I don't know what it is about you." He kissed her again.

Cass knew she should stop him, knew this was going too far, too fast, but instead she found her hands braced on his chest, her fingers digging into the fabric of his shirt. As his arms tightened around her, she melted against him, conscious of nothing but the taste of him. His warmth.

His strength.

Thunder rumbled overhead and the spatter of raindrops hardened into a shower, but neither of them pulled away. Something shifted in Cass as lightening crackled across the sky, and need inundated her like the rain coursing toward the ground. She'd thought she'd had it under control. She'd thought she'd liked doing everything herself. But as Brian's kiss intensified she realized she'd only been holding her needs in check by the barest thread.

She wound her arms around his neck and clung to him as thunder rolled across the ranch and echoed through her. Brian tightened his hold on her, crushing her against his body. Desire sparked a flame inside her no amount of rain could put out. When lightning shot down from the sky again, hit the earth somewhere close by, far more powerful than any of her tame explosions, her nerves resonated with it, thrilling to life as Brian caressed her and she opened her mouth to let him deepen the kiss. She didn't want the controlled, barren existence she'd planned for herself. She didn't want to keep everything she felt inside all the time. She slid her hands over his shoulders, and clung to him as another wave of longing swept over her, leaving her breathless and gasping, wanting to be closer to Brian as the rain soaked her hair and turned her clothing sodden.

Brian was murmuring something in between his kisses. Endearments. Prayers. Lightning struck again, closer this time—like her fireworks, but so much better—because the lightning wasn't a substitute for her feelings; each bolt that struck the earth echoed the electric sensations jolting through her body. Cass fumbled with the buttons of his shirt, her mouth on his and when she couldn't get them open, she pulled with all her might. Buttons popped. Fabric tore. She splayed her hands over his muscled chest.

Good. He felt so good.

"Cass—are you—"

She wasn't here for conversation. Lightning shattered the sky and Cass tugged her own shirt over her head. She reached behind for the catch of her bra and found Brian's hands there before her. When it came free, her breasts spilled out of the cups and she tossed it away, eager for his touch. He didn't disappoint her.

Palming one and then the other, he leaned down to take a sensitive nipple into his mouth.

Cass gasped and arched back, reveling in the sensation as Brian went on a sensual journey with his mouth, teasing her, tugging, nipping and laving until she thrummed like a string pulled tight on a bow. She reached for the button of his jeans, got it open, reached in and closed around him.

Yes.

Lightning crashed again. Dimly, Cass realized the danger. They were out in a storm. The rumble of the thunder echoed overhead only moments later. But when Brian kicked off his boots, tugged his pants off and tossed them aside, all thoughts of leaving flew from her mind. He slowed down as he shucked off his boxer briefs, however, as if wanting to give her time to change her mind.

She wasn't going to change it. She kicked off her boots, slid off her shorts and panties, and let him get a good, long look. Her skin was hot despite the rain and she ached for him.

"Protection?" he asked. Standing face to face in the pouring rain, only a step between them, stripped bare, Cass thought she'd never felt so alive. Brian's body was a masterpiece of long lines and sharp planes. She didn't think she'd ever seen a man so shaped by his trade. If war had been a cruel mistress, Brian had been an excellent student.

"I'm not... I'm not on the Pill." She never could stand the headaches it gave her.

"I don't have… anything."

The rain poured down in rivulets off his short hair, down the ridge of his nose and over his lips. Cass knew they gone much too far to stop now.

It's okay not to be careful, she heard Alice say again in her mind.

"I'm clean," she whispered. She didn't know if he heard her over the rumble of thunder.

"I'm clean, too, but without protection this is more than sex, Cass." He stepped forward. Put his hands on her hips. "It's a promise. A promise we're in it for the long haul. Forever. Are you going to be my wife? Because otherwise the answer is no."

Cass knew she needed to stop. She needed to think.

But her body had already made up its mind.

She placed her hands on his chest again, her heart thundering against her ribs. She was right where she wanted to be, despite the dangers. Brian's touch had cracked her heart wide open and she couldn't stop what he had started. She couldn't go back. She wanted to touch him. Wanted to feel… everything.

Brian met her with open arms and swept her into a crushing embrace.

Lightning crashed again as their mouths met and to the accompaniment of the rumbling thunder, Brian lifted her up and stumbled forward until they slammed against the stone. Cass wrapped her legs around his hips, hungry for him—desperate to feel him inside. When he shifted and pressed against her, she tipped her head back and closed her eyes, letting the raindrops wash her face as he pushed slowly into her.

It felt so good, Cass was helpless to do anything but take him in. Lightning danced in the sky above her. Thunder rolled and echoed across the pastures, but she was lost in a rhythm she'd craved without realizing what she'd been missing. Making love to Brian was like careening down a rushing river, no boat, no life-preserver—lost to the current, nothing to do but surrender to it and hope to survive.

As her longing increased, so did the care Brian lavished on her. As their bodies fell into a rhythm all their own, his hands teased her, his mouth tasted her and he stoked her desire to the breaking point. Brian increased his pace, the rain beating an erotic dance on her breasts when he leaned back to fill her full. She wanted him so badly— wanted him right where he was, forever; inside her. Making her blaze with need. Pushing her to the edge of ecstasy. He pushed in again with a long, strong stroke and Cass cried out, crashing over the edge in an explosion of feeling. The afterburn of the lightning streaked across the inside of her eyelids as she shut them, blind to everything but the bliss that enveloped her. Wave after wave of ecstasy washed through her. Cass could only hold on and ride them out, the riot of feelings inside her unlike anything she'd known before.

Brian followed soon after, his thrusts pressing her against the warm, wet stone as he gasped out his release. She kissed his neck, tasting the salt of his skin mixed with rainwater, and rode with him as he pulsed inside her, thrilling with the feeling of him. When it was over, they stayed like that, Brian's strong legs bracing them, his arms holding her, Cass wrapped around him, until their breathing slowed down. When she finally pulled away and untangled herself from him, it felt more like a loss than a simple, necessary action. Brian didn't let go of her, though.

"Tell me you're okay."

When had the rain begun to slow? Even as they stood there it lessened to a soft patter, the lightning moving farther off, the thunder rumbling but nowhere near as strong as before. "I'm fine." Unsteady, but more than fine. Glorious.

Cass shivered a little in a breeze that lifted a long strand of her hair. She could only imagine what she looked like—ravaged by the storm.

By Brian.

Cass smiled, and Brian searched her face. "I don't regret this," he said. "No matter what happens."

No matter—

Cass understood with a shock, and she dropped a hand to her flat belly. She hadn't thought about the consequences at all, she who thought of consequences all the time.

It's all right not to be careful…

But—

He'd asked her to marry him.

She'd said—

She hadn't said anything, had she?

She'd given her body to him without holding back. She'd taken a risk on starting a family with him.

"I—" Cass didn't know what to say as the enormity of what she'd done overwhelmed her. She'd as good as said she'd marry him.

Was she ready to take that step with Brian?

Too late to turn back now, her conscience told her. She'd made love to him without protection—

Brian distracted her with a kiss that sizzled through her veins all the way down to her toes.

Much more of that and she'd do it all over again, Cass thought wildly. She was insatiable where Brian was concerned. Unable to think rationally—

In over her head.

"I don't regret it," he said again, his hand cupping her cheek. He bent to find their clothing, separating it as he went. Cass automatically took her blouse, jeans, bra and panties from him, but didn't relish stepping into the sodden items. She didn't know what to think about what had happened, and decided not to think about it at all for the moment. First she needed to get her bearings.

And get dressed.

"If there's a child, I'll welcome him—or her," Brian went on. "I'd do anything for you, Cass—you know that. I've always wanted a family. I've always wanted a ranch like this."

Cass froze, about to step into her panties. A family—and a ranch. Why were those two always linked when Brian was speaking?

Was that why he'd made love to her without protection?

To solidify his claim on this land?

"Nothing like climbing into wet clothes," he joked, making a face as he pulled on his boxer briefs. "I guess if we walked back without them on there'd be questions, though."

"Yes, there would," Cass said slowly, her head spinning, as she drew her panties on. Did he want her? Or Two Willows?

Did he love her at all?

"Cass? Something wrong?"

She couldn't find the words to ask him, suddenly so cold she had goose bumps all over.

"Hey, you're freezing. Let's get you back inside." But as Brian reached for her, Cass batted his hand away. Memories of Bob overwhelmed her. The way he'd courted her. Used her. Had sex with her.

Stolen from her.

Tried to take control of the ranch.

Brian reached for her again. She slapped his hand away again. "Don't touch me." She needed to think this through. She took a step back, pulling on the rest of her clothing quickly.

"Cass—"

She remembered the way she'd told Bob her secrets. Trusted him with her heart. Let him smash it to pieces. What made her think Brian was any different?

He doesn't want you—he wants the ranch, she heard Bob say in her mind. Hadn't Brian all but admitted it?

What had she done?

"Cass—"

"Don't! Stop pretending to want me. Why are you

here?" She had to know right now, before another moment passed. If he was going to eviscerate her, let it happen right now.

"I already told you—your father sent me—"

"Sent you to screw me? To get control of the ranch? Is that why you came? Did you think you could marry me and take over?" Pain lanced through her as she realized she'd been fooled again. How was Brian any different from Bob really? Because he was better spoken? Better looking?

A Navy SEAL?

Cass staggered back as the truth washed over her. She'd made the same mistake—twice. She'd allowed her heart to lead her head—and she knew better than that.

What if she was pregnant? How would she ever escape Brian? She'd walked right into another trap. For a moment she'd thought she'd found a partner, but she'd been wrong. She'd thought there'd be someone to share her burdens with, but there wouldn't. Brian wanted what every man wanted—control of her. Control of the land. No one wanted her for herself.

No one.

She'd be alone forever. Just like she'd always been since the day her mother died.

Pain lanced through her chest and she pressed her hands to her heart, trying to keep it from splitting in two. This was everything she'd tried to avoid. Her feelings were clawing at her like ravenous dogs. She had to hold them back. Had to clamp them down. Because if she let them loose, she'd remember—she'd remember—

Images of her mother's limp body flooded her mind, and Cass doubled over with a cry. She'd been at Amelia's side when she'd passed—when she'd slipped away to a world where Cass couldn't reach her—leaving her in charge—of everything.

Her father had never stepped foot on the ranch again, and she'd missed—she'd missed h—

"Cass—"

She'd missed having someone to turn to. Someone who knew what to do when things broke, sisters fought, hired hands rebelled—

"Cass—"

Someone who could help when hearts got broken, men lied, and she couldn't—couldn't—

"Cass!"

Someone who'd loved her once—she knew he had—before she'd screwed up, before she'd let him down—before he'd come to hate her for being alive when his wife had died—

Cass batted Brian away from her, sobbing in great, awful gasps that left her choking, aching, fighting for breath. This was why she didn't feel. This was why she locked it all away. It hurt so bad.

Loving hurt so bad.

"Sweetheart, I'm not going to lie to you. The idea of getting to live on this ranch is pretty intoxicating."

Somehow she was on her knees, Brian crouched next to her, trying to take her in his arms. She kept fighting him. She couldn't let him win. Couldn't let him take what little she'd managed to hold on to for this long.

"I've wanted a ranch like this all my life. It's why I went into the Navy; to save up for a chance to buy a spread one day. But I got kicked out too soon, and my brother needed my help," Brian was saying. "I sent him nearly all of my savings. I didn't want him to lose the woman he loves. I don't have enough to buy a ranch of my own, so yes, Two Willows got a hold of my heart, but not like you have. Never like you have."

Cass fought her way back to her feet and lurched into the nearest pathway, Brian on her heels. She could barely see through her tears, but she knew was she had to get away. From Brian. From the standing stone.

From the General.

From everything.

"I love you; you've got to know that!" Brian called after her.

She broke into a run, darted into the nearest pathway, through several grassy corridors, but she must have taken a wrong turn; where the exit was supposed to be was only another blank wall of green. "Damn it!"

"Cass, I—"

Brian was still behind her. Cass sped up, racing through the twists and turns, around corners and down passages, putting distance between them until she finally left him behind. Where was the stupid exit? Cass wanted out. She wanted all this to be done. She wanted real distance between herself and Brian—not just a few green pathways—a distance she could see.

Once she thought she heard him call out, but his voice was so far away, it was quickly lost before she could even tell from what direction it had come. Her labored breathing became the only sound, loud and harsh in her ears as the dregs of the storm shredded to the southeast.

Cass kept running. Running away from the pain. From the past. She wanted to put it all behind her. Wanted to be by herself. Wanted everything to go back to the way it was—

Except no—that wasn't any good either, she realized as she sprinted around another turn. She'd been losing the ranch out of her own incompetence. Losing her sisters to men who would have led them into lives of misery.

She wanted to go back further—to when her mother was alive, to when her father had loved them. To when Two Willows was safe—

And if that wasn't possible, she wanted—she wanted—

"Mom, take me with you!" The cry—the one she'd held in so long—tore from her throat.

And quiet fell over her with an almost audible shock.

Cass stopped her in her tracks and—frightened by the sudden lack of sound—spun around.

Shivers prickled down her spine.

No matter which way she turned, walls of green confronted her, hemmed her in. She'd never been lost in the maze before.

Never.

Where was she?

Cass's breathing rasped in the absolute quiet.

Where was she?

She couldn't hear anything. Not a voice. Not a bird. Not even the lowing of cattle in the distance.

Where was Brian?

Her sisters?

It was as quiet as if she was the only one alive.

As if she wasn't alive.

Panic threaded through Cass. Despite what she'd said, she wasn't ready to leave the world. She had a job to do: protect her sisters. She wasn't done with that yet. And then there was Brian. She didn't know if being with him was right or wrong—but she wanted to find out.

She took another breath and felt the rush of air into her lungs.

Not dead yet, then. But far from home, as familiar as these green walls were.

"Mom?"

Her mother wasn't here, of course. No one was, and Cass spun around again. When was the last time she'd been alone? There was always someone with her. Someone to pretend to. A reason to keep up the façade that all was well. Even when it wasn't.

But there was no one here now. No one but her, the tall green walls and the clearing sky high overhead.

The great, gulping sobs she'd spilled out in front of Brian had drained her, leaving her chest sore and her body hollow. Cass, too tired to run anymore, sat down in the damp grass and admitted to herself that the maze wasn't going to let her go. And that all wasn't well.

Far from it.

She was lonely, and scared. She missed her parents. She missed their love—and approval.

And Brian—

"I fell in love with him," she admitted out loud. "I wanted to marry him. I wanted to raise my family here."

A whisper of wind lifted a tendril of hair from her face, as gently as her mother's touch had once been. A sense of peace filled Cass as she breathed out all her pain and let it go. Maybe it was okay to admit what she'd wanted.

Maybe Wye was right and the world wouldn't end if she cried now and then. Maybe feeling her feelings wouldn't kill her.

She was alive now.

At least, she thought she was.

Leaning back on her hands, she examined the sky high above her. The last traces of clouds were gone, leaving a sky so blue it spoke of infinite possibilities. With each deep breath, she relaxed a little more.

Maybe it was okay to take a break. Maybe that's what she needed. Time to figure this out.

When had she stopped doing this? Sitting still once in a while and taking in how beautiful the world was? She was always so busy rushing around and solving problems. Or trying to prevent them.

Trying to control everything. But what if she couldn't control any of it? Would it all come crashing down? Would she die, too?

This time when her tears came, they were hot, but silent, and they eased her heart instead of hurting it.

"I'm sorry, Mom," she said out loud. "I'm sorry I haven't done better." She'd tried. And in the end that was all she could do, wasn't it? No one was around, but she didn't feel alone as she cried. She felt the grass, the maze, the sky sympathizing. She was human, after all. No worse or better than anyone else. "What do I do now?" she asked the emptiness around her when her tears dried up again. If only her mother could answer her.

Should she be with Brian? Or should she remain alone?

With a rush like an indrawn breath, the world came alive again. Birds chirped in the hedges. Cattle lowed in the distance.

"Cass!" Brian's voice was still far away, but this time she heard his call distinctly. She cocked her head. Was that an answer? Was her mother saying she should trust him?

Cass didn't know.

But as she slowly got to her feet, she knew she couldn't control Brian. She didn't think she wanted to. Life was so much more exciting when a man like him came along and swept you off your feet.

Messy. Unpredictable. Painful, sometimes.

But exhilarating, too.

Maybe that was the answer, she thought—that there was no answer. She wasn't in control of everything and some problems she couldn't solve. Maybe she didn't need to know today if she'd be with Brian. Maybe she needed to wait and see.

Peace didn't only come from making decisions; it could come from knowing you still needed time to take in all the information.

From what she'd seen, Brian was caring, loving and honest. But he also had his own past to sort out. His own wounds to overcome.

She wouldn't drive him off the ranch. And she wouldn't give her heart to him today—although she had to admit, he possessed most of it already.

She would wait. She'd learn more about him—and herself.

She'd discovered something truly momentous today: the world didn't stop turning, or end in a fiery explosion, if she felt her feelings—even strong ones. No matter how much she had cried, or raged, or ran, the storm had passed, and now the sun shone in a glorious blue sky.

And she hadn't even set off an M-80.

No matter what happened next, she'd be okay.

She'd still have that sky.

She'd still be Cass.

That would have to be enough.

"CASS!" BRIAN COULDN'T understand how he could lose a whole woman in a little hedge maze.

Okay, a big hedge maze, but still.

Why wasn't she answering him? Was she hiding

from him in there? Had she escaped to the house by some back entrance he didn't know about?

He'd gone to look, couldn't find her there, either, and had come back to try the maze again. He was just about to call Cab for reinforcements when she strode out of the hedge entrance and came to a stop in front of him.

Brian, frantic enough to be ready to lose his temper, stopped short when he took her in. She was still soaked through, her hair in wild, wet tendrils, her eyes huge in her face.

"Where *were* you?"

"I don't know."

Her simple answer sent chills running down his spine. He'd never seen anyone look like—

Brian didn't know what she looked like.

As if she'd stepped into a vortex and come back trailing traces of some foreign world. He wanted to touch her. Bring her back down to earth. Make sure she knew how he felt about her.

"Damn it, I don't care about the ranch, Cass. I care about you. I love you."

After a moment, she nodded. But she kept walking toward the house.

"Cass?" He wasn't sure if she'd heard him. Wasn't sure if she was back from wherever she'd gone in the maze. He'd never seen her cry like that. She usually held her emotions in such a tight check, he hadn't known she was capable of it.

Her tears didn't scare him, though. He'd been

through tough times and he knew they came to an end eventually. The way he figured it, the two of them could work together to weather the storms life threw at them. He hoped she knew that was what he wanted. If it meant giving up Two Willows and the rest of his goals, he'd do it in a heartbeat if that's what it took to have her in his life.

She headed for the house, and he wondered whether to follow her or give her some time. He was still trying to figure that out when a silver truck roared up the access road from the barns, past the house and out toward the highway, zipping past so close to him Brian had to jump back.

"Hey!" he called after it, but the truck didn't slow down and Brian didn't recognize it. He watched it turn toward town and sighed. Was everyone off their rocker around here?

A movement down the track the way the truck had come caught his eye and Brian turned to see a figure lurch into view, waver and sink to its knees.

"Lena!"

He ran toward her, too late remembering his pledge to meet her at the Park. What time was it? Surely it couldn't be that late—

He sped up, dread knotting his stomach. Lena had needed him, and he'd forgotten all about her, too busy with Cass—

There was no time for recriminations. Not with Lena slumped on the ground, one hand to her face.

"Lena? Lena!" Brian raced for her, dropped to one

knee when he reached her, took her shoulders and peered into her face, swearing when he saw the bruise that swelled one eye shut. "Who did this? Scott?"

"He said… he said…" Lena's words were slurred, and Brian lifted her to her feet. "Keep my nose… out of his business."

"Where were you? At the Park?"

Lena nodded, her eyes glassy with tears, something Brian never thought he'd see. The two strongest Reed women, both in tears in the course of an hour. This had to stop.

"What do you think… think… his business is on my ranch?" Lena spoke as slowly and thickly as if she'd been drinking rather than tangling with a man who had seventy pounds on her at least.

Brian burned for retribution, and he'd have it as soon as he could. First he had to get Lena to her sisters. He threw an arm under her shoulder and helped her the rest of the way. Alice met them in the doorway, her face pale and her eyes wide.

"What did you do to Cass? I think she—" She took in the state of Lena's face. "Oh, my God. It was Scott, wasn't it? I knew you shouldn't be with him."

"Keep them safe," Brian told her. "Both of them. Don't let them out of your sight."

He couldn't wait another minute.

Scott was going to pay for this—right now.

Soon he was gunning his own truck down the track that led to the highway. Scott had a few minutes' head start, but there was only one road to town from here. If he could cut him off before Scott reached it, he was golden.

He was well past the speed limit when he spotted the silver truck far ahead of him and put the pedal to the floor to catch up. Scott must have noticed him in the rearview mirror, because he gunned his engine, too. Brian wasn't going to lose this race, though. He had plenty of experience handling high speed activity under far worse conditions. When he drew alongside Scott, he yelled through the open passenger side window, "Get over!"

"Fuck off!" Scott tried to pull ahead, but Brian matched him, keeping one eye out for traffic ahead.

"I said, get over before I run you off the road!"

Scott lunged away from him, reaching for something. The glove compartment? Brian wouldn't be at all surprised to find he had a weapon in there. He slammed a hand on the horn and Scott jerked, lost control of the wheel for a moment—just long enough for his front tire to catch on the dirt shoulder and drag the rest of the truck off the road. Brian slammed his brakes, then hit the gas again, keeping alongside him, using his truck to prevent Scott from finding a way back on to the macadam. The shoulder was running out, and Scott had no choice but to swerve to a stop. Brian hit the brakes again, boxing him in. He didn't wait for Scott to find that weapon. He unbuckled his seat belt, lunged across the front seat, through the window and into Scott's truck, landing on top of the man.

"What the fuck?" Scott managed to get the glove

compartment open, but Brian grabbed the pistol inside and tossed it out of the passenger side window. He slammed his fist into the man's face, but Scott wasn't going to go down easy. As they grappled in the seats awkwardly, the armrests and central console getting in the way, Scott managed to open the far door and slither toward freedom. Brian went with him and together they slid out of the truck and onto the ground in a heap.

Brian scrambled to his knees first, grabbed Scott by the shirt and lifted him as he surged to his feet. His fist connected with Scott's cheekbone.

"You fucker!" Scott swung back at him, but his punch didn't land. Brian dimly heard a siren approaching as he struck Scott again. Scott staggered, and Brian followed up with another right hook. His fist hitting Scott's face felt much too good. Scott shoved him away and they staggered apart just in time for Cab to appear around the tail of the silver truck.

"You boys having a good time?" Cab said jovially, his hand on his holster.

"It'll be better when someone picks up that pistol Scott dropped." Brian pointed, keeping his gaze on Scott, ready to grab the man if he went for it.

Cab nodded, sauntered over to where it lay on the ground, pulled out a handkerchief and picked up the weapon. "Shouldn't leave these things lying around. Never know who'll find them."

"Safety first," Brian agreed. "Right, Scott?"

"Fuck you—" Scott began, took a look at Cab and subsided.

"Any more of these I should know about?" Cab asked them.

"Nope," Brian said.

Scott shook his head.

"Then I'll be on my way. Enjoy yourselves, gentlemen."

Brian cocked an eyebrow at Scott. "Now's the time to ask the kind sheriff for help if you need it."

"I don't need it."

They waited until Cab's door slammed, the cruiser's engine started and he drove off.

Then Brian lunged for Scott again.

"How could I have been so stupid?" Lena asked again, a bag of frozen peas pressed to the side of her face. Cass was grateful she'd sharpened up in the minutes since Brian had brought her into the kitchen. She wanted to take Lena to the hospital but so far her sister had refused to go.

"You aren't stupid," Cass told her. "You thought Scott cared about you."

"Which makes me stupid," Lena said. She, Cass and Alice were sitting in the living room. Sadie came in with a pot of tea and cups on a tray, set them on the coffee table and began to pour one for each of them. These days she was back to her jeans and boots, her face devoid of makeup. Cass thought she looked more herself again. "How many guys have I seen him beat up? He's a violent asshole. He's never been a nice guy. I didn't want him to be. I thought he was hot because he rode motorcycles and got into bar fights. Fuck!" she added when she tried to take a sip of the tea Sadie handed her and lifted a hand to her split lip.

"You thought he'd never hit you. What kind of a man punches a woman?" Cass said. For a moment— just a moment—she had the urge to head to her shed and scoop up an armload of fireworks. How could anyone do this to her sister? But gunpowder and explosions wouldn't fix Lena. She needed something else. To talk about it. To know she wasn't alone.

"What kind of a woman doesn't see it coming? God, I want to rip him a new one. I want to beat the crap out of him. I wish I was a man," Lena burst out, and winced, pressing the peas to her face again. "I've always wished I was a man."

"Lena—"

"No. Don't give me that crap about how it's better to be a woman, because it isn't. Let's face it; everything would be different if we were men. Howie wouldn't have used Alice's truck to run his druggie errands. Mark wouldn't have convinced Sadie to be part of his crew, Bob wouldn't have made our lives miserable and Scott wouldn't have decked me, because if I'd been a man I would have stomped his ass into the ground. None of this would have happened, because the General would have handed over the ranch and left us the fuck alone!"

Cass couldn't deny it. But she didn't want to hate who she was, and she didn't want Lena to feel that way, either.

"I think Mom gave us a good example of what a

woman can do—" she began, but faltered as Lena's expression grew outraged.

"Mom? Mom gave us a good example? Mom sat here on this ranch and waited for her husband to spare her a moment or two when he wasn't too busy. She martyred herself for this place. For him! And now we're doing it, too. So don't talk to me about Mom. Don't talk to me at all!" Lena set down the teacup with a thump that rattled it in its saucer, stood up and strode toward the stairs. "I'm done with men," she shouted over her shoulder. "And that includes the General. This is my ranch now and I'm running it as I see fit. I don't care who the General sends."

Ten seconds later they heard her bedroom door slam.

Cass turned to Alice and shook her head. "I don't think I can take much more of this day."

"Go upstairs and take a nap. I'll hold down the fort," Alice said. "Get some sleep. You need it. But Cass," she added, almost as an afterthought, as both of them rose to their feet. "Where did you go this afternoon? When you were in the maze?"

All Cass could do was shrug. "I really don't know."

It was the same answer she'd given Brian, and she knew in the morning, she'd have to face what they'd done. She'd have to sort out her feelings for him. Decide what to do next. They'd taken such a chance. She'd never let passion get the better of her that way before.

"I don't think you were… here," Alice said. "I don't

know where you went, either."

"It was… peaceful," Cass told her. "I felt… safe."

"I'm glad." Still, Alice followed her. "It's going to get better now, isn't it? Without Howie and Mark and Scott. Maybe it'll be like it used to be—just us."

"I don't know about that." Sean was still hanging around Jo, and she knew Bob would be back. There was the missing money and the constant threat that the General would take away the ranch. It seemed to Cass there were too many problems to ever sort out.

"Cass…" Alice trailed her to the base of the stairs. "If you tried to follow Mom out there in the maze, I understand why you'd want to. But please—" she touched Cass's hand where it rested on the bannister "—don't go. I don't think… I don't think we can do this without you."

Cass swung around to catch Alice in a fierce hug. Alice was right; for one moment she'd been weak and she'd wanted to go, but not anymore. She could never leave her sisters behind. "I'm not going anywhere. I think—I think Mom gave me a reprieve. Time out of time to catch my breath—that's all. I'm here now, and I won't do that again. I promise."

Alice nodded and took a breath when Cass finally let her go. "There's more coming. I don't want to say that, but it's true. We're not out of the worst of it yet."

Of course they weren't. Bob was still prowling around telling people they were getting married. Scott was still out there, a free man even after he'd hit Lena. They were short thirty thousand dollars and their father could take the ranch away at any time. Not to mention the chance she'd taken making love to Brian.

Exhaustion bowed Cass's head as she made her way upstairs. When she finally crawled into bed, she pulled her sheet up over her head, despite the sticky heat of the day. She'd face the world later.

Right now she wanted to forget everything.

THE HOUSE WAS quiet when Brian entered the kitchen late that night. He'd come home from his altercation with Scott with busted knuckles and a sore hand but when he'd found out that Cass had gone to bed, he'd headed down to the stables to muck them out, because the bloodlust he'd felt when he went after Scott still hadn't abated. He'd known he had to calm down before he could be with Cass again. It had taken hours and a lot of hard work but he finally felt in control of himself.

Cass had to know they were meant to be together, especially after making love in the maze. She'd wanted him as badly as he'd wanted her—and she wanted the kind of life he wanted, too.

The only thing standing between them was her fear, and he couldn't fight that with his fists; he had to prove to her he could be the kind of husband she could depend on.

He ran the knuckles of his right hand under water for a long time, knowing it was too late to stop the swelling. Knowing, too, it had been worth it.

As a local hard-ass, Scott hadn't proven to be much of an opponent, despite the fact he had several inches and twenty pounds on Brian. Sometimes his SEAL training came in handy, Brian told himself. This was one of those times.

In deference to Cab's career, he hadn't flattened Scott, but he'd given him a good drubbing before dropping him off in front of the sheriff's office. Let Cab take it from there. He doubted the man would give any more trouble to the women at Two Willows.

Tomorrow he'd have to sort things out with Cass. He wished he could do it tonight, but he wasn't at his best, and he figured neither was she. A good night's rest and everything would come clear.

Time to get some sleep. But as he headed toward the stairs, Brian stiffened as a cry rang out and was instantly muffled upstairs.

What the hell—?

Once again he was moving before he even thought about the consequences. He took the stairs two at a time and paused, trying to trace the sound. Cass's bedroom door was shut, but even as he reached for the knob the sound came again from the end of the hall, where Jo's white cat, Tabitha, paced impatiently in front of another closed door. It wasn't the cat who'd made that noise, though. It had been a woman—Jo—and she didn't sound happy.

He dimly realized he might be about to barge in on Jo and her boyfriend—what was his name? Steve? Sean?—before his shoulder hit the door, crashed it open, and he slid into the room. Tabitha streaked past him. Brian took in Jo sitting in a chair, a laptop with a webcam propped on a stool in front of her, Sean standing behind her, his hands working at the buttons of her shirt while she squirmed and fought, trying to stop him.

"We'll make good money," Sean was growling at her.

"I don't want to!"

Sean never saw Brian's fist until it connected with his nose. Brian winced as his sore knuckles connected with skin and bone again. Sean fell with a cry on Jo's bed, scrambled to his feet and raced for the door, blood streaming from his mouth down his chin. Brian lunged for him again, missed and decided to let the man get away. He wasn't sure he trusted himself to stop once he got started raining vengeance on him. Besides, Jo had her knees tucked under her chin and she was crying, Tabitha weaving around the legs of the chair.

He knocked the laptop off the stool, not wanting to stop and figure out how to cut the video feed. The webcam went flying and smashed to pieces against the wall. Brian scooped Jo up, sat on her bed and cradled her in his arms.

"Shh, I've got you. You're safe now."

As her tears wet his shoulder, Brian decided enough was enough. He would call the General tonight. Tell the sonofabitch to come home and help his daughters. He hadn't even had time to process why Scott, who had no affiliation with Two Willows besides dating Lena, would come after her for going to sort out some problem with the hands at the Park. What was his connection to them?

He was missing something here. Something that would make it all make sense.

"Why did Sean want you to strip on camera?" he asked Jo.

"For the money," she sobbed. "He said I could make more flashing my... going topless... than he could ever make. He said we were in this together and I should do it for him. I told him no. He just wouldn't listen."

That didn't make sense to Brian. There was so much porn on the internet he doubted something so tame as Jo's breasts could make a decent amount of money. Either Sean had wanted to lure Jo into doing much, much more—

Or he thought he could control her once she'd exposed herself.

He thought of Scott punching Lena. Howie and Mark working together—bringing Sadie along in Alice's car. Bob trying to marry Cass.

Control tactics. It was all about control. All of it aimed at keeping the women silent.

About what?

"Shh," he said again as Jo buried her face in his shoulder. "It's going to be okay."

He was going to stop whatever was happening at Two Willows once and for all.

WHEN CASS WOKE it was dark outside and she sat up, thoroughly confused, sure she'd heard a noise. Glancing at her bedside clock, she realized she'd slept through the afternoon, through dinner and into the night. An engine racing outside brought her out of bed and to the window in time to see taillights disappearing around the house. Had that been Sean's truck? He seemed in an awful hurry to leave.

Even at night the ranch was beautiful, Cass thought as she drew the curtains. She couldn't blame Brian for falling in love with it. She only wished he'd fallen for her that way. He said he had, but after everything that had happened, how could she tell if he was speaking the truth?

She couldn't help but think about making love to Brian earlier. Who knew sex could feel like that, like all the walls between them had dissolved to allow them to come together in a searing stroke of heat?

Could he have faked all that passion? Was it simply something men knew how to do? Cass wondered if there was some secret code when it came to men that she'd never find the key to unlock. Their motivations mystified her.

But not Brian's. His were plain and simple. Understandable.

He wanted a home. Her home.

He'd do what it took to get it.

He wanted her, too. But which did he want more? Did it matter?

It did to her.

She knew she wouldn't sleep again anytime soon. Might as well get up and look over the ranch's accounts.

But when she stepped out of her room, she was surprised to see Lena, Sadie and Alice in the hall, and a light shining from Jo's room past the shattered remains of her door.

"What happened?"

"I don't know. I heard voices. Someone running," Alice said.

Cass pushed past them all to get to Jo, but when she reached her sister's room, nothing could prepare her for the scene that met her eyes. Brian sat on Jo's bed, legs wide, Jo balanced on his lap in his embrace, her arms wrapped around him tightly, her face buried in his neck.

Cass let out a choked sound, and when they sprang apart she could see that Brian had managed to get her sister's shirt half unbuttoned. Pain seared her breath from her lungs as her other sisters crowded around her.

Brian and Jo? Not hours after he'd been inside her?

"Cass!" Jo clutched her shirt together.

Brian held a hand her way. "Cass, don't—"

"Out," she managed to say. "Get… out! Get out!" Her voice rose with every word. Jo began to cry, but Cass didn't care. This was too much. The last straw. "Get out! I mean it!"

Brian opened his mouth, opened his hands wide as if in supplication, then seemed to realize there was nothing he could say. "All right; I'm getting out. But it's not what you think, and I'll be back." He shouldered his way out of the room as her sisters stepped back, open-mouthed with shock.

"Cass, I didn't—it wasn't—" Jo began.

Cass didn't want to hear any explanations. As Brian disappeared down the stairs, his footsteps thunderous on the wooden boards, rage welled up in her throat and came out as a feral cry. "I don't want to hear any more! I'm done! Just—done!" She pushed past the others out of the room, picked up speed and dashed to her own room down the hall. Inside, she slammed the door so hard its hinges rattled, and that felt so good she nearly opened it and did it again.

How much was she expected to stand in one night? Cass paced her room wildly. How treacherous could one man be? How much pain could one life hold? She rushed to the window to look out at her shed. Nothing it contained was big enough to express her anger.

"It's too much!" Cass's tears came hot and fast. She'd cried more in one day than she had in a decade, and she couldn't stand it anymore. She didn't want to feel like this. She craved another storm—one with enough thunder and lightning to broadcast her fury, but the night remained clear.

She scrubbed her cheeks angrily, but more tears came, as if the ache in her heart was leaking straight from her eyes. Cass knew she wouldn't be able to stop it. She'd failed at every turn. She hadn't kept anyone safe, least of all herself. She'd already begun to come to terms with the idea that Brian wanted her land more than he wanted her, but now he'd set her own sister against her.

And her sisters were all she had.

Cass stepped back from the window, defeated by

the clear night sky. No storm would wash these feelings away. No fireworks were wild enough to express them.

She sank down on her bed, tucked her feet underneath her and curled into a ball. For eleven years she'd feared the day the General would take the ranch away from her. She'd never once feared the real catastrophe. If she lost her sisters, she'd lose herself.

The door slipped open and Alice glided in on silent feet, shutting it firmly behind her again. She sat next to Cass on the bed, and pulled her into her arms. "You haven't lost anyone." Cass shut her eyes and rested her head on Alice's shoulder, grateful for her sister's strength. When Lena joined them a few minutes later, she, too, knelt on the bed and wrapped her arms around both of them.

Sadie joined them next, and took a position on the bed near Cass's feet. The door opened a fourth time, and Cass knew it had to be Jo.

She stiffened. A moment later, the mattress sunk, as Jo sat down.

"It was Sean," she said quietly. "He tried to get me to take my top off while he was filming me. He wanted money. He said we should share everything; even my body. Brian stopped him—"

Cass thought she'd run out of tears but she was wrong. So wrong.

She'd failed again.

She'd failed everyone.

She turned and lifted herself to her knees, reaching for her sister. Jo leaned into her embrace, and clung to her. "I thought he loved me," Jo said. "I thought—"

"I know. I know, honey." Cass held on to her for dear life as the others leaned in, too. "I'm so sorry."

"Brian decked him and Sean ran like the house was on fire." Jo laughed amidst her tears, a painful sound. "If he hadn't come right then, I don't know what would have happened. Sean wouldn't stop."

"I'm glad Brian was there," Cass said. She'd have to apologize in the morning. It shamed her that she'd read the situation so wrong. She'd looked for pain when there was only love.

"He got my car back, you know," Alice said. "I didn't have the guts to stand up to Howie, even though I sensed what he was doing was wrong."

"Look at this." Lena held up her phone. Cass wiped her eyes on her sleeve and squinted to make out the photo. "That's Scott," Lena clarified. "That's his face after Brian got done with him. Ella Hall saw him in town. Now I can say, *you should see the other guy.*" Her laugh was all bravado, but Cass's heart squeezed with gratitude toward Brian. She wasn't one for violence— usually. But Scott was a bully who'd beaten up plenty of men—and probably women, she thought now—over the years. Maybe now he'd think twice about it.

"Brian stopped me before I got myself in real trouble," Sadie said softly. "I'm so ashamed of myself I can hardly look at him, but that doesn't mean I don't appreciate what he did. He's a man, and a meddling SEAL, and the General's lackey, but he's saved our bacon, hasn't he?"

"I guess he has," Cass admitted.

Jo gave her a final squeeze and pulled back. Tabitha jumped up onto the bed and Jo scooped her into her lap.

"Speaking of bacon... I'm hungry."

Cass laughed, but when her stomach growled, she admitted, "Yeah, me, too."

"Do you think Brian would get us some more pizza?" Lena asked.

Another chuckle escaped Cass, but so did a few more tears. "After tonight? I doubt it." But even as she was saying it, Cass thought he probably would. If they asked.

If a pizza place was open at one in the morning in Chance Creek.

"Come on down to the kitchen. I'll whip something up." She hesitated. "We'd better discuss the new order of things around here, too, while we're at it."

"What do you mean?" Alice asked as they climbed off the bed and headed for the door.

"I mean Lena's right; we're done taking orders. No more fooling around when it comes to the General. This is our ranch now and we'll run it as we see fit. First thing tomorrow, those hands are going to go. We'll kick them off together," she told Lena. "We'll all pitch in to help with the cattle until we can hire new help. We'll all fix the roof together, too. I have a confession to make," she added, straightening her clothes. "Bob stole quite a bit of money from us. We're going to have to operate on a shoestring, but I have no doubt if we work together, we can get back on track."

"I'm in," Sadie said quickly. "All I want to do is get back to work on the gardens, but I'll help with everything else, too, and put all my sales money into the kitty."

"I'm in," Jo agreed. "I'll do whatever it takes to keep this place running."

"Are you saying I can be overseer?" Lena asked as they entered the hall.

"That's exactly what I'm saying," Cass told her.

"Then I'm in. All the way."

"Me, too," Alice said. "Sales have been good this year. If you need more money, all you have to do is ask."

Cass squeezed her. "Thank you. You four are all I need, you know."

"You're all we need, too," Jo said, and led the way downstairs.

Chapter Nine

"D IDN'T TAKE YOU long to thoroughly screw things up," Logan said when Brian shut himself in the General's office and patched together a video call early the next morning with the men he'd left back at USSOCOM. He'd spent most of the rest of the night pacing the maze, telling himself he had to give Cass time to calm down and give Jo a chance to explain what had happened. He knew once she did, Cass would see her mistake. But then what? She still thought he wanted Two Willows, not her.

He'd fallen asleep on the bench near the standing stone. At daylight he'd gone back inside to find the house quiet, but the kitchen a disaster, as if the Reed women had cooked a full-course meal in the middle of the night.

Maybe they had.

"I didn't mean to. I thought I was making progress. It's these assholes the Reeds are dating."

"Sounds like you got rid of them," Connor said with a grin. "Good work on that front."

"Yeah, there's that," Brian said tiredly. He'd never

forget the look on Cass's face when she'd walked in on him and Jo. That stark horror and betrayal had etched its lines on his heart at knifepoint, and the scars would always be there. He never wanted her to look at him like that again. He was afraid her regard for him had turned right then into something hard and dark—something he wouldn't be able to melt into love again.

He had well and truly screwed things up. Taken her passion and turned it to dust. Taken her trust and twisted it into a knot he'd never be able to undo.

"Don't you think you can give up now, wuss," Jack snapped at him. "I see that *poor me* expression on your ugly mug. It's a fucking disgrace. You're a SEAL. You're on a mission. You don't fold at the first sign of trouble."

"She thinks I did her sister," Brian protested.

"She thinks you held Jo on your lap. Which is all that happened. So get back there and tell her that."

"Cass doesn't want to see me—"

"Cass doesn't want to see me," Jack parroted. "Are you kidding me? That's your defense? Buck the fuck up, sailor. Get back into the fray and do your duty."

"Fix the house," Hunter said in more measured tones. "That's why you're there, right? Let things calm down and do your job. Jo's going to tell her what really happened, right?"

"I guess so." He figured Hunter was right; Jo would tell her sister what Sean had done—and what he'd done to get rid of the bastard. He wasn't sure it was enough to change Cass's mind about him, though. The intimacy they'd shared in the maze seemed so far gone he wasn't sure they could ever recover it.

It didn't matter if he'd meant to let her down or not; in her mind he had.

"Just get to work," Hunter said again. "And don't stop."

That made sense. He knew how to work, and there was a lot to get done on the ranch. "Will do."

"Fix this, Lake," Logan said. "We're counting on you."

The others nodded, and Brian felt the weight of their dependence on him. Just one more burden to bear, he told himself. He'd go make himself as useful as possible.

Hopefully that would be enough.

"THAT'S A LOT of shingles," Wye said as she and Cass stood in the kitchen watching Brian help the delivery crew unload them onto the back lawn. "You really going to get on that roof and fix it?"

"That's the plan," Cass said. It had been well over a week since the night she and her sisters had huddled together on her bed. The day had dawned warm and it was going to be a hot one before it was all over. She still hadn't apologized to Brian for her mistake, and he'd kept his distance from her, eating most of his meals in town. He woke the earliest of all of them and was always out of the house by the time she came down to make breakfast. He worked far into the night, too. Lena said they'd created a list of repairs and chores around the ranch, and he was working his way through it, checking them off one by one.

He'd kicked the remainder of the hands off the ranch the day after his altercations with Scott and Sean, before she and Lena could take that on. Cass didn't mind. It was clear none of the men were loyal to the ranch, and she'd dreaded the job. She'd meant to thank Brian for that—and apologize to him too, but somehow the moment never seemed right and with each day that passed, she wondered if her chance was slipping away.

Jo and Sadie were helping Lena and Brian with the cattle, and they'd already begun the hiring process for a new bunch of hands. Now that the shingles were here, and Brian would fix the roof, Cass would see him far more often, though.

She couldn't decide how she felt about that.

Since that awful night, she'd had a lot of time to think about everything he'd done, and she realized in every case except making love to her, he'd put the interests of her family and her ranch ahead of every-thing else.

He truly had helped each of her sisters—preventing them from going further down the dangerous trajecto-ries they'd been taking. Things would have been so much worse if he'd never come to Chance Creek.

It was hard to admit a man could do so much good. At first Cass had balked at giving him the credit, until she'd decided it wasn't a man/woman thing. It was a distance thing. As an outsider coming into their home, he'd seen all the things their blind spots hadn't allowed them to see. The strength of his arm had helped now and then, for sure, and she was glad it was him and not a female friend like Wye who'd gone after Scott after what he did to Lena. But mostly he'd been someone to talk to, someone to confide in. Someone to go to for advice.

She couldn't fault him for being a good friend to all of them. The realization left her more confused than before.

In the end, she decided the most important thing they'd all learned was how their anger at the General had left them ripe for exploitation by other men.

Still, she hadn't been ready to talk about it with Brian. She'd thought her heart would never mend after that day of heartbreak, but work was smoothing the way toward healing. She'd begun a top to bottom spring cleaning of the house, even if it was mid-summer, and the strenuous exercise had pumped enough endorphins through her brain that she found more reasons to hope than to sigh.

"Have you told Brian you're afraid of heights?" Wye asked her.

"No. Of course not."

"No, because that would be far too easy," Wye echoed.

"It's not about easy. It's about... pride." Cass turned away from the window. "This is my home. I want to be the one to care for it."

"It could be Brian's home, too. You said he wants it to be." Wye lifted her eyebrows, and Cass was afraid she'd betrayed something with her expression. "What?" Wye challenged her. "What happened between you and Brian?"

"I told you what happened with him and Jo," Cass hedged. She'd told Wye everything—except what had happened in the maze.

"But you're holding something back. I can tell. What's going on with you and that SEAL? Did you sleep with him?"

Cass shushed her. "For God's sake, keep your voice down. No one knows."

"You did sleep with him!" Wye raised an eyebrow. "Spill it. Everything. Right now."

Cass gave in. She told Wye how they'd met in the maze. How they'd made love. As she recounted the story, her heart throbbed with regret for what might have been.

"Well, that's a twist," Wye said when she was done.

"It's crazy, isn't it?" Cass sighed.

"For two single people who are totally hot for each other to meet up in a rainstorm and make love? Yeah, doubt that's ever happened before."

"Be serious." Cass moved to the sink, grabbed a cloth, wet it and began to wipe down the already clean counters.

"I am being serious."

"Well, it doesn't matter anyway. All that's over."

Wye took the rag from her hand and hung it up again. "Why? Why does it have to be over just because the two of you had a little misunderstanding? The way I see it the Universe just handed you a gift, so enjoy it! For once in your life don't ask questions, don't make plans, don't second guess what your instincts are telling you. Just… enjoy a romance with a sexy guy."

"A sexy guy who wants to marry me in order to get my land!"

"That wouldn't be cool—if it's true," Wye admitted. "But do we know it's true? No."

"He said it."

"He said he'd do anything to live on a ranch like this," Wye countered. "That's a throwaway line. People say that about everything. *I'd do anything to have hair like that. I'd do anything to be able to sing like a superstar. I'd do anything to lose ten pounds.* But they don't mean it. Brian wants a ranch like Two Willows. So, sue him."

When she put it that way, Cass had to admit maybe she'd overreacted. She'd done that a lot. "He is kind." The more she thought about what he'd done for her sisters, the clearer that had become.

"He sounds kind."

"Did I tell you about the bench he put in the maze?" She recounted how she'd found him installing it to make up for what he'd said to Alice.

"Which is how you got in trouble," Wye said with a wicked grin.

"Let's hope not."

Wye's grin vanished. "What's that supposed to mean?"

With a sigh, Cass confessed the risk she'd taken when they'd made love. Wye's humor disappeared in an instant.

"You know better than that, Cass Reed."

"I *do* know better than that. I can't explain it. I wasn't drunk. I've got no excuse, except…"

"Except a hot, kind Navy SEAL who's after your heart and your land came on to you and didn't pack a condom."

"I should be on the Pill. Any other self-respecting twenty-six-year-old woman would be." Cass swiped at the counter again, then dropped the cloth in the sink and pulled out a glass.

"What would you do if you got pregnant?"

"Have the baby," Cass said automatically as she poured a drink for Wye and then another for herself. "I have a home, resources, a family to help me, and I want to be a mother."

"What are you going to do if you get an STD?"

"Cry."

Wye shook her head. "Like that'll help. Don't ever do that again."

"I won't."

"At least it wasn't with Bob."

Cass spit out the sip of water she'd just taken. "Eww!"

Wye cracked a smile and Cass relaxed a little, feeling like she'd been to confession and could now move forward with a clear conscience.

"I worry about you, though," Wye went on. "You've held in so much for so long. Now you're losing control every which way, and while it's my personal belief you've found a good man to lose control with, you've got to keep your head on your shoulders."

Cass mopped up the water. "It's not like it'll happen again. Brian's only here to finish up the job the General gave him. He hasn't come near me in days."

"And you wish he would?" Wye prompted gently.

Cass struggled with her answer and finally nodded. "I really blew it, Wye."

"I don't think so."

"What if he… leaves… without giving me another chance?"

"Don't think like that." Wye touched her arm. "There are a lot of reasons for him to stay, you know. You're smart and pretty and a good friend. And you've got a ranch," she added with a grin.

"Thanks," Cass said wryly.

"Any time."

THERE HAD BEEN a ladder leaning against the side of the house since Brian had arrived, as if Cass had been inspecting the roof, although he'd never seen her climb it. Brian was moving it to a better location when Cass and Wye exited the house. Cass walked her friend to her Beetle and waited for her to drive away. Brian came to intercept her.

"Afternoon. Now that the shingles have been delivered, I'm getting set to start tearing off the old ones. The weather's supposed to be good all week. I figure we better get a move on."

Cass shaded her eyes as she gazed up at the roof. "I

wonder what Mom would think of the way we're fixing up the place?"

It was the perfect opening for a longer conversation, and Brian jumped on it. "What was she like? You've never told me much about her." He wondered if Cass would find an excuse to head back inside, but instead she considered his question.

"I think she was always a homebody, but like I said before, once the General joined the Army, she never left the ranch unless he was home on leave. Like Sadie, she spent a lot of time in the gardens. She had a green thumb. She read like anything. Could talk on any subject with anyone who came calling. She said since people had to visit Two Willows to see her, it was up to her to stay interesting."

"She didn't belong to any clubs, or a church or anything?"

"She contributed to lots of them, but she never wanted a fuss made about her and her refusal to leave the ranch, so she didn't join anything like that. Reverend Halpern visited every week. He used to tease her and say that if all his other parishioners made him give them personal sermons, his work would never be done. I think he wanted her to try leaving. Superstition doesn't really jibe with the church, you know? But he didn't push her, and he never stopped coming until she died."

"What does he think of the stone?"

Cass smiled impishly. "We don't talk about it much when he's around."

"I wish I'd met your mother." Brian shaded his eyes

and looked up at the roof. He was thankful its pitch wasn't too steep because it was high enough to make the job dangerous.

"She would have appreciated everything you've done for my sisters."

"I know my mother would have liked you. She died when I was too young for us to have talked much about women, but she used to say that I should find a wife who was better than me." He shrugged. "Maybe that was a thinly veiled message to my father."

Cass ignored his reference to marriage. "What did she like to do?"

"She was a nurse. She was a little shy, but a very hard worker. She believed in right and wrong. She also believed people could change, which I think is why she stuck with my dad even after things began to go badly."

"Sounds like a lovely person."

"You know what I miss most? Holidays." Brian couldn't believe he was telling Cass this. He'd never talked about it with anyone. Most conversations about his mom stopped when he mentioned she'd gotten shot. "She was so big on holidays. Christmas, Easter, Halloween. She made the best costumes."

Cass was nodding. "I know exactly what you mean. Holidays for us have never been the same since my mother died. I try—but there are only the five of us to celebrate now—plus a few ne'er-do-wells."

"Did you just use ne'er-do-wells in a sentence?"

"I did. Ten points for Gryffindor."

Brian grinned. He was searching for a new topic

when Cass suddenly said, "Could you help me with something?"

"Sure." Brian perked up. Given how seldom Cass asked for help, this had to be a good sign. "What do you need?"

"Come to my shed. I want to show you something." She led the way to the small structure at the far side of Sadie's gardens. When she took out a key to unlock the door, Brian understood he was being allowed into her inner sanctum.

Inside, she flicked on a light, which illuminated a small, rectangular room. Brian spotted the kiln at the far end. "You do pottery?"

"I used to. Mom and I did; it's been a while since I made anything. That isn't what I wanted to show you, though." She gestured him over near a set of shelves where a few mismatched pieces of pottery sat as if they'd never been moved after they'd been fired. "This is my stash."

For one second, he thought she was referring to drugs, and he tensed all over, but quickly realized she meant her fireworks. She sure had a lot of them. When Brian took in the assortment on the floor-to-ceiling shelves, he whistled. "I'm glad you keep that door locked."

"I let things get out of control," she agreed, and smiled wryly. "Which is ironic, since I've always used them to feel like I was keeping things under control."

"How'd that work for you?" Brian figured he'd ask for more details someday, but not today. He scanned the shelves and relaxed a little when he confirmed she only had fireworks—not explosives. He'd been beginning to wonder how deep this habit went.

"Not too well. I want to save a few of these for the Fourth of July, but I think I'm ready to get rid of the rest. I'm just not sure how. Do you think I should call Cab?"

"I think that's a start. I'll help you figure it out." He wanted to reach out and touch Cass, but this fragile truce between them was good enough for today. "You didn't buy all these at a fireworks stand. I'm pretty sure some of this stuff has been outlawed for years."

"Where there's a will there's a way," Cass said simply. "I don't have the will anymore, though."

"Glad to hear it. I'm glad you trusted me enough to tell me about it, too."

Cass reached out to adjust a bottle rocket so it lined up with the others. "I see the good in you, Brian."

"I'd like to start over. Try dating." He shifted closer to her, wanting her to remember how good they'd been together.

"The thing is," she said sadly, "I'm still not confident you'd want me if I didn't come with a ranch. Until I am, I can't be with you." She wouldn't meet his gaze. "But I'm going to talk to the General and tell him how much you've helped us. I'm going to tell him he should offer you a permanent job. I'll tell him to build you a house on the property somewhere, rather than putting you in one of those damn trailers in the Park. That way when you find the right woman you'll have a home to offer her."

When he found the right woman? Brian shook his head. Her words had the kick of a bullet to the heart. Didn't she understand how he felt about her?

He guessed not. He'd lost her trust.

He'd lost her.

"The thing is, Cass, the only woman for me is you."

CASS WAS STILL replaying that sentence in her head the following afternoon as she did up the lunch dishes when her phone buzzed in her pocket. It was Lena.

"Cass? We've got a problem. A big one."

"What is it?"

"Come down to the stables—and be ready to ride. You've got to see this."

Cass slipped the phone back into her pocket, found her boots and shoved her feet in them, then hurried out the door and jogged down the track, wondering if the hands had come back and were making trouble. Lena hadn't sounded like she was in imminent danger, but Cass couldn't help wishing that Brian was around for backup. He'd gone into town to get more supplies for the roofing job. Pretty soon she was going to have to face her worst fear and help him up there.

She wasn't looking forward to that at all.

The day before, he'd left the shed soon after he told her she was the only woman he wanted. Cass hadn't known what to say to that. Words were words. They didn't mean anything—as much as she wished they did.

When she met Lena at the stables, her sister had two

horses saddled and ready to go. Cass ached when she realized how long it had been since she'd ridden.

"What's wrong?"

"Bob was here. I spotted his truck in the distance, but I couldn't catch up to him. So I followed his tire tracks to see where he'd come from. You're never going to believe this."

Lena mounted her horse and set out down the track. Cass scrambled to mount, too, and catch up with her.

"Where are we going?"

"Come on!" Lena didn't slow down as she cut past the Park, past the pastures and into a part of the ranch Cass rarely went to these days.

Drier, stonier, unfit for cattle, this corner of the ranch wasn't good for much. Cass knew the track they were taking led to a canyon.

"Why was Bob heading this way?"

"Take a look."

Lena led the way down a steep grade. They'd camped here once or twice as kids, liking the feeling of being hidden away from the world, but now its isolation unnerved Cass. Why would Bob want to come here?

Not for any good reason, she figured.

Cass gasped when she rounded a bend in the track and had a clear view of the canyon floor. "You've got to be kidding me! He was living here the whole time?" The dilapidated trailer Bob said he'd hauled to the dump sat square in the middle of the flat, barren ground.

"Not living. Working." Once again Lena led the way. She dismounted and Cass followed suit, leaving her horse with Lena's a dozen yards from the trailer. When they drew near, Lena veered off for a moment to grab a battered folding lawn chair sitting outside the trailer and set it under one of the windows that used to be boarded up. Cass took in the fat padlock on the door, the square of plywood on the ground and the screwdriver sticking out of Lena's back pocket. "I got that piece off," Lena confirmed. "We need to hurry though; who knows when Bob will be back. Take a look."

Cass climbed up on the chair as Lena steadied it. It took a minute for her eyes to adjust to the relative dimness of the trailer. Most of the other windows were still boarded up. One or two small ones had curtains over them. As her vision cleared, she sucked in a breath. "Oh… fuck. Is that… is that what I think it is?"

"A whole hell of a lot of drugs," Lena confirmed. "Like… a whole hell of a lot of drugs, from what I can tell. And I don't like the look of that equipment."

"Is he cooking meth… here?"

"I don't think so—yet. I did a quick search online and there was a list of things to look for. I don't see any of the ingredients or telltale signs that they've been cooking it here. Sure looks like that was the plan, though. Maybe you disrupted that when you fired Bob. Maybe they just hadn't moved their operation yet. Meanwhile, they're storing everything here before they ship it off."

Cass tried to identify what was in the various packages. "Why didn't they at least cover everything up?"

"Who's going to see it here? They thought they were

safe, so they didn't bother. They're coming in and out on the back roads, but they obviously don't think we're much of a threat."

"No wonder…" Cass climbed down off the chair. "No wonder they've all been after us. No wonder Bob moved all his people in like he did. It was all part of a bigger plan."

"Of course it was. You realize why he was doing it here, don't you?"

"What do you mean?" Cass was still in shock. She surveyed the clearing, wondering if anyone was watching them now. Would Bob leave such a large stash unguarded? "We should get going."

"We can't just leave this stuff," Lena contradicted her. "Don't you get it? We're their cover. Anything happens, it's our fault. If the stash gets found—it looks like it's ours."

"That's ridiculous," Cass stammered, but a cold shock slid through her veins. If the drugs were found. If the authorities thought they were theirs…

They'd lose Two Willows for sure.

"We have to call Cab." Cass reached for her phone.

"No way. Get up there again and look through that window. Notice anything familiar?" Lena demanded.

"Like what?"

"Look!" Lena wasn't going to back down.

When Cass reluctantly did so, she leaned farther into the window and sucked in a breath. "That's… that's the manual you couldn't find. Sitting right there on the counter."

"And your cast-iron pan."

"Wait, those are Sadie's missing garden clogs. All the stuff we've been looking for—it's all here."

"All the stuff we never reported missing, and a lot more we didn't even notice was gone," Lena said. "That trailer is full of our stuff. Anyone stumbles onto it— they'd think we're the ones storing the drugs. What do you bet there's more in the drawers and cabinets."

"Cab wouldn't think that."

"Wouldn't he? Cass, if they've done this much to frame us, what else have they done? Think about it. Think about all those hired hands who answered to Bob. We've got nothing on them. As far as we know they didn't do anything out of line while they were here except mouth off to us. We didn't file any complaints about them. Bob's got them in his pocket. If we call Cab and say Bob and the others are storing drugs on our ranch, he's got five upstanding citizens to testify on his behalf. Citizens who lived here. Who watched us. Who would know exactly what we do."

"So they'd testify Bob had nothing to do with the trailer. That doesn't mean anyone would believe them." Cass hopped off of the chair. "Besides, we fired them."

"Which makes it look worse. Think about it," Lena said again. "What if that's not all they do? What if they testify that we're the ones who moved the trailer from the Park, and we're the ones who've been in and out of it all the time?"

A cold shiver ran down Cass's spine. Even if the charges didn't stick… their reputations would be dragged through the mud.

"The General," Cass whispered. "It doesn't matter how this goes, does it? The General is going to freak when he hears about this." She tried to think through all the possible ways this disaster could play out.

In the end, it was all the same.

He would decide once and for all they weren't capable of running the ranch right. He'd install a new round of overseers and hands... maybe he'd even follow through on his threat to kick them out for good.

Standing with Lena next to a trailer whose contents represented the end of everything they'd worked for, Cass had never felt so helpless. The General would never understand how things had gotten this bad. Even if she tried to explain, he'd point out all the mistakes they'd made along the way.

The worst of it was, he'd be right.

They'd been too gullible. Too trusting. Too blind to the problems mounting up all around them. Anger, pure and clear, burned through her. All they'd ever wanted was to be left alone to live their lives. Why did everyone need a piece of them?

"We are not going to let them ruin things for us," she said to Lena.

"We have to get rid of the trailer," Lena said. "We could hitch it up to my truck and drive it out of town. Leave it somewhere."

"What if someone sees us? That seems like a perfect way to get caught." Cass thought fast. "No one can know about this. No one." It felt like old times; the two of them against the world. How many times had she and Lena concocted a plan to fight back when things seemed unfair? Adrenaline coursed through her veins as she considered the options. They needed to get rid of the evidence, even if they hadn't committed the crime. There was one way to do that: an action commensurate with the fury that was building in her heart.

Lena waited for her to say more, and Cass knew her sister knew exactly what was running through her mind, but every time she opened her mouth to utter the words, she found she couldn't say them. She remembered making love to Brian, opening her heart to the feelings that had coursed through her as they moved together. She remembered the tears she'd cried later, the sobs that had wracked her, but left her feeling… peace. She didn't want to backtrack now. She didn't want more secrets—more reasons for her family to live apart from everyone else. She didn't want to have to hide her feelings again.

Finally, when Cass didn't speak, Lena began, "We could blow it—"

"No. We can't," Cass said, coming to her senses. She put up a hand to forestall Lena's arguments. "Absolutely not. There's a big difference between setting off a bottle rocket and blowing up a trailer. We can't do that."

"I know you could rig something big enough to do the job. Come on, you've got to admit you want to." Lena was furious, too, and Cass understood her need for revenge.

"Of course I want to," she snapped, "but that doesn't make it right."

"So, you're done with all that? Forever?"

Her sarcastic tone assured Cass she didn't believe it. "I'm not saying I won't set off a firecracker or two now and then," she said. "But I am saying an explosion, no matter how safe or how small, can't stand in for my feelings. That's heading down a path I never wanted to go. And I'm not going to do it anymore; I already asked Brian for help disposing of the rest of the fireworks." She stopped, as the answer became clear. "And that's what we need to do now. Ask him for help."

"A man?" Lena said scornfully.

"Yes. A man." It was a new idea to Cass, too, and she was just as uncomfortable with it as Lena seemed to be.

"I asked him for help before, you know. With the hands. He didn't come."

Shame twisted Cass's gut. "That's my fault," she said. "He was with me. I distracted him."

Lena looked at her askance. "Distracted him? Like... distracted him, distracted him?" She waggled her eyebrows, and Cass appreciated that in the middle of this calamity, her sister could still find time for humor.

"Yes," she admitted.

"So... was it big?"

Cass shoved her. "Get serious."

"I am. Like, this big?" Lena held her hands apart.

Cass shoved her again. "Anyway, I know he'll help this time."

Lena sighed. "That's not how we used to do things."

"How we used to do things got us right here." Isolated. Vulnerable.

She understood Lena's reluctance to involve Brian. Every fiber of her body rebelled against the idea of asking for help.

Even from someone who said he loved her.

"He'll tell the General." But Lena sounded more discouraged than angry, and Cass wondered if she was secretly relieved at the thought of bringing in reinforcements.

"I don't think so. I think... I think he's on our side." Cass realized it was true as she spoke the words. As far as she knew, he hadn't told the General about any of their mistakes. Instead, he'd worked hard to fix them and get the ranch back on track. "Brian wants to marry me." It was a revelation to say it out loud. "He wants to be part of our family—and the ranch. He doesn't want to lose it, either. I think... I think maybe we should give him a chance."

"I think you're right." Lena looked about as surprised as Cass felt. "Which kind of makes me feel sick to my stomach."

Cass laughed. "I know what you mean. A man... who helps. It's a novel concept."

"Do you think there are more like him?" Lena asked as Cass pulled out her phone.

"We could ask the General," Cass joked as she called Brian.

Lena shuddered. "Let's not. We got lucky once, but

lightning doesn't strike the same place twice."

Cass couldn't say why another chill ran down her spine as she waited for Brian to pick up his phone.

"CASS?" BRIAN HAD just pulled up and parked behind the house when his phone buzzed.

"We could use some help. Head down toward the stables and we'll meet you there."

"Sure thing," he said when he found his voice again. Cass, asking for help for a second time in two days? That was new. "Be right there." He started the engine and put the truck in gear. Might as well drive down and save some time. He wanted to reach Cass before she changed her mind.

After what she'd said yesterday, he'd been hard put to feel confident about his chances to fix things with her, but now things were looking up. All the way down the track toward the stables he wondered what the problem was, but nothing prepared him for what Cass and Lena showed him when they met up, stabled the horses they'd been riding, climbed into his truck and directed him toward the canyon, heading down a track to a barren scoop of land. He mentally scanned the map of the ranch he'd memorized back at USSOCOM where it hung on the wall, and shook his head; there was nothing down this way.

At least, there never used to be.

Now there was; a beater of a trailer straight out of the seventies. "What's that?" he asked warily as he climbed out of the truck.

"Take a look," Cass said, climbing out, too, and pointing to the folding chair.

He crossed the clearing, and hoped the spindly thing would hold his weight, but when he climbed up on it and peeked in, he realized the state of the chair was the last thing he needed to worry about.

"Bob moved it here," Lena said when he stepped down again. "We've got to get it out of here before anyone finds out about it. I think we should tow it away and leave it somewhere."

"And I think that's a good way for us to get caught with it. A bunch of our things are in there. We think Sean stole them. He's the one who's always sneaking into the house with Jo. If they're still in there and someone finds the trailer, we'll be implicated."

"We can break in and get them out," Lena argued.

"But someone could still see us move it—and then we'd really look guilty."

Brian held up a hand. "Give me a minute to think this through." He paced a tight circle, his mind flipping through all the facts at hand. A trailer full of drugs and the kind of equipment used to cook meth. Bob trying to marry Cass. Mark providing Howie with drugs to deliver.

"If the General finds out about this, he'll take the ranch for sure," Cass said quietly.

Once again, Brian thought of how much pain this family could have been spared if only there had been true communication between the different factions. When he thought of the General back as USSOCOM taking all the time to set up this elaborate plan, he had to shake his head. Why didn't the man pick up the phone and talk to Cass and the others? Better yet, why not visit them?

"You said Bob was here? Today?"

"That's right. There are several places you can access our property from the highway. Those gates are locked, but of course Bob had the key—still does; he never gave it back. And anyway, a good pair of snips will cut through any padlock we might use."

"Bob orchestrated everything. He found a place to store his inventory and potentially cook meth where no one would think to look," Brian mused. "Cab said Mark's a chemist, so he's probably behind some of that stash—and the equipment. That pot could be home-grown or shipped up from somewhere else."

"Howie was the delivery man," Cass said.

"Scott was the muscle," Lena put in.

"And Sean was in the house watching us, and stealing things to incriminate us," Cass said. "They were working together all along."

"We need to let them know they can't use Two Willows for a home base anymore," Lena said. "I say we blow that trailer up."

Cass was shaking her head. "I already said no to that. It isn't safe."

"See what you've done?" Lena said to Brian. "You've made her... reasonable."

"What should we do?" Cass asked him, ignoring her sister's jibe.

A plan occurred to Brian. One that made him smile.

"I'm with Lena. Let's blow it sky high."

"ARE YOU SURE you want to do this?" Cass asked Wye for the tenth time as they walked up the street toward the Dancing Boot that evening. The light was fading from the sky and her nerves were keyed up tight. The plans they'd made were risky in the extreme and she still had her doubts they'd manage to pull them off.

"Are you kidding? I've never done anything so exciting. I'm all in." Wye definitely seemed excited; she had a bounce in her step that Cass envied.

"You'll have to distract Howie for at least an hour. Two is better."

"Trust me. I was born for this undercover stuff." As the bar came into view, Cass slowed her pace until Wye grabbed her arm and pulled her along. "Come on. Let's do this."

"How can you be so calm?" Cass asked her. "I can't believe I'm about to steal a car."

"Borrow it, you mean. Isn't that what Howie always told Alice when he took hers? Turnabout is fair play, right?"

Cass took in her friend's high heels, tight mini and the plunging neckline of her top and wondered again how she'd let Brian talk her into bringing Wye into this. Her normally calm, no-nonsense friend was practically giddy at the thought of playing her part.

"Wye is going to be our distraction and our lookout," Brian had said back when he'd laid out the plan in the gazebo that afternoon. "She'll keep Howie busy while you take his truck."

"I don't know how to hotwire a truck," she'd protested.

"He keeps a spare key under the mat," Alice had said blithely. "Chance Creek is a small town, after all. There's no crime here." She had shrugged with an impish smile that made Cass breathe a little easier about Alice's recovery. She'd hated to see her sister so brought down by Howie's duplicity. If Alice was willing to make jokes, her heart had to be on the way to healing.

Unlike Wye, Cass was dressed all in black, her hair tightly braided and tucked under a dark baseball cap. When they reached the club, she hung back. "Call me when you've landed the quarry," she said. "But Wye, if anything goes wrong, just bail."

"Don't worry about me. I'll be perfectly safe. When I'm done, I'll head over to Fila's." She named a popular restaurant in town. "I'm spending the night at her place. She and her husband will drive me there. Do you see Howie's truck?"

"Right over there." Cass pointed to the far side of the lot where Howie had parked on the diagonal, hogging two spots. She hoped it was true that Wye would be safe. If anything happened to her while she was helping them, Cass would never get over her remorse. She watched her friend disappear into the bar, made her way over to the far side of the lot and leaned against a nearby tree, trying to keep out of sight of the bar's patrons.

It was nearly a half an hour before Wye texted her a message. *Got him*. Cass texted Brian, who was back at the ranch with her sisters preparing for the next step in their plan, and scanned the lot again. So far, so good. This side had filled up early and most people were parking at the back of the bar now. She slid between the vehicles, opened the door to Howie's truck and carefully climbed inside.

It was the work of a moment to find the key Alice had told her about. Cass slid it in the ignition, debated whether or not to buckle up her seat belt and finally did, then turned the key.

The engine roared to life and Cass ducked, sure that Howie would be able to hear it from inside the bar, as silly as that was. It would be impossible to hear anything on a normal night. Tonight, with a live band playing, he'd go home with his ears ringing.

She set the truck in reverse, inched the massive vehicle out of the space it occupied and tapped on the gas. It lurched forward once, twice, until she got a feel for the engine. She exited the parking lot as quickly as she could and headed out of town.

Cass didn't breathe easily until she'd left Chance Creek behind, but even on the country highway leading to Two Willows, her heart was beating fast. She kept both hands on the wheel and checked her rearview mirror every couple of seconds. When she saw headlights behind her she thought she would throw up, but the vehicle turned off well before Two Willows came into view.

When she turned into her own driveway, Cass didn't think she'd ever been so happy to arrive at home, but this was only the start of the plan. She carefully drove Howie's truck down the rutted track toward the canyon where the small storage trailer sat, and was rewarded when she found Brian and her sisters ready for her, everything unloaded from the trailer and sitting in piles on the dirt outside.

"It's all going smooth as silk," Brian assured her. "I called in every Navy SEAL favor I could. It's lucky there are a few of them in town. Boone Rudman's got Sean cornered playing pool at Rafters. Mason Hall found Bob at the hardware store and convinced him to visit Westfield. He told him he was looking for an overseer to run their cattle operation, and the idiot fell for it."

"What about Howie?" He and Mark were still waiting for their court dates. Cass hated to think about them roaming free in Chance Creek. She'd hoped they would simply skip town, but so far that hadn't happened.

"We didn't even have to do anything about him," Lena said. "He got into a fight with Luke Matheson."

"He didn't," Cass said, appalled at Scott's stupidity. After getting licked by Brian she'd have thought he'd avoid getting into another fight. Luke was a scrapper. Scott had picked the wrong man to bait.

"He's already at the sheriff's office," Brian added.

"We separated everything that's ours out from their crap," Lena told her. "It's already all back at the house. Mark's the only wild card now. We can't get a bead on him. We're hoping he's out of town."

Cass didn't like the sound of that. "Let's get going, then, just in case."

BRIAN HAD TO hand it to Cass and her sisters: they knew how to work. With four of them helping, Howie's truck bed was full in no time. Brian closed the tailgate and they tied a tarp firmly in place to cover it.

Alice was poised in her car out on the highway, keeping watch for any unexpected visitors to the ranch, but so far she hadn't called to warn them about anyone coming near it. Brian hoped their luck would continue, but he wasn't counting on it. That's why he'd demanded that the women all leave the ranch when he did.

Brian ordered them into Lena's truck and told them to drive up the track a ways before he got to work installing the explosives he'd improvised from Cass's collection of fireworks and various solvents and chemicals he'd found around the ranch. Luckily his training had covered all sorts of scenarios—but he'd never thought he'd use his knowledge like this.

When he was done, he hopped back into Howie's truck and caught up with them farther down the track. They'd debated who should drive Howie's truck back into town, but Brian had overridden all Cass's protests. "If anyone gets caught, it needs to be me. The General will vouch for me," he'd said, and Cass had subsided.

"Have you checked in with Alice?" he asked through the window when he pulled up alongside them.

"She's anxious. She can't get a good read on things,

but for now everything is still clear. I only wish we could implicate the rest of the men somehow," Cass said. "It doesn't seem fair Howie will take the rap for what they all did."

"I bet Howie gives them up," Lena said. "He won't go down alone."

Brian hoped they realized it would be naïve to think any of the men would get out of the business no matter what happened tonight. The most they could hope was that the troublemakers would leave Chance Creek, or at any rate, stay away from Two Willows. They were taking a chance doing this, but unlike the women, Brian knew soon there'd be four more men to protect the ranch. He was banking on that being enough.

"Let's get this show on the road," Brian said. He passed her the cell phone he'd rigged to ignite the explosion remotely. She'd been very impressed when he'd shown her how he planned to set it all up. Discussing the blast radius, potential contamination of the soil beneath the trailer, containment ideas and more with Cass had proven to be far more arousing than it had ever been back in the Navy. But that was all due to the company.

"You give me a five-minute head start, set off that explosion and get the hell out of here."

"We've got it."

"Don't backtrack, whatever happens," he warned them. "Even if the damn thing doesn't blow. You get the hell off the ranch and stay off until we meet up in town."

"Brian—we've got it," Cass said.

"Okay. Be safe. Don't drive like a bat out of hell," he warned Lena.

"I won't."

"Get going," Cass chastised him. She pulled out her own phone. "Alice? All clear?" She gave Brian a thumbs-up.

Brian took a deep breath. "All right. See you on the other side" He hated having Cass out of his sight, even for a moment, but they'd be together again in less than an hour.

"Wait!" Cass hopped up on the passenger seat of Lena's truck and leaned out the window. She reached for Brian.

"What is it?" He put Howie's truck in park and leaned out to take her hand.

"Brian, be safe. You need to come home when this is done. I... I need you to come home."

Brian swallowed in a suddenly dry throat. *Home*. His heart swelled at the word and its implications. Damn right he was coming home. He pushed his upper body out the window, closed the gap between them as best he could and kissed her. "I will. I swear. And then we're going to talk about marriage again."

"O...okay." She sat back down.

Heart soaring, Brian did the same and pressed on the accelerator, feeling invincible. They were going to take down the bad guys. He was going to win the girl. He pulled out and set off up the track, frequently looking back in his mirror. He was past the house and almost to the highway when an explosion lit the night behind him.

A nice, controlled explosion—where it couldn't cause any harm.

A message to their friends.

Two Willows was no longer home to the drug trade. It wouldn't ever be home to the manufacture of meth.

Time to make sure Mark and the others understood that loud and clear.

He toggled his phone. "Cass? Everything all right?"

"It's perfect!" Her excited voice rang out. "Did you see it? It went up like a torch!"

"You women all right?"

"We're fantastic!" She was breathless, almost giddy. Brian suppressed a smile.

That was his girl. "See you in town." He cut the call and focused on the road.

The plan was simple: The women would wait several minutes to give him a head start, then drive into town all together in Lena's truck. Once Brian had dropped off Howie's vehicle, they'd meet at the rendezvous point, and head back to the ranch.

Brian set a good pace, but he kept his wits about him as he drove into town, knowing that at any moment Howie could realize his ride was missing and contact his friends. He took a circuitous route to the sheriff's office that didn't pass through the busiest streets of the small town. Not that the streets were particularly busy, even on a Friday night, but he didn't want to push his luck.

When he was still some blocks from his destination,

Brian pulled up the hood of his jacket to shade his face. Reaching the station, he pulled around back to where the department vehicles were parked when not in use, cut the engine and carefully climbed out, hoping to escape notice until he was ready. He undid one corner of the tarp and distributed several bags of pot and pills—and meth—on top of it where anyone could see.

Taking one last look to make sure no one else was around, he leaned inside the truck's open window, pushed on the horn for all he was worth and then booked it out of the parking lot at high speed. His mad dash through the neighborhood was worthy of an action sequence in the best spy movie, he thought as he leaped a fence and nearly tangled himself in a swing set. Several blocks away, he spotted Lena's truck, just where it was supposed to be.

But when he pulled open the door to climb inside, his heart dropped. Alice was driving it.

"Where the hell are Cass and Lena?" he demanded, climbing in.

Alice gunned the engine and turned back toward Two Willows. "You know we can't all leave the ranch at once. Cass stayed to keep the General safe. Lena stayed to protect Cass. And there's trouble coming. I can feel it. We need to get home." Sadie and Jo watched him silently from the backseat.

Brian swore.

He'd never even thought of that stupid superstition, and Cass hadn't mentioned it once.

He thought of Lena taking potshots at the target.

He thought of Mark unaccounted for.

"Hell. Floor it," he demanded.

Alice did as she was told.

CASS JUMPED WHEN her phone buzzed in her pocket. She and Lena had split up, the better to keep watch for trouble, Lena at the front of the house and Cass at the back. She wondered if Brian had discovered she and Lena had stayed at the ranch, and what his reaction had been. It didn't matter, she told herself; they'd be together again soon enough. She leaned against the back porch railing, sweeping her gaze in all directions at intervals. Now she pulled out her phone, and her heart sank when she saw it was Wye.

"Lost him," Wye said without preamble. "I did the best I could, I'm sorry. He got a call and was out of there like a shot."

"That's just fine," Cass said, although anxiety crawled through her gut and into her throat. Brian and the others were still in town. Who knew where Howie would go next?

Was he on the way here even now?

"I slipped out the back as soon as he left. I didn't want him to ask me questions when he realized his truck was missing."

"Where are you now?" Cass strode through the house and gestured to Lena in the darkened front room. "It's Wye—Howie's flown the coop," she hissed.

"I'm at Fila's restaurant, just like we planned," Wye said. "I'm going home with Fila and Ned, and I'll spend the night at the Double-Bar-K."

Cass breathed a sigh of relief she was out of danger. "Terrific. I'll let you know what happens."

"Is Brian back yet?"

"Not yet, but he will be soon." She hoped.

"Cass, I'm worried. Do you want me to call the sheriff?"

"No. So far it's all working perfectly. We'll be fine, I swear."

Wye sighed. "Call me as soon as Brian gets there."

"Will do."

Cass cut the call and joined Lena by the window. "Now there's two of them out there somewhere. Pretty soon there'll be more."

"I'd hoped we wouldn't need these, but looks like we will." Lena reached behind the couch, lifted a shotgun out and handed it to Cass. "Remember how to use this?"

"Of course." The General might not want them to serve, but he wouldn't stand for his girls to be ignorant around firearms. Every foreman had been tasked with making sure their skills were up to par.

"I've got my Glock. And another shotgun, too. I grabbed all the ammunition I could find—and everything else I thought might be of use." She passed a number of cartridges to Cass, who pocketed them. "Shout if you see something."

"You, too."

The shotgun was heavy when she carried it to the back porch, and her heart was heavy, too, at the thought of violence coming to Two Willows, but this was her home and it meant the world to her.

She'd defend it if necessary.

THE CALLS CAME one after another on the drive back to Two Willows. Brian fielded them as Alice drove as quickly, calmly and terrifyingly fast as a Formula One racer.

"Sean bailed on me," Boone said. "Got a text and bolted for the door. I tried to stop him but the place was crowded. He was gone before I could get outside."

"Bob hightailed it out of here," Mason said. "We did our best to detain him, but short of force, there wasn't much we could do."

"One of the deputies just came into Fila's," Wye hissed when Brian picked up her call. "He said Scott made bail a half-hour ago. Tell Cass I'm still fine; I'm on my way to the Double-Bar-K, but I thought you'd want to know. You know Cass and Lena are at the ranch, don't you?"

"We're on our way there," Brian told her. He cut the call. "Drive faster," he told Alice.

She didn't answer. Just took a turn at a speed that made Brian grab the armrest.

Just a few more minutes, he told Cass in his mind. *Just stay safe a few more minutes*. He went to call her, but decided to hold off. She needed to keep her wits about her right now, not be distracted by the phone.

He'd never forgive himself if she came to any harm. He'd promised himself he wouldn't drag a woman down with him like his father or brother had. He'd thought he could help Cass, but now his plan could be the death of her.

Hold on, he told her again in his mind. *Just hold on long enough for me to make this right.*

BACK ON THE porch, the minutes ticked away slowly, giving Cass hope that Brian would make it home before Howie put two and two together and came to confront them. With all the lights off in the house, the sweep of the pastures was clear in the distance. A beautiful night.

A dangerous one.

Her phone trilled again. Lena appeared like a ghost in the doorframe. "What is it?"

"Wye just texted. Scott's out on bail."

"He's probably on his way here. They probably all are by now."

"Okay," was all Cass could manage. Her fingers curled around the barrel of the shotgun. So this was what it was like to go war, she thought. No wonder her father had been consumed by his career. Tonight she had a purpose that guided every thought and movement. It set her heart thumping and her mind into overdrive. It was as if a machine had replaced her brain; one capable of processing far more items of data than usual.

Real life receded. The moment was all that mattered. She scanned the backyard, gardens and distant pastures again.

And again.

"I'll be out front," Lena said and slipped away.

Cass nodded but didn't stop looking for trouble.

When the men came, there was little warning. Just the bounce and flash of headlights from a truck moving fast over uneven ground from the direction of the barns and Park.

"Lena! Here they are," Cass shouted. In an instant, Lena was at her side.

The truck's engine roared as it raced up the hill and swerved in close to the house. Cass stood her ground. So did Lena.

"What the fuck?" Bob yelled, sticking head and shoulders out of the truck. "You blew up our stuff? Are you fucking kidding me?"

"I'll blow up my trailers whenever I feel like it," Cass shouted back.

The passenger door opened, and Howie and Scott spilled out. "Where's my truck, bitch?" Howie yelled, advancing on them.

"Gone—and it isn't coming back!"

"Hold it right there," Lena warned. "One more step and you'll feel it."

"Don't you threaten me." Scott surged forward, then danced back with a curse when Lena took a potshot at him with her pistol. She was aiming short, Cass saw. The bullet ricocheted off the dirt five feet in front of him. Lena never missed by five feet.

All the men ducked back into the truck. It swerved away, then circled back, although this time Bob stopped farther away.

"You aren't the only one who can shoot," Scott yelled from the safety of the truck. When a bullet zipped past and buried itself in the cladding of the house, Cass grabbed Lena and pulled her inside.

"Jesus, we can't get in an old-fashioned shootout."

"Too late. We already are." Lena slammed the door shut and locked it, then crossed to the kitchen window, opened it, batted the screen away and took another potshot, aiming for the truck this time. "The only thing these assholes understand is force."

"I'm calling Cab. The drugs are gone; we've got nothing to worry about now," Cass said. She didn't wait for her sister to agree. A moment later she had her phone out and the sheriff on the line.

"We're taking fire, Cab," she said when he picked up. "I've got five men in a truck taking potshots at my house."

"What the hell's going on down there?"

"Come quick!"

"This got anything to do with—"

Cass cut the call, moved to the window at the other end of the room, cracked it open and set the shotgun on the sill. When Scott took another shot at the house, she aimed high, not wanting to hurt anyone if she could help it, and pulled the trigger. "Fuck! That's got a kick," she said to Lena, who just laughed.

"You've been slacking on your practice."

That was true. She hadn't handled a firearm in months.

It wasn't like you forgot, though.

She racked another cartridge and took aim.

"Maybe I scared them off," she said when nothing happened for a long moment.

"Don't get cocky," Lena said, just as Howie leaned out of the truck's window.

That wasn't any shotgun he was holding, Cass realized. "Down! Get Down!" She dropped to the floor.

Lena ducked as the world exploded in gunfire, round after round chewing up the wooden siding of the house. When the windows shattered, they both rolled over and pressed their faces to the ground. Still the firing went on with a rat-a-tat-tat Cass had only ever heard in war movies.

"Where'd they get automatic weapons?" she cried, but she didn't expect an answer. As the bullets pinged and zipped and thwacked through the windows and buried themselves in the wall across the room, Cass hugged her arms over her head and fought to keep from sliding into panic.

Lena was yelling something she could hardly hear. "…works. Fireworks!"

"They're in the shed," she yelled back, then pressed herself back to the ground as another glass pane shattered, sending shards spinning and twisting through the air in a dangerous waterfall.

"No. No!" Lena's voice was hard to make out over the gunfire. "Right there!" She pointed to the cabinet Cass was huddled up against. Cass couldn't understand how her fireworks had gotten inside, but when she pulled the door open, there they were—a collection of bigger ones, including a pile of M-80s. Lena must have grabbed them earlier when she rounded up everything that might be handy. "Hold them back," Lena was yelling. "Scare them! They're circling around."

Cass held her breath. If the men came in from both sides of the house at once, she and Lena didn't stand a chance. She shifted the shotgun to her left hand, grabbed the bag of fireworks in her right and turned back to Lena, who stopped trying to communicate with words and switched to the set of military hand gestures they'd all learned as little girls.

Cass let out a laugh that was nearly a sob as she took in what Lena was saying. She needed to get into the front room and get ready. If… no, *when…* the men stormed the front door, the M-80s might be a big enough surprise to keep them at bay a little while longer.

She hadn't army-crawled in years and almost immediately her muscles protested at the strange movements. She inched forward until she reached the end of the wall of cabinets. Looking across the gap made by the back door, she gasped when she saw its thick, wooden expanse had splintered. The kitchen windows had all shattered. She took in the broken dishes, the papers strewn across the floor and glanced back at the door as it buckled under a new round of fire.

"I can't get past," she screamed to Lena. She'd have to if she wanted to make it into the front room. But any second that door would give. She pictured a barrage of bullets slamming into her as she scooted across. Rooted in place, she couldn't make herself go any farther.

"Yes, you can. Now! Hurry!"

Cass shook her head. She couldn't do it. Couldn't—

"They're destroying the house!"

Cass blinked. Lena was right. They were ruining it. *Her house.*

Cass surged across the gap, slithered right past Lena and bolted for the front room.

"Matches," Lena screamed and tossed her a box she pulled out of a drawer by the sink.

Cass grabbed them, too, scrambled her way into the front room and shoved the sofa away from the inner wall to make a diagonal barricade facing the front door. Crawling behind it, hoping it would offer a little cover, she set the shotgun aside and pulled the M-80s out of the bag with shaking hands. She set them up in a row and prepared the matches. Now all she could do was wait.

In a sudden silence, she heard Bob shouting orders. "Cass, you're dead meat!" he yelled.

She prayed that wasn't true.

Where the hell was Brian? Where was Cab? What was taking so long?

She had no idea if minutes or hours had passed since she'd called the sheriff.

She heard voices circling around the front of the house, considered standing up and looking, but was glad she hadn't when the windows exploded inward a second later as gunfire filled the air again.

Wait, she told herself, pressing against the couch for safety. *Wait for it.*

Another lull. More voices.

"Now!" a man yelled. Was that Bob?"

Cass lit a match, dropped it, stamped it out with her bare hand on the floor and lit another one as fast as she could. This time she succeeded in keeping it lit and she held it to each fuse in turn of three M-80s.

There was nothing for it now. She had seconds before she had to throw them or risk blowing off her own hands. *Come on*, she willed at the front door. *Come on!*

She heard a scream from the kitchen, and the front door burst open simultaneously. Everything slowed down.

Cass picked up the M-80s one by one and hurled them at the men spilling into the front hall.

Gunfire ricocheted all over and Cass ducked, pressing against the sofa again, covering her head with her hands.

The world exploded, the M-80s deafening in the close quarters. Suddenly Cass felt like she was underwater; sounds and sensations came from every angle, but made no sense. She grabbed for the shotgun, rolled over and waited for the next attack.

"DANGER!" ALICE YELLED, suddenly swerving across the road into the other lane. Brian grabbed the steering wheel and tugged the truck back into line. "Danger! Danger!"

"Alice, calm down. Snap out of it!" There wasn't time for visions. Brian already knew Cass and Lena were in trouble. "Drive the truck."

Alice gripped the wheel tighter, her breath coming in harsh pants. She floored the gas and Brian fell back his seat.

"Are they okay? What's happening?" Sadie shrieked from the backseat.

"No visions! Just drive," Brian countermanded, keeping a hand ready to grab the wheel again. Thank God they were near the ranch. Just another minute or two.

But minutes were endless during a battle. Brian knew that all too well.

Alice's head dropped forward, and Brian swore, nearly straddling the console between them as he fought to get control of the wheel. She snapped up again, slapped his hand away and drove, her face white, her mouth in a tight line, an Alice he'd never seen before.

Brian glanced back, took in Sadie's and Jo's terrified expressions. They were holding hands as if they'd seen what Alice had.

"No," he said. "No, we're not too late."

"Not yet," Alice said. "Not yet."

WHO WAS SCREAMING?

Cass's hearing came back with a rush and snap that had her rolling over and staggering to her knees. That sound—who? Lena?

A peep over the couch showed a confusion of bodies in the doorway, but male voices yelling told her it was only a matter of time before the shooting began again.

Still, that screaming went on and on. On and—

Cass shut her mouth, doubled over and nearly retched on the floor. She'd been the one screaming. Because she was the one who couldn't believe what was happening around her.

The living room was destroyed. The couch's stuffing embedded by bullets into the wall behind it. Bullets that could just have easily hit her.

Where was Lena?

What was she supposed to do now?

She still had the shotgun. Tucking it under one arm, she moved to the end of the couch to peep around and see the path to the kitchen. If she was going to die, she wanted to see Lena one more time.

"God damn it, Cass!"

Cass froze.

Bob.

Still alive. Still coming after her.

"You stupid bitch! Why'd you have to screw it all up? But then that's what you do, isn't it? You're such a screw-up your own father hates you."

She held her breath. *He's trying to draw you out*, she told herself. He was trying to play with her emotions— get her so riled up she went off half-cocked. Well, she wasn't afraid of her feelings anymore and he couldn't trip her up that way.

But what did it matter? He was going to get her anyway. Mere feet bridged the distance between them. It would take a single shot to end her life.

This was it.

She'd run out of time.

Her thoughts flew to her mother. Would she be waiting for her if the worst happened?

She remembered her mother's face the last time she saw her, as she slipped away from this world to the next. She had seemed peaceful when she went—as if the transition to the next world wasn't so hard after all.

Cass hoped that was true. Hoped if Bob shot her, the end would come quick. At least then she'd be done with all the pain and worry. She'd be with the one person who had ever made her feel safe—

A sound from the kitchen arrested her. A moan.

Lena.

Bob's low laugh hit her square in the gut. "That's one of them," he said quietly to one of the other men. "You go finish Lena off. I'll take care of Cass."

No.

No one was going to finish Lena off.

Not on her watch.

She wasn't done with her job yet. She had four sisters to watch over. A ranch to protect.

A father to keep safe.

Wait for me, Mom; I'm going to be a little longer.

Cass stood up and pulled the trigger.

"THERE THEY ARE!" Sadie yelled from the backseat as Alice swerved around the house and hit the brakes. The truck lurched to a stop, but Brian had already leaped out of it, racing toward the sound of gunfire.

Sean was on the ground, half propped against Bob's

dusty truck. Brian saw the glint of a weapon in his hand and kicked the pistol into a long arc before Sean could use it. It fell somewhere in Sadie's garden and Sean sagged back, slipping into unconsciousness. He must be hurt bad, but Brian didn't care.

He kept on going, leaped the back steps and barged into the kitchen to find Scott bent over Lena's body. He disposed of the man with a sharp kick to the face before Scott could even react, grabbed the man's semi-automatic and hit him with it—hard. When he was sure Scott was down for the count, he bent over Lena.

"Go... go," she hissed at him, although her face was covered with blood.

Brian made a game time decision. First he had to secure the premises. Then he could issue first aid. "I'll be back."

The blast of a shotgun had him pressing up against the wall, but a man's shout and a woman's scream—Cass's scream—brought him racing into the living room. Coming around the corner, his instincts made him pull the trigger, and he shot the weapon out of Howie's hand. He brought Sean's pistol to bear on Bob. The man had sunk to his knees and was swearing up a blue streak, pressing both hands to his forehead, where blood streamed from multiple wounds into his eyes.

Behind him a man raised a gun. With a fluid move-ment, Brian brought his weapon to bear and shot twice, and the man crumpled.

That was Mark. Brian swept the room with his gaze again. Sean, Scott, Bob, Mark. Where was Howie?

"Cass, behind me."

She moved as if she was in a dream, shotgun lowered, but still in her hand. He pivoted to cover her, lifting a hand to hold her back as he peeked into the kitchen again. Scott still lay on the floor unarmed, but Lena lifted a hand and pointed.

Howie must be hiding around the corner.

"Stay back," he murmured to Cass. He whipped around the corner, and took his shot. When Howie crashed to the floor, writhing in pain, Brian disarmed him.

"Get your sister," he said to Cass, making sure Howie didn't have another weapon.

Cass bent down with a cry over Lena's battered body, gathered her into her arms and did her best to raise her up. Once again Brian acted as a shield as they worked their way toward the back door. He pivoted one way, then the other, trying to watch for danger from all sides at once.

Outside, Sadie and Jo had bound Sean's hands with gardening twine. Alice rushed to help carry Lena. Gunfire erupted behind him as they made it around the tail of Bob's truck.

"Everyone back. Get down!"

As the women scurried to huddle around him, Brian did his best to take stock of the situation. Cass and Alice bent over Lena. Sadie and Jo pressed close to them.

They were pinned down. Low on ammunition. Bob had staunched his wound and was back on his feet, aiming for them from the back door. There were plenty of weapons left in the house for him to use.

Brian's mind raced as he tried to come up with a new plan. He should have called Cab. He should have kept Cass and Lena with him the whole time. He—

"Give it up, Lake," Bob called from the house. "You're outnumbered and outgunned. Should have shot me when you had the chance! I'm going to kill you. Then I'm going to take great pleasure in killing the rest of those bitches. But not Cass. I've got other plans for her."

Brian didn't realize he'd broken cover and started toward the house until Cass grabbed him.

"Brian!"

Her voice brought him back to reality. This was what Bob wanted; what he was counting on. But Brian wasn't some hotheaded kid anymore, rushing in when wisdom called for caution. He was going to marry Cass. Her sisters would be part of his family.

And he'd do whatever it took to protect them— including looking before he leaped. He waved Cass back and held his ground, waiting for Bob to make a mistake. He didn't have much ammunition. He needed to get it right the first time.

"You call yourself a Navy SEAL? What kind of hero hides among a passel of girls?"

A smart one, Brian decided when Bob opened the door wider and slid the nose of his gun outside. Brian waited patiently until he saw the glint of Bob's eyes in the moonlight. Bob fired off a round in their direction, but Brian fired, too.

And his shot found its mark. Bob dropped to the ground just as Alice stiffened again.

"Incoming!"

Sirens reached Brian's ears only moments later and relief washed through him. He let out the breath he'd been holding, and turned. "Who called Cab?"

"Me." Cass bent low over Lena. "Hang on, honey. Help's coming. Just hold on," she pleaded with her sister.

Alice touched Lena's arm. Sadie and Jo formed a ring around them. Cass leaned down to kiss Lena's forehead. "That's it. Stay with us."

"They mess'd up the house," Lena slurred.

"Don't you worry about that," Cass told her. "I've got all the help I need to fix it up again." She glanced at Brian, gratitude shining in her eyes.

"That's right." He had to clear his throat as the sheriff and his deputies pulled in, and spilled out to take command of the scene. "I'll be here every step of the way. The house will be good as new before you know it."

"Marry her," Lena said, her eyes closing again.

A minute later, medics swarmed around them, and Brian had to step back to give them access to Lena's bloodied form.

"I will," he promised her. "I will."

Chapter Ten

"**S**O YOU DON'T have any idea how a truckload of drugs ended up behind the sheriff's department a half-hour before your ex-overseer and his cronies started shooting up your house?" Cab asked again the following morning.

Cass shook her head tiredly. They were seated at the table in what was left of her kitchen, and she was having a hard time holding back the emotions that kept threatening to swamp her. She and her sisters had made so many wonderful memories in this room. Now the cabinets were splintered, the windows shattered, and even the battered old table she loved so much had gouges and grooves from the bullets.

And Bob was gone. Dead. He'd never bother her anymore.

Cass wasn't sure how she felt about that. Relieved that he wouldn't come back for her again. Pained to know someone had died because of her.

They'd never find the thirty grand he'd stolen from her; she was sure of that. She wasn't sure if she cared. Brian was with her now. They'd all work together to recoup their losses.

Lena was resting comfortably in her room. She'd been treated and released from the hospital, and Cab had already questioned her, but he hadn't pushed her to answer and Lena had remained closemouthed about most of it. A shot had creased her cheekbone, and she was bruised all over, but apart from a headache and some stitches, she was fine. The same couldn't be said for the men who'd invaded their home last night. Bob was dead. Mark had two bullets in his thigh. Sean had one in his shoulder, and Howie had been shot in the gut. Scott had gotten off easiest with a broken wrist and bruised testicles. Cass knew it was important to answer Cab's questions, but she was finding it hard to concentrate. Finding it hard to care much about the injuries sustained by the men who'd tried to kill them, too.

Cab had sent Brian and her other sisters from the room, saying he wanted to talk to her alone. Brian had hesitated, but in the end he'd done what Cab had asked. So had Alice, Sadie and Jo.

"Cass? You have anything else you want to say? Why'd your overseer come and shoot up your house?" Cab asked her again.

"I don't know. Maybe because I fired him?" The sheriff wasn't going to get her to admit that the drugs in Howie's truck had anything to do with Two Willows. Maybe she was overreacting; maybe by some miracle the General wouldn't jump to conclusions if he heard the hands had been using the ranch to cover up their operation. After all, as Brian had pointed out to her earlier, the General was the one who'd hired Bob.

But Cass knew better than to count on the General behaving rationally when it came to the ranch. He was far more likely to go off half-cocked and evict them from the property. She couldn't allow that to happen, which was why she couldn't cooperate with Cab.

"And why'd you do that?"

"He never listened to me." That was the truth, even if it wasn't the whole truth. All Bob had ever cared about was himself, and if she could have seen that right off, none of this would have happened.

"I thought the General did all the hiring and firing at Two Willows."

Cass straightened in her seat and focused. She should have seen that coming. "He does."

"But Bob let you run him off the ranch."

Damn it, she needed to keep her story straight. Cass tried to think clearly, but she'd been up for nearly twenty-four hours and her need to sleep was getting desperate. "Let's just say I knew something Bob didn't want to get out." That he'd stolen more than thirty grand. It still galled her that Bob thought she was so stupid he'd been surprised when she'd figured it out. All she could guess was that he'd thought he'd manage to marry her before she did. Thank God that hadn't been the case, or she would really have been in a fix.

"So you blackmailed him." Cab sat back in his seat and waited for an answer.

Blackmail? That didn't sound good. She shook her head slowly. "I politely suggested he find another place to work, or I would take it as approval for me to spread the word." Too bad Bob had quickly realized she wouldn't follow through on her threat.

"Just what was his secret?"

"Sheriff, I don't want to speak ill of the dead."

Cab tapped his pen on the table, the only sign of impatience he'd betrayed so far. "I can do this all day, Cass," he said finally.

So can I, she wanted to say, but she only looked at him. She'd been interrogated countless times by the General back when the stakes were even higher; when leaving the ranch would have meant the breakup of her family into foster homes around the state. It didn't matter that those interrogations had taken place over the phone or on a video chat. Cab might be a formidable man when he wanted to be—but the General was far worse—even long distance.

Cab rubbed his nose with the back of his hand. "Let's play a game. I'm going to describe a hypothetical situation. And you describe—completely hypothetically—what you would do about it."

Cass kept quiet. It was a trick, and not a very sophisticated one.

"You know, before we start I'd like to point out we're on the same side here," Cab added.

"Maybe. Maybe not."

"You don't trust me?"

"Sheriff, don't take this personally, but you are a man. On the whole, men haven't made much of an impression on me."

Cab heaved a sigh. "I guess I can understand that. Ready for that game?"

She shrugged.

"I'll take that as a yes." He shifted in his chair. "Hypothetically, is it possible that when Bob hired on at Two Willows he came here for other reasons than to run the ranch?"

"Hypothetically," she said. She'd give him that much.

"And hypothetically, did he maybe dip his fingers into the ranch's earnings, and that's why you escorted him off the property, so to speak?"

The sheriff was a little savvier than she'd thought. Cass considered her answer. "Hypothetically, if an overseer had stolen money from me, I would have found a way to run him off."

"Instead of reporting the theft."

"Keeping the ranch is more important than a little hypothetical cash, Cab."

"You think the General would have taken it away?" His furrowed brow told her he didn't understand. Cass didn't blame him. No one understood that the General had dangled that possibility over her head for years to try to keep her in line. She simply couldn't take the chance he wasn't bluffing. Only someone who'd lived like she had—so insecure in her place in the world— would understand that.

"I know he would take it away if he thought I'd messed up so badly. So if Bob had stolen cash from me, and if one of the General's spies let him know that happened, my sisters and I would be up a creek without a paddle."

Cab had the grace to wince, confirming what Cass had always suspected—that he was indeed one of the General's spies. Not the only one, though. Not by a long shot.

"So why did Bob come back?"

She wasn't going to get caught out like that. "Apparently, to shoot up my kitchen." She gave Cab a serene smile.

He didn't smile back. "Before he went postal on your kitchen."

"Hypothetically?"

"Hypothetically. Could it have something to do with the truckload of drugs in my parking lot?"

Cass chose her words carefully. "Hypothetically, the drug trade is alive and well in Chance Creek. And hypothetically, my ex-overseer might have seen fit to use Two Willows as a conduit. And hypothetically I might have needed to put a stop to it."

"But Brian was the one who put a stop to it, wasn't he? He was the one who took down Bob. You missed," Cab pointed out.

Cass bristled. That was a low blow. When a wave of vertigo washed over her, she clutched at the table to steady herself. She'd nearly killed a man—that was enough. She'd nearly died herself.

"You're right; I missed," she repeated. With a shotgun at nearly point-blank range. The General would be disappointed.

"I'm glad to find out you and your sisters aren't masterminding the local drug trade," Cab told her. "But next time something goes wrong at this ranch, you call and tell me." He tapped the table twice with his finger. "And next time someone tries to kill you, you pull that trigger faster. And hit the damn target this time. I don't ever want to explain to the General he needs to come home and bury one of his girls. Nearly killed him to bury his wife."

Cass looked up at him, taken aback. How could he know what the General felt? She had the sense Cab wanted her to ask, but Cass couldn't go there. Not now.

"Shouldn't you be figuring out who owns that truck-load of drugs?" she asked him, suddenly exhausted.

"Oh, we've figured it out. And Howie's already talking. Those guys can't give each other up fast enough."

"Well, that's some good news. I guess it's time for us to start cleaning this place up."

"Not so fast." Cab held up a hand. "I have one more question. Did you ladies have some kind of accident out here lately? With a trailer?"

She didn't even blink. If Cab thought he was half as good at this game as the General was, he was sorely mistaken. "I'm not sure what you mean."

Cab sighed again. "Sean told us about the trailer they were using to store their drugs. He said he was last in it yesterday. Said something had happened to it. I went and check out the canyon where he said it was parked. Lo and behold, there'd been an explosion. Not much of that trailer left."

"Bob hauled away an old trailer from the Park about a month ago," she said truthfully. "Said he brought it to the dump. If it didn't leave my property, he'd be the one to ask."

"If he was alive." Cab held her gaze.

"If he was alive." Cass didn't blink.

"Why the hell didn't you join up?" Cab said finally. "Would have made a damn good operative. Look at you, cool as a cucumber, lying to the authorities."

Cass wished to God she could tell him everything. He was a good man, a man she'd always trusted. Now there'd be all this between them. "This house and my sisters are all I have," she said. "They're my whole world. Do you understand that?"

After a long moment, Cab nodded. "Yeah, I do. But you and your sisters have stirred up a hornet's nest. I hope you realize that. Is that Navy SEAL going to stay?"

"I hope so," she confessed.

"I hope so, too. Next time, you call me. You don't handle it yourself no matter what happens. You call me, you got that?"

It was Cass's turn to nod. "Sheriff," she said as Cab rose to his feet. "I wish things were different."

He softened. Touched her shoulder. "Cass Reed, your father—if he wasn't such a God-damn ass and came around once in a while—would be proud of you for the way you defended your home—and your family. And as much as it makes my job harder, he'd be proud of you for knowing when to talk and when to keep mum. But if you think that's all I've got when it comes to questioning, you're underestimating me. If it suits me—and next time it *will* suit me—we won't stop until I know your innermost fears and dreams. You got that?"

"Yes, sir." She got it.

"Take care of yourself. Take care of Lena and the others. And that SEAL? He's a keeper. Don't toss him away because of a couple of hard cases and a distant father. Hear me?"

"Yes, Sheriff."

He crossed his arms. "Damn it, when women like you get all docile, it's downright frightening. I mean it, Cass. Marry the man and let him help you get this ranch back in shape."

"Yes, Sheriff."

With a grunt of exasperation, Cab jammed his hat back on his head, just as Brian leaned into the kitchen.

"You all finished in here?"

"I'm leaving," Cab told him on his way past. A moment later they heard him say good-bye to Sadie and Jo.

"Time to fix everyone some lunch," Cass said to Brian. "If there are any dishes left." She surveyed the room sadly.

"Is it my imagination, or did I hear the sheriff putting in a good word for me?" He approached and rested his hands on her hips.

She rolled her eyes. "You might have."

"He's a smart man. And I'll help you rustle up some lunch in a minute. But first, let's go outside. I want to stretch my legs."

"I need to check on Lena."

"Alice is with her." He didn't wait for her to acquiesce. Instead, he tugged her out the back door and headed for the maze.

"You've got a question for the stone?" she said when they drew near, wondering what it could be. She hadn't gone back into the maze since they'd made love. Surely he didn't think they were going to fool around now?

"Something like that. Now, I think I know the way. I managed to get to the center last time." For the next few minutes, Brian bumbled through the maze and Cass followed, smiling despite everything that had happened in the past twenty-four hours. He made a wrong turn or two, but found his way without too much trouble. When they reached the center, Cass felt the sense of calm the stone always worked on her. Brian led her to the bench and gestured for her to sit.

When he knelt in front of her, she held her breath in surprise.

"Cass, I came here looking for a future after all my plans were blown to hell by my own impatience. I wanted to meet the beautiful woman whose photo I'd been staring at for weeks, and I hoped maybe there would be a place for me at Two Willows…" He trailed off and started again. "Even though I was afraid I could never be the kind of man who deserved a woman like you, some small part of me hung on to the hope there was a future *with you* for me here at Two Willows. But nothing—" He squeezed her hand. "Nothing prepared me for what I felt when I first saw you. You took my breath away, and the moment I stepped into your house I knew you were the woman for me. Not because of the ranch. Not because Two Willows could be my home. But because of you. Two Willows is Two Willows because of you. When I walked into the house, the love and care you lavished on it shone from every surface. It isn't just a place where people sleep and eat—it is a place where people live and dream. I haven't had a home like that since I was a child. I didn't know how much I'd missed it."

"Brian—"

"No, let me finish. Cass, I love you because of the way you love your family. I love how you take the time to do the little things for everyone. I love how the round of chores and events of each day don't faze you one bit; you simply do them to the best of your ability. I love how you keep an eye on everyone you care about. I love the way you still have time for your friends. I love the way you feel in my arms, and how I feel when I'm near you. I swear I will always come when you need me. I will do everything I can to help you keep Two Willows and your sisters safe. Cass, would you do me the great honor of marrying me?"

Cass swallowed, hardly daring to believe this moment had come. She could barely breathe the way her heart was pounding in her chest. But surprisingly there was little to think about or debate in her mind. Previously, their situation had seemed so complicated.

Now it was simple.

She loved him. Loved everything about him. She loved spending time with him. Loved working on the house with him. Loved contemplating a life they might make together.

She'd seen the care he'd spent on fixing the house so far. She'd heard from Lena that he was knowledgeable about ranching and had a good seat on a horse. There was no question of him taking her away from Two Willows.

He wanted to be here as much as she did.

She'd received the blessing of her sisters, her best friend—and even the local sheriff. Everyone except the General had weighed in, and he'd been the one to send Brian here in the first place, hadn't he?

What would the General think about her marrying his Navy SEAL?

She didn't care.

Because Brian had proved once and for all he truly loved her. When the chips were down he'd come to save her. He'd helped her sisters, protected them—put his life on the line for them. Gone were any fears about his intentions. Brian was a real man—an honest man. An honorable one. And she'd be proud—so proud—to be his wife.

"Yes," she said to Brian. "Yes, I'll marry you."

As his arms closed around her, she leaned in to meet his kiss. This was exactly where she belonged, she thought, melting against him. At the heart of her ranch, giving her heart to the man she loved.

When he pulled back and rose to his feet, she said,

"Where are we going?" She was a little disappointed he'd cut the occasion short.

"To town. We'll pick up lunch on the way home, but first there's something we have to do."

As Brian drove through his adopted town, he wanted to roll down the window of his truck and shout the news through the streets.

Cass had said yes.

He was going to stay at Two Willows. He was going to repair their home and do whatever it took to shore up the cattle operation.

He wasn't ever going to let her down.

Still, when he pulled in to park near the little jewelry store Alice had told him about, he felt uneasy. It had seemed like a good idea before to allow Cass to pick out her own engagement ring and get the seal of approval from Rose Johnson, whom Alice had said could tell about these things.

Now the moment was here, he wasn't so sure about that. But Cass was already climbing out of the truck, and her face had lit up with happiness when she saw the jewelry store.

No going back now.

Brian hurried around to take her hand. "I wanted you to choose for yourself." It sounded right when he said it out loud. He knew too much about Cass's past to ever want her to feel like he was dictating to her.

"I'd like that," she said simply.

Inside, they moved slowly among the glass display

cases until they found a selection of rings. They were bent over the case, pointing out different rings to each other, when a petite woman came out of the back and greeted them.

"Morning, Cass. It's good to see you off the ranch. What brings you in today? And who is this?"

"This is Brian Lake. My... fiancé." Cass blushed prettily when she said it, and Brian's chest swelled with pride.

"We're here for a ring," he said.

"I'm so glad." Rose rushed to pull out a few trays. "Try as many as you like."

Cass tried on several, but Brian noticed there was one she kept looking at, but didn't pick out. He plucked it out of the velvet case and handed it to her. The band was delicate, tapered near the rosette-shaped diamond. As he slid it on her finger, it felt right.

"Is that the one?" he asked softly.

Cass nodded, her eyes shining. "It's beautiful."

"We'll take it." He slid it off her finger again. "Don't worry; we'll have it back on there in a jiffy." First, he needed to know for sure it was right. He handed it to Rose, who took it and held it in the palm of her hand for a moment. She closed her eyes and tightened her fingers around it. When she opened them again, she handed the ring back to Cass.

"The two of you will be very, very happy," she said, as misty-eyed as Cass became when she heard her words.

"Thank you." Cass held up the ring. "It really is

beautiful."

Brian slipped it back on her finger and kissed her soundly. "So are you."

CASS WAS GRATIFIED by her sisters' reaction when she showed them her new ring and announced the date of her wedding in three weeks' time. Crowded around Lena's bed, Jo threw her arms around Cass, and her other sisters, barring Lena, weren't far behind. Cass stooped down to give Lena a careful hug while the others congratulated Brian.

"Do you still approve?" she whispered.

"I do. I think you two will do fine. Think Brian can keep the General from sending another overseer?"

"I hope so."

The next half-hour was spent sharing around the lunch they'd bought, reliving the events of the night before, and making plans for the restoration of the house, but when the meal was over, Brian told the others, "Cass and I will be back later."

He led her from Lena's room, but instead of heading downstairs, he tugged her into the bedroom he'd been staying in at the other end of the hall. He shut the door, locked it, scooped her up and carried to her the bed. Sitting down, still cradling her in his lap, he trailed searing kisses down her neck. "Finally. We're alone."

Cass laughed. "Have you been waiting?"

He answered with another kiss. "Haven't you?"

She nodded, her pulse tripping in anticipation.

"We have a bed this time and everything," he said.

"What do you say?"

She couldn't resist him when he looked at her like that.

"Heck, yeah." Cass gave in, fumbled with his shirt, then leaned back while he stripped it off, the muscles in his arms and chest rippling with his movements. She didn't know what she wanted to touch first; the hard planes of his chest, his bulging biceps or the flat washboard of his stomach. She reached for the buttons of her blouse. Brian gently pushed her hands away and did it for her. As each button slid free of its hole, exposing more of her to view, Cass felt no trepidation. She had no secrets left. Brian had seen them all and accepted her for who she was. She couldn't wait to bare her body to him. She wanted him to touch her even more. She moaned when her blouse fell open and he shifted her on his lap so he could bend down and trail warm kisses along the edge of her bra cups.

Still perched there, she slipped out of her jeans and Brian helped her out of her panties. He slid them down and helped untangle her legs from them, an acrobatic feat that left them both laughing in between kisses. He stood up, lifting her easily, and she wrapped her legs around his waist while he unbuttoned his jeans and shucked them off. His boxer briefs followed and when he sat down again, shifting her to cover his hardness, they both moaned.

Brian cupped her bottom and settled her more firmly against him, then slid his hands up to unhook her bra and peel it off. Cass moaned again, wanting him to touch her, but instead he buried his fingers in her long hair. Tugging her head gently back he kissed her, exploring her fully, tasting her and allowing her to taste him. Cass wanted more. Her nipples tingled every time they scraped against his chest. Now that they were engaged, any amount of space between them seemed like too much. She shifted, wanting him inside her, but Brian caught her around the waist and held her in place. His kisses left her reeling and when he finally brought his hands to cup her breasts and run his thumbs over her sensitive nipples, she thought she might lose control right there. She leaned back and allowed him access. He bent to kiss first one and then the other and then gave himself over to laving and playing with them until Cass could barely breathe.

"Has anyone ever told you you're magnificent?" he murmured against her skin.

She whimpered with need, wrapping her legs tighter around his waist, and he finally took pity on her.

"We'll use a condom this time," he grunted into her hair as he shifted, lifting her along with him, and reached into a pocket of his bag, pulling one out after a fumbling search.

Condom?

Cass hadn't thought about what had happened at the stone in days.

Speaking of days… She began to count, but there was no time to think the equation through. Brian ripped the packet open with his teeth, eased it out and tossed the wrapper aside. He got it on one-handed after a bit of swearing, then sat up straight again, positioning Cass over him. "Ready?"

"What?" Cass was still counting, but as he gripped her hips and moved her into place she forgot about everything but him. She braced her knees on the edge of the bed and eased down, closing her eyes as she slowly took him inside her. Brian groaned, his muscles flexing as he lifted her up and then coaxed her down again. Soon they worked together, moving in tandem. The position allowed him deep access and Cass clung to him as he picked up speed. She didn't think she'd be able to hold on long, but at the same time she wanted their lovemaking to go on forever. Her hands sliding over his skin, she leaned forward to press kisses against his neck and over his shoulder. Every inch of him turned her on and she wanted to touch him everywhere.

Brian sped up again and soon all she could do was hold on as he thrust into her. Slick and wet and aching she leaned back and gasped when Brian took one nipple into his mouth. One of his hands on her bottom, the other cupping her neck, he laved and nipped at her breasts until Cass couldn't hold back anymore. She came with a cry and moments later, Brian grunted, bucking against her, his fingers digging into her skin until he came, too, shuddering against her. His last thrusts filled her, coaxing more tremors from her until he collapsed back onto the bed, pulling her with him to lay against his chest.

Cass listened to the pounding of his heart, smiling to know she'd made it race. It felt so right to be with

Brian this way.

And she'd be with him forever.

Whether or not she was pregnant.

"YOU CALL YOURSELF a Navy SEAL?" the General thundered late that afternoon. "You are a disgrace to your uniform. I sent you there to solve problems, not drag my daughters into a shootout. I oughtta—"

"What's done is done. The important part is your daughters are safe and the men who came after them won't bother them anymore. I'll see to it that there's no more trouble, but it's time you came home and saw the lay of the land for yourself."

"You don't watch the news much, do you? The shit's hitting the fan all over the world and you want me to come home and play nursemaid? You're the one who lost control of the operation. You get it back on track."

"This isn't an operation," Brian told him. "These are your daughters and they've been through a frightening ordeal. They need their father!"

"They haven't needed me since they were little girls," the General retorted. "You're trying to cover up the mess you made there by blaming me. I wasn't born yesterday. Get my house in order and get my girls in line. Now!"

He was about to sign off. Brian knew he had to stop him. He'd thought the General would question him carefully on all aspects of what had happened, but now he had the sense the man had heard the details about the shootout already from someone else. Didn't the

General care about his daughters at all? When he'd filled in the other men back at USSOCOM about what had happened, they'd fallen all over each other asking questions.

"You might want to get a plane ticket anyway," he said quickly. "Because Cass and I will be getting married—in about three weeks." Neither of them had wanted to put it off now that they'd decided. They were looking around at their options for a venue, but as Cass had said, "They shot up the house, not the gardens. We can always hold it outside."

The General hesitated. "Married?"

"That's right—married. You'll need to be here to walk Cass down the aisle. And you need to know that marrying Cass puts me on her side, not yours. I won't spy for you anymore. But I will love and care for your daughter. I'll fight for her until I take my last breath."

The General rubbed his chin, the first time Brian had ever seen him so uncertain. His gaze shifted somewhere off the screen and Brian thought he was looking at the photograph of his wife he always kept close by.

"It's her mother she'll miss at her wedding," the General said softly.

"She'll want you there."

The General shook his head. "I doubt that. Besides, these are uncertain times, and she knows how busy it gets here."

Brian couldn't believe what he was hearing. "General—"

The other man muttered something. Brian caught the words "crisis" and "leadership" and "duty."

"General, wait—"

The screen cut out, leaving a logo behind. Brian stared at it for several long minutes.

The General wasn't going to come. He was going to break Cass's heart all over again.

"Brian? What's wrong? I thought I heard voices."

He started. Turned to see Cass framed in the doorway and was struck again by that mixture of sweetness and beauty that was unique to her. He would do anything to protect her from harm, but he was helpless to protect her from her father's cruelty.

"Just talking to… someone I know."

What could he say? He realized he was going to have to be more to this wonderful woman than just a husband. He had to make up for the gaps in her life, as she was already making up for the gaps in his. He swallowed past a lump in his throat. "I love you. You know that, right?"

She smiled uncertainly. Brian stood up. "I just want you to know, I'm going to be the man worthy of you. I swear."

"Of course. You already are—"

"And when we have children I will be there for them when they wake up in the morning and I will be there when they go to bed. I'm not going to miss… anything." He crossed the room and pulled her into an embrace. "I love you, and that's forever," he said again, and kissed her. "You understand that, right?"

She nodded and buried her head in his neck. When her words came they were muffled. Breathless. And everything he'd ever wanted.

"I love you, too."

Brian took a deep breath, told his future bride her father wouldn't make it to her wedding, and held her while she cried.

CASS THOUGHT DINNER would never end. Brian's words rebounded in her mind as she ate, but it wasn't his declarations of love that made her dizzy with shock or the news that the General couldn't make it to the wedding. She'd had her cry and the world hadn't ended. It was what Brian had said about children. Lovely words she could barely remember now because—

Cass counted back. Counted again.

Could she be…?

She'd wondered more than once since they'd first made love. But then things had gotten so crazy she hadn't had a chance to check. Enough time had passed that a test should be able to answer the question once and for all.

When Brian and Lena went to check on the cattle after their evening meal, she called Wye, told her about the errand she needed to run and met her a half-hour later in town.

"Do you really think you're pregnant?" Wye whispered as they hurried down the aisles of the local drugstore.

"I don't know. I feel a little… funny. Here, put this

in the basket, too." Cass added mouthwash, several toothbrushes, a package of disposable razors and a serving platter shaped like a sunflower.

"What do you need that for?" Wye pointed to the platter as she steered her toward the pregnancy tests, scanned the packages and chose one.

"I don't want anyone to notice I'm getting a test," Cass hissed. "I'm going to camouflage it among the other things I'm buying."

"It's not going to work."

It didn't. The cashier definitely paused when she reached the pregnancy test and scanned Cass's face. Luckily, Cass didn't recognize the teenager and evidently it was mutual. The cashier went back to ringing up her other purchases.

Wye followed Cass home. Upstairs, Cass sequestered herself in the second-story bathroom and followed the box's directions. Stuffing the test stick into the bag she'd brought it home in, she washed her hands, opened the door to find Wye pacing the hall, and led her downstairs and out to the maze. The sun was low in the west, but it was still warm.

"It takes two minutes," Cass told her.

Wye pulled out her phone and started a timer. "What I really don't understand is why aren't you doing this with Brian?" she asked as they walked the grassy paths of the maze.

"I don't know. Everything has been so crazy. Being with him without protection was crazy. That's not how I am. I'm not ready to face him with this, and if I'm not pregnant, then we can wait to talk about it some other time."

"Have you talked about kids at all?"

Cass nodded. "He says he wants them."

"Good."

They reached the center of the maze and sat together on the bench.

"Ten seconds," Wye said. "Nine, eight…"

Waiting for the results was excruciating. Cass could barely breathe.

"Zero. Take a look," Wye said.

Cass opened the bag, checked the test, and her eyes filled when she read the results.

"I'm going to have a baby."

Wye wrapped her in a hug and bounced up and down on the bench. "Oh my God! I'm going to be Aunt Wye! I'm so happy for you!" She pulled back from Cass. "Are you happy?"

Cass clung to her, still too dazed to take it in. She was going to be a mother.

A mother.

Feeling faint, she braced her hands on her knees. Visions of her own mother filled her mind. Amelia teaching her to cook, to ride, to read and write. Digging in her gardens. Presiding over family dinners. Stopping everything to listen to what her girls had to say. Cass's throat thickened with a longing to see her again.

"Are you okay? Cass, what is it?"

"I'm okay. I'm just… overwhelmed," Cass said. "My mother left me so early. I wish I could tell her. I wish she was here."

"You know what? I think she is here," Wye said, hugging her again. "I think she always has been. And I think she's so proud of you, Cass."

A tear slid down Cass's cheek, and then another. "I feel her sometimes. Especially here."

Wye hugged her again. "Remember how many people love you. I know you think you're alone sometimes, but you're not."

Cass nodded. That was true—she was beginning to believe it.

"I think I need to be alone for a minute, though." She straightened and wiped her eyes. "Before I tell Brian."

Wye nodded, patted her shoulder and stood to leave. "I'll find him and send him along, but I'll take my time walking out, okay?"

"Thank you."

Alone with the stone, Cass stared at its tall, impassive flank, and wondered what would come next. When her daughter was born—and somehow she knew it would be a daughter—her name might be Lake, but she would still be a Reed. Which meant she'd give her heart and soul—her blood—to Two Willows.

She'd grow to take her place in the line of women who'd tended the cattle, worked the soil, kept the house, protected the property.

It was a good life, she decided. One she'd be proud to pass on to a child.

Especially now she had a partner to share it all with.

She sat back on the bench and let the evening enchant her. Took in the birdsong around her, the summer smells of fresh grass and flowers. A soft breeze caressed her cheek.

Mom, is that you?

Wye was right; she felt her mother's loving presence everywhere on the ranch. And now that Brian was marrying her—and the General seemed to condone that, even if he couldn't make it to the wedding—she felt more secure about her future here. It still hurt to know her father wouldn't break his self-imposed exile from the ranch in order to come, but now that she loved Brian, she thought she understood—at least a little. The traces of her mother's presence here soothed Cass—but she thought they caused her father pain. He couldn't face what he had lost. And he couldn't see that by not facing it, he was losing even more.

"Cass?"

She didn't need to turn to know that Brian had come to find her. He touched her arm. Sat next to her on the bench.

"Wye told me you were here."

"I'm pregnant," she said without preamble. She didn't want to soften the words. She wanted to know how he really felt about it.

Brian drew in a breath. "Pregnant?" When he reached for her with both hands and kissed her, Cass had her answer, but there was still one more thing she needed to know.

"You don't know how unbelievably good that

sounds." Brian kissed her again. "My wife. My baby."

"Brian—"

"I'm going to treat you like a queen. You'll be the most spoiled bride—" He pulled back suddenly. "Are you all right with this?"

She nodded. "I think so. But… I'm afraid," she admitted.

"Because of the General… and your mother?"

"Yes."

"Because you're wondering if I'll leave?"

She couldn't believe he could know her worst fears without even being told.

"I will never leave." He braced her shoulders with his hands. "Never. God, Cass, do you know how badly I've always wanted everything you're giving me now? How badly I want to wake up to you, make love to you and spend my day out on this ranch creating a life for you and our children? How badly I want to work with horses and cattle, outside in all weather, running this spread? How honored I'll be to work beside Lena because I know she'll give that job her heart and soul, too? Do you have any idea what I'd do to keep the rest of your sisters safe and happy? You've given me a whole life. Everything I've always wanted. And now you're giving me a baby, too?" He swallowed. "Honey, that's more than I ever hoped for."

"But how do I protect her?" Cass ached for him to understand. "How do I protect my sisters? What if we open our hearts to a man—to you—and you let us down?"

"I won't do that," he assured her. "I'm not your father. And I'm not Bob, or any of the others. I guess you just have to trust that." But he didn't seem satisfied, and neither was she. Brian scrubbed his hand over his mouth, scanned the ground in front of them and raised his gaze to the stone. "Ask it," he demanded, pulling her to stand before it. "Ask it if I'll stay. You said it's always right."

His words seared through her. He was right; she'd get an answer one way or the other, just as she had before. The stone had said she'd marry him. Rose had said she'd be happy. But neither had said how long that would last.

Did she really want to know?

Cass stared up at the stone, debating the answer. Then she stepped forward and placed both hands on its rough surface. Why not take the bull by the horns and find out once and for all? "Will Brian stay with me—until I die?"

The wind whipped up, swirled around her until her hair danced into her eyes. The hedges rustled with the passing breeze.

"Oh!"

Cass flinched when something struck the back of the head. She reached back to untangle it from her hair—a sprig of tiny yellow roses.

"My mother's favorite," she whispered to Brian, holding the sprig up for him to see.

She was here. Her mother was answering. Cass's lips trembled. She tilted her head back and tried to hear her words in the wind. What did the flowers mean? Was that all the answer she would get? It was too ambiguous.

Mom, she called inside her mind, but her mother's presence was already slipping away again.

"What did your mother used to say about love and marriage?" Brian asked softly.

Cass laughed, a sharp sound, as tears filled her eyes. "She always said…" She fought to swallow a sob, blinking back the wetness that threatened to spill over her eyelids. "She always said a successful marriage took three things: a decision, a leap of faith and a whole lot of cussedness." She searched his face. "I guess this is where the leap of faith comes in."

Brian wrapped his arms around her. "Lucky for you, I'm one stubborn cuss. I'm not going anywhere, Cass. I said it before and I'll say it again. I'll say it until I die. You're not getting rid of me."

"Good." Cass pressed a kiss to the base of his neck and gave in. Maybe the real message was that she couldn't control the future—that none of us ever truly knew where our lives would lead. But that Brian was here with her now, and he loved her, and that was worth the leap of faith marriage represented.

It would have to be good enough, Cass decided.

Because she wasn't going to let Brian go again.

THREE WEEKS LATER, Cass stood in the front hall at Two Willows and waited for the musical signal that would send Jo out the door to lead the procession toward the garlanded bower where Brian waited.

Holding her wedding on Two Willows's front lawn felt more right than Cass could say. With the house anchoring the scene, as it had anchored her all her life, and her friends and family celebrating her happiness, her marriage would start off on the right foot.

It would take some time before it was put to rights again, though. She'd started on the interior. Brian was nearly done with the roof. Once he learned she was pregnant, he'd refused to allow her up there to help. She'd graciously accepted his decision, and her fear of heights was still safely her secret. Someday she'd tell him and they'd have a good laugh over it, but for now she'd allow him to think she'd grown excessively agreeable.

She saw reminders of her mother everywhere she looked, from the flowers she held in her hands that came from the gardens her mother had first planted, to her sisters' faces, happy for her despite the cares and heartaches each of them still struggled with, to her own reflection in the mirror Wye held up for her for one final check. She wore her mother's wedding gown, which Alice had altered to fit her thinner frame. Her mother's veil, too. With her hair pinned up and her mother's pearls around her neck, she looked like Amelia had when she'd posed for her wedding photo.

The only thing missing was her father. She still remembered how gently Brian had told her he wouldn't be coming. How he'd held her while she cried. She remembered how he'd whispered over and over that he'd never leave. The way that Brian cherished her was already changing the way she felt about the world. Her father might not be here today, nor her mother, but she was still surrounded by family. Friends. A community she was proud to be a part of.

Cass swallowed hard. She was happy. So happy.

The music swelled. Wye and her sisters straightened and got in line.

"Ready?" Jo asked.

Cass's phone erupted from the side table in a burst of tinny music, and she wondered who on earth could be calling now. Everyone she knew in the world was sitting outside waiting for her.

"Ignore it," Lena urged her. "We have to go."

Something made Cass reach for it, though, and when she saw who it was, her heart skipped a beat. "It's the General."

Her sisters stared back at her. "Answer it," Wye said. She grabbed it from Cass's hand, swiped to accept the call and held it to Cass's ear.

Cass took it. "H—hello?"

"Cass."

"Mm-hmm." Her voice squeaked a little. She swallowed again.

"Wish I could be there. Got tied up. You know how things are." His voice was gruff and he sounded older. It had been so long since they'd really spoken. Cass clung to the phone.

"I know." Her heart was pounding in her chest. Had he really called her on her wedding day?

It was far more than she'd expected, and she found she couldn't be angry with him, even though she knew she should be. He should be here.

But at least he'd called.

"I bet you're every bit as beautiful as your mother was."

"I don't know about that." Her voice quavered with emotion. She only wanted to honor her husband to the same extent her mother had honored the General. Amelia was a fine role model, and Cass meant to do her best to live up to her standards.

"I do. You were always something, Cass. You've done well."

"I wish you could be here." The words escaped her mouth despite her best intentions. Wye put an arm around her. Cass leaned on her.

Her father cleared his throat. "Me, too. Say hello to that SEAL of yours. Tell him to watch his step."

"I will."

"Tell your sisters... well, tell them..."

She waited for him to finish his sentence. Ached for him to do so.

"Well, tell them to behave."

Cass bit back her disappointment, but when he went on, her heart squeezed again. "I'm proud of all of you. A man couldn't ask for better girls."

Jo gestured to her. "We have to go," she whispered.

"They're... waiting for me," Cass said. She didn't want to end the call. Regret for all the years of hardness between them pressed against the back of her throat.

"You'd better go, honey. Be strong. Be true to yourself. You've got this."

"Okay."

He was gone, and Cass realized she hadn't told him about the baby, but as the music swelled again and Jo stepped out of the house to begin the walk down the aisle, followed by Sadie, Alice, Lena and Wye, Cass decided she'd worry about one thing at a time. First she'd get married. Then she'd fix her family. There was enough time—and enough love—to do both.

WHEN THE MUSIC swelled, Brian set his gaze on the front door of Two Willows and waited to see the woman he loved walk toward him to become his bride. First Jo would appear, then her sisters, then Wye and Cass, of course, but as the music played on, no one exited the house at all.

The people gathered in the white folding chairs he'd helped set up on the lawn this morning began to murmur when more seconds passed and still no one came.

"What's happening?" he asked Cab, who'd agreed to stand up with him. His brother sat in the audience with his wife and kids, as did his father. Brian loved both of them—always would—but he'd decided he needed someone reliable to be by his side when he took Cass for his wife. Most of the others who'd come for the wedding were Cass's friends, but there were familiar faces in the audience and he knew that soon he'd feel at home in Chance Creek. Soon enough the other men back at USSOCOM would join him, too.

As seconds stretched into a minute and then more,

people craned their necks to see what was going on back at the house. When Jo finally stepped out into the sunlight in a spring green sheath dress and matching shoes, the audience let out a collective breath and ah-ed over how beautiful she looked. All of Cass's sisters were pretty in their wedding finery, and so was Wye, but when Cass stepped over the threshold, he had eyes for no one but her. The fitted bodice of her gown set off her figure, while its full skirt made her look like something out of a fairy tale. When she met his gaze, she smiled tremulously, and Brian's heart caught in his throat. He'd never seen her so beautiful. He watched her walk down the aisle, so lovely and graceful he couldn't believe she would soon be his. When she reached his side, he took her hand and squeezed it. She squeezed back.

"You're stunning," he whispered. "I love you."

"I love you, too."

Brian barely heard the words of the ceremony. He couldn't see anything but Cass, his beautiful Cass, as she said the words that made her his wife. When the reverend finally said, "You may kiss the bride," Brian lifted her veil and kissed her long and hard until the audience erupted in cheers. As they faced the gathered company as man and wife, Brian held up a hand to silence the clapping. "We have one more announcement. I hope you'll be as happy for us as we are. I know it's not conventional to announce this at a wedding, but I can't keep this a secret. We're having a baby. Due in March. It's time for a new beginning here at Two

Willows. Come and grab some grub and let's get dancing. We've got a lot to celebrate!"

Walking up the aisle with Cass at his side, friends thronging them on all sides offering their congratulations, Brian knew that life would keep throwing curve balls at him, and that there was no way to predict the future. He also knew that with Cass by his side, he could face anything. He'd finally found a home with Cass.

And he meant to stay with her forever.

Epilogue

SADIE HAD JUST run through the back door into the house to fetch another tray of appetizers when a pounding on the front door made her jump and press a hand to her heart. Wondering who had come so late to the wedding, she rushed to welcome them, but was surprised to find a stranger on the steps when she swung open the door.

The words she was about to say died on her lips when she took in the handsome features of the man in front of her. Tall, broad-shouldered, with hair so dark brown it was almost black, and piercing blue eyes that seemed to dance with mischief, she was struck by the dimple that indented one cheek when he smiled.

"Well, hello there, lassie," he said in an outrageously fake Irish brogue. "You must be Sadie Reed. I'm Connor O'Riley. The General sent me."

Be the first to know about Cora Seton's new releases!
Sign up for her newsletter here!
www.coraseton.com/sign-up-for-my-newsletter

Other books in the Brides of Chance Creek Series:

Issued to the Bride One Airman
Issued to the Bride One Marine
Issued to the Bride One Sniper
Issued to the Bride One Soldier

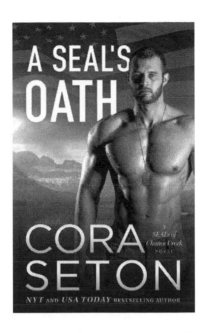

Read on for an excerpt of Volume 1 of **The SEALs of Chance Creek** series – *A SEAL's Oath.*

NAVY SEAL BOONE Rudman should have been concentrating on the pile of paperwork in front of him. Instead he was brooding over a woman he hadn't seen in thirteen years. If he'd been alone, he would have pulled up Riley Eaton's photograph on his laptop, but three other men ringed the table in the small office he occupied at the Naval Amphibious Base at Little Creek, Virginia, so instead he mentally ran over the information he'd found out about her on the Internet. Riley lived in Boston, where she'd gone to school. She'd graduated with a fine arts degree, something which confused

Boone; she'd never talked about wanting to study art when they were young. She worked at a vitamin manufacturer, which made no sense at all. And why was she living in a city, when Riley had only ever come alive when she'd visited Chance Creek, Montana, every summer as a child?

Too many questions. Questions he should know the answer to, since Riley had once been such an integral part of his life. If only he hadn't been such a fool, Boone knew she still would be. Still a friend at least, or maybe much, much more. Pride had kept him from finding out.

He was done with pride.

He reached for his laptop, ready to pull up her photograph, whether he was alone or not, but stopped when it chimed to announce a video call. For one crazy second, Boone wondered if his thoughts had conjured Riley up, but he quickly shook away that ridiculous notion.

Probably his parents wondering once again why he wasn't coming home when he left the Navy. He'd explained time and again the plans he'd made, but they couldn't comprehend why he wouldn't take the job his father had found him at a local ranch.

"Working with horses," his dad had said the last time they talked. "What more do you want?"

It was tempting. Boone had always loved horses. But he had something else in mind. Something his parents found difficult to comprehend. The laptop chimed again.

"You going to get that?" Jericho Cook said, looking up from his work. Blond, blue-eyed, and six-foot-one inches of muscle, he looked out of place hunched over his paperwork. He and the other two men sitting at the table were three of Boone's most trusted buddies and members of his strike team. Like him, they were far more at home jumping out of airplanes, infiltrating terrorist organizations and negotiating their way through disaster areas than sitting on their asses filling out forms. But paperwork caught up to everyone at some point.

He wouldn't have to do it much longer, though. Boone was due to separate from the Navy in less than a month. The others were due to leave soon after. They'd joined up together—egging each other on when they turned eighteen over their parents' objections. They'd survived the brutal process of becoming Navy SEALs together, too, adamant that they'd never leave each other behind. They'd served together whenever they could. Now, thirteen years later, they'd transition back to civilian life together as well.

The computer chimed a third time and his mind finally registered the name on the screen. Boone slapped a hand on the table to get the others' attention.

"It's him!"

"Him, who?" Jericho asked.

"Martin Fulsom, from the Fulsom Foundation. He's calling me!"

"Are you sure?" Clay Pickett shifted his chair over to where he could see. He was an inch or two shorter than Jericho, with dark hair and a wiry build that concealed a perpetual source of energy. Even now Clay's foot was tapping as he worked.

Boone understood his confusion. Why would Martin Fulsom, who must have a legion of secretaries and assistants at his command, call him personally?

"It says Martin Fulsom."

"Holy shit. Answer it," Jericho said. He shifted his chair over, too. Walker Norton, the final member of their little group, stood up silently and moved behind the others. Walker had dark hair and dark eyes that hinted at his Native American ancestry. Unlike the others, he'd taken the time to get his schooling and become an officer. As Lieutenant, he was the highest ranked. He was also the tallest of the group, with a heavy muscular frame that could move faster than most gave him credit for. He was quiet, though. So quiet that those who didn't know him tended to write him off. They did so at their own peril.

Boone stifled an oath at the tremor that ran through him as he reached out to accept the call, but it wasn't every day you got to meet your hero face to face. Martin Fulsom wasn't a Navy SEAL. He wasn't in the military at all. He'd once been an oil man, and had amassed a fortune in the industry before he'd learned about global warming and had a change of heart. For the last decade he'd spearheaded a movement to prevent carbon dioxide particulates from exceeding the disastrous level of 450 ppm. He'd backed his foundation with his entire fortune, invested it in green technology and used his earnings to fund projects around the world aimed at helping him reach his goal. Fulsom was a force of nature, with an oversized personality to match his incredible wealth. Boone liked his can-do attitude and his refusal to mince words when the situation called for plain speaking.

Boone clicked *Accept* and his screen resolved into an image of a man seated at a large wooden desk. He was gray-haired but virile, with large hands and an impressively large watch. Beside him stood a middle aged woman in a severely tailored black suit, who handed him pieces of paper one at a time, waited for him to sign them and took them back, placing them in various folders she cradled in her arm.

"Boone!" The man's hearty voice was almost too much for the laptop's speakers. "Good to finally meet you. This is an impressive proposal you have here."

Boone swallowed. It was true. Martin Fulsom—one of the greatest innovators of their time—had actually called *him*. "It's good to meet you, too, Mr. Fulsom," he managed to say.

"Call me Martin," Fulsom boomed. "Everybody does. Like I said, it's a hell of a proposal. To build a fully operational sustainable community in less than six months? That take guts. Can you deliver?"

"Yes, sir." Boone was confident he could. He'd studied this stuff for years. Dreamed about it, debated it, played with the numbers and particulars until he could speak with confidence about every aspect of the community he wanted to build. He and his friends had gained a greater working knowledge of the fallout from climate change than any of them had gone looking for when they joined the Navy SEALs. They'd realized most of the conflicts that spawned the missions they took on were caused in one way or the other by struggles over resources, usually exacerbated by climate conditions. When rains didn't come and crops failed, unrest was sure to follow. Next came partisan politics, rebellions, coups and more. It didn't take a genius to see that climate change and scarcity of resources would be two prongs spearheading trouble around the world for decades to come.

"And you'll start with four families, building up to ten within that time frame?"

Boone blinked. Families? "Actually, sir…" He'd said nothing about families. Four *men*, building up to ten. That's what he had written in his proposal.

"This is brilliant. Too brilliant." Fulsom's direct gaze caught his own. "You see, we were going to launch a community of our own, but when I saw your proposal, I said, 'This man has already done the hard work; why reinvent the wheel? I can't think of anyone better to lead such a project than someone like Boone Rudman.'"

Boone stifled a grin. This was going better than he could have dreamed. "Thank you, sir."

Fulsom leaned forward. "The thing is, Boone, you have to do it right."

"Of course, sir, but about—"

"It has to be airtight. You have to prove you're sustainable. You have to prove your food systems are self-perpetuating, that you have a strategy to deal with waste, that you have contingency plans. What you've written here?" He held up Boone's proposal package. "It's genius. Genius. But the real question is—who's going to give a shit about it?"

"Well, hell—" Fulsom's abrupt change of tone startled Boone into defensiveness. He knew about the man's legendary high-octane personality, but he hadn't been prepared for this kind of bait and switch. "You yourself just said—"

Fulsom waved the application at him. "I love this stuff. It makes me hard. But the American public? That's a totally different matter. They don't find this shit sexy. It's not enough to jerk me off, Boone. We're trying to turn on the whole world."

"O-okay." Shit. Fulsom was going to turn him down after all. Boone gripped the arms of his chair, waiting for the axe to fall.

"So the question is, how do we make the world care about your community? And not just care about it—be so damn obsessed with it they can't think about anything else?" He didn't wait for an answer. "I'll tell you how. We're going to give you your own reality television show. Think of it. The whole world watching you go from ground zero to full-on sustainable community. Rooting for you. Cheering when you triumph. Crying when you fail. A worldwide audience fully engaged with you and your followers."

"That's an interesting idea," Boone said slowly. It was an insane idea. There was no way anyone would spend their time watching him dig garden beds and install photovoltaic panels. He couldn't think of anything less exciting to watch on television. And he didn't have followers. He had three like-minded friends who'd signed on to work with him. Friends who even now were bristling at this characterization of their roles. "Like I said, Mr. Fulsom, each of the *equal* participants in the community have pledged to document our progress. We'll take lots of photos and post them with our entries on a daily blog."

"Blogs are for losers." Fulsom leaned forward. "Come on, Boone. Don't you want to change the world?"

"Yes, I do." Anger curled within him. He was serious about these issues. Deadly serious. Why was Fulsom making a mockery of him? You couldn't win any kind of war with reality television, and Boone approached his sustainable community as if he was waging a war—a war on waste, a war on the future pain and suffering of the entire planet.

"I get it. You think I'm nuts," Fulsom said. "You think I've finally blown my lid. Well, I haven't. I'm a free-thinker, Boone, not a crazy man. I know how to get the message across to the masses. Always have. And I've always been criticized for it, too. Who cares? You know what I care about? This world. The people on it. The plants and animals and atmosphere. The whole grand, beautiful spectacle that we're currently dragging down into the muck of overconsumption. That's what I care about. What about you?"

"I care about it, too, but I don't want—"

"You don't want to be made a fool of. Fair enough. You're afraid of exposing yourself to scrutiny. You're afraid you'll fuck up on television. Well guess what? You're right; you will fuck up. But the audience is going to love you so much by that time, that if you cry, they'll cry with you. And when you triumph—and you *will* triumph—they'll feel as ecstatic as if they'd done it all themselves. Along the way they'll learn more about solar power, wind power, sustainable agriculture and all the rest of it than we could ever force-feed them through documentaries or classes. You watch, Boone. We're going to do something magical."

Boone stared at him. Fulsom was persuasive, he'd give him that. "About the families, sir."

"Families are non-negotiable." Fulsom set the application down and gazed at Boone, then each of his friends in turn. "You men are pioneers, but pioneers are a yawn-fest until they bring their wives to the frontier. Throw in women, and goddamn, that's interesting! Women talk. They complain. They'll take your plans for sustainability and kick them to the curb unless you make them easy to use and satisfying. What's more, women are a hell of lot more interesting than men. Sex, Boone. Sex sells cars and we're going to use it to sell sustainability, too. Are you with me?"

"I…" Boone didn't know what to say. Use sex to sell sustainability? "I don't think—"

"Of course you're with me. A handsome Navy SEAL like you has to have a girl. You do, don't you? Have a girl?"

"A girl?" Had he been reduced to parroting everything Fulsom said? Boone tried to pull himself together. He definitely did not have a *girl*. He dated when he had time, but he kept things light. He'd never felt it was fair to enter a more serious relationship as long as he was throwing himself into danger on a daily basis. He'd always figured he'd settle down when he left the service and he was looking forward to finally having the time to meet a potential mate. God knew his parents were all too ready for grandkids. They talked about it all the time.

"A woman, a fiancée. Maybe you already have a wife?" Fulsom looked hopeful and his secretary nodded at Boone, as if telling him to say yes.

"Well…."

He was about to say no, but the secretary shook her head rapidly and made a slicing motion across her neck. Since she hadn't engaged in the conversation at all previously, Boone decided he'd better take her signals seriously. He'd gotten some of his best intel in the field just this way. A subtle nod from a veiled woman, or a pointed finger just protruding from a burka had saved his neck more than once. Women were crafty when it counted.

"I'm almost married," he blurted. His grip on the arms of his chair tightened. None of this was going like he'd planned. Jericho and Clay turned to stare at him like he'd lost his mind. Behind him Walker chuckled. "I mean—"

"Excellent! Can't wait to meet your better half.

What about the rest of you?" Fulsom waved them off before anyone else could speak. "Never mind. Julie here will get all that information from you later. As long as you've got a girl, Boone, everything's going to be all right. The fearless leader has to have a woman by his side. It gives him that sense of humanity our viewers crave." Julie nodded like she'd heard this many times before.

Boone's heart sunk even further. Fearless leader? Fulsom didn't understand his relationship with the others at all. Walker was his superior officer, for God's sake. Still, Fulsom was waiting for his answer, with a shrewd look in his eyes that told Boone he wasn't fooled at all by his hasty words. Their funding would slip away unless he convinced Fulsom that he was dedicated to the project—as Fulsom wanted it to be done.

"I understand completely," Boone said, although he didn't understand at all. His project was about sustainability. It wasn't some human-interest story. "I'm with you one hundred percent."

"Then I've got a shitload of cash to send your way. Don't let me down."

"I won't." He felt rather than heard the others shifting, biting back their protests.

Fulsom leaned so close his head nearly filled the screen. "We'll start filming June first and I look forward to meeting your fiancée when I arrive. Understand? Not a girlfriend, not a weekend fling—a fiancée. I want weddings, Boone." He looked over the four of them again. "Four weddings. Yours will kick off the series. I can see it now; an empty stretch of land. Two modern pioneers in love. A country parson performing the ceremony. The bride holding a bouquet of wildflowers the groom picked just minutes before. Their first night together in a lonely tent. Magic, Boone. That's prime time magic. *Surviving on the Land* meets *The First Six Months*."

Boone nodded, swallowing hard. He'd seen those television shows. The first tracked modern-day mountain men as they pitted themselves against crazy weather conditions in extreme locations. The second followed two newlyweds for six months, and documented their every move, embrace, and lovers' quarrel as they settled into married life. He didn't relish the idea of starring in any show remotely like those.

Besides, June first was barely two months away. He'd only get out of the Navy at the end of April. They hadn't even found a property to build on yet.

"There'll be four of you men to start," Fulsom went on. "That means we need four women for episode one; your fiancée and three other hopeful single ladies. Let the viewers do the math, am I right? They'll start pairing you off even before we do. We'll add other community members as we go. Six more men and six more women ought to do it, don't you think?"

"Yes, sir." This was getting worse by the minute.

"Now, I've given you a hell of a shock today. I get that. So let me throw you a bone. I've just closed on the perfect piece of property for your community. Fifteen hundred acres of usable land with creeks, forest, pasture and several buildings. I'm going to give it to you free and clear to use for the duration of the series. If—and only if—you meet your goals, I'll sign it over to you lock, stock and barrel at the end of the last show."

Boone sat up. That was a hell of a bone. "Where is it?"

"Little town called Chance Creek, Montana. I believe you've heard of it?" Fulsom laughed at his reaction. Even Walker was startled. Chance Creek? They'd grown up there. Their families still lived there.

They were going home.

Chills marched up and down his spine and Boone wondered if his friends felt the same way. He'd hardly even let himself dream about that possibility. None of them came from wealthy families and none of them would inherit land. He'd figured they'd go where it was cheapest, and ranches around Chance Creek didn't come cheap. Not these days. Like everywhere else, the town had seen a slump during the last recession, but now prices were up again and he'd heard from his folks that developers were circling, talking about expanding the town. Boone couldn't picture that.

"Let me see here. I believe it's called… Westfield," Fulsom said. Julie nodded, confirming his words. "Hasn't been inhabited for over a decade. A local caretaker has been keeping an eye on it, but there hasn't been cattle on it for at least that long. The heir to the property lives in Europe now. Must have finally decided he wasn't ever going to take up ranching. When he put it on the market, I snapped it up real quick."

Westfield.

Boone sat back even as his friends shifted behind him again. Westfield was a hell of a property—owned by the Eaton family for as long as anyone could remember. He couldn't believe it wasn't a working ranch anymore. But if the old folks were gone, he guessed that made sense. They must have passed away not long after he had left Chance Creek. They wouldn't have broken up the property, so Russ Eaton would have inherited and Russ wasn't much for ranching. Neither was his younger brother, Michael. As far as Boone knew, Russ hadn't married, which left Michael's daughter the only possible candidate to run the place.

Riley Eaton.

Was it a coincidence that had brought her to mind just moments before Fulsom's call, or something more?

Coincidence, Boone decided, even as the more impulsive side of him declared it Fate.

A grin tugged at his mouth as he remembered Riley as she used to be, the tomboy who tagged along after him every summer when they were kids. Riley lived for vacations on her grandparents' ranch. Her mother would send her off each year dressed up for the journey, and the minute Riley reached Chance Creek she'd wad up those fancy clothes and spend the rest of the summer in jeans, boots and an old Stetson passed down from her grandma. Boone and his friends hired on at Westfield most summers to earn some spending money. Riley stuck to them like glue, learning as much as she could about riding and ranching from them. When she was little, she used to cry when August ended and she had to go back home. As she grew older, she hid her feelings better, but Boone knew she'd always adored the ranch. It wasn't surprising, given her home life. Even when he was young, he'd heard the gossip and knew things were rough back in Chicago.

As much as he and the others had complained about being saddled with a follower like Riley, she'd earned their grudging respect as the years went on. Riley never complained, never wavered in her loyalty to them, and as many times as they left her behind, she was always ready to try again to convince them to let her join them in their exploits.

"It's a crime," he'd once heard his mother say to a friend on the phone. "Neither mother nor father has any time for her at all. No wonder she'll put up with anything those boys dish out. I worry for her."

Boone understood now what his mother was afraid of, but at the time he'd shrugged it off and over the years Riley had become a good friend. Sometimes when they were alone fishing, or riding, or just hanging out on her grandparents' porch, Boone would find himself telling her things he'd never told anyone else. As far as he knew, she'd never betrayed a confidence.

Riley was the one who dubbed Boone, Clay, Jericho and Walker the Four Horsemen of the Apocalypse, a nickname that had stuck all these years. When they'd become obsessed with the idea of being Navy SEALs, Riley had even tried to keep up with the same training regimen they'd adopted.

Boone wished he could say they'd always treated Riley as well as she treated them, but that wasn't the truth of it. One of his most shameful memories centered around the slim girl with the long brown braids. Things had become complicated once he and his friends began to date. They had far less time for Riley, who was two years younger and still a kid in their eyes, and she'd withdrawn when she realized their girlfriends didn't want her around. She still hung out when they worked at Westfield, though, and was old enough to be a real help with the work. Some of Boone's best memories were of early mornings mucking out stables with Riley. They didn't talk much, just worked side by side until the job was done. From time to time they walked out to a spot on the ranch where the land fell away and they could see the mountains in the distance. Boone had never quantified how he felt during those times. Now he realized what a fool he'd been.

He hadn't given a thought to how his girlfriends affected her or what it would be like for Riley when they left for the Navy. He'd been too young. Too utterly self-absorbed.

That same year he'd had his first serious relationship, with a girl named Melissa Resnick. Curvy, flirty and oh-so-feminine, she'd slipped into his heart by slipping into his bed on Valentine's Day. By the time Riley came to town again that last summer, he and Melissa were seldom apart. Of all the girls the Horsemen had dated, Melissa was the least tolerant of Riley's presence, and one day when they'd all gone to a local swimming hole, she'd huffed in exasperation when the younger girl came along.

"It's like you've got a sidekick," she told Boone in everyone's hearing. "Good ol' Tagalong Riley."

Clay, Jericho, and Walker, who'd always treated Riley like a little sister, thought it was funny. They had their own girlfriends to impress, and the name had stuck. Boone knew he should put a stop to it, but the lure of Melissa's body was still too strong and he knew if he took Riley's side he'd lose his access to it.

Riley had held her head up high that day and she'd stayed at the swimming hole, a move that Boone knew must have cost her, but each repetition of the nickname that summer seemed to heap pain onto her shoulders, until she caved in on herself and walked with her head down.

The worst was the night before he and the Horsemen left to join the Navy. He hadn't seen Riley for several days, whereas he couldn't seem to shake Melissa for a minute. He should have felt flattered, but instead it had irritated him. More and more often, he had found himself wishing for Riley's calm company, but she'd stopped coming to help him.

Because everyone else seemed to expect it, he'd attended the hoe-down in town sponsored by the rodeo that last night. Melissa clung to him like a burr. Riley was nowhere to be found. Boone accepted every drink he was offered and was well on his way to being three sheets to the wind when Melissa excused herself to the ladies' room at about ten. Boone remained with the other Horsemen and their dates, and he could only stare when Riley appeared in front of him. For once she'd left her Stetson at home, her hair was loose from its braids, and she wore makeup and a mini skirt that left miles of leg between its hem and her dress cowboy boots.

Every nerve in his body had come to full alert and Boone had understood in that moment what he'd failed to realize all that summer. Riley had grown up. At sixteen, she was a woman. A beautiful woman who understood him far better than Melissa could hope to. He'd had a fleeting sense of lost time and missed opportunities before Clay had whistled. "Hell, Tagalong, you've gone and gotten yourself a pair of breasts."

"You better watch out dressed up like that; some guy will think you want more than you bargained for," Jericho said.

Walker's normally grave expression had grown even more grim.

Riley had ignored them all. She'd squared her shoulders, looked Boone in the eye and said, "Will you dance with me?"

Shame flooded Boone every time he thought back to that moment.

Riley had paid him a thousand kindnesses over the years, listened to some of his most intimate thoughts and fears, never judged him, made fun of him or cut him down the way his other friends sometimes did. She'd always been there for him, and all she'd asked for was one dance.

He should have said yes.

It wasn't the shake of Walker's head, or Clay and Jericho's laughter that stopped him. It was Melissa, who had returned in time to hear Riley's question, and answered for him.

"No one wants to dance with a Tagalong. Go on home."

Riley had waited one more moment—then fled.

Boone rarely thought about Melissa after he'd left Chance Creek and when he did it was to wonder what he'd ever found compelling in her. He thought about Riley far too often. He tried to remember the good times—teaching her to ride, shoot, trap and fish. The conversations and lazy days in the sun when they were kids. The intimacy that had grown up between them without him ever realizing it.

Instead, he thought of that moment—that awful, shameful moment when she'd begged him with her eyes to say yes, to throw her pride that single bone.

And he'd kept silent.

"Have you heard of the place?" Fulsom broke into his thoughts and Boone blinked. He'd been so far away it took a moment to come back. Finally, he nodded.

"I have." He cleared his throat to get the huskiness out of it. "Mighty fine ranch." He couldn't fathom why it hadn't passed down to Riley. Losing it must have broken her heart.

Again.

"So my people tell me. Heck of a fight to get it, too. Had a competitor, a rabid developer named Montague."

Fulsom shook his head. "But that gave me a perfect setup."

"What do you mean?" Boone's thoughts were still with the girl he'd once known. The woman who'd haunted him all these years. He forced himself to pay attention to Fulsom instead.

Fulsom clicked his keyboard and an image sprung up onscreen. "Take a look."

Letting his memories go, Boone tried to make sense of what he was seeing. Some kind of map—an architect's rendering of a planned development.

"What is that?" Clay demanded.

"Wait—that's Westfield." Jericho leaned over Boone's shoulder to get a better look.

"Almost right." Fulsom nodded. "Those are the plans for Westfield Commons, a community of seventy luxury homes."

Blood ran cold in Boone's veins as Walker elbowed his way between them and peered at the screen. "Luxury homes? On Westfield? You can't do that!"

"I don't want to. But Montague does. He's frothing at the mouth to bulldoze that ranch and sell it piece by piece. The big, bad developer versus the environmentalists. This show is going to write itself." He fixed his gaze on Boone. "And if you fail, the last episode will show his bulldozers closing in."

"But it's our land; you just said so," Boone protested.

"As long as you meet your goals by December first. Ten committed couples—every couple married by the

time the show ends. Ten homes whose energy require-
ments are one-tenth the normal usage for an American
home. Six months' worth of food produced on site
stockpiled to last the inhabitants through the winter.
And three children."

"Children? Where do we get those?" Boone couldn't
keep up. He hadn't promised anything like that. All he'd
said in his proposal was that they'd build a community.

"The old-fashioned way. You make them. No cheating; children conceived before the show starts don't
count."

"Jesus." Fulsom had lost his mind. He was taking
the stakes and raising them to outrageous heights…
which was exactly the way to create a prime-time hit,
Boone realized.

"It takes nine months to have a child," Jericho
pointed out dryly.

"I didn't say they needed to be born. Pregnant bel-
lies are better than squalling babies. Like I said, sex sells,
boys. Let's give our viewers proof you and your wives
are getting it on."

Boone had had enough. "That's ridiculous, Fulsom.
You're—"

"You know what's ridiculous?" Fulsom leaned forward again, suddenly grim. "Famine. Poverty. Violence.
War. And yet it never stops, does it? You said you
wanted to do something about it. Here's your chance.
You're leaving the Navy, for God's sake. Don't tell me
you didn't plan to meet a woman, settle down and raise
some kids. So I've put a rush on the matter. Sue me."

He had a point. But still—

"I could sell the land to Montague today," Fulsom said. "Pocket the money and get back to sorting out hydrogen fuel cells." He waited a beat. When Boone shook his head, Fulsom smiled in triumph. "Gotta go, boys. Julie, here, will get you all sorted out. Good luck to you on this fabulous venture. Remember—we're going to change the world together."

"Wait—"

Fulsom stood up and walked off screen.

Boone stared as Julie sat down in his place. By the time she had walked them through the particulars of the funding process, and when and how to take possession of the land, Boone's temples were throbbing. He cut the call after Julie promised to send a packet of information, reluctantly pushed his chair back from the table and faced the three men who were to be his partners in this venture.

"Married?" Clay demanded. "No one said anything about getting married!"

"I know."

"And kids? Three out of ten of us men will have to get their wives pregnant. That means all of us will have to be trying just to beat the odds," Jericho said.

"I know."

Walker just looked at him and shook his head.

"I get it! None of us planned for anything like this." Boone stood up. "But none of us thought we had a shot of moving back to Chance Creek, either—or getting our message out to the whole country." When no one answered, he went on. "Are you saying you're out?"

"Hell, I don't know," Jericho said, pacing around the room. "I could stomach anything except that marriage part. I've never seen myself as a family man."

"I don't mind getting hitched," Clay said. "And I want kids. But I want to choose where and when to do it. And Fulsom's setting us up to fail in front of a national audience. If that Montague guy gets the ranch and builds a subdivision on it, everyone in town is going to hate us—and our families."

"So what do we do?" Boone challenged him.

"Not much choice," Walker said. "If we don't sign on, Fulsom will sell to Montague anyway."

"Exactly. The only shot we have of saving that ranch is to agree to his demands," Boone said. He shoved his hands in his pockets, unsure what to do. He couldn't see himself married in two months, let alone trying to have a child with a woman he hadn't even met yet, but giving up—Boone hated to think about it. After all, it wouldn't be the first time they'd done unexpected things to accomplish a mission.

Jericho paced back. "But his demands are—"

"Insane. I know that." Boone knew he was losing them. "He's right, though; a sustainable community made only of men doesn't mean shit. A community that's actually going to sustain itself—to carry on into the future, generation after generation—has to include women and eventually kids. Otherwise we're just playing."

"Fulsom's the one who's playing. Playing with our

lives. He can't demand we marry someone for the sake of his ratings," Jericho said.

"Actually, he can," Clay said. "He's the one with the cash."

"We'll find cash somewhere else—"

"It's more than cash," Boone reminded Jericho. "It's publicity. If we build a community and no one knows about it, what good is it? We went to Fulsom because we wanted him to do just what he's done—find a way to make everyone talk about sustainability."

"By marrying us off one by one?" Jericho stared at each of them in turn. "Are you serious? We just spent the last thirteen years of our lives fighting for our country—"

"And now we're going to fight for it in a whole new way. By getting married. On television. And knocking up our wives—while the whole damn world watches," Boone said.

No one spoke for a minute.

"I sure as hell hope they won't film that part, Chief," Clay said with a quick grin, using the moniker Boone had gained in the SEALs as second in command of his platoon.

"They wouldn't want to film your hairy ass, anyway," Jericho said.

Clay shoved him. Jericho elbowed him away.

"Enough." Walker's single word settled all of them down. They were used to listening to their lieutenant. Walker turned to Boone. "You think this will actually do any good?"

Boone shrugged. "Remember Yemen. Remember what's coming. We swore we'd do what it takes to make a difference." It was a low blow bringing up that disaster, but it was what had gotten them started down this path and he wanted to remind them of it.

"I remember Yemen every day," Jericho said, all trace of clowning around gone.

"So do I." Clay sighed. "Hell, I'm ready for a family anyway. I'm in. I don't know how I'll find a wife, though. Ain't had any luck so far."

"I'll find you one," Boone told him.

"Thanks, Chief." Clay gave him an ironic salute.

Jericho walked away. Came back again. "Damn it. I'm in, too. Under protest, though. Something this serious shouldn't be a game. You find me a wife, too, Chief, but I'll divorce her when the six months are up if I don't like her."

"Wait until Fulsom's given us the deed to the ranch, then do what you like," Boone said. "But if I'm picking your bride, give her a chance."

"Sure, Chief."

Boone didn't trust that answer, but Jericho had agreed to Fulsom's terms and that's all that mattered for now. He looked to Walker. It was crucial that the man get on board. Walker stared back at him, his gaze unfathomable. Boone knew there was trouble in his past. Lots of trouble. The man avoided women whenever he could.

Finally Walker gave him a curt nod. "Find me one, too. Don't screw it up."

Boone let out the breath he was holding. Despite the events of the past hour, a surge of anticipation warmed him from within.

They were going to do it.

And he was going to get hitched.

Was Riley the marrying kind?

RILEY EATON TOOK a sip of her green tea and summoned a smile for the friends who'd gathered on the tiny balcony of her apartment in Boston. Her thoughts were far away, though, tangled in a memory of a hot Montana afternoon when she was only ten. She'd crouched on the bank of Pittance Creek watching Boone Rudman wade through the knee-deep waters, fishing for minnows with a net. Riley had followed Boone everywhere back then, but she knew to stay out of the water and not scare his bait away.

"Mom said marriage is a trap set by men for unsuspecting women," she'd told him, quoting what she'd heard her mother say to a friend over the phone.

"You'd better watch out then," he'd said, poised to scoop up a handful of little fish.

"I won't get caught. Someone's got to want to catch you before that happens."

Boone had straightened, his net trailing in the water. She'd never forgotten the way he'd looked at her—all earnest concern.

"Maybe I'll catch you."

"Why?" She'd been genuinely curious. Getting overlooked was something she'd already grown used to.

"For my wife. If I ever want one. You'll never see me coming." He'd lifted his chin as if she'd argue the point. But Riley had thought it over and knew he was right.

She'd nodded. "You are pretty sneaky."

Riley had never forgotten that conversation, but Boone had and like everyone else he'd overlooked her when the time counted.

Story of her life.

Riley shook off the maudlin thoughts. She couldn't be a good hostess if she was wrapped up in her troubles. Time enough for them when her friends had gone.

She took another sip of her tea and hoped they wouldn't notice the tremor in her hands. She couldn't believe seven years had passed since she'd graduated from Boston College with the women who relaxed on the cheap folding chairs around her. Back then she'd thought she'd always have these women by her side, but now these yearly reunions were the only time she saw them. They were all firmly ensconced in careers that consumed their time and energy. It was hard enough to stay afloat these days, let alone get ahead in the world—or have time to take a break.

Gone were the carefree years when they thought nothing of losing whole weekends to trying out a new art medium, or picking up a new instrument. Once she'd been fearless, throwing paint on the canvas, guided only by her moods. She'd experimented day after day, laughed at the disasters and gloried in the triumphs that took shape under her brushes from time to time. Now she rarely even sketched, and what she produced seemed inane. If she wanted to express the truth of her situation through her art, she'd paint pigeons and gum stuck to the sidewalk. But she wasn't honest anymore.

For much of the past five years she'd been married to her job as a commercial artist at a vitamin distributor, joined to it twenty-four seven through her cell phone and Internet connection. Those years studying art seemed like a dream now; the one time in her life she'd felt like she'd truly belonged somewhere. She had no idea how she'd thought she'd earn a living with a fine arts degree, though. She supposed she'd hadn't thought much about the future back then. Now she felt trapped by it.

Especially after the week she'd had.

She set her cup down and twisted her hands together, trying to stop the shaking. It had started on Wednesday when she'd been called into her boss's office and handed a pink slip and a box in which to pack up her things.

"Downsizing. It's nothing personal," he'd told her.

She didn't know how she'd kept her feet as she'd made her way out of the building. She wasn't the only one riding the elevator down to street level with her belongings in her hands, but that was cold comfort. It had been hard enough to find this job. She had no idea where to start looking for another.

She'd held in her shock and panic that night and all the next day until Nadia from the adoption agency knocked on her door for their scheduled home visit at precisely two pm. She'd managed to answer Nadia's questions calmly and carefully, until the woman put down her pen.

"Tell me about your job, Riley. How will you as a single mother balance work and home life with a child?"

Riley had opened her mouth to speak, but no answer had come out. She'd reached for her cup of tea, but only managed to spill it on the cream colored skirt she'd chosen carefully for the occasion. As Nadia rushed to help her mop up, the truth had spilled from Riley's lips.

"I've just been downsized. I'm sorry; I'll get a new job right away. This doesn't have to change anything, does it?"

Nadia had been sympathetic but firm. "This is why we hesitate to place children with single parents, Riley. Children require stability. We can continue the interview and I'll weigh all the information in our judgement, but until you can prove you have a stable job, I'm afraid you won't qualify for a child."

"That will take years," Riley had almost cried, but she'd bitten back the words. What good would it do to say them aloud? As a girl, she'd dreamed she'd have children with Boone someday. When she'd grown up, she'd thought she'd find someone else. Hadn't she waited long enough to start her family?

"Riley? Are you all right?" Savannah Edwards asked, bringing her back to the present.

"Of course." She had to be. There was no other option but to soldier on. She needed to get a new job. A better job. She needed to excel at it and put the time in to make herself indispensable. Then, in a few years, she could try again to adopt.

"Are you sure?" A tall blonde with hazel eyes, Savannah had been Riley's best friend back in school, and Riley had always had a hard time fooling her. Savannah had been a music major and Riley could have listened to her play forever. She was the first person Riley had met since her grandparents passed away who seemed to care about her wholeheartedly. Riley's parents had been too busy arguing with each other all through her childhood to have much time left over to think about her. They split up within weeks after she left for college. Each remarried before the year was out and both started new families soon after. Riley felt like the odd man out when she visited them on holidays. More than eighteen years older than her half-siblings, she didn't seem to belong anywhere now.

"I'm great now that you three are here." She wouldn't confess the setback that had just befallen her. It was still too raw to process and she didn't want to bring the others down when they'd only just arrived. She wasn't the only one who had it tough. Savannah should have been a concert pianist, but when she broke her wrist in a car accident several years after graduation, she had to give up her aspirations. Instead, she had gone to work as an assistant at a prominent tech company in Silicon Valley and was still there.

"What's on tap for the weekend?" Nora Ridgeway asked as she scooped her long, wavy, light brown hair into a messy updo and secured it with a clip. She'd flown in from Baltimore where she taught English in an inner-city high school. Riley had been shocked to see the dark smudges under her eyes. Nora looked thin. Too thin. Riley wondered what secrets she was hiding behind her upbeat tone.

"I hope it's a whole lot of nothing," Avery Lightfoot said, her auburn curls glinting in the sun. Avery lived in Nashville and worked in the marketing department of one of the largest food distribution companies in North America. She'd studied acting in school, but she'd never been discovered the way she'd once hoped to be. For a brief time she'd created an original video series that she'd posted online, but the advertising revenue she'd generated hadn't added up to much and soon her money had run out. Now she created short videos to market low-carb products to yoga moms. Riley's heart ached for her friend. She sounded as tired as Nora looked.

In fact, everyone looked like they needed a pick-me-up after dealing with flights and taxis, and Riley headed inside to get refreshments. She wished she'd been able to drive to the airport and pick them up. Who could afford a car, though? Even when she'd had a job, Riley found it hard to keep up with her rent, medical insurance and monthly bills, and budget enough for the childcare she'd need when she adopted. Thank God it had been her turn to host their gathering this year. She couldn't have gotten on a plane after the news she'd just received.

When she thought back to her college days she realized her belief in a golden future had really been a pipe dream. Some of her classmates were doing fine. But most of them were struggling to keep their heads above water, just like her. A few had given up and moved back in with their parents.

When she got back to the balcony with a tray of snacks, she saw Savannah pluck a dog-eared copy of *Pride and Prejudice* out of a small basket that sat next to the door. Riley had been reading it in the mornings before work this week as she drank her coffee—until she'd been let go. A little escapism helped start her day off on the right foot.

"Am I the only one who'd trade my life for one of Austen's characters' in a heartbeat?" Savannah asked, flipping through the pages.

"You want to live in Regency England? And be some man's property?" Nora asked sharply.

"Of course not. I don't want the class conflict or the snobbery or the outdated rules. But I want the beauty of their lives. I want the music and the literature. I want afternoon visits and balls that last all night. Why don't we do those things anymore?"

"Who has time for that?" Riley certainly hadn't when she was working. Now she'd have to spend every waking moment finding a new job.

"I haven't played the piano in ages," Savannah went on. "I mean, it's not like I'm all that good anymore—"

"Are you kidding? You've always been fantastic," Nora said.

"What about romance? I'd kill for a real romance. One that means something," Avery said.

"What about Dan?" Savannah asked.

"I broke up with him three weeks ago. He told me he wasn't ready for a serious relationship. The man's thirty-one. If he's not ready now, when will he be?"

"That's tough." Riley understood what Avery meant. She hadn't had a date in a year; not since Marc Hepstein had told her he didn't consider her marriage material. She should have dumped him long before.

It wasn't like she hadn't been warned. His older sister had taken her aside once and spelled it out for her:

"Every boy needs to sow his wild oats. You're his shiksa fling. You'll see; you won't get a wedding ring from him. Marc will marry a nice Jewish girl in the end."

Riley wished she'd paid attention to the warning, but of course she hadn't. She had a history of dangling after men who were unavailable.

Shiksa fling.

Just a step up from Tagalong Riley.

Riley pushed down the old insecurities that threatened to take hold of her and tried not to give in to her pain over her lost chance to adopt. When Marc had broken up with her, it had been a wake-up call. She'd realized if she waited for a man to love her, she might never experience the joy of raising a child. She'd also realized she hadn't loved Marc enough to spend a life with him. She'd been settling, and she was better than that.

She'd started the adoption process.

Now she'd have to start all over again.

"It wasn't as hard to leave him as you might think." Avery took a sip of her tea. "It's not just Dan. I feel like breaking up with my life. I had a heart once. I know I did. I used to feel—alive."

"Me, too," Nora said softly.

"I thought I'd be married by now," Savannah said, "but I haven't had a boyfriend in months. And I hate my job. I mean, I really hate it!" Riley couldn't remember ever seeing calm, poised Savannah like this.

"So do I," Avery said, her words gushing forth as if a dam had broken. "Especially since I have two of them now. I got back in debt when my car broke down and I needed to buy a new one. Now I can't seem to get ahead."

"I don't have any job at all," Riley confessed. "I've been downsized." She closed her eyes. She hadn't meant to say that.

"Oh my goodness, Riley," Avery said. "What are you going to do?"

"I don't know. Paint?" She laughed dully. She couldn't tell them the worst of it. She was afraid if she talked about her failed attempt to adopt she'd lose control of her emotions altogether. "Can you imagine a life in which we could actually pursue our dreams?"

"No," Avery said flatly. "After what happened last time, I'm so afraid if I try to act again, I'll just make a fool of myself."

Savannah nodded vigorously, tears glinting in her eyes. "I'm afraid to play," she confessed. "I sit down at my piano and then I get up again without touching the keys. What if my talent was all a dream? What if I was fooling myself and I was never anything special at all? My wrist healed years ago, but I can't make myself go for it like I once did. I'm too scared."

"What about you, Nora? Do you ever write these days?" Riley asked gently when Nora remained quiet. When they were younger, Nora talked all the time about wanting to write a novel, but she hadn't mentioned it in ages. Riley had assumed it was because she loved teaching, but she looked as burnt out as the rest of them. Riley knew she worked in an area of Baltimore that resembled a war zone.

Her friend didn't answer, but a tear traced down her cheek.

"Nora, what is it?" Savannah dropped the book and came to crouch by her chair.

"It's one of my students." Nora kept her voice steady even as another tear followed the tracks of the first. "At least I think it is."

"What do you mean?" Riley realized they'd all pulled closer to each other, leaning forward in mutual support and feeling. Dread crept into her throat at Nora's words. She'd known instinctively something was wrong in her friend's life for quite some time, but despite her questions, Nora's e-mails and texts never revealed a thing.

"I've been getting threats. On my phone," Nora said, plucking at a piece of lint on her skirt.

"Someone's texting threats?" Savannah sounded aghast.

"And calling. He has my home number, too."

"What did he say?" Avery asked.

"Did he threaten to hurt you?" Riley demanded. After a moment, Nora nodded.

"To kill you?" Avery whispered.

Nora nodded again. "And more."

Savannah's expression hardened. "More?"

Nora looked up. "He threatened to rape me. He said I'd like it. He got... really graphic."

The four of them stared at each other in shocked silence.

"You can't go back," Savannah said. "Nora, you can't go back there. I don't care how important your work is, that's too much."

"What did the police say?" Riley's hands were shaking again. Rage and shock battled inside of her, but anger won out. Who would dare threaten her friend?

"What did the school's administration say?" Avery demanded.

"That threats happen all the time. That I should change my phone numbers. That the people who make the threats usually don't act on them."

"Usually?" Riley was horrified.

"What are you going to do?" Savannah said.

"What am I supposed to do? I can't quit." Nora seemed to sink into herself. "I changed my number, but it's happening again. I've got nothing saved. I managed to pay off my student loans, but then my mom got sick... I'm broke."

No one answered. They knew Nora's family hadn't

had much money, and she'd taken on debt to get her degree. Riley figured she'd probably used every penny she might have saved to pay it off again. Then her mother had contracted cancer and had gone through several expensive procedures before she passed away.

"Is this really what it's come to?" Avery asked finally. "Our work consumes us, or it overwhelms us, or it threatens us with bodily harm and we just keep going?"

"And what happened to love? True love?" Savannah's voice was raw. "Look at us! We're intelligent, caring, attractive women. And we're all single! None of us even dating. What about kids? I thought I'd be a mother."

"So did I," Riley whispered.

"Who can afford children?" Nora said fiercely. "I thought teaching would be enough. I thought my students would care—" She broke off and Riley's heart squeezed at Nora's misery.

"I've got some savings, but I'll eat through them fast if I don't get another job," Riley said slowly. "I want to leave Boston so badly. I want fresh air and a big, blue sky. But there aren't any jobs in the country." Memories of just such a sky flooded her mind. What she'd give for a vacation at her uncle's ranch in Chance Creek, Montana. In fact, she'd love to go there and never come back. It had been so long since she'd managed to stop by and spend a weekend at Westfield, it made her ache to think of the carefree weeks she spent there every summer as a child. The smell of hay and horses and sunshine on old buildings, the way her grandparents used to let her loose on the ranch to run and play and ride as hard as she wanted to. Their unconditional love. There were few rules at Westfield and those existed purely for the sake of practicality and safety. *Don't spook the horses. Clean and put away tools after you use them. Be home at mealtimes and help with the dishes.*

Away from her parents' arguing, Riley had blossomed, and the skills she'd learned from the other kids in town—especially the Four Horsemen of the Apocalypse—had taught her pride and self-confidence. They were rough and tumble boys and they rarely slowed down to her speed, but as long as she kept up to them, they included her in their fun.

Clay Pickett, Jericho Cook, Walker Norton—they'd treated her like a sister. For an only child, it was a dream come true. But it was Boone who'd become a true friend, and her first crush.

And then had broken her heart.

"I keep wondering if it will always be like this," Avery said, interrupting her thoughts. "If I'll always have to struggle to get by. If I'll never have a house of my own—or a husband or family."

"You'll have a family," Riley assured her, then bit her lip. Who was she to reassure Avery? She could never seem to shake her bad luck—with men, with work, with anything. But out of all the things that had happened to her, nothing left her cringing with humiliation like the memory of the time she'd asked Boone to dance.

She'd been such a child. No one like Boone would have looked twice at her, no matter how friendly he'd been over the years. She could still hear Melissa's sneering words—*No one wants to dance with a Tagalong. Go on home*—and the laughter that followed her when she fled the dance.

She'd returned to Chicago that last summer thinking her heart would never mend, and time had just begun to heal it when her grandparents passed away one after the other in quick succession that winter. Riley had been devastated; doubly so when she left for college the following year and her parents split. It was as if a tidal wave had washed away her childhood in one blow. After that, her parents sold their home and caretakers watched over the ranch. Uncle Russ, who'd inherited it, had found he made a better financier than a cowboy. With his career taking off, he'd moved to Europe soon after.

At his farewell dinner, one of the few occasions she'd seen her parents in the same room since they'd divorced, he'd stood up and raised a glass. "To Riley. You're the only one who loves Westfield now, and I want you to think of it as yours. One day in the future it will be, you know. While I'm away, I hope you'll treat it as your own home. Visit as long as you like. Bring your friends. Enjoy the ranch. My parents would have wanted that." He'd taken her aside later and presented her with a key. His trust in her and his promises had warmed her heart. If she'd own Westfield one day she could stand anything, she'd told herself that night. It was the one thing that had sustained her through life's repeated blows.

"I wish I could run away from my life, even for a little while. Six months would do it," Savannah said, breaking into her thoughts. "If I could clear my mind of everything that has happened in the past few years I know I could make a fresh start."

Riley knew just what she meant. She'd often wished the same thing, but she didn't only want to run away from her life; she wanted to run straight back into her past to a time when her grandparents were still alive. Things had been so simple then.

Until she'd fallen for Boone.

She hadn't seen Uncle Russ since he'd moved away, although she wrote to him a couple of times a year, and received polite, if remote, answers in turn. She had the feeling Russ had found the home of his heart in Munich. She wondered if he'd ever come back to Montana.

In the intervening years she'd visited Westfield whenever she could, more frequently as the sting of Boone's betrayal faded, although in reality that meant a long weekend every three or four months, rather than the expansive summer vacations she'd imagined when she'd received the key. It wasn't quite the same without her grandparents and her old friends, without Boone and the Horsemen, but she still loved the country, and Westfield Manor was the stuff of dreams. Even the name evoked happy memories and she blessed the ancestor whose flight of fancy had bestowed such a distinguished title on a Montana ranch house. She'd always wondered if she'd stumble across Boone someday, home for leave, but their visits had never coincided.

Still, whenever she drove into Chance Creek, her heart rate kicked up a notch and she couldn't help scanning the streets for his familiar face.

"I wish I could run away from my dirty dishes and laundry," Avery said. Riley knew she was attempting to lighten the mood. "I spend my weekends taking care of all my possessions. I bet Jane Austen didn't do laundry."

"In those days servants did it," Nora said, swiping her arm over her cheek to wipe away the traces of her tears. "Maybe we should get servants, too, while we're dreaming."

"Maybe we should, if it means we could concentrate on the things we love," Savannah said.

"Like that's possible. Look at us—we're stuck, all of us. There's no way out." The waver in Nora's voice betrayed her fierceness.

"There has to be," Avery exclaimed.

"How?"

Riley wished she had the answer. She hated seeing the pain and disillusionment on her friends' faces. And she was terrified of having to start over herself.

"What if... what if we lived together?" Savannah said slowly. "I mean, wouldn't that be better than how things are now? If we pooled our resources and figured out how to make them stretch? None of us would have to work so hard."

"I thought you had a good job," Nora said, a little bitterly.

"On paper. The cost of living in Silicon Valley is outrageous, though. You'd be surprised how little is left over when I pay my bills. And inside, I feel... like I'm dying."

A silence stretched out between them. Riley knew just what Savannah meant. At first grown-up life had seemed exciting. Now it felt like she was slipping into a pool of quicksand that she'd never be able to escape. Maybe it would be different if they joined forces. If they pooled their money, they could do all kinds of things.

For the first time in months she felt a hint of possibility.

"We could move where the cost of living is cheaper and get a house together." Savannah warmed to her theme. "With a garden, maybe. We could work part time and share the bills."

"For six months? What good would that do? We'd run through what little money we have and be harder to employ afterward," Nora said.

"How much longer are you willing to wait before you try for the life you actually want, rather than the life that keeps you afloat one more day?" Savannah asked her. "I have to try to be a real pianist. Life isn't worth living if I don't give it a shot. That means practicing for hours every day. I can't do that and work a regular job, too."

"I've had an idea for a screenplay," Avery confessed. "I think it's really good. Six months would be plenty of time for me to write it. Then I could go back to work while I shop it around."

"If I had six months I would paint all day until I had enough canvasses to put on a show. Maybe that would be the start and end of my career as an artist, but at least I'd have done it once," Riley said.

"A house costs money," Nora said.

"Not always," Riley said slowly as an idea took hold in her head. "What about Westfield?" After all, it hadn't been inhabited in years. "Uncle Russ always said I should bring my friends and stay there."

"Long term?" Avery asked.

"Six months would be fine. Russ hasn't set foot in it in over a decade."

"You want us to move to Montana and freeload for six months?" Nora asked.

"I want us to move to Montana and take six months to jumpstart our lives. We'll practice following our passions. We'll brainstorm ideas together for how to make money from them. Who knows? Maybe together we'll come up with a plan that will work."

"Sounds good to me," Avery said.

"I don't know," Nora said. "Do you really think it's work that's kept you from writing or playing or painting? Because if you can't do it now, chances are you won't be able to do it at Westfield either. You'll busy up your days with errands and visits and sightseeing and all that. Wait and see."

"Not if we swore an oath to work on our projects every day," Savannah said.

"Like the oaths you used to swear to do your homework on time? Or not to drink on Saturday night? Or to stop crank-calling the guy who dumped you junior year?"

Savannah flushed. "I was a child back then—"

"I just feel that if we take six months off, we'll end up worse off than when we started."

Savannah leaned forward. "Come on. Six whole months to write. Aren't you dying to try it?" When Nora hesitated, Savannah pounced on her. "I knew it! You want to as badly as we do."

"Of course I want to," Nora said. "But it won't work. None of you will stay at home and hone your craft."

A smile tugged at Savannah's lips. "What if we couldn't leave?"

"Are you going to chain us to the house?"

"No. I'm going to take away your clothes. Your modern clothes," she clarified when the others stared at her. "You're right; we could easily be tempted to treat the time like a vacation, especially with us all together. But if we only have Regency clothes to wear, we'll be stuck because we'll be too embarrassed to go into town. We'll take a six-month long Jane Austen vacation from our lives." She sat back and folded her arms over her chest.

"I love it," Riley said. "Keep talking."

"We'll create a Regency life, as if we'd stepped into one of her novels. A beautiful life, with time for music and literature and poetry and walks. Westfield is rural, right? No one will be there to see us. If we pattern our days after the way Jane's characters spent theirs, we'd have plenty of time for creative pursuits."

Nora rolled her eyes. "What about the neighbors?

What about groceries and dental appointments?"

"Westfield is set back from the road." Riley thought it through. "Savannah's right; we could go for long stretches without seeing anyone. We could have things delivered, probably."

"I'm in," Avery said. "I'll swear to live a Regency life for six months. I'll swear it on penalty of... death."

"The penalty is embarrassment," Savannah said. "If we leave early, we have to travel home in our Regency clothes. I know I'm in. I'd gladly live a Jane Austen life for six months."

"If I get to wear Regency dresses and bonnets, I'm in too," Riley said. What was the alternative? Stay here and mourn the child she'd never have?

"Are you serious?" Nora asked. "Where do we even get those things?"

"We have a seamstress make them, or we sew them ourselves," Avery said. "Come on, Nora. Don't pretend you haven't always wanted to."

The others nodded. After all, it was their mutual love of Jane Austen movies that had brought them together in the first place. Two days into their freshman year at Boston College, Savannah had marched through the halls of their dorm announcing a Jane Austen film festival in her room that night. Riley, Nora and Avery had shown up for it, and the rest was history.

"It'll force us to carry out our plan the way we intend to," Savannah told her. "If we can't leave the ranch, there will be no distractions. Every morning when we put on our clothes we'll be recommitting to our vow to devote six months to our creative pursuits. Think about it, Nora. Six whole months to write."

"Besides, we were so good together back in college," Riley said. "We inspired each other. Why couldn't we do that again?"

"But what will we live on?"

"We'll each liquidate our possessions," Savannah said. "Think about how little most people had in Jane Austen's time. It'll be like when Eleanor and Marianne have to move to a cottage in *Sense and Sensibility* with their mother and little sister. We'll make a shoestring budget and stick to it for food and supplies. If we don't go anywhere, we won't spend any money, right?"

"That's right," Avery said. "Remember what Mrs. John Dashwood said in that novel. 'What on earth can four women want for more than that?—They will live so cheap! Their housekeeping will be nothing at all. They will have no carriage, no horses, and hardly any servants; they will keep no company, and can have no expenses of any kind! Only conceive how comfortable they will be!'"

"We certainly won't have any horses or carriages." Savannah laughed.

"But we will be comfortable, and during the time we're together we can brainstorm what to do next," Riley said. "No one leaves Westfield until we all have a working plan."

"With four of us to split the chores of running the house, it'll be easy," Avery said. "We'll have hours and hours to devote to our craft every day."

Nora hesitated. "You know this is crazy, right?"

"But it's exactly the right kind of crazy," Riley said. "You have to join us, Nora."

Nora shook her head, but just when Riley thought she'd refuse, she shrugged. "Oh, okay. What the hell? I'll do it." Riley's heart soared. "But when our six months are up, I'll be broke," Nora went on. "I'll be homeless, too. I don't see how anything will have improved."

"Everything will have improved," Savannah told her. "I promise. Together we can do anything."

Riley smiled at their old rallying-cry from college. "So, we're going to do it? You'll all come to Westfield with me? And wear funny dresses?"

"And bonnets," Avery said. "Don't forget the bonnets."

"I'm in," Savannah said, sticking out her hand.

"I'm in," Avery said, putting hers down on top of it.

"I guess I'm in," Nora said, and added hers to the pile.

"Well, I'm definitely in." Riley slapped hers down on top of the rest.

Westfield. She was going back to Westfield.

Things were looking up.

End of Excerpt